The Fascinating Story of Muhammad

The Fascinating Story of Muhammad

Simplified & de-mystified from the original narration and the Qur'an

by

Ahmad Shameem

Based on the Qur'an and the earliest records by
Ibn Ishaq, Ibn Hisham, Ibn Sa'ad, and al Tibri

AuthorHouse™ UK Ltd.
1663 Liberty Drive
Bloomington, IN 47403 USA
www.authorhouse.co.uk
Phone: 0800.197.4150

© 2014 Ahmad Shameem. All rights reserved.

No part of this book may be reproduced, stored in a retrieval system, or transmitted by any means without the written permission of the author.

Published by AuthorHouse 12/28/2013

ISBN: 978-1-4918-8900-8 (sc)
ISBN: 978-1-4918-8902-2 (hc)
ISBN: 978-1-4918-8901-5 (e)

Library of Congress Control Number: 2013923478

Any people depicted in stock imagery provided by Thinkstock are models, and such images are being used for illustrative purposes only. Certain stock imagery © Thinkstock.

Because of the dynamic nature of the Internet, any web addresses or links contained in this book may have changed since publication and may no longer be valid. The views expressed in this work are solely those of the author and do not necessarily reflect the views of the publisher, and the publisher hereby disclaims any responsibility for them.

The painting on the title of this book is one of many miniatures commissioned by the Turkish Ottoman ruler Murad III (1574-1595) to illustrate the epic "Siyar-i-Nabi" (The Life of the Prophet). The epic was completed by Mustafa Darir around 1388 CE in Turkish language, upon the wish of Sultan Barquq, the Mamluk ruler in Cairo, Egypt.

Scions of the Quraysh Tribe from which Muhammad, his opponents, and his adherents originated

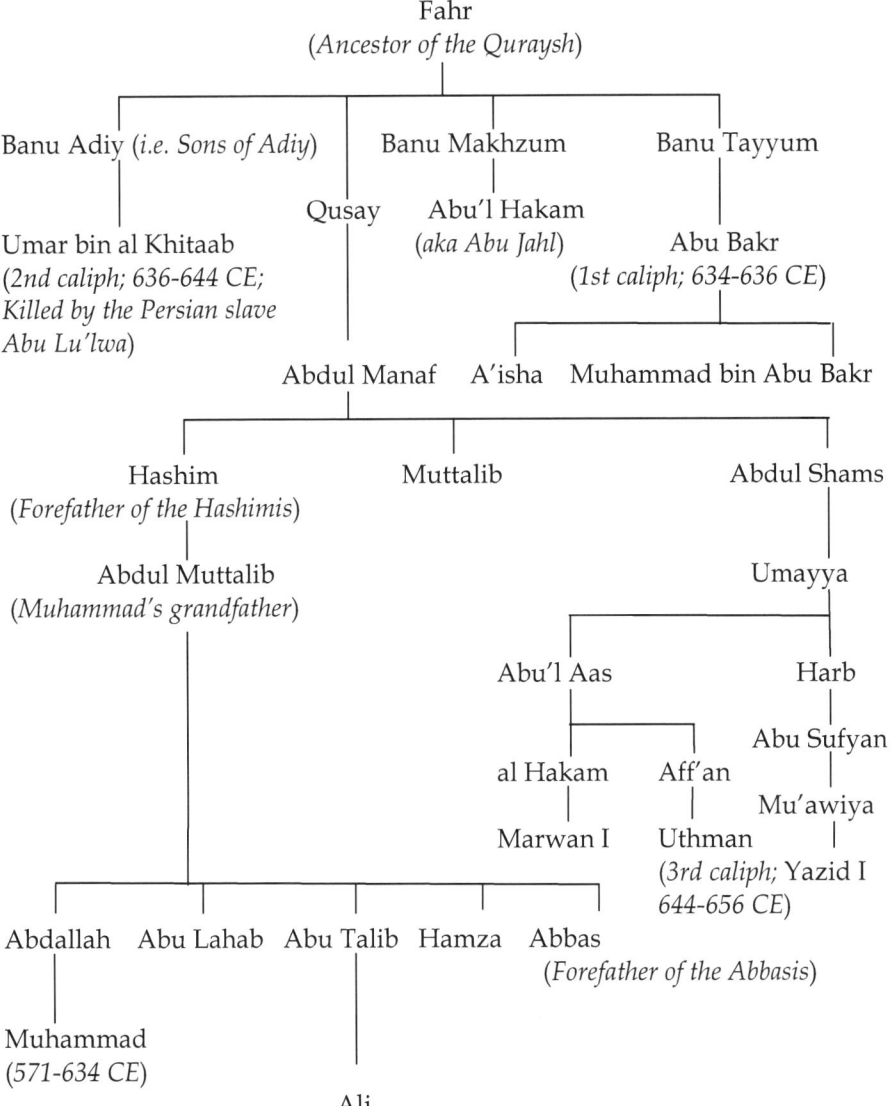

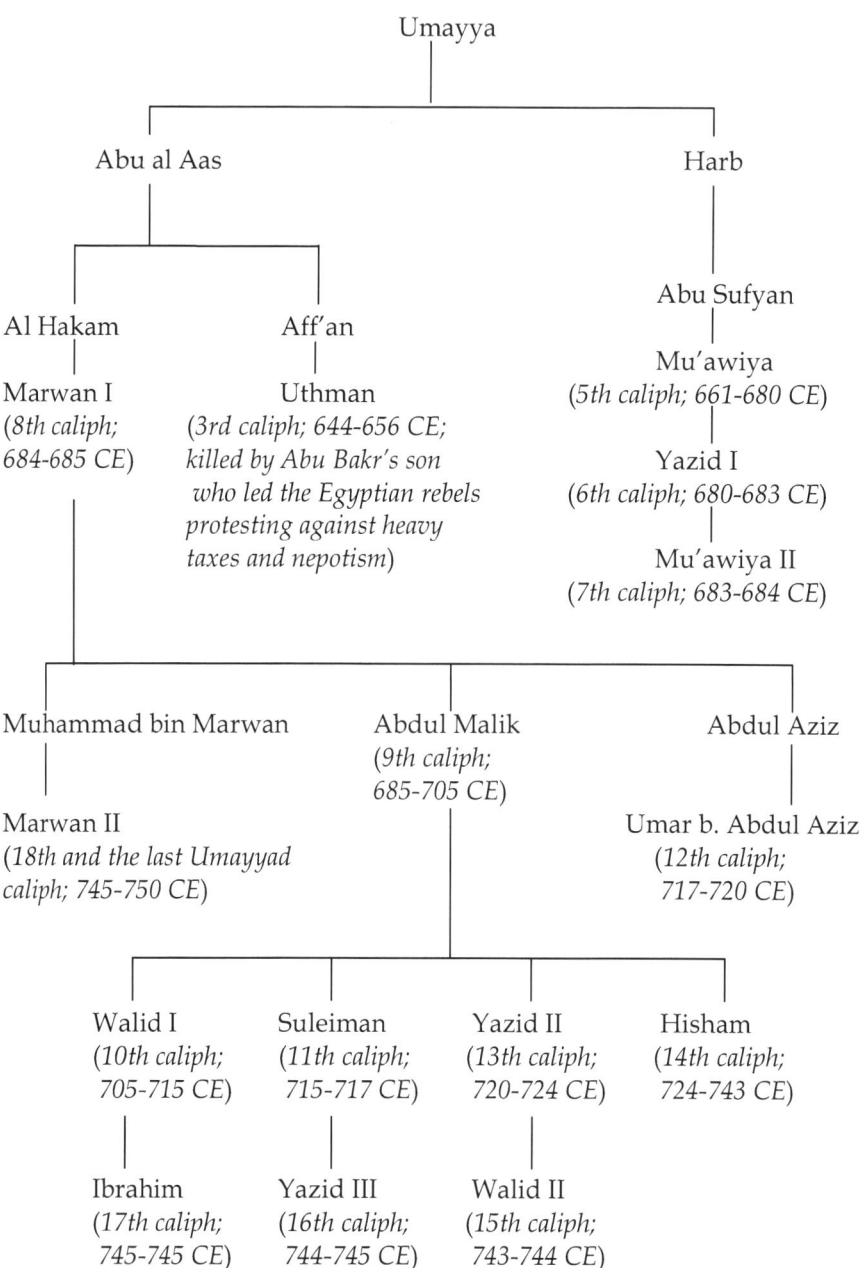

ix

Banu Abbas (The Sons of Abbas)

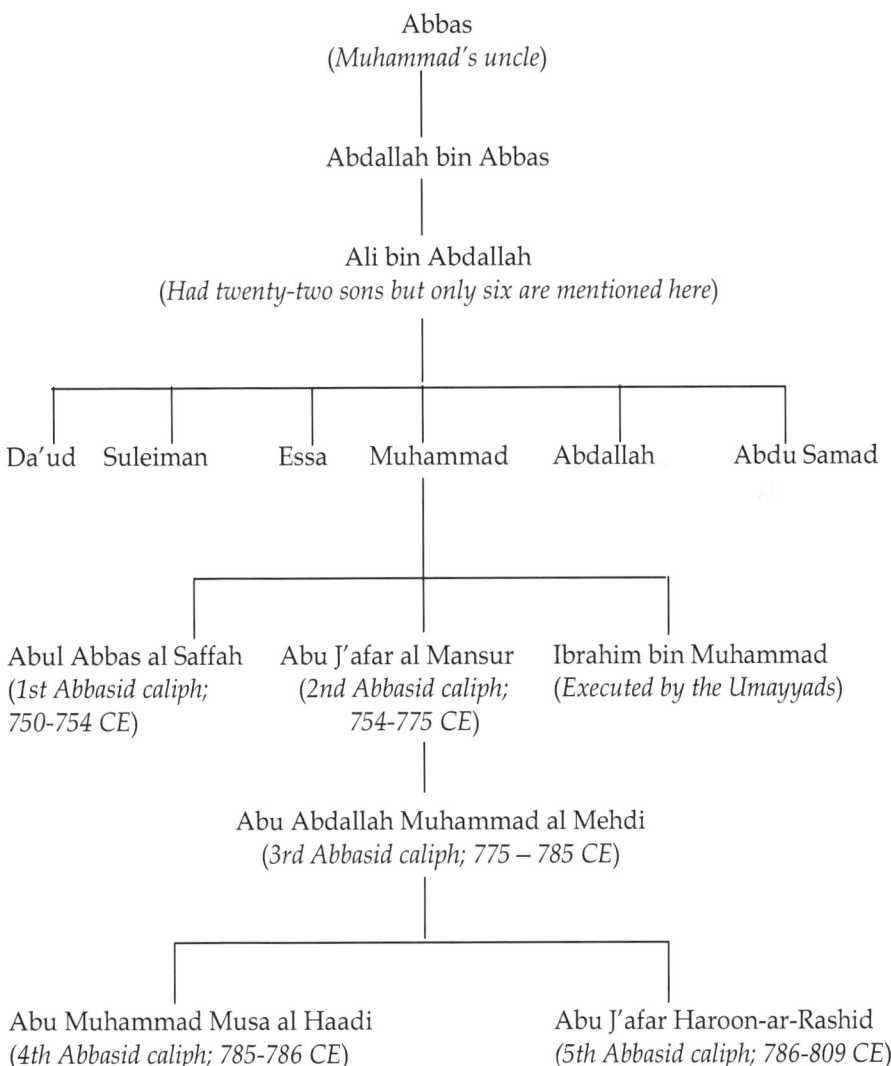

Ali, his progeny and the Shiite spiritual leaders (Imams)

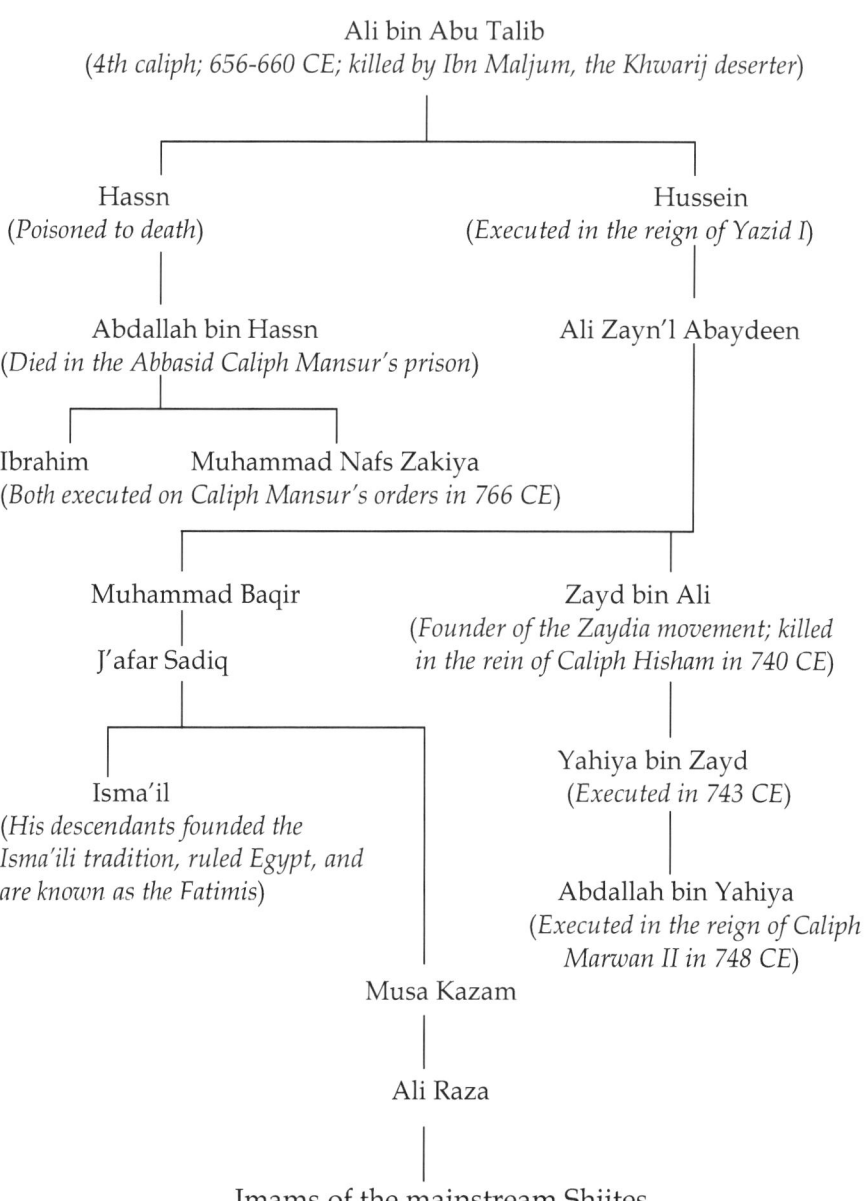

Contents

INTRODUCTION 1

MUHAMMAD AND HIS SOCIETY
IN THE LIGHT OF THE EARLIEST ARAB RECORDS 3
    Many sacred houses competed as income generating businesses 6
    Why Abraha came to attack Mecca 6
    Muhammad grows amidst the Quraysh tribes
    competing to take charge of the pilgrim business 9
    Muhammad invites his Hashimi clan to follow him 19
    The myth of the general persecution of Muhammad
    and his followers in secular Mecca 42
    Muhammad rides a super-speed winged horse
    and flies to the heavens to meet God and the prophets 55
    The boycott of the Hashimis, and its annulment:
    Muhammad responds with more insults for his elders 62
    Muhammad travels to Ta'if
    to solicit support from the Thaqif 69
    Muhammad persuades the tribes of Medina
    and conspires against their Jewish neighbours 74
    Muhammad begins to split the multi-faith society
    of Medina: The Covenant of Medina 91
    Muhammad preaches from the Torah and beguiles
    the Jews into respecting him as a leader 96
    Muhammad recruits the poor by
    sheltering, feeding and training them 99
    The testimonies to robberies and assassinations 101
    The slave trade 104
    Muhammad preaches to the people of Medina 106
    Muhammad preaches to the Jews of Medina 108
    Secret assassinations of critics in Medina 113
    Muhammad develops a pretext for maligning
    the Jews and breaking with them 119
    Muhammad trains his men in religion and robbery
    to raid the Meccan caravans and weaker tribes 124
    Physical cleanliness and moral depravation:
    How were the jihadis disciplined? 128
    The raid on the Mustalaq tribe and
    the kidnapping of its chief's daughter 133

THE ISSUE OF ADULTERY	135
THE TRANSMUTATION BETWEEN RELIGIOUS AND BANDITRY-RELATED TERMS	139
THE FIRST RAID ON A MECCAN TRADE CARAVAN, TAKING BOOTY AND PRISONERS FOR RANSOM	141
THE BATTLE OF BADR	144
MUHAMMAD PROVOKES MORE HATRED AGAINST THE JEWS	160
SECRET ASSASSINATIONS OF THE JEWISH LEADERS BEGIN	167
THE EXPULSION OF THE BANU QAYNUQA AND CONFISCATION OF THEIR LANDS	170
MUHAMMAD KEEPS INCITING ANTI-JEWISH SENTIMENTS AND STEPS UP RAIDS ON MECCAN CARAVANS	175
ABU SUFYAN WINS AT UHUD, SPARES MUHAMMAD'S LIFE AND MUHAMMAD GLORIFIES DEATH IN JIHAD	176
THE EXPULSION OF THE BANU NADIR AND CONFISCATION OF THEIR LANDS	185
THE BATTLE OF THE ALLIES (AHZAAB), AND WAR BY DECEIT	189
THE MASSACRE OF THE BANU QURAYZA, CONFISCATION OF THEIR LANDS, AND ENSLAVEMENT OF THEIR WOMEN AND CHILDREN	197
MUHAMMAD SENDS AN ASSASSIN TO MECCA TO KILL ABU SUFYAN	203
THE TRUCE OF HUDAYBIYA	204
THE MASSACRE AND ENSLAVEMENT OF THE KHYBER JEWS	210
SAFFIYA – THE BEST OF THE BOOTY: REGULATING THE DISTRIBUTION OF CAPTURED WOMEN AND BOOTY	214
THE SETTLEMENT OF THE KHYBER LANDS	218
MUHAMMAD'S WIVES QUARREL AND CONSPIRE IN JEALOUSY: A'ISHA IS ACCUSED OF ADULTERY	219
MUHAMMAD MARRIES THE WIFE OF HIS FOSTER SON AND ABOLISHES THE TRADITION OF TREATING FOSTER CHILDREN AS ONE'S OWN	228
MUHAMMAD PREPARES TO FORM AN ALLIANCE WITH THE "UNBELIEVER" MECCANS	236
MUHAMMAD LAUNCHES A PROPAGANDA CAMPAIGN IN ORDER TO POPULARIZE THE HASHIMIS	239
MUHAMMAD FINDS HIS EXCUSE AND TAKES MECCA	240
THE MURDERS OF THE CRITICS AND APOSTATES IN MECCA	246
THE RAIDS ON THE TRIBES SETTLED AROUND MECCA	253
THE BATTLE OF HUNAYN	256
THE REASONS FOR THE RELATIVES FIGHTING EACH OTHER, AND THE NON-QURAYSH FIGHTING FOR THE SUPREMACY OF THE QURAYSH: ECONOMIC CHAOS AND STARVATION	264

Muhammad's tribal wars to enable his largely
"unbeliever" Quraysh tribe to rule all Arabs 269
The "law of revenge" among the believers...................................269
The raid on Ta'if 272
Insider traitors used to raid their own tribes 273
The siege of Ta'if 273
The distribution of the booty from Hawazin
and coercing people to become believers...................................... 275
Continual persecution, buying traitors,
and harassing the critics 281
Muhammad maligns the Christians, as
a pretext to raid their settlements on route to
Damascus, and punishes the pacifists 283
Back in Medina, and the social boycott of the pacifists............. 296
The details of Muhammad's taxes
and the means of extortion 298
The besieged people of Ta'if are divided,
lured, and made to surrender, one by one................................... 301
The persecution of the remaining secular Meccans 303
Do not attend the funerals of the unbelievers 308
More tribes are brought to Muhammad's rule 309
The myths of "God's protection" and "God's curses" 310
Muhammad rules an Arabia run by bandits................................312
More revenue collectors and more prophets 316
Muhammad sanctifies the pagan rituals 317
As Muhammad grows old, he
forbids men from seeing his wives..319
Muhammad falls ill and dies, while his
associates fight amongst themselves for power........................321

APPENDIX I: ARAB-ISLAMIC IMPERIALISM SUMMARIZED HIGHLIGHTS OF THE KHILAFA DESPOTISM OF MUHAMMAD'S RELATIVES............................331

Abu Bakr, the first caliph (634-636 CE) ignores
the murder of Sa'ad bin Ubaada 331
Umar, the second caliph (636-644 CE): The beginning
of the colonization of Bilaad al Shaam and Persia....................332
The Umayyads enslave the Syrians, Egyptians,
Iraqis, and Persians in the name of Islam 334
(644 CE) An oppressed Persian slave stabs and kills Umar........ 336

UTHMAN, THE THIRD CALIPH (644-656 CE), BEGINS
BY DISREGARDING THE ISLAMIC LAW OF REVENGE 336
(651 CE) UTHMAN ASSEMBLES AND EDITS THE QUR'AN 338
(656 CE) ABU BAKR'S SON MURDERS UTHMAN 340
ALI AND MU'AWIYA BECOME RIVAL CALIPHS (656-660 CE) 341
A'ISHA LEADS AN ARMY AGAINST ALI:
TALHA AND ZUBAYR ARE KILLED 342
ALI AND MU'AWIYA FIGHT FOR POWER 342
(660 CE) THE KHWARIJ TURN INTO BANDITS AND MURDER ALI 344
MU'AWIYA (661-680 CE) EXECUTES ABU BAKR'S SON
AND CONDEMNS THE SHIITES 345
THE SIXTH CALIPH YAZID (680-683 CE) AND THE
SLAUGHTER OF MUHAMMAD'S GRANDSON 346
THE CALIPH'S ARMY PLUNDERS MEDINA AND MECCA 348
CALIPH ABD AL MALIK (685-705 CE) PLANS
TO CONSTRUCT ANOTHER KA'BA IN JERUSALEM 349
HAJJAJ BIN YOUSSEF 350
HAJJAJ USES CATAPULTS TO BOMBARD THE KA'BA 351
WALID BIN ABD AL MALIK (705-715 CE): FURTHER
PERSECUTION OF THE ABBASIDS AND ALAWITES 351
UMAR BIN ABD AL AZIZ, A RARE NOBLE CALIPH (717-720 CE)
IS POISONED BY HIS OWN FAMILY 352
THE ABBASIDS SEIZE THE CALIPHATE FROM THE UMAYYADS 352
AL SAFFAH, THE FIRST ABBASID CALIPH (750-754 CE)
SLAUGHTERS THE ALAWITES OF MOSUL 353
SHI'A ISLAM 355
THE LEGACY OF MUHAMMAD AND HIS RELATIVES 356

APPENDIX II:
THE FALLACIES OF "ISLAMIC HISTORY" 357

APPENDIX III:
WHAT CAN GOOD-NATURED MUSLIMS DO? 363

EPILOGUE: WAS MUHAMMAD A MAN OF GOD? 365

NOTES ON RESEARCH, REFERENCES, AND TRANSLATIONS
FROM ARABIC AND URDU TEXTS TO ENGLISH 371

ACKNOWLEDGEMENTS 371

ABOUT THE AUTHOR 373

SELECTED BIBLIOGRAPHY 375

REFERENCES AND NOTES 379

Introduction

Upon the suggestion of Prometheus, I sent the first draft of this book for evaluation to Ali Sina and Ibn Warraq. On 22nd June 2005, Ali Sina replied, "This is a great book. I read the first 30 pages and I could not stop. This book must be translated in all the languages and become available to all ..." On 9th August 2005, Ibn Warraq replied, "If Prometheus agree to publish it, I shall indeed review it." This was encouraging from these leading experts on Islam but it took me eight more years to verify that everything I had quoted in this book from the Qur'an and earliest Arab records met the best standards of research and historiography.

The earliest Arab history, written in the 7th and 8th centuries by al Waqidi, al Tibri, Ibn Ishaq, Ibn Hisham, and Ibn Sa'ad, supported by relevant verses of the Qur'an, is greatly differentiable in length and analyses from the modern Islamic propaganda history. The Islamists teach short, purged, and grossly exaggerated versions to produce preachers, jihadis, and propagandists to spread Islam but the earliest history, based on hundreds of thousands of gathered reports and narrations of the people of the period, contemporary poetic-prose, and analyses provides more detailed and realistic account.

The earliest historians portray a picture of Muhammad with attributes of a 6th-7th century Arabian leader, called "the messenger of Allah," in a tribal Arabia where it was not rare for articulate men and women to use similar titles in order to influence people. From among these earliest records, Muslim and non-Muslim scholars agree that Ibn Hisham's compilation of Ibn Ishaq's (704-767 CE) biography of Muhammad is the most complete. Ibn Ishaq painstakingly gathered reports from people over decades. He travelled extensively to get first-hand knowledge of the past, and collect accounts from people who had heard of events from those who had lived with Muhammad, or were alive in his time.

These earliest books show that modern Islamic propaganda does not reflect the reality of the Arab society and culture of Muhammad's period. There are glaring contradictions between the earliest Arab records and modern Islamic myths. This book tells the story of Muhammad, Islam, the Qur'an, and the Arabian society of the period as truthfully and originally as the available records make it possible.

Muhammad and his Society
In the light of the earliest Arab records

The "Ka'ba" (meaning "the cube") was the central and holiest shrine of Arabs of many faiths. Among varying reports about what it housed, some state that it was decorated with paintings of the prophets Abraham and Ishmael (*Isma'il*), a mural of Jesus (*Essa*) and Mary (*Mariam*), and the sacred black stone. It also housed a treasure that consisted of donations from the pilgrims.[1] People of all faiths, including Jews and Christians, visited the Ka'ba and respected it because the concept of a sanctuary or protected place had existed in Jewish and Christian traditions too.

In the Middle East, a person's identity relates to his ancestral background followed back to the originator of the clan. This might have been influenced by the Middle Eastern religions such as the Gospel of Mathew names Jesus with a long list of his antecedents starting from Abraham and David. Ancestors are venerated along with the great saints and imams whose graves are turned into shrines to satisfy the human longing to belong to a collective group, to gather there, weep, pray, venerate and feel safer as part of a community.

At the time of Muhammad's birth, the Ka'ba was a relatively modest structure of stone and clay walls, the height of a man, with a roof made of palm fronds draped with cloth. The Arabs also called it "the Arish," which was the ancient Semitic name for the structure built in the wilderness by the Israelites under Moses as a protected place holding the spirit of God. For God they used the word "al Lah," literally meaning "the high one" like its Hebrew equivalent Elohim or the more ancient Mesopotamian El – the one supreme deity reigning above all lesser tribal gods and totems.[2]

For decades Muhammad's tribe, the Quraysh, had been ruling Mecca and living in relative safety and prosperity because of people's respect for Mecca, donations, and pilgrim-based trade such as selling pilgrim's cloaks (ahram), water and food, fodder for their camels, donkeys and horses, and animals for sacrifices. In the Ka'ba, they stored pilgrims' non-consumable donations such as gold, silver and precious stones. There was a law prohibiting donations earned through usury, exploitation or unfair means, which shows that usury was considered immoral long before Muhammad declared it so.

The Quraysh had spread word that a snake guarded the treasure and, because people were superstitious, none dared to steal the treasure. However, once someone broke into the Ka'ba and stole the treasure. After carrying out a search, the Quraysh found the treasure with a slave of the Banu Maleeh tribe. They amputated the slave's hand though he pleaded that a noble man of the Quraysh had stolen the treasure and he was only guarding it.[3]

The event shows that amputation of hands as a punishment dates to a pre-Muhammadan era, which the Islamists call "the period of ignorance" without realizing that Muhammad went even further and sanctified amputation for theft as part of "God's law."

The Quraysh then decided to raise the walls of the Ka'ba and put a roof on it so that no one could break in. Arabs of all faiths held superstitious beliefs that donations and animal sacrifices at the Ka'ba would save them from sickness, war, and other evils, or would increase their wealth, fertility, and so on. However, Ka'aba was not the only shrine. People offered donations and prayed at other shrines and temples as well for these were closer to their tribal lodgings. When the population of Mecca outgrew the town, and many tribes moved out, they took a stone from the sacred area to honour it. Wherever they settled, they set it up and would walk around it the way they went round the Ka'ba.[4]

It was not possible for people far from Mecca to come to pray at the Ka'ba except for the annual pilgrimage, "hajj," and so they had to have their own consecration stones. Among these, Suva was the totem stone of the Hudhayl tribe and its custodians were the Banu Lehan sub-tribe.[5] Laat was the totem stone of the people of Ta'if. Quraysh had a totemic stone called Hubal, located by a well near Ka'ba, and two more, Asaaf and Na'ila, near the Zamzam spring, and they sacrificed animals beside them. Muhammad's wife A'isha once said, `We always heard that Asaaf and Na'ila were a man and women of Jurham who had copulated in the Sacred Ka'ba and God had transformed them into two stones as a punishment.'[6]

Some Quraysh tribes, the Kinana and al Mudar, venerated Uzz'a, which was located at Nakhla at a mile's distance from Mecca. Manat, another totem stone, was located seven miles from Medina. Like the other stones, it was un-carved and when the Medinian tribes Aus, Khazraj, and Azd travelled to the Ka'ba, they would wear their pilgrim's cloaks (ahram) and shave their heads near it. Upon return from the hajj, they took off their cloaks at the same location. Just as all these tribes jointly venerated the Ka'ba and sacrificed animals and offered donations, the Meccans too respected their temples and offered sacrifices and donations when they passed by them. Generally, the Arabs had mutual respect for faiths, known in modern times as secularism; it was a multi-faith society.

The hajj consisted of showing respect for the Ka'ba, walking around it while reciting prayers, staying in Arafat and Muzdalfa, sacrificing animals, and feeding the pilgrims. People of all faiths were welcomed to attend.

In modern times, only Muslims are allowed to perform hajj though they do it in the same manner as pre-Islamic people did. The only stones now considered sacred are the black stone and those used in the construction of the Ka'ba. Nearly a billion Muslims believe that they are not "idolaters" and that the hajj is purely an Islamic tradition. They believe that the pre-Islamic Arabs worshipped idols and Muhammad converted them to believe in God alone. However, the earliest records show that the Meccan totem stones were not "idols;" no one bowed to them or prayed to them. They acted not as gods but as tribal totems, as a place to gather for sacrifices and prayers to God. Effectively, it was the same as wearing a cross or respecting the black stone, which Muhammad used to kiss and place his head on. People knew that God was separate from these stones and when they went for hajj, they made this clear in their prayers:

> We are present in front of you O God; we are present
> You have no partners except one whom you own (*the idol*)
> You own it and what it owns (*donations*)
> And the idol is not the Lord.[7]

When Muhammad abolished the use of totemic stones, there was no need to mention the idols. Hence, the pre-Islamic hajj prayers were shortened as follows:

> We are present in front of you O God; we are present
> We are present for You Who has no partners.

Many sacred houses competed as income generating businesses

The Quraysh were not the only people who solicited pilgrims. There were many sacred houses all over Arabia and in the neighbouring regions, which competed to attract pilgrims and generate income. For example, there was one sacred house (*bayt al haram*) in Yemen constructed by the Yemeni king Taban, also called Tab'a. Long before Muhammad was born, the Yemeni king Tab'a had come to attack and plunder Medina in revenge for the murder of his son but two Medinian Jewish scholars convinced him to refrain from pillage. As a price to save their town, these Jewish Medinians agreed to help him construct his sacred house in Yemen. Whilst returning from Medina towards Yemen, Tab'a passed by Mecca. Some men of the Banu Hudhayl tribe, who were jealous of the Meccans' income from the Ka'ba, approached him and tried to lure him to attack the Ka'ba by telling him that there was a treasure hidden in it. The king sought advice from the said two Jewish scholars who said, `O king do not attack the Ka'ba because it is a holy place of worship for God.' The Yemeni king prayed there, sacrificed animals, donated a precious covering and a door for the building, and advised its custodians to keep it clean and tidy. On his return to Yemen, the king converted to Judaism and later so did his Yemenite subjects.[8]

It is noteworthy that while the earliest Arab history states that the said Jewish scholars had been instrumental in saving the Ka'ba from plunder, in modern Saudi Arabia, a Jew would hardly dare enter the country – albeit in disguise.

Why Abraha came to attack Mecca

Negus, the Christian king of Abyssinia, was once angry at the disobedience of his governor Abraha. He swore that he would drag Abraha by his forelocks and trample his lands under his feet. In turn, Abraha begged forgiveness and wrote back that he had fulfilled the king's oath by shaving off his head, and would send a pot full of clay from his lands so that the king could trample it under his feet.

Negus forgave Abraha at which Abraha wrote back stating that he was constructing a grand Cathedral to honour the king and to divert the pilgrims from Mecca towards the Cathedral. When the Quraysh heard this, they sent an agent who, finding an opportunity, defecated in the Cathedral to show that it was not a sacred house. The Quraysh did not like anyone trying to diminish their pilgrim-based income.

Abraha found out that the miscreant was an agent of the custodians of the Ka'ba and he swore that he would attack Mecca and demolish the Ka'ba. He gathered an army but the Quraysh too declared *jihad* (war) and sent a group of *jihadis* (warriors) to fight him on his way. Abraha was able to defeat the Arab warriors and arrest their leader, called Zunafar.

On their way to Mecca, Abraha's army passed by the town of Ta'if. The people of Ta'if had always been rivals to Mecca. Their Temple of Laat competed with the Ka'ba in attracting pilgrims and donations and, in turn, the Quraysh used to attack them. Hence, they were pleased to see Abraha's army going to raid Mecca. They honoured Abraha and assigned a man to guide him to Mecca.

In those days, the chief of Mecca was Muhammad's grandfather Abd al Muttalib. Abraha sent his commander to meet Abd al Muttalib with the message that it was not his intention to kill the inhabitants of Mecca but only to destroy the Ka'ba. Abd al Muttalib went to meet Abraha at the latter's request. Abraha treated him with respect and asked if he wanted anything. Abd al Muttalib complained that Abraha's men had taken two hundred of his camels and he wanted them back. Abraha was amazed and said, `You are worried about your camels and not about the House of God whom you worship?' Abd al Muttalib replied, `I own the camels and I am concerned about them. God owns the Ka'ba and He will protect it.'[9]

When Abd al Muttalib had received his camels, he decided that his people should vacate Mecca, and they escaped to the surrounding mountains where one could find as many stones as one wanted. This was a very clever military strategy because when Abraha and his army passed through the difficult mountainous terrain, with Abraha seated on his elephant, they faced a heavy barrage of stones from the mountaintops, which killed most of them.

The Quraysh spread myths that God had sent birds carrying stones in their beaks and paws, which they threw at Abraha's men. These stones had the effect of wounding like arrows and spears; blood and pus poured out of the sores and the men turned into mutilated corpses. Abraha's breast exploded and his heart burst out. Those who survived had to beg in Mecca for food.[10] The Qur'an celebrates this victory as follows:

> Did you not see what your God did
> To the People of the Elephant?
> Did He not lead them to worse humiliation?
> And sent birds who threw stones at them
> Turning them into chewed fodder. (Sura al Feel – *The Elephant*)

The myths augmented the superstitious value and business potential of the Ka'ba. More and more pilgrims poured in with their donations and prayers. With enhanced reverence for the Ka'ba, the Quraysh were safe from banditry as well: Because many bandits were afraid of the curses which the custodians of the Ka'ba could pass on them, they would not attack their trade caravans. The Qur'an tells this as follows:

> The Quraysh are greatly revered
> They are safe in their journeys in autumn and spring
> They should obey the Lord of this House,
> Who gives them food when others are hungry
> And keeps them in peace when others are afraid.
> (Sura al Quraysh)

The verses reflect the socio-economic conditions in which, when people were afraid of famine and hunger, they donated at the Ka'ba, and bandits did not attack the trade caravans of the Quraysh because of the superstitious value of the Ka'ba.

Many Meccans were great merchants and traders. They used to send trade caravans, which were camel trains up to two thousand camels, towards Damascus in spring and towards Yemen in autumn. These carried leather, wool, small amounts of gold and silver extracted in the mountains of Hejaz, and the most profitable of their goods, myrrh and frankincense grown in Yemen, Ethiopia and Somalia. Rich people all over the Middle East used myrrh as a precious perfume while vast amounts of frankincense were burned in both the Byzantine churches and the sacred Zoroastrian fires. Various spices of frankincense, and myrrh in both oil and crystal form could be sold for many times more their original cost after paying tolls, protection money to territorial chiefs, and customs and taxes imposed by the imperial rulers. In this trade, three major Meccan clans played key roles in the cartels and syndicates, depending upon their investment and wealth. These clans were the Banu Umayya (Umayyads), the Banu Makhzum, and the Banu Hashim (Hashimis).

However, travelling in trade caravans was not an easy task. People regularly died in the caravan journeys over hundreds of miles of desert. Other than the scorching sun, its heat magnified by sand, stone, and dust, there were risks of sickness, scorpion sting, snakebite, accidents, bandits, and Bedouin raiders. When Muhammad's father Abdallah was returning from Damascus with a trade caravan, they stopped in Medina and had ten more days to reach Mecca, but he fell ill and died. His great grandfather Hashim, Abd al Muttalib's father, too had died at Gaza during a caravan journey. It was much safer to make money by controlling the businesses in Mecca which profited from the thousands of pilgrims who came to pray at the Ka'ba.

Muhammad grows amidst the Quraysh tribes competing to take charge of the pilgrim business

In the beginning, the Jurham tribe possessed the Ka'ba; then the tribes of Kinana and Khuza'a got possession and expelled Jurham out of Mecca. At that time, the Quraysh, who had migrated from Yemen, lived in scattered settlements and tents, dispersed among their people.

The Khuza'a possessed the Ka'aba and passed it from son to son until Qusayy bin Kilaab, a Quraysh chief, claimed that Quraysh were the noblest offspring of Ishmael, the son of Abraham, and had better claim to possess the Ka'ba. After protracted negotiations and battles, Qusayy defeated the Khuza'a, drove them out of Mecca, and gained possession of the Ka'ba for Quraysh.

Now the population of Quraysh had outgrown their resources, and the income from the Ka'ba was not enough to support all of them. The tribe had begun with their ancestor Fahr whose sons and grandsons led the sub-tribes Ghalib, Ka'ab, Lu'ayy, Kalab, Qusayy, and Hashim, to name a few. Tribal pride forced them to be generous and wasteful when they had plenty. Instead of careful use and equitable distribution, wealth was concentrated among the custodians of the Ka'ba, the moneylenders, traders and merchants. This led to bouts of proud generosity and waste, followed by periods of starvation. In times of famine, many had little more than breadcrumbs to eat.[11] At times, some tribes would loot and plunder the other tribes in and around Mecca.[12] The three prominent Quraysh sub-tribes, Banu Hashim, Banu Makhzum and Banu Umayya, jealously rivalled each other[13] in their bid to control the Ka'ba. Fights among these to seize the pilgrim business and the associated prestige had taken place several times[14] though each side based its claims on its greater piety and the rival's impious conduct.

Tribal wars also took place over the control of water resources, territorial grazing rights, and the authority to levy taxes, protection money, or tolls on those living in or passing through a tribal territory.

Abd al Muttalib had nine sons of whom Abdallah was the youngest. Abdallah died a few months before his son Muhammad was born around 570 CE. Thus, Muhammad and his mother Amina came under the protection of Abd al Muttalib. According to the custom, the infant was sent away with a foster nanny, Halima, to be breast-fed and to live with her family in a rural settlement among the dessert Bedouins, around fifty miles from Mecca.

Readers who are interested in a detailed study of Muhammad's childhood and the contemporary Meccan social and economic life may find Lesley Hazleton's book "The First Muslim" very helpful. About the social conditions of Mecca and, generally, of the world in the 6th century, she states:

> …in the city, any child's chances of survival into adulthood were not good unless he could be sent away to a wet nurse. In fact, to survive infancy at all before the age of modern medicine was itself an achievement. At the height of Rome's power, for instance, only one third of those born in that city made it to their fifth birthday, while records for eighteenth-century London show that well over half of those born were dead by age sixteen. Whether in Paris or Mecca, something as simple as a rotten teeth or an infected cut could kill you. Between disease, malnutrition, street violence, accidents, childbirth, bad water, and spoiled food, not to mention warfare, only ten per cent made it beyond age forty-five. It wasn't until the early twentieth century, when the role of germs became clear and antibiotics were first developed, that life spans began to increase to what we now take for granted… however… infant survival was higher in rural areas than in cities. If the specific reasons weren't understood, the concept of fresh air was.

…Sixth century Mecca was no different. At the height of summer, when daytime temperatures regularly reached well over a hundred degrees Fahrenheit, the air was barely breathable. Fumes from cooking fires were held in by the ring of mountains around the city, and vultures wheeled above the dung heap on the edge of the town, a noxious dump where refuse rotted and fermented, earning it the name "mountain of smoke." Hyenas snuffed and scavenged there by night, and narrow alleys echoed with their howls. With no sewage system or running water, infections spread rapidly. Earlier that same year of Muhammad's birth, there had been one of the localized outbreaks of the smallpox that ravaged the Middle East… Cities were dangerous places for new-borns …[15]

When Muhammad was around three, an event took place that forced Halima to return him to Mecca. Halima reported this event as that Muhammad and his brother (Halima's son) were with the lambs behind the tents when his brother came running and said to us, `Two men clothed in white have seized that Qurayshi brother of mine, thrown him down, opened up his belly, and are stirring it up.' They ran towards him and found him standing up and very angry. They asked him what happened and he reported exactly what his foster brother had told earlier. Halima's husband said, `I am afraid that this child has had a stroke so take him back to his family before the result appears.'

When they took him back to Amina, she asked why they had brought him back when they had been so keen to keep him. Halima said, `God has let him live so far and I have done my duty. I am afraid that ill will befall him so I have brought him back as you wished.'

Halima reported, `Amina asked what had happened and gave me no peace until I told her. When she asked if I feared a demon possessed him, I replied that I did. She retorted that no demon had any power over her son and that when she was pregnant with him, a light went out from her, which illumined the castles of Syria. When he was born, he put his hands on the ground and lifted his head towards the heavens.'

It is not hard to find mothers defending their children with all sorts of exaggerated claims when they perceive that one has disparaged or slighted their children – the mildest example being mothers shouting at schoolteachers for not giving high marks to their children in school tests.

The Meccans were well aware of the miracle stories about the birth of Jesus, and some of them, starting with Amina, concocted very similar stories about the birth of Muhammad. Just as God had sent an angel to Mary to foretell the birth of Jesus, a popular story states that a voice said to Amina, `You are pregnant with the lord of this people and when he is born say, "I put him in the care of the One from the evil of every envier; then call him Muhammad."

In Jesus's story, a star had pointed the three kings to the birthplace of Jesus. Likewise, Muhammad's spin-doctor poet Hassan bin Thabit invented a story about him, stating, `I was a boy of seven or eight when I heard a Jew calling out at the top of his voice from the top of a fort in Yathrib (Medina), `Tonight has risen a star under which Ahmad is to be born.' Ahmad was Muhammad's other name.

Muhammad himself enjoyed the propagation of these miracle stories. Similar to that which Jesus had said, that his father was up in the heavens, he told the following to his companions:

> I am what Abraham my father prayed for and the good news of my brother Jesus. When my mother was carrying me, she saw a light proceeding from her, which showed her the castles of Syria. I was suckled among the Banu Sa'ad bin Bakr (Halima's tribe) and while I was with a brother of mine behind our tents shepherding the lambs, two men in white garments seized me, opened my belly, extracted my heart, and thoroughly cleaned it…

Behind this miracle story was the trivial incident that the two men probably manhandled the child and, not wanting to dwell upon it, the adults quickly euphemised it as stated above – a deflection strategy that was as common in ancient cultures as it is in modern ones.

Contrary to the miracle stories, Amina had a very ordinary end. When Muhammad was six, she travelled to Medina to see her tribal relatives, the Banu Najjar, where she caught a disease and died on her return journey at a place between Medina and Mecca.

Abd al Muttalib took in the orphaned Muhammad and looked after him. When Muhammad was eight, Abd al Muttalib too died and he came to live with his uncle Abu Talib and cousins, Abu

Talib's sons, Ali, Aqeel, Talib, and J'afar, and daughter Fakhita. It is not clear if Fakhita was later called Umm Hani (the mother of Hani) or if Umm Hani was Abu Talib's another daughter. Although Muhammad lived with Abu Talib, his other uncles, Hamza, Abu Lahab and Abbas also cared for him. When Muhammad was born, Abu Lahab had sent his slave woman to breastfeed him until he was sent away with Halima.

Growing up in the company of his grandfather, uncles, and other Quraysh elders, Muhammad observed the awesome power of religion and rituals that forced the superstitious to travel to the various temples from far corners of Arabia and offer donations. As an insider, he observed his elders' negotiating the distribution of the offerings, and jostling for positions of status within the religious hierarchy. He saw how they used religion to their advantage, to obtain power and prestige, and to make money. Subconsciously, he was learning ways of interpreting the religious paraphernalia around him and trying to find his own place in it.

After the death of Abd al Muttalib, the Umayyads and the Banu Makhzum seized control of the Ka'ba and denigrated the Hashimis to lower positions such as arranging water canisters for the pilgrims.[16] Some Hashimis earned enough from their other businesses and belonged to the elite Meccans. Muhammad's uncle Abbas and the new Meccan chief Walid bin Mughira were moneylenders. These thrived on usury.[17] Abu Talib did some trade and had some commercial dealings but he had a large family to support and was poor.[18] Abu Lahab had once stolen a golden statue of a deer from the Ka'ba and sold it to make money[19] but, because he was a Quraysh dignitary, they had not punished him.

Because of Abu Talib's poverty, Muhammad took other people's goats for grazing at a small wage.[20] Then he drove Abu Talib's trade camels to nearby regions. As an adult, he tried to make a living through trade but one cannot start a trade without some capital and young Muhammad had none. His desperation to make some money reflects in one commercial deal with Abdallah bin abi Hamsa: Muhammad reached an appointed place to make a deal and found that Abdallah was not there. He was so desperate that he kept waiting for him for three days and when Abdallah remembered his promise and reached the appointed place, he found that Muhammad was not angry at all.[21]

When Muhammad had gained Abu Talib's trust as his trade apprentice, he requested the hand of Fakhita in marriage but Abu

Talib wanted his daughter to marry someone from the Meccan elite and he quickly married her off to a rich man of the Banu Makhzum.

In those days, among the richest persons in Mecca was Khadija bint Khuyald, Muhammad's distant cousin from the powerful Banu Asad. She was educated, and her cousin Waraqa bin Noufal was reputed to be an expert of both the Hebrew and Greek bibles. Some state that he was Christian while others state that he was a rabbi.[22] From her two previous husbands, Khadija had sons called Harith, Hind,[23] and Abdallah, and a daughter called Zaynab.[24] Khadija had inherited her wealth from her second husband. She met young Muhammad and fell in love with him at first sight.[25]

Many historical events show that, in pre-Muhammadan Arabia, women of higher status had the freedom to choose their husbands. They could also solicit desirable men to make love. For example, a woman who was the sister of Waraqa bin Noufal had once offered a number of camels to Muhammad's father Abdallah, a day before his marriage to Amina, to lure him to make love to her.[26] After marrying Amina and consummating his marriage, Abdallah went to see the woman who had proposed to him, asked her if her offer was still open, and she replied, `The light that was with you yesterday, has left you and I no longer need you.' Another report quotes her words as, `No! When you passed by me yesterday, there was a white blaze between your eyes and when I invited you, you refused me and went to Amina, and she has taken it away.'[27] The Islamists give a spin to this event of plain feminine jealousy, stating that the light the woman had seen was the light of God. Abdallah passed it to Amina and then she conceived Muhammad – the apostle of God.

In the year 625, Khadija hired Muhammad to take her trade caravan to Syria for a fee that was double that she used to pay to others. Three months after he returned from his trip to Syria, she asked him to marry her, to which he agreed.[28] At that time, Muhammad was around twenty-three while Khadija was forty. Because Arab women were often married at the age of twelve or even less, he would be her son's age.

Muhammad's uncle Hamza formally asked on his behalf, and his other uncles and prominent family members attended the wedding. A report states that Khadija had arranged for a feast, plied her father with wine and made him drunk, and then sent for Muhammad and his relatives. Her drunken father did not object to what was going on but later, when he sobered up and found that his rich middle-aged daughter had married a poor young man, he was furious and declared that this wedding was a mismatch because she had married down in wealth and social status. However, because it was her choice, the marriage was accepted. One does not find freedom for women to such an extent in modern Islamic societies.

After his marriage, Muhammad lost interest in Khadija's trade and she relieved him of business duties[29] but kept supporting him morally and financially. She also gave him a slave boy named Zayd bin Haritha[30] and adopted Ali, the son of Abu Talib, to come and live with them. Abu Talib's trade was faltering and he had many children to provide for. He had fostered Muhammad, and so the newlyweds repaid this kindness by adopting his son Ali.

Khadija named their first child Abd al Uzz'a (the slave of the idol Uzz'a) Qasim but he died in infancy. Yet Muhammad kept the title "Abu'l Qasim" (the father of Qasim). Muhammad too had once sacrificed a goat in the name of Uzz'a but later, when he abandoned the idols, he used to argue with Khadija about her bedtime prayers to Laat and Uzz'a. In turn she would say, `Just ignore my prayers and ignore the idols.'[31]

When Muhammad would leave the city to contemplate in the Cave of Hira, Khadija would send him food. He had learned the tradition of solitary meditation, called *tahannut* from the "Ahnaf" – those who followed the "Hanifi" faith (*Deen-a-Hanifi*). The Ahnaf considered this faith as the faith of Abraham, the common father of Jews and Arabs. They avoided sectarianism and divisiveness that was rife in the Middle East and has been rife until today. They did not venerate idols and totem stones and recognized one God whatever its name, El, Elohim, Allah, Allahuma, Yahweh, or Ahura Mazda – the Zoroastrian god of light and wisdom. Still, like the other Meccans, they maintained that Abraham was the founder of Mecca where Hagar had fled and given birth to Ishmael, and then Abraham and Ishmael had built the Ka'ba as the House of God. Generally, people respected them, and they were free to preach and train others.[32]

Among the Ahnaf, other than Khadija's cousin Waraqa bin Noufal, were Muhammad's clansmen, Abdallah bin Jahsh, Uthman bin al Huwayrith, and Zayd bin Amr.[33] According to reports, the first three converted to Christianity while the fourth, Zayd, left for Syria in search of a true religion and met Christian and Jewish leaders. Zayd and Umayya bin abi Asalat, the famous Arab poet and ruler of Ta'if – a town near Mecca – finally resolved on the Hanifi faith. Zayd became a social reformer and used to foster the daughters of those who did not want to keep them.

The famous orators of the time, Qis bin Sa'ada, Qays bin Nashba, and Abuzar Ghifari had abandoned the use of idols and totem stones long before Muhammad did so.

The followers of many religions and creeds lived side by side in Mecca, Medina, and all of Arabia. Even within one tribe, one could find believers and unbelievers of the many faiths and creeds. In Muhammad's tribe, the Quraysh, Waraqa bin Noufal cherished his Bible and the sub-tribe Tamim, as a tribe, were Zoroastrians. The Banu Harith in Najran were Christians. The tribes Rabi'a, Ghassan, Qada'a, Banu Hanif in Yamama, and some of the Banu Ta'iy in Yemen were also Christians. The tribes of Himyar, the Banu Kinana, the Banu Harith bin Ka'ab and the Kinda were Jews.[34]

XXX

Historians state that Khadija was so rich that when the Meccan merchants would send their trade caravans, her share in the goods used to be larger than many. However, seventeen years into her marriage with Muhammad, her wealth dwindled so much that when he was forty, the couple and their children could barely survive. They had their daily rations provided by her relatives. Muhammad sought a share from his well-off tribal relatives but little came from them and this enraged him. He was now afraid of poverty, as his following prayers demonstrate, `God I beseech thee not to turn me back to poverty, humility and low life.'[35]

The verses Muhammad said during this period reveal that he was so unsure about his status and position that he had begun to identify himself with the poor and the orphans shunned by the rich:

Have you seen the man who lies about the due (*deen*)?
The one who pushes the orphan away
And does not offer food to the poor?
Destruction will come to those who ignore their prayers
Who show off but do not lend a petty item of use. (Sura 107)

The Islamists interpret the "due" (*deen*) in these verses to mean "the due on the Day of Judgement." They argue that Muhammad was angry with his relatives not for denying him a share in worldly wealth but denying the Day of Judgement. However, repeatedly one finds in the Qur'an, analogous to Muhammad's behaviour, a juxtaposition of life after death with life in this world. As subsequent events show, Muhammad wanted donations in this world from his followers and promised to recompense in paradise after the Day of Judgement. That is why his uncle Abu Lahab had said, `Muhammad makes many promises but all to be fulfilled after our deaths.'

Khadija and her relatives had provided for Muhammad and his daughters for around seventeen years and he saw it his right to live off other people's provisions. When his wealthy tribal relatives refused to pay for him, rightly or wrongly, he construed it as their denial of the Day of Judgement itself.

The Quraysh claimed that they spent the income from the Ka'ba on religious causes and Muhammad could not take a share unless he had a strong religious claim. It was then that he claimed that he was God's messenger. This is a highly presumptuous and questionable attitude and if one adds to it what Muhammad did later, in terms of his raids and booty taking, the situation becomes highly questionable. Similar behaviour is found among a vast majority of religious preachers, in several countries, who gather donations in the name of God but consume a major portion of these on their own upkeep, often to scandalous levels.

People would not see Muhammad as God's messenger unless he uttered something poetic and wise, and claimed that these were God's messages, but Muhammad hated poetry and poets. In his lengthy solitary meditations, when he realized that he had no other choice and uttered his first verses, he felt so disgusted with himself that he thought of killing himself. But instead of committing suicide, he believed that the Angel Gabriel had come to him with these verses. His state of mind at what happened was reported by Ibn Zubayr and A'isha in his words as follows:

> The angel appeared to me and said, `Recite in the name of thy Lord Who created; created man out of a clot of blood; thy Lord is the most bountiful who taught by word that which man did not know.' I recited and the angel left. I woke up and felt that the words had been engraved on my heart. There was none I

hated more than a poet or a madman; I could not bear to look at poets or madmen yet it seemed to me that I had either become a poet or gone mad. I decided to jump down from the mountain cliff and kill myself. But when I reached the mountain top, I heard a voice from heaven saying, `Muhammad you are the messenger of God.'

Muhammad told this to Khadija and she sought advice from the most senior among the Ahnaf scholars, her cousin Waraqa. Waraqa listened carefully and said that the spirit that had come to Mohammad was the same spirit which had come to Moses, and that he believed that Muhammad would be the prophet of his people.
However, it was too much for Muhammad to bear. Until this time, he had never lied in his life and was known as "the truthful." He felt that he could not carry on producing "messages from God." He lost confidence and got very depressed. His lessons in Biblical prophets, Abraham, Moses, Aaron, David, Jesus and others had taught him that poetic and semi-poetic communication of words of wisdom to people had been the first requirement in every prophet's career. To be part of the "Abrahamic tradition," the ability to communicate in a sublime manner was essential. Once the communication had been established, those prophets who had picked the sword and fought, such as David, had succeeded in their lifetimes. Those who had not done so, such as Jesus, had either been exterminated or side-lined. But Muhammad had faltered at the very first step.
For two years, no "revelation" appeared. Finally, he realized that the process of issuing messages had to continue. His fear that God had abandoned him, because he had not been truthful, is evident from the second "revelation" that appeared around two years after the first:

> By the dawn and by the dusk
> Your Lord has not forsaken you
> And He does not detest you
> The end will be better than the beginning
> Soon your Lord will reward you and make you happy
> Did He not find you an orphan and give you shelter?
> Did He not find you astray and guide you?
> Did He not find you poor and enrich you (*Khadija's wealth*)?

Hence, do not shun the orphan and chide the poor
And keep speaking about His blessings. (Sura 93)

Muhammad invites his Hashimi clan to follow him

After another year, when Muhammad had memorized a number of his poems, called *suras*, he invited his tribesmen to a meal prepared of wheat, mutton, and milk. The surviving sons of Abd al Muttalib, his uncles, came including Abu Lahab, the half-brother of Abu Talib. Abu Lahab, which means "father of flame," had earned his nickname because of his red face and fiery temperament. Some forty men came to the feast and when they had eaten to their contentment, Muhammad recited his suras in a majestic voice. The tribesmen sat entranced. It seemed they were impressed but either the recitation went on for too long or Abu Lahab had some urgency he needed to attend, he stood up angrily and left saying, `Muhammad has cast a spell on you.' As people were leaving, Muhammad asked them to come for the same meal the next day saying that he had an important announcement to make.

The next day Abu Lahab was not present. Muhammad again recited his suras after the meal, and then said, `Sons of Abd al Muttalib, I have brought to you the best of what any Arab has ever brought. God has commanded me to invite you to the best of this world and the hereafter. Which of you will follow me in this matter?' Ali later reported this event as follows:

> They all sat quiet and although I was the youngest and weakest, I said, `I will follow you O' messenger of God.' Muhammad put his hand on my shoulder and said, `He is my representative and successor among you. Listen to him and obey him.' The older men burst into laughter and stood up, saying to Abu Talib, `Muhammad has ordered you to obey your son.'

According to the Arab values whereby sons obey their fathers, Muhammad had turned the situation upside down. The tribal elders found it insulting and arrogant on part of Muhammad to ask them to follow and obey the young, believing that he was a *majnoon* (mad) or possessed by a *jinn* (ghosts or spirits made of fire) but many young Hashimis were impressed and they began to follow him. These were called *mu'umineen,* which means "believers."

Muhammad and his believers (*mu'umineen*) began to pray together in a different way, forehead and palms on the ground and hump in the air. This posture, known as *sajda*, had traditionally been the posture of prisoners made to kiss the feet of the victorious kings and found in the ancient Assyrian murals – captives prostrating in front of the conqueror. Whilst walking in a valley, Abu Talib once saw them praying in in this different way and was amazed. `Nephew! What is this religion that you follow?' he asked, and Muhammad invented a quick reply, `This is the religion of our ancestor Abraham. I invite you to join us.' Abu Talib said, `Nephew, I cannot abandon the ways of our fathers. I cannot adopt this religion but you are free to pray the way you like and follow your faith. As long as I live, I will ensure that no one stops you from it.'[36]

More shrines meant fewer donations for the Quraysh: Muhammad declares it the greatest sin and takes up issue with his tribe

Muhammad declared that if the Quraysh elders would follow him as God's messenger, he would lead them to close all other temples and destroy all other faiths, and, hence, there would be more donations and greater prosperity for the Quraysh. In his greed to capture all of the donations, he uttered the followings verses and left evidence now found in the Qur'an:

> God produces animals and crops in fields
> Some of which people donate in God's name
> And some they keep to donate to their idols,
> Whom they call, "partners of God in donations."
> That which they donate to the idols does not reach God
> And that which belongs to God is donated to the idols
> It is an evil decision these people make. (Sura 6, verse 136)

In order to understand Muhammad's motivation in denouncing the *mushraykeen* (those who allowed shrines, secular, multi-faith), one needs to look at the facts known about his early life. First, he had no father to discipline him but only a grandfather and uncles who did support him but they had other responsibilities too. From around the age of twenty-three, he lived off Khadija's wealth without doing much real work, and so, as usually happens with those who live off other people's money, he believed that others should provide for him. Add to this the lowly position in the control and governance of the Ka'ba to which the Hashimis had been pushed, and one can see why he started his process of subjugating people to his will. He declared that he wanted all to obey God but because he claimed to be God's sole interpreter, and stopped any criticism of his actions through open and secret assassinations (described in the following pages) it may well be that he used the name of God to achieve his own ambitions.

Muhammad began to criticize the idols, temples, and every religion that kept people from bowing to Mecca and bring their donations to its custodians. The question is, did God need these donations or was it just Muhammad who wanted all donations to come to Mecca? Why would God need a house and ask people all over the world to come to visit Him there when it is told that God is present everywhere? If this house was symbolic, then why criticize the use of idols as symbols of God? After all, both the idols and the house were made of stone.

To this day, the Saudis do not allow any grave or temple within their reach that could attract veneration and hence reduce the income generating power of the Ka'ba. Recently, when Iraq was freed from Sadam's regime and it turned out that the Shiite shrines in Iraq attracted as many pilgrims as the Ka'ba did, the Saudi Wahhabis expressed serious concerns. The subsequent bomb blasts at many Shiite shrines cannot be dissociated from these concerns. Later, the Wahhabi Taliban blew up the statues of Buddha in Bamyan, Afghanistan. The Wahhabis have also been bombing the Sufi shrines in Pakistan, killing hundreds. The al Shabab Wahhabis in Somalia too have destroyed many shrines and offended those who sought spiritual solace in these shrines. The spirit of Muhammad is very alive in modern times – even after fourteen centuries.

XXX

Not only a house, the Qur'an states, God once had a she-camel (*naqa-t'llah*) too for whose sake God destroyed a whole tribe. Interpreting the below quoted verses, Islamic scholars state that the Thamood tribe were given God's she-camel and, to take care of it, God appointed an apostle. This sacred she-camel had alternate days reserved to drink water from a well while the tribe had the other day. God's apostle told the Thamood not to drink water when it was the day of the she-camel but the tribe rebelled. Though it was only one man who tied the camel's feet, God destroyed the whole tribe.[37]

> The apostle of God said to the Thamood:
> 'It is God's she-camel, so observe her turn to drink water!'
> But they disobeyed him, and they tied her feet.
> So God destroyed them for their sin
> And levelled their dwellings to the ground.
> And He fears not the consequences of His actions.
> (Sura 91, verse 13-15)

Here the Qur'an actually testifies that God ordered people to revere a she-camel. Islamic scholars do not reflect upon the need for such an order to people who were already short of drinking water and could not idly stand by while a "sacred she-camel" benefitted from it.

As to how modern Muslims unsuspectingly believe in such blasphemous stories, one needs referring to the psychology of religion. There is hardly any logic when it comes to many religious beliefs. The abovementioned case is most likely to be that of some deceitful and arrogant man wanting to collect donations in the name of the "sacred she-camel of God." Likewise, the ruling clique of the Quraysh grew fat on the income of the Ka'ba as the "Sacred House of God" and spread myths, which we now find in the Qur'an.

XXX

Muhammad declared that all should follow him as God's messenger but the well-off chiefs of the Quraysh found no reason to believe in him. Hence, when he began to issue statements such as that the idols were just stone which could not benefit men, some of the Quraysh elders in turn said:

> Muhammad! We see you struggling for a living the way we ordinary humans do. Our idols give us nothing but why does your god not give you some more respect and value than you have now? We live in a town narrowed by mountains and we

are usually short of water: Could you ask your god, who has made you his messenger, to remove these mountains and give us more space? Or bless us with streams and rivers such as we find in Iraq and Syria? If you are the messenger, could you raise our elders from dead? Could you bring back Qusayy bin Kilaab who was our truthful great grandfather? If you do not want to bless us, ask your god to give you something like an angel perhaps who could accompany you to confirm that you are the messenger; or ask your god to give you gardens, palaces, and treasures of gold and silver to save you from standing in the market all day the way we do.[38]

Instead of seeing the point that, in performing miracles, his god was as useless as the idols, Muhammad perverted the argument and tried to win sympathy through his "divine revelations:"

> They say they will not believe in me unless I bring
> Streams of water, palm trees, grapes, gardens and spring
> Or bring God and his angels for chastisement
> Or drop the sky upon them as punishment
> Or bring a house of gold from the heavens
> Or ascend myself to the heavens
> Or bring a book, which they could follow.
> Say, `My God is great but I am human
> And a human messenger you must follow.' (Sura 17, verses: 90-93)

Muhammad used to speak about his arguments against their claims and their arguments against his claims, and his scribes used to memorize and write it down for him. The Qur'an is replete with the narrations of what others said to him, what he said to them, and what he said about them. Some of these verses are as follows:

> They have made gods other than God who create nothing but are created; these have no power over their lives and deaths, their profit and loss, and their resurrection.
> The unbelievers say, `These verses are fabrications in which others have helped him.' Thus they commit atrocities and tell lies.
> They also say, `These are scriptures of previous religions, which he has got written by others who keep reading them to him day and night.'

Tell them, these have been sent by God who knows the secrets of earth and heavens. He is kind and forgiving.

And they say, `What kind of messenger is he who eats and does business in the markets? Why is there no angel with him to warn? Why does God not give him a treasure or a garden to eat from?'

See how they hurl silly metaphors at you and they are not capable of reformation. God is generous and if He had wanted, He would have given me several gardens better than those they speak about; gardens with streams and several palaces.

They think that the Day of Judgment is a lie. For such people, we have prepared a blazing fire. They will hear it roaring in anger from afar.

When they will be tied up and thrown in the tightest corners of hell, they will want to die and it will be said to them, `Do not seek one death today but many deaths.' (Sura 3, verses: 3-14)

Because the Meccans generally believed in freedom of speech and faith, they did not stop Muhammad from preaching and gathering followers. When he criticized their idols and cursed their beliefs, they still allowed him to pray in the Ka'ba.

XXX

There were many reasons for the Quraysh not wanting to follow Muhammad. Firstly, he insulted their dead elders by saying that they were all in hell as unbelievers – though these were his own elders too. Secondly, most of the Quraysh did not want to fight against people of other faiths though Abu Talib tried to persuade them that war was the only means to obtain domination, and said that people did not dare stand up to warriors, insult or humiliate them.[39]

Many Hashimis did support Muhammad when Abu Talib invited them to show tribal loyalty to him. Out of jingoism, these Hashimis called Muhammad, "the Pride of the Proud Hashimis," and taunted the other Quraysh tribes.[40] With their support, Muhammad began to proselytize and gather more followers. His early followers, such as Khabbab, Ammar, Abu Fukayha, Yasaar, and Suhayb were either poor[41] or those who could not hope for a better status in Mecca. For example, Yasaar was a freed slave (*mawaali*) of Safwan bin Umayya. When Muhammad would take these men to the Ka'ba, the well-off Meccans used to jeer at them and say to one another, 'Are these the men whom God has chosen to bless instead of us? If what Muhammad has brought were a good thing, these fellows would not have been the first to get it, and God would not have put them before us.'[42] Muhammad heard about this and issued the following verses:

> Thus We (*God*) tempt some so that they may say,
> 'Are these the men whom God has favoured among us?'
> Does not God know best who of his men is grateful?
> (Sura 6, verse 52)
> Apostles have been ridiculed before you
> And those who ridiculed were overpowered
> By that which they derided.   (Sura 6, verse 10)

Objections to Muhammad's claims would infuriate him and, as the later events showed, he used to dream of torturing those who criticized him. He was particularly vengeful against the rich and in many verses warned them:

> Woe to every slandering backbiter
> Who stores wealth and keeps counting it
> He thinks his wealth will last forever
> No! He will be thrown into a devouring fire
> And what do you think it is?
> It is a fire, kindled by God, which mounts over the hearts
> It shall be like a vault over them in columns. (Sura 104)

In those days of animosity between the rich and the poor, a poet named Abu Qays had warned the Quraysh:

> Gangs of needy and vengeful people are stalking your homes.[43]

As the later events showed, Muhammad had plans to use the poor and vengeful people to attack the rich. Hence, he began to sit with them and relate to their feelings of deprivation with such of his verses as follows, also showing his own grief at being denied his inheritance:

> As for man, when his Lord gives him honour and gifts,
> He boasts, 'My Lord has honoured me.'

But when He restricts his subsistence,
In despair he says, `My Lord has humiliated me!'
No! You do not honour the orphans!
And you do not encourage one another to feed the poor!
And you devour all the inheritance with greed,
And you love wealth excessively!
No! When the earth will be pounded to powder,
And your Lord will come with His angels, rank upon rank,
And hell, that day, will be brought closer,
On that day man will remember,
But how will that remembrance profit him? (Sura 89, verses 14-23)

Truly, man is ungrateful to his Lord;
And to that he testifies (*by his deeds*);
And he is extremist in his love of wealth.
Does he not know, when the graves will spill out their contents,
And that which is hidden in chests will be exposed,
That their Lord will know them well on that day?
(Sura 89, verses 6-11)

To reply to the taunt that he had no son, Muhammad issued many verses like these; "The life of this world is a temporary competition in obtaining wealth and sons" (57:20); "Righteous deeds, not wealth or sons will bring you closer to God" (34:37), and the following sura:

We (*God*) have granted to you the fountain of abundance
Therefore, praise your Lord and sacrifice
Those who insult you will have no future (Sura 108)

However, naively, he admitted that having daughters in place of sons was unfair:

Have you considered Laat, Uzz'a, and the third Manat?
(*Known as the daughters of God*)
What! For you sons, and for Him (*God*), daughters?
Such would be indeed a most unfair distribution!
(Sura 53, verses 19-22)

During the seventeen or so years Khadija had kept Muhammad at her expense and let him pursue religious education, he had been regularly attending the lectures of the famous Christian orator Qis bin Sa'ada, and often sat at Marwa with a young Christian named Jabr who was a slave of the Banu Hadrami. Jabr remembered large sections of the *Injeel*, the local Bible, by heart and would recite these to those who came to see him. Muhammad liked those ideas of the Bible that favoured the poor, such as "Blessed are the poor for they shall inherit the earth," in the Gospel of Matthew, and made his own verses such as the following:

> We (*God*) wished to be gracious to those who were oppressed in the land, to make them leaders and heirs.   (Sura 28, verse 5)

> The bounty of God and His blessings are better than any wealth they hoard.   (Sura 10, verse 58)

He also quoted biblical stories, albeit with some distortions, in his Qur'anic suras, such as the stories of Mary (*Maryam*), Joseph (*Youssef*), Jonah (*Younas*), Abraham (*Ibrahim*), the Israelites (*Bani Israel*), and Noah (*Nuh*). Some Meccan nobles noted this and said, `The one who teaches Muhammad most of what he brings is Jabr, the Christian slave of the Banu Hadrami.' Muhammad heard this and, in his following verses, implicitly implied that he had been translating parts of the biblical scriptures and presenting them as God's messages sent to him:

> We are well aware that the unbelievers say, `A man teaches him.'
> The one they point to actually speaks in the Ajmi language
> But this (*Muhammad's*) language is plain Arabic.
>   (Sura 16, verse 103)

The result of Muhammad's Christian education was evident: When he recited to the Christians, he would selectively recite verses to suit their inclination. He mellowed the hearts of the Christian pilgrims from Najran by reciting such verses and many wept with emotion.[44] Muhammad mentioned this in his verses:

> Those to whom We (*God*) sent the book before you (*Muhammad*)
> They believe in it. And when our verses are read to them

> They say they believe in them; it is the truth sent by God
> And we are already believers   (Sura 28, verse 53)

> The closest friends of the believers are among those
> Who say, 'We are Christians'
> This is because there are priests and monks among them
> And because they are not proud.
> When they listen to the messenger's revelations
> You see their eyes overflowing with tears.
> Because they recognize the truth, they say, 'Our Lord! We believe.
> So write us among those who testify.'   (Sura 5, verses 82-83)

When these Christians were leaving after their meeting with Muhammad, a number of Quraysh nobles intercepted them and said, 'God, what a wretched group you are! Your people at home sent you to bring information about this fellow, and as soon as you sat with him, you renounced your religion and believed in what he said. We do not know a more naïve and stupid group than you.'

They answered, 'Peace be upon you, we will not engage in foolish controversy with you. We have our faith and you have yours.' Muhammad found out about this too and added it to his verses:

> And when they hear nonsense, they stay away from it
> And say, 'We have our deeds and you have your deeds
> Peace be upon you. We do not argue with the ignorant.
>   (Sura 28, verse 55)

XXX

Tribal affiliations have always played a major role in the Arab political decision-making. This is still true of much of modern Arabia. Even whilst deciding which prophet to follow, the Arabs used to evaluate the tribal links of one or the other prophet. This is shown in statements, such as, one follower of Musaylima (described later) had said, 'I know that Musaylima is a fake prophet but the liar of the Rabi'a tribe is better than the honest of the Mudhir tribe.' Likewise, a Ghatfan chief once said in support of another prophet named Taliha, 'By God I prefer to follow a prophet from my allied tribes than to follow one from the Quraysh.' Accordingly, the Umayyad and the Banu Makhzum saw Muhammad's claim of being the messenger as a Hashimi conspiracy to seize control of the pilgrim business.

In those days, the chief of the Makhzum tribe was Walid bin Mughira whose nephew, Abu'l Hakam bin Hisham, held a high position among the custodians of the Ka'ba.[45] During their childhood, Muhammad had beaten him up, giving him a permanent wound mark on his leg.[46] When Abu'l Hakam barred a slave from following Muhammad, he vented out his anger against his childhood rival as follows:

> Have you seen him who forbids a slave from praying?
> Have you considered if he was on the right path?
> Was he ordering to be pious or rejecting and turning away?
> Does he not know that God does see?
> If he will not desist, we shall drag him by his forelocks;
> The wrongful liar's forelocks.   (Sura 96, verses 9-16)

"Drag one by one's forelocks" was a traditional Arab pledge, which meant, "to severely humiliate." Muhammad also changed his name Abu'l Hakam (meaning "father of wisdom") to a derogatory Abu Jahl (meaning "father of ignorance"). The name was to symbolize him forever and now Islamic textbooks name Abu'l Hakam as Abu Jahl and curse him as the enemy of Islam. His original name is not used. However, evidence from the earliest Arab books shows that Abu'l Hakam was not only tolerant but also scared of Muhammad.[47] The Meccans knew this well and therefore, once, when he refused to pay to one of his creditors, some Meccans told the creditor to seek Muhammad's help. When Muhammad knocked at his door with the creditor by his side, Abu'l Hakam immediately made the payment.[48]

A man named Nadr bin al Harith knew many Persian fables such as the stories of Rustam, Isfandyar and the kings of Persia. He said, `Muhammad cannot tell a better story that I; he tells only old fables which he has copied as I have.' Muhammad heard about this and he issued the following verses:

> The unbelievers say that these are fabricated tales
> And others have helped him (*in copying them*)
> They have grossly transgressed
> And they say, `These are ancient fables which he has copied

And these are read to him morning and evening' (*to memorize*)
Tell them that God has sent these
And he knows the secrets of heaven and earth
(Sura 25, verses 4-6)

When our verses are read to them, they say,
`We have heard it all, and we can utter similar verses if we want
These are nothing but what was told by earlier people.'
(Sura 8, verse 31)

Woe to those who cheat in measuring (*what they sell*)
They obtain it (*commodities*) in full measure
But they give it in lesser measures
Do they not fear the day of resurrection
When the unbelievers will face punishment?
When our verses are read to them
They say, "These are fables of the ancient people"
Their deeds have rusted their hearts. (Sura 83, verses 1-14)

For those who found faults with his verses, Muhammad said:

Woe to every sinful liar
When he hears God's verses, he struts in pride
As if he heard nothing
Give him the news of a painful punishment
And when he understands something in our verses
He makes fun of it
For these will be a grievous punishment in hell.
(Sura 45, verses 7-10)

One day Muhammad sat with Walid bin Mughira in the mosque, and Nadr bin al Harith came with some other Meccan elders and sat in the assembly. Muhammad spoke, Nadr interrupted him, but Muhammad kept speaking and silenced him. Then he read to them:

Surely, you and those to whom you pray (*idols*) other than God are the fuel of hell. You will go there. If these had been gods, they would not have come to it, but you all will be in hell forever. There will by wailing and crying but they will not be able to hear.

(Sura 21, verse 98-100)

Then Muhammad left and Abdallah bin al Ziba'ra al Sahmi came and sat down. Walid said to him, `By God Nadr could not stand up to Abdul Muttalib's grandson just now as he alleged that we and our gods are fuel for hell.'

Abdallah said, `If I was here I would have refuted him. Ask Muhammad "Is everything which is worshipped besides Allah in hell with those who worship it?" We worship the angels; the Jews worship Ezra; and the Christians worship Jesus Son of Mary. Will all these be in hell?' Abdallah's point was that God could not throw all the Christians, Jews, and almost all other people on earth in hell. Walid and the others in the assembly agreed that Muhammad was making impossible claims, and they thought that Abdallah had argued convincingly. Men told Muhammad about this argument and he changed his stance by stating that while Christians and Jews of the past would be forgiven, in future they would have to obey him:

Those who have received kindness from God in the past
Will be removed far from hell and will not hear its sound.
(Sura 21, verse 101-102)

In other words, Jesus and Ezra and those rabbis and monks who had lived in obedience to God, would be kept far from hell. He added that Jesus and all the other prophets were "God's honoured slaves:"

And they say the Merciful (*God*) has begotten a son,
No, they are but honoured slaves,
They do not speak before He speaks,
And they carry out His commands
And any of them who says, I am God as well as He,
We (*God*) shall repay him in hell
Thus do We punish the sinful ones. (Sura 21, verses 26-30)

The Meccans saw the Christians' worship of Jesus as a justification for keeping many faiths. Muhammad replied to it as follows:

> The example of Mary's son pleases your people
> And they say, `Is he better or those to whom we pray?'
> They just want to dispute for they are a belligerent nation
> Jesus was nothing but a slave to whom We (*God*) showed favour
> And made him an example to the Israelites
> If We had wished We could have made you angels
> To act as vice-regents in the earth
> In (*the life of*) Jesus there is knowledge of the (*last*) hour
> So doubt not about it but obey me. (Sura 43, verses 57-61)

Al Akhnas bin Shariq was a respected leader of the Thaqif. People listened to him respectfully but because he criticized Muhammad, the latter issued the following insulting verses about him:

> Do not follow every feeble oath-taker,
> Mean, slanderer, backbiter
> He obstructs virtue and encourages debauchery
> He struts in pride though born of adultery (*zanim*)
> Boasting of his wealth and sons
> When our verses are read to him, he spurns
> Saying that these are ancient people's scriptures
> We shall brand with smouldering embers
> His nose – resembling an elephant's trunk. (Sura 68, verses 10-16)

Ubayy bin Khalf took to Muhammad an old crumbling bone and said, `Muhammad, do you allege that God can revivify this after it has decayed?' Then he crumbled it in his hand and blew the pieces in Muhammad's face. Muhammad answered, `Yes, I do say that. God will raise it and raise you after you have become like this. Then God will throw you in hell.' Then he issued the following verses about this argument:[49]

> Does man not know that We (*God*) created him from sperm
> Then man became impetuous and petulant
> He (*Ubayy*) gave us a parable and forgot how he was conceived

Saying, 'Who will revivify bones which are rotten?'
Say, 'He who gave them life in the first place will revivify them.'
He knows all about creation. (Sura 36, verses 77-79)

Walid bin Mughira said, 'If God was to send down revelations, He would not have preferred Muhammad over me, for I am the greatest chief of Quraysh, or Abu Mas'ud Amr bin Umayr, the chief of Thaqif, we two being the great ones of Ta'if and Mecca.' Muhammad was angry with Walid[50] and he expressed his anger in many verses including the following where, in his customary fashion, the narrator switches between Muhammad and God:

Leave me (*God*) to deal with him, whom I alone created,
And granted to him lots of wealth,
And sons to be by his side, and a comfortable life,
Yet he is greedy and wants me (*God*) to give him more.
No. He rejects my verses
On him, I shall impose a fearful doom.
He reflected upon (*the verses*) and he evaluated them
May he be killed for how (*little*) he valued them
Then killed again for how (*little*) he valued
He looked askance, frowned, and scowled
Then he turned back, sneered, and said,
'This is nothing but fables copied from the old;
These are human fabrication.'
I (*God*) shall throw him in hellfire.
Do you know what hellfire is?
It leaves nothing, spares nothing, and scorches people's skin.
Nineteen angels supervise it. (Sura 74, verses 11-30)

Muhammad sent one of his followers to recite these verses to the Quraysh elders. After listening, Abu Jahl said, 'These verses state that there will be nineteen angels to burn us in hell but we, the unbelievers, number into thousands; surely we can overpower these nineteen supervisors in hell.'[51]

Muhammad replied to this in the next verses by explaining that he had given the number of angels only to test the unbelievers; the verses strengthen the faith of the believers while those who disbelieve would ask, 'What does God mean by this?' In other words, if one asked for explanation, one was surely an unbeliever. And he added, 'This is the way by which God guides and misguides people according to His choice. No one but God knows the exact number of His troops.' Thus, Muhammad not only gave a false figure "nineteen" and then denied it, but also insulted God by saying the He practised favouritism and discrimination.

Obviously, people did not like to hear that God and his angels were sadistic tormentors. When they would turn away from listening to Muhammad, he would issue yet more verses:

Why do they turn away from my warnings?
And run like asses fleeing in fear of a charging lion.
(Sura 74, verses 49-51)

XXX

The evidence showing that Muhammad had borrowed many of his religious concepts from the contemporary Arab poetry and the Hanifi faith comes from a comparison of these with the poetry of Zayd bin Amr. Zayd's poetry was very popular in Arabia and it contains many themes that later appeared in the Qur'an, such as the following:

- Recommendation to worship God alone;
- Not making partners or associates to God;
- Rejecting the idols;
- Praying to receive God's blessings;
- References to angels, Moses, Abraham, Aaron, Jonah and the Pharaohs;
- Seeking examples in the destruction of earlier nations;
- Calling God the most Merciful and Forgiving;
- Seeking to be pious;
- The pious will go to paradise while unbelievers will burn in hell after humiliation in this world;
- Warnings to people to save themselves from destruction;
- Seeking examples of God's existence in the creation of the earth, sky, sun and moon, the growth of plants from seeds, etc.[52]

It is not hard to see that the nobler themes of the Qur'an resemble, in both content and form, those found in pre-Muhammadan Arab poetry.

As said earlier, Zayd had migrated to Syria. He heard from merchants that Muhammad had declared himself God's messenger, and when he heard some of his verses, he realized that these were not different from his poems. He started his journey back to Mecca to meet Muhammad but when he had just a few days left to reach Mecca, bandits killed him.

In addition, a comparison of the poetry of Qis bin Sa'ada and Umayya bin abi Asalat with many Qur'anic themes and verses also shows a remarkable similarity between them. Muhammad was greatly impressed with Qis bin Sa'ada's oratory and he copied his style of saying, *Amma ba'd* (meaning, "About what comes after this") in sermons.[53] Many scholars have shown that Muhammad's earliest short poems (*Suras*), now present in the Qur'an, follow Qis bin Sa'ada's literary style. Similarly, parts of the poetry of Umayya bin abi Asalat resemble those found in the Qur'an.[54]

Umayya bin abi Asalat, the great poet, was a tribal chief of Ta'if, a town near Mecca. His cousin Utaba was the Umayyad chief of Mecca. Because Muhammad's men later murdered Utaba, Umayya was so grieved that even after Muhammad's conquest of Mecca he refused to believe that Muhammad was God's messenger. He could recognize that Muhammad was imitating his poetry in his Qur'anic verses.

The Arabs were fond of scholars, storytelling and folklore. At night, they would gather and listen keenly to Christian, Jewish, and other scholars, storytellers and poets, at times for the whole night. As for around seventeen years, from the age of twenty-three to forty, Muhammad lived off the property and resources of his older wife Khadija, he had enough time to learn from these narrations and remember them in his own words. In a moment of honesty, he admitted that many of his verses were present in older scriptures:

> Verily this is a revelation from the Lord of the Worlds:
> The Faithful Spirit has descended with it upon your heart
> So that you may be a warner, in plain Arabic speech
> And most surely the same is in the scriptures of the ancients.
> (Sura 26, verses 192-196)

Muhammad also admitted that not all that he said was correct:

> He (*God*) it is Who has revealed the Book to you
> Some verses in here are doubtless

These are the "mother of the Book";
Others are doubtful (*mutashabihatun*).   (Sura 3, verse 7)

The question arises, if Muhammad's verses were from God, Who by definition is perfect, how He could possibly send, "doubtful verses?" Using a devious argument, Muhammad implied that the "doubtful verse" were sent so that the unbelievers could use them to reject faith in God:

Those in whose hearts is perversity
Follow the doubtful in these verses
They seek to create trouble; they seek their logic
But no one knows their logic except Allah. (Sura 3, verse 7)

When Muhammad pestered people with his warnings of horrible punishments, some would challenge him to bring forth those punishments. Because he was unable to do so, he would cleverly state that God had deferred the punishments:

And then they challenged us and said,
`O God! If it is right of you, then rain down stones on us
Or send on us a gruesome punishment!'
But God will not punish them
While you (*Muhammad*) are among them
Nor will He punish them while they may seek forgiveness.
(Sura 8, verses 32-33)

He wanted the Hashimis to take control of the Ka'ba under his leadership, but the Umayyads and Banu Makhzum would not allow this. The following Qur'anic verses reflect this:

Why should God not punish them
When they keep us from taking the Ka'ba?
Though they are not fit to be its custodians
Only the truly pious can be the custodians
But most of them do not understand
Their prayers around the Ka'ba is clapping and whistling
Now taste the gruesome punishment for your rejection.
(Sura 8, verses 34-35)

XXX

Many of Muhammad's revelations presented the ancestors of the Quraysh as belonging to the age of jahiliya (ignorance) for which they would be burned and tortured in hell. There was no pardon for *mushraykeen* (secular/multi-faith people), and because the dead could not return to life and accept Muhammad as their saviour, the ancestors of Quraysh, Muhammad's own ancestors, were doomed.

Abu'l Hakam took a delegation of the Banu Makhzum to meet Abu Talib. He said to Abu Talib, `By God, we can no longer bear this vilification of our fathers and ancestors, making fun of our values and regular insults to what we hold sacred. Stop Muhammad from condemning our ancestors or let us stop him. Because you are not his follower, we believe you are one of us so let us stop him if you cannot.'

Abu Talib knew that a non-Hashimi would not hurt Muhammad because that would mean a declaration of war on the Hashimi clan. Without Abu Talib's permission, no one could attack a Hashimi and so he ignored Abu'l Hakam's heated talk, telling him that he would speak with his nephew.

When Abu'l Hakam left, Abu Talib pleaded with Muhammad, asking him to moderate his tone against the "unbelievers." Muhammad found the occasion right to emotionally blackmail his old and frail uncle, and burst into tears. `By God,' he said whilst crying, `if they put the sun in my right hand and the moon in the left, I will not abandon this path even if I die in the course of it.' In traditional terms, it meant, `Go on Uncle, expel me from the clan and get me killed.'

Abu Talib too began to cry and stopped Muhammad from leaving the house, `Come back nephew. Say whatever you want. By God I will always protect you.'

Another report suggests that, afterwards, Abu Sufyan led the Umayyad delegation, which met Abu Talib and offered him to adopt their strongest and brightest young man named Umara as his son, in exchange for Muhammad. Abu Talib was outraged and he replied, `What an evil scheme; you want me to feed and raise your son so that you could kill my nephew? By God this will never happen.' However, this event seems highly unlikely because, later in the battle of Uhud, Abu Sufyan spared Muhammad's life and Muhammad seldom said anything against him though he cursed Abu'l Hakam and Abu Lahab; Much later, Muhammad even married Abu Sufyan's daughter, Umm Habiba.

Abu Talib called upon the Hashimis and his brothers to support Muhammad and they all agreed, except Abu Lahab.

When they saw that Muhammad's followers were increasing and multiplying, a number of leading men of every clan of Quraysh, such as Utaba bin Rabi'a, his brother Shayba, Abu Sufyan, Abu'l Bakhtri, Walid bin Mughira, al Aas bin Wa'il, Umayya bin Khalf and Abu'l Hakam spoke directly to him. They asked him to stop insulting tribal totem stones, stop saying that the tribal ancestors were hell bound unbelievers, and they would give him whatever he wanted, `If you want money, we will gather it for you. If you want honour, we will make you our chief. And if you are under the spell of some ghost or jinn, which comes to see you, we will find the best hakim (quack) and get you cured.' Muhammad replied that he had no such intentions because God had appointed him and commanded him to be an announcer and a warner. They could either accept this or wait for God's judgement, and he snubbed them with verses such as follows:

> When you recite the Qur'an, We (*God*) put an invisible veil between you and those who do not believe in the hereafter. And We cover their hearts lest they should understand the Qur'an, and We instill deafness into their ears. When you praise your Lord only, they turn their backs and flee.
> (Sura 17, verses 45-46)

It was not difficult to see why people with common sense fled when they heard Muhammad's Qur'an. There were serious problems with its verses. For example, Surah 15, verses 57-74, while telling the story of how God decimated the nation of Prophet Lot, end up in a serious blunder as follows:

When Allah sent angels as his envoys to destroy the people of Prophet Lot, they first met Abraham. Abraham said to them, `Why have you come O envoys?' The angels said, `We have been sent to destroy this nation of sinners. We will save the family of Lot except his wife who will be among those left behind.' The wife would be killed because she too participated in homosexual acts.

Then the angels went to Prophet Lot and said to him, `We have brought to you that which is inevitable. You must travel by night with your family members and tell them not to look back. And we are telling you that those left behind will be dead by the morning.'

The angels then appeared as pretty boys whom Lot's people found very attractive, and they came running with joy to molest them. Lot tried to stop his people and said, as the Qur'an states:

> Lot said, `These are my guests.
> Don't disgrace me; fear Allah, and do not shame me.
> If you must do this act (*sodomy*), here are my daughters.'
> But those people wandered to and fro, wild with intoxication
> And the devastation came upon them before morning,
> And We (God) turned the towns upside down,
> And rained down on them brimstones hard as baked clay.
> (Sura 15, 68-74)

People with common sense would find it hard to understand how Prophet Lot could offer his daughters to those alleged rapists to stop them from raping the angels. A third of the Qur'an consists of many of the Jewish and Christian biblical narratives but these older scriptures tell these tales rather differently and when Jews and Christians, whom Muhammad called "people of the book," would point at errors in Muhammad's verses, he would accuse them of what he was doing himself:

> O people of the book, why do you mix truth with untruth, and hide the truth that you know? (Sura 3, verse 71)

The Qur'an is so full of repetitions of curses for the unbelievers, and glad tidings for the believers that if all these appeared only once, it would not leave too much to read. The theme of God "covering the hearts of the unbelievers with a veil," and Muhammad trying to remove the curtain (i.e. against God's will) appears again as follows:

> We send the apostles only to give glad tidings and warnings: But the unbelievers dispute with vain argument to weaken the truth, and they make fun of our verses and warnings. And who is crueler than one who hears the verses of the Lord, but turns away... Surely We have veiled their hearts lest they should understand, and deafened their ears. If you will call them to guidance, even then they will not accept it. (Sura 18, verses 56-57)

The naïve among Muhammad's followers would ask why God did not punish the unbelievers and Muhammad would reply that God sent punishment only at appointed times – neither before nor after:

> If He were to punish them for their deeds, then surely He would have hastened their punishment: but they have their appointed time, beyond which they will find no refuge.
> We destroyed populations when they committed iniquities but we fixed a time for their destruction. (Sura 18, verses 58-59)

Then the critics asked why God sent verses in bits and pieces; why did He not send the entire Qur'an all at once? Muhammad replied that he would ask God and, after a few days, replied as follows:

> We have sent the Qur'an bit by bit
> So that you could recite it to people
> In parts and gradually　　　　(Sura 17, verse 106)

Some followers of Muhammad have left oral records, which contradict each other; for example, one of them reports that Abdallah bin Masud wanted to recite the Qur'an in the Ka'ba. The believers warned him that because of his low social background, the Quraysh would beat him up, and it would be safe if upper class men were to recite. However, Abdallah went to the Ka'ba and very loudly recited Qur'anic verses for which the Quraysh did beat him up. Conversely, another believer reports that Abu Sufyan, Abu Jahl, and al Akhnas bin Shariq were so keen to listen to the Qur'an that they used to hide outside Muhammad's house and listen to him loudly practicing his recitations all night. Muhammad used to practice in order to decide if he should deliver his sermons loudly or in lower voice and he mentioned this as follows:

> Recite neither too loud nor very quiet
> Find a way between these two.　(Sura 17, verse 110)

After listening to Muhammad for three consecutive nights, al Akhnas asked Abu Sufyan what his opinion was. Abu Sufyan said, 'Parts of what I heard, I already know and I know their meaning but there were other parts that I did not understand.' al Akhnas replied, `I feel exactly the same.' Then he went to see Abu Jahl and asked him the same. Abu Jahl said:

> What did I hear! The Hashimis and we have always been rivals for status and prestige. When they are generous and hospitable to people, we try to excel. When they pay large sums in blood money, we do the same. Our situation is like two horses running at the same speed. We are in tough tribal competition and now they claim they have a prophet who receives revelations from the heavens. Now we will have to do the same but when shall we attain something like that? By God, we will never believe that he is right and we will not accept a subservient position to a Hashimi.[55]

Utaba bin Rabi'a once listened to Muhammad's verses respectfully and carefully. He then went to the other Quraysh leaders and said to them, `Take my advice and do as I do. Leave this man alone for, I swear by God, the words that I have heard will be blazed abroad. If other Arabs kill him, they will have rid you of him; if he wins them over, his sovereignty will be your sovereignty, his power your power and you will be prosperous through him.'

They said, `He has bewitched you with his tongue,' and he replied, `I have given you my opinion, you do what you think fit.'

Time would show how correct Utaba was in his prediction; after the final truce between Muhammad and the Quraysh, Muhammad would bring his Ansar jihadis from Medina and help the Quraysh to rule Arabia for many centuries to come. However, in his early days of apostolate in Mecca, Muhammad had no military might and little to show besides his semi-poetic verses.

Once, Muhammad had a long discussion with the Meccan elders. After the discussion was over, Abdallah bin abu Umayya walked with him and said, `By God I will never believe in you until you get on a ladder, reach the sky and bring down four angels with you to testify that you are telling the truth. And by God, even if you do that, I do not think I should believe you.'

Abu Jahl did even worse. When Muhammad left the meeting, he swore to the clan leaders that the next day he would bring a very heavy stone and when Muhammad would prostrate in his prayers, he would crush his skull with it. `Betray me or defend me,' he said, `let the Hashimis do what they like afterwards.' The others said that they would never betray him and that he could carry on with his project. The next day he brought a heavy stone and as Muhammad prayed facing Syria and the clan leaders waited for Abu Jahl to carry out his promise, Abu Jahl walked towards Muhammad, then returned and dropped the stone. When asked what had happened, he said, `When I went near him, I saw a ferocious camel in my way baring its teeth in fury as if it would eat me.'

Someone told this to Muhammad and he said, `That was Gabriel. If Abu Jahl had come near me, Gabriel would have seized him.'

The myth of the general persecution of Muhammad and his followers in secular Mecca

The Islamists repeatedly slander the *mushraykeen* (secular/multi-faith people) for "persecuting Muhammad and his followers." However, when one looks at the events of the said persecution, one finds that it was hardly the persecution that justified such violence as Muhammad was to perpetrate. On the contrary, one finds numerous examples of how the Meccans supported and fed Muhammad and his converts because of the Arabian tribal ethics of hospitality despite difference of faith. For example, the non-believer Ibn al Dughunna supported the believer Abu Bakr, and the non-believer chief of Mecca Walid bin Mughira supported the believer Uthman bin Mad'un.[56]

In order to attract people to his faith, Abu Bakr made a mosque by the door of his house among the Banu Jumah where he starting praying and reading the Qur'an with emotions and tears in his eyes. Youths, slaves and women used to stand by him astonished at his demeanour. Some men of Quraysh went to Ibn al Dughunna saying, `Have you given this fellow protection so that he could create problems for us? Lo, he prays and reads what Muhammad has produced, and his heart becomes soft and he weeps. And he has a striking appearance so that we fear he may seduce our youths and women and weak ones. Go to him and tell him to go to his own house and do what he likes there but do not upset us.'

Ibn al Dughunna went to Abu Bakr and said, `I did not give you protection so that you might hurt your people. They dislike the place you have chosen and suffer hurt therefrom, so do it in your house where you can do what you like.' Abu Bakr refused to budge and renounced his protection. Ibn al Dughunna told the Quraysh that Abu Bakr was no longer under his protection.

Abu Bakr was going to the Ka'ba and one of the loutish fellows of Quraysh threw dust on his head. Either Walid bin Mughira or al Aas bin Wa'il passed him and he said, `Do you see what this lout has done to me?' He replied, `You have done it to yourself (by renouncing Ibn Dughunna's protection)!'

In order to improve their lives, many Meccans used to migrate to other countries. Historically, this used to happen long before Muhammad launched his campaign. However, the Islamists falsely assert that the migrations during Muhammad's life were a result of the "persecution of Muslims," thus ignoring the facts that most migrants were unbelievers, many returned as well, and even more people migrated when Muhammad established his rule over Mecca and Medina. By these false claims, the Islamists actually want to turn the attention of the students of history from the well-documented persecution of non-Muslims, particularly the Jews, after the believers' takeover of Mecca and Medina, which led to the migration of tens of thousands out of central Arabia. During the caliphate (*Khilafa*) rule, after the death of Muhammad, tens of thousands migrated out of Mecca and Medina because of the tribal bloodshed between the Umayyads, Abbasids, Ansar, and Alawis.

The fact is that concerned relatives protected and tried their best to stop the believers from leaving Mecca;[57] when a member of a certain tribe would convert, his other tribesmen still protected him. Tribal protection was available to fellow tribesmen regardless of their faith. For example, Abu Jahl once asked an unbeliever to allow his tribe, the Makhzum, to teach a lesson to the latter's believer younger brother. The elder brother replied, `Do teach him a lesson but if you killed him, I swear by God, I will kill the noblest of you to the last man.' Abu Jahl went away. To add insult to injury, one of his own relatives provided a house to the believers to gather, and they started having meetings right next to his house. Muhammad's uncle Hamza, a famed warrior, also joined the community of believers. Because of his fearsome reputation as the strongest and most irritable man of the Quraysh, it was hard for one to persecute a believer. Abu Jahl once criticized Muhammad, speaking spitefully of his religion and trying to bring him into disrepute. A woman told Hamza how Abu Jahl had insulted Muhammad and that the latter had not said a word. Filled with rage, Hamza started running towards the mosque where Abu Jahl sat among his tribesmen. He went up to him, stood over him, lifted up his bow and struck him a violent blow with it, saying, `Will you insult him when I follow his religion and say what he says? Hit me back if you dare.' Some of the Banu Makhzum got up to support Abu Jahl but he said, `Let Hamza alone for, by God, I insulted his nephew deeply.'

Another violent and ill-tempered man who, like Hamza, loved to get drunk on potent date wine was Abu Jahl's nephew Umar. His father, al Khitaab, was the stepbrother of the previously mentioned Zayd bin Amr who had criticized the use of idols, went to live in Syria and died at the hands of bandits on his return journey. About Umar's obstinacy, someone had once said, `Umar will not become a believer until al Khitaab's donkey does.'

Once, after heavy drinking, Umar picked up his sword and angrily said to his friends, `I am going to kill the apostate Muhammad who has split up the Quraysh, made mockery of our traditions, and insulted our faith and our forefathers.' One of his friends reminded him of the law of retaliation, `You deceive yourself Umar. Do you think the Hashimis will allow you to continue walking upon the earth after you have killed Muhammad? Why don't you start with your own family? Your sister, her husband, and your nephew have become Muhammad's followers.'

Umar went to his sister's house, heard them reciting Muhammad's verses and was furious. He beat her and wounded her but he saw blood on her face, he felt sorry for her and demanded that she give him the sheet of paper from which she was reading. When he read the verses, he was so impressed that he went to see Muhammad and became a believer (*mu'umin*).

Umar's son Abdallah reported that after his conversion, Umar went to a man called Jameel who had the loudest voice, and asked him to announce his conversion. Jameel shouted at the top of his voice, `Umar has apostatized.' Umar shouted back, `He is a liar; I have become a believer (*mu'umin*) and I testify that there is no God but Allah and Muhammad is His apostle.'

A number of men gathered around Umar and they began to fight with him until Umar was tired and weary and he sat down while the men stood around him. Al Aas bin Wa'il al Sahmi, a sheikh of the Quraysh, wearing a Yemeni robe and embroidered shirt came up and inquired what the matter was. When told that Umar had apostatized, he said, `Why should not a man choose a religion for himself, and what are you trying to do? Do you think that Banu Adiy (Umar's clan) will surrender their man to you thus? Let the man alone.'

In this incident, one witnesses the freedom of conscience among the Arabs, which Muhammad destroyed forever because in any modern Islamic country, people are very likely to kill the one who shouts in a public place that one has apostatized from Islam. Muslims have killed many just on suspicions that the latter had apostatized.

The next day, Umar decided to rub his conversion in the face of his uncle Abu Jahl, and he knocked at his door. Abu Jahl opened the door and said, `The best of welcomes, nephew, what has brought you?' Umar answered, `I have come to tell you that I believe in God and His apostle Muhammad and I regard as true what he has brought.' Abu Jahl slammed the door in Umar's face and said, `God damn you and damn what you have brought.'

Muhammad's companion Khabbab bin al Aratt was an ironsmith who made swords. He sold some to the abovementioned al Aas bin Wa'il and then went to demand payment. Al Aas said to him, `Does not Muhammad, your friend whose religion you follow, allege that in paradise there is all the gold and silver and clothes and servants that his people can desire?' `Certainly,' said Khabbab. `Then give me time till the day of resurrection when I enter paradise and pay your debt there; for by God, I will have no less share and influence with God than you and Muhammad.' Upon hearing about this, Muhammad issued the following verses:

> Have you seen the one who disbelieves my verses?
> And says he will be given wealth and sons
> Does he have knowledge of the unseen?
> Or has he received a promise from God?
> No. We shall note what he says and enhance his punishment
> We will take from him the things he speaks about
> And he will come to us empty-handed. (Sura 19, verses 77-80)

Abu Jahl met Muhammad and said to him, `Muhammad, by God, if you did not stop cursing our gods we will curse the god you serve.' Muhammad then stopped cursing their idols and issued the following verses, which state that idol-worship happens because God does not want to stop it:

Ignore those who make partners to God
If God had so willed, they would not have made His partners
We (*God*) have not made you (*Muhammad*) their warner
And you have no authority over them
So do not curse those to whom they pray other than God
Lest they curse God through lack of knowledge
This is how We (*God*) make every nation cherish its deeds
When they will return to their God
He will tell them what they used to do. (Sura 6, verses 106-108)

After Umar's conversion, the believers began to pray in the Ka'aba more often because no one could dare oppose Hamza and Umar. Umar's conversion shows that even the staunchest opponents of Muhammad, such as Abu Jahl, could not stop their family members from becoming believers. When Abu Jahl would hear that a man had become a believer, if he was a man of social importance and had relations to defend him, he would reprimand him saying, `You have forsaken the religion of your father who was better than you. We will declare you a blockhead and brand you as a fool, and destroy your reputation.' If the believer was a merchant, Abu Jahl would say, `We will boycott your goods and reduce you to beggary.' If the believer was a person of no social importance, he would beat him and incite people against him.[58]

Weaker men and slaves were vulnerable on both sides. Bilal's owner, Umayya bin Khalf, would not accept his conversion and he would leave him in scorching heat with a heavy stone on his chest. Waraqa bin Noufal once passed by and saw Bilal in this state shouting, `One God, one.' He went to Umayya and said to him, `I swear by God that if you killed him in this way, I will turn his grave into a shrine.'

Abu Bakr once passed by and said to Umayya, `Have you no fear of God that you treat this poor fellow like this? How long is it to go on?' Umayya replied, `You are the one who corrupted him, so save him from his plight that you see.' `I will do so,' said Abu Bakr; `I have a black slave, tougher and stronger than he is, and he is not a believer. I will exchange him for Bilal.' Abu Bakr exchanged his slave for Bilal and freed him but when one reads about the killings and atrocities Bilal committed later, one loses sympathy for him.

Abu Bakr's other slave, Amir bin Fuhayra, fought in the battles of Badr and Uhud for the believers and was killed at the battle of Bi'r Ma'una.

When Umar was an unbeliever, he had flogged some, including a female slave, for following Muhammad.[59] Abu Bakr once passed by Umar's house and found him beating his slave girl mercilessly until he was tired and said, `I have stopped beating you only because I am tired.' She replied, `May God treat you in the same way.' Abu Bakr bought the girl and freed her. However, Umar retained his habit of being merciless to slaves, and the girl's curse took effect decades later when, as the second caliph of the believers, Umar was stabbed and killed by a Persian slave, Abu Lu'lwa, who then committed suicide.

The Islamists quote events like this as evidence of the non-believers' persecution of the believers but when they read that Umar participated in the large-scale massacres, loot, and plunder of unbelievers, they hail these atrocities as heroic acts. Taking sides with the believers, they ignore events such as the Meccan chief Umayr bin Wahb's torturing the unbelievers in Mecca to convert them to Islam, which defies the dogma that the Meccans generally expelled or tortured the believers.[60]

One basis of the Islamists' said dogma is that the *mushraykeen* (secular/multi-faith people including Muhammad's uncle Abu Lahab and many relatives) have been cursed scores of times in the Qur'an as the enemies of God. On deeper examination, these curses turn out to be no different from the typical inter-tribal and intra-tribal rivalries, intrigues and power struggles that go on even now in all-Muslim Arabia and many other countries where socio-political interaction originates from tribal rivalry and hatred. This showed recently (2011-13) in the Iraqi, Libyan and Syrian inter-tribal bloodsheds and horrible massacres, which Muslims inflicted on each other.

For around thirteen years, Muhammad taunted and ridiculed the Meccan leaders and though they answered back, it tells that he was not really threatened. His follower Sa'ad bin abi Waqqas was the first to attack and wound an unbeliever.[61]

Then Muhammad took his forty followers to the Ka'ba and very aggressively and loudly demanded the dismantling of the idols, which was an attack on the multi-faith society. A fight took place between opposing groups leading to the death of Harith bin abi Hala – the unbeliever son of Khadija from her former husband.[62]

XXX

Increasingly, Muhammad began to seek support from outside of Mecca. Before instructing his followers to gradually migrate to Medina and prepare the local people to accept him as their prophet, he sent eighty-three men, women and children to Abyssinia where they obtained permission from its Christian king, the Negus to live there. The Islamists claim that these believers migrated because of oppression but the fact that most of these later returned to Mecca when it was still in the hands of the seculars, defies their propaganda. In addition, the list of names of the migrants includes men from such powerful tribes as Umayya, Makhzum, Asad, and Abd al Shams – more likely to oppress than be oppressed. Among these were Uthman and his wife Ruqayya, Muhammad's daughter. Uthman was one of the richest men in Mecca and was never oppressed let alone persecuted.

The Quraysh still saw the believers as one of them. Hence, they dispatched two envoys, Abdallah bin abu Rabi'a and Amr bin al Aas, with valuable gifts, which they presented at the king's court and requested him to send the migrants back home. The Negus called in the migrants and asked them what their religion was for which they had forsaken their people without accepting Christianity or any other religion. J'afar bin abu Talib very cleverly mixed many obvious lies with some half-truths and answered as follows:

> O King, we were an uncivilized people, worshipping idols, eating corpses, committing abominations, breaking natural ties, treating guests badly, and our strong devoured our weak. Thus we were until God sent us an apostle whose lineage, truth, trustworthiness, and clemency we know. He summoned us to acknowledge God's unity, to worship him, and to renounce the stones and images which our fathers and we formerly worshipped. He commanded us to speak the truth, be faithful to our engagements, mindful of the ties of kinship and kindly hospitality, and to refrain from crimes and bloodshed. He forbade us to commit abominations and to speak lies, to devour the property of orphans and to vilify chaste women. He commanded us to worship God alone and not associate anything with Him, and he gave us orders about prayer, almsgiving, and fasting. We followed him in what he had brought from God, we treated as forbidden what he forbade, and as lawful what he declared lawful. Thereupon our

people attacked us, treated us harshly and seduced us from our faith to try to make us go back to the worship of idols instead of the worship of God, and to regard as lawful the evil deeds we once committed. So when they treated us unjustly and circumscribed our lives, and came between us and our religion, we came to your country, having chosen you above all others. Here we have been happy in your protection, and we hope that we shall not be treated unjustly while we are with you, O King.[63]

The Negus asked if they had with them anything that had come from God. When J'afar said that he had, the Negus commanded him to read it to him. He cleverly selected and read to him a passage from biblical scriptures which Muhammad had learned from the Meccan Christians and retold in his verses as follows:

Speak of the mercy of your Lord to His servant Zachariah.
He prayed to his Lord in secret, `O my Lord! My bones are weak and the hair of my head glisten grey but whenever I have prayed to you, you have blessed me. Now I fear what my relatives will do after me but my wife is barren, so give me such an heir as will represent me and the posterity of Jacob, and make him one with whom you are well-pleased!'
His prayer was answered: `O Zachariah! We give you good news of a son. His name shall be Yahiya and we have not conferred distinction on this name before.'
He said, `O my Lord! How shall I have a son, when my wife is barren and I have grown quite decrepit from old age?'
The Lord said, `That is easy for me: I did indeed create you before from nothing!'
Zachariah said, `O my Lord! Give me a Sign.'
The Lord said, `The Sign shall be that you shall not speak to any man for three nights, although you are not dumb.'
So Zachariah came out to his people from him chamber. He told them by signs to celebrate God's praises in the morning and in the evening.
The Lord said to Yahiya, `O Yahiya! Take hold of My Book with might.'
And We (*God*) gave him wisdom even as a youth, and piety and purity. He was devout and kind to his parents, and he was not

overbearing or sinner. So peace on him the day he was born, the day that he dies, and the day that he will be raised up to life again.

In this Book, We also tell the story of Mary, when she withdrew from her family to a place in the East and placed a screen to hide from them. Then We sent her our angel, and he appeared before her as a man in all respects.

She said, `I seek God's protection from you if you do fear God.'

He said, `No, I am only a messenger from your Lord to bring to you the gift of a holy son.'

She said, `How shall I have a son, seeing that no man has touched me, and I am not unchaste?'

He said, `So you are but your Lord says, "That is easy for Me, and We wish to appoint him as a sign to men and a mercy from Us. It is a matter so decreed."'

So she conceived him, and she retired with him to a remote place. And the pains of childbirth drove her to the trunk of a palm tree. She cried in anguish, `I wish I had died before this and become a thing forgotten and out of sight!'

But a voice cried to her from beneath, `Grieve not for your Lord has provided a rivulet beneath you; and shake towards yourself the trunk of the palm tree and it will let fall fresh ripe dates upon you. So eat and drink and cool your eye. And if you see any man, say, "I have vowed a fast to God Most Gracious, and this day I will not enter into talk with any human being."'

At last she brought the baby to her people.

They said, `O Mary! Truly an amazing thing you have brought! O sister of Aaron! Your father was not a man of evil and your mother was not an unchaste woman!' But she pointed to the baby.

They said, `How can we talk to a child in the cradle?'

The baby said, `I am indeed a servant of God. He has given me revelation and made me a prophet and He has made me blessed where ever I be, and He has enjoined on me prayer and charity as long as I live. He has made me kind to my mother, and not overbearing or cruel. So peace is on me the day I was born, the day that I die, and the day I shall be raised to life.'

Such was Jesus the son of Mary. It is a statement of truth, about which they doubt in vain. (Sura 19, verses 2-34)

The Negus and his bishops found these verses familiar, in one or the other form. J'afar had preached to them their own religion but cunningly stopped before the next verse which states, "It does not befit God to have a son."

The biblical verses moved the Negus and his bishops and they reportedly wept until their beards were wet. Then the Negus said, `Truly, this and what Jesus brought have come from the same source. By God, I will never give them up to them and they shall not be betrayed.'

When Abdallah and Amr went back to where they were lodging, Amr said, `Tomorrow I will tell the king something that will uproot these migrants.' Abdallah, who was the more God-fearing of the two said, `Do not do it, for they are our relatives though they have gone against us.' Amr said, `By God, I will tell him that they assert that Jesus, son of Mary, is just a creature.' He went to the king in the morning and told him that the believers said a dreadful thing about Jesus, son of Mary, that he should send for them and ask them about it. The king did so. The migrants gathered asking one another what they should say about Jesus. They decided that they would say what Muhammad had brought, come what may. So when they went into the royal presence and the question was put to them, J'afar answered, `We say about Jesus that which our prophet brought, saying, he is God's apostle, and his spirit, and his word, which he cast into Mary the blessed virgin.' Because "the spirit of God" actually has the same meaning as "the spiritual son of God," the Negus took a stick from the ground and said, `By God, Jesus, son of Mary, does not exceed what you have said by the length of this stick.' His generals round about him snorted when he said this, and he said, `Though you snort, by God! Go, for you are safe in my country.'

The migrants stayed by posing as almost Christians. In time, Muhammad would use the same trick with the Jews of Medina. He would pray with them facing Jerusalem, and use Torah to guide his men. The Jews would think that Muhammad had become a Jew until his men would grow in numbers and strength, and start killing and exiling them one by one – one Jewish tribe at a time. Later, they would start attacking the Christians.

XXX

The secular Meccans repeatedly tried to pacify the believers and allowed them to pray their own way in the Ka'ba as long as the other pilgrims were not disturbed.[64] They even offered to combine the prayers.[65] Al Aswad bin al Muttalib, Walid bin Mughira, Umayya bin Khalf and al Aas bin Wa'il, men of reputation among their people, met Muhammad and said, `Muhammad, come let us worship what you worship, and you worship what we worship. You and we will join in this matter. If what you have is better than what we have we will take a share of it, and if what we have is better than what you have, you can take a share of that.' But Muhammad was not interested in multi-faith prayers and he replied that he did not need to pray their way because God would reward him in paradise while those who would not follow him would be made to drink molten metal in hell.[66] He then issued his "God-sent revelations:"

> Say, O unbelievers,
> I do not worship what you worship,
> And you do not worship what I worship,
> And I will not worship what you worship,
> And you will not worship what I worship;
> You have your religion and I have mine. (Sura 109)

These verses implied a promise that the others could keep their religions but, after his total victory, as will be described, Muhammad totally banned all other faiths in Arabia. In the coming centuries, his followers, largely through coercion, almost eliminated the other faiths from the regions they conquered.

For a short period, Muhammad regretted saying what he said in Sura 109 above because he saw that his people turned their backs on him. Their estrangement pained him and he longed to make a message from God that would reconcile his people to him. He meditated on the project and came up with the following:

> By the star when it sets
> Your friend has neither erred nor gone astray
> He speaks not from his own desire
> But receives revelations from heavens. (Sura 53, verses 1-4)

When he reached the seventeenth verse, he added the following in praise of the three main idols of the Meccans:

> Surely, he has seen some signs from the Lord's major signs
> Have you considered Laat, Uzz'a, and the third Manat?
> (*Quraysh called these "the daughters of God"*)
> These are the exalted angels whose intercession God approves.

When Quraysh heard this, they were delighted at the way in which Muhammad spoke of their gods and they listened to him. The blindly following believers did not wonder why Muhammad had abandoned his stance for "one God." They did not suspect a mistake or a slip as Muhammad recited it. When he reached the end of the Sura and prostrated, the believers prostrated confirming him, and the secular/multi-faith people who were in the mosque prostrated when they heard about the idols. Everyone in the mosque, believer and unbeliever, prostrated except Walid bin Mughira who was too old and frail to prostrate, so he took a handful of earth and bent over it. Then the people dispersed and Quraysh went out, delighted at what Muhammad had said about their gods, saying, `Muhammad has spoken of our gods in splendid fashion. He alleged in what he read that they are the exalted angels whose intercession is approved.'

News reached the migrant believers in Abyssinia that Quraysh had reconciled with Muhammad and many started to return to Mecca. However, because of his aggressive nature, Muhammad could not stomach this environment of peace and friendship. He invented another story to resume hostilities. He said that Gabriel had come to him and said, `What have you done, Muhammad? You have read to these people something I did not bring from God and you have said what He did not say to you.' Muhammad said that God had told him that every prophet and apostle before him had desired as God desired but Satan had interjected something into their desires:

> Every prophet and apostle that We sent before you
> Desired something in which Satan intervened
> But God removes Satan's adulteration
> And establishes His truth
> And God is all-knowing and wise. (Sura 22, verses 52)

Therefore, said Muhammad, God had annulled those verses that Satan had suggested and sent new verses as follows:

Have you considered Laat, Uzz'a, and the third Manat?
What! For you sons, and for Him (*God*), daughters?
Such would be indeed a most unfair distribution!
They are nothing but names your fathers gave them
God has given them no authority. (Sura 53, verses 19-23)

To further insult their female identity, Muhammad added:

There are many angels in the heavens
Their intercession does not bring profit
Those who do not believe in the Day of Judgement
Give female names to angels. (Sura 53, verses 26-27)

Meanwhile, the migrants to Abyssinia had begun to return and thirty-three men were already back. Those who feared that they will be reprimanded for leaving Mecca sought protection from their secular relatives which the latter happily provided. Abu Talib protected his sister's son, Abu Salama, and Walid bin Mughira protected his nephew Uthman bin Mad'un but when the latter realized that he was not in any danger, he publicly renounced Walid's protection. Upon Walid's request, he came to the mosque and announced, `I have found Walid loyal and honourable in his protection but I don't want to ask anyone but God for protection; so I give him back his promise.' A secular man, Labid bin Rabi'a of the Kilaab tribe liked Uthman's fortitude and recited a verse:

Everything but God is vain,
And everything lovely must inevitably cease

Uthman perceived this as an insult and shouted, `You lie! The joys of paradise will never cease.' Labid said, `O men of Quraysh your friends never used to be such ill-mannered.' One of the listeners answered, `This is one of those louts with Muhammad who have abandoned their religion. Take no notice of what he says.' Uthman reacted so harshly that the man rose to his feet and hit him in the eye so that it became black. This upset Walid and he said to Uthman, `Nephew, had you kept my protection, your eye would not have suffered this way.' Uthman retorted, `My good eye needs to suffer too and I am under the protection of One who is more powerful than you.' Walid said, `Come nephew, my protection is always open to you,' but Uthman shunned him.

Some men of Banu Makhzum came to Abu Talib and said, `We understand your offering protection to Muhammad but why are you protecting our tribesman Abu Salama?' Abu Talib replied, `Abu Salama asked for it and he is my sister's son too. If I do not protect my sister's son, how can I protect my brother's son?'

Abu Lahab supported his brother Abu Talib and warned the Makhzum men, `You have continually attacked this sheikh for protecting his own people. By God if you do not stop, we will stand with Muhammad until he gains his objective.' They said that would not do anything to annoy Abu Talib and went away.

The concerned relatives of some of these, out of love, even locked them up for fear that they would leave again. For example, Hisham bin al Aas bin Wa'il was held in Mecca and was allowed to join Muhammad only after the three major battles, which he fought from Medina, were over. Likewise, Ayyash bin abu Rabi'a went to Medina with Muhammad but his maternal brothers, Abu Jahl and al Harith, followed him and brought him back to Mecca where they held him until the three major battles were over. Being not able to understand the concern of these relatives for their kin, the Islamists propagate that these were imprisoned because they had become believers.

Muhammad rides a super-speed winged horse and flies to the heavens to meet God and the prophets

The opposition he faced in Mecca enhanced Muhammad's belief that people would follow him in the Byzantine and Persian empires. He now felt that he was in league with Abraham, Moses, Jesus, and other prophets, and that is what he saw in his dreams. One day, he told his followers that in the middle of the night, Gabriel had come and lifted him onto a white animal, half mule half donkey with wings. This animal, called *Buraaq*, strode with lightning speed and took him to the ancient temple of Aelia in Jerusalem. This Jewish temple stood at the location of the stone slab where Abraham had tried to slaughter his son in the name of God and instead slaughtered a lamb. Muslims would later build a mosque at this place and call it *Masjid al Aqsa* meaning, "the farthest mosque."

According to Muhammad, the winged mule then took him to meet God in heavens where angels greeted him. Then he climbed a ladder and ascended through seven levels of heaven meeting the prophets Adam, Jesus, John, Joseph (*Youssef*), Enoch (*Idris*), Aaron (*Haroon*), Moses and finally, at the highest level, Abraham. Some reports suggest that Muhammad met these prophets in the Jerusalem temple where they had all assembled, and he led them in prayers. Then they offered him to choose to drink wine, water, or milk. Muhammad reported:

> I heard a voice saying: If he takes the wine, he and his people will go astray; if he takes the water, he and his people will be drowned; and if he takes the milk, he and his people will be rightly guided. So I took the vessel containing milk and drank it. Gabriel said to me, 'Muhammad, you have been rightly guided and so will your people be.'

In plain words, Muhammad took a bogus test in which "a voice" provided him with the right answer beforehand.

Getting messages from God in dreams was not new. The Bible is full of such stories. Yahweh (God) had said to Aaron and Miriam: "If there is a prophet among you, I will come to see him and speak to him in a dream." Joseph's gift of dream interpretation had enabled him to become an advisor to the Pharaoh. Abraham, Jacob, Solomon, Saint Joseph, Saint Paul, all saw God in their dreams but Muhammad claimed that his night journey was real. A'isha later explained this journey by saying that the messenger's body remained where it was but God removed his spirit by night.

Although Muhammad's disciples tried to stop him from telling others about his "night journey," fearing that the others would laugh at him, Muhammad went ahead with an open declaration.

'By God this is plain absurdity,' some people said in response, 'A camel takes a month to reach Syria and another month to return. How did Muhammad made his journey in one night?' Many believers too were ashamed when they heard this ridiculous story from Muhammad's mouth, and they abandoned him; some went to Abu Bakr and said, 'What do you think of your friend now, Abu Bakr? He alleges that he went to Jerusalem last night and prayed there and came back to Mecca.' At first Abu Bakr replied that Muhammad could not say such a thing but when they told him that he was in the mosque at that very moment telling people about it, Abu Bakr said, 'If he says so then it is true; and what is so surprising about it? He tells me that communications from God come to him in an hour of a day or night and I believe him, and that is more extraordinary than this!'

Abu Bakr then went to Muhammad and asked if these reports were true, and when Muhammad said they were, he asked him to describe Jerusalem to him. Muhammad explained what Jerusalem was like and whenever he described a part of it Abu Bakr said, 'That is true. I testify that you are the apostle of God.' Then Muhammad said, 'And you, Abu Bakr, are the *Siddiq* (verifier).'

To put pressure on the suspecting believers, Muhammad added that God had made him see the vision of the night journey only to test who would believe him and who would turn away. It was no different from God telling Abraham to slaughter his son and then Abraham had said to his son, 'O my son, verily I saw in a dream that I must sacrifice you,' and then acted accordingly. Muhammad added, 'Revelation from God comes to the prophets waking or sleeping. My eyes sleep but my heart is awake.'

To convince his companions that he was not lying, Muhammad described Abraham, Moses, and Jesus, as he saw them that night, saying, 'I have never seen a man more like myself than Abraham. Moses was a ruddy faced man, tall, thinly fleshed, curly haired with a hooked nose. Jesus, Son of Mary, was a reddish man of medium height with lank hair with many freckles on his face as though he had just come from a bath. One would suppose that his head was dripping with water, though there was no water on it. The man most like him among you is Urwa bin Mas'ud al Thaqafi.'

Muhammad's cousin Umm Hani, daughter of Abu Talib, reported the following:

> The apostle went on no night journey except while he was in my house. He slept that night in my house. He prayed the final night prayer, then he slept and we slept. A little before dawn he woke us, and when we had prayed the dawn prayer he said, 'O Umm Hani, I prayed with you the last evening prayer in this valley as you saw. Then I went to Jerusalem and prayed there. Then I have just prayed the morning prayer with you.'
>
> Then he got up to go out and I grabbed his robe and laid bare his belly as though it were a folded Egyptian garment. I said, 'Don't talk to people about it for they will call you a liar and insult you.' He said, 'By God, I certainly will tell them.'

I said to a Negress slave of mine, 'Follow him and listen to what he says to the people, and what they say to him.'

The apostle did tell the people and they were amazed and asked what proof he had. He replied that he had passed by the caravans of so-and-so in such-and-such a valley and the animal he bestrode scared them and a camel bolted. Then he said, 'I carried on until in Dajanan I passed by a caravan of the Banu so-and-so and found the people asleep. They had a jar of water covered with a lid. I took the covering off, drank the water, and replaced the lid. The proof of that is that their caravan is this moment coming down from the pass of al Tan'im, led by a dusky camel loaded with two sacks, one black and the other multihued.'

The people hurried to the pass and the first camel they met was as he had described. They asked the men about the vessel and they told them that they had left it full of water and covered it and that when they woke it was covered but empty. They asked the others too, who were in Mecca, and they said that it was quite right: they had been scared and a camel had bolted.

Umm Hani's use of the title "the apostle" instead of "Cousin Muhammad" shows that she reported this story after Muhammad's takeover of Mecca, which happened thirteen years later, when she had become a believer. Being a member of the then victorious Hashimi tribe, she was bound to support whatever Muhammad said but she went further than that and claimed that he had left for the heavens whilst living in their house. Actually, when the event of the night journey happened, Muhammad was living with Khadija, and Umm Hani was married to Hubayra, an unbeliever man of the Banu Makhzum – the tribe of Abu Jahl. Muhammad could not have possibly slept the night at her house.

To distract people from thinking more about the impossibility of the super-speed night journey, Muhammad quickly spun the following horror stories and described his ascent to heaven as follows:

> After I had prayed in Jerusalem, a ladder was brought to me, finer than any I have ever seen. It was that to which the dying man looks when death approaches. Gabriel mounted

it with me until we came to one of the gates of heaven called the Gate of the Watchers. An angel, Isma'il, was in charge of it. Under his command were twelve thousand angels each of them having twelve thousand angels under his command. When Gabriel brought me in, Isma'il asked who I was, and when he was told that I was Muhammad he asked if I had been given a mission, and on being assured of this, he wished me well. All the angels who met me when I entered the lowest heaven smiled in welcome and wished me well except one named Malik who said the same greetings but did not smile or show that joyful expression which the others had. When I asked Gabriel the reason he told me that he does not smile because he is the keeper of hell. I said to Gabriel, `Will you not order him to show me hell?' And he said, `Certainly! O Malik, show Muhammad hell.'

Malik removed hell's covering and the flames blazed high into the air until I thought that they would consume everything. So I asked Gabriel to order him to send them back to their place, which he did. I can only compare the effect of the withdrawal of flames to the falling of a shadow when Malik placed their cover on them.

When I entered the lowest heaven, I saw a man sitting there with the spirits of men passing before him. To one he would speak well and rejoice in him saying, `A good spirit from a good body' and of another he would frown, saying, `An evil spirit from an evil body.' In answer to my question Gabriel told me that this was our father Adam reviewing the spirits of his offspring; the spirit of a believer raised his pleasure, and the spirit of an infidel raised his disgust so that he said the words just quoted.

Then I saw men with lips like camels; in their hands were pieces of fire like stones, which they used to thrust into their mouths and they would come out of their posteriors. I was told that these were those who sinfully devoured the wealth of orphans.

Then I saw men with such large bellies as I have never seen; treading over them were camels maddened by thirst when they were cast into hell, and the men were unable to move out of the way. These were the usurers.

Then I saw men with good fat meat before them side by side with lean stinking meat, eating of the latter and leaving the former. These men are those who forsake the women permitted by God and go after those God has forbidden.

Then I saw women hanging by their breasts. These women were those who had fathered bastards on their husbands. Great is God's anger against a woman who brings a bastard into her family; the bastard deprives the true sons of their portion and learns the secrets of the female quarters.

Then I was taken up to the second heaven and there were the two maternal cousins Jesus, Son of Mary, and John, son of Zachariah. Then to the third heaven and there was a man whose face was as the moon at the full. This was my brother Joseph, son of Jacob. Then to the fourth heaven and there was prophet Idris (*Enoch*) exalted to a lofty place. Then to the fifth heaven and there was a man with white hair and a long beard, never have I seen a more handsome man than him. This was the beloved among his people, Aaron son of Imran. Then to the sixth heaven, and there was a dark man with a hooked nose. This was my brother Moses, son of Imran. Then to the seventh heaven and there was a man sitting on a throne at the gate of the immortal mansion. Every day seventy thousand angels went in not to come back until the resurrection day. Never have I seen a man more like myself. This was my father Abraham. He took me to Paradise and there I saw a pretty woman with dark red lips and I asked her to whom she belonged, for she pleased me much when I saw her, and she told me that she belonged to Zayd bin Haritha.

Thus Muhammad gave Zayd, his slave turned foster-son, the good news about this pretty woman whose name was Zaynab. In future, he would get Zayd marry a certain Zaynab in real life; then Zayd would divorce her and he would marry her himself. This affair of Zayd, Zaynab and Muhammad will be described later in this book.

To keep people from suspecting him, Muhammad used the technique of spinning tale upon tale until it would become too much to analyse and refute. He added more details to his ascent to the heavens. When Gabriel took him up to each of the heavens and asked permission to enter, he had to say whom he had brought and whether he had received a mission, and the dwellers would say, 'God grant him life, brother and friend!' until they reached the seventh heaven and met God. In this meeting, God laid upon

Muhammad's nation the duty of performing fifty prayers a day. Muhammad said:

> On my return after meeting God, I passed by Moses and what a fine friend of believers he was! He asked me how many prayers had been laid upon me and when I told him fifty, he said, 'Fifty prayers a day are a weighty matter and your people are weak, so go back to God and ask him to reduce the number of prayers.'
> I did so and God took off ten. Again I passed by Moses and he said the same again; and so it went on and each time God took off ten and then five until I was left with five prayers a day. Moses again gave me the same advice. I replied that I had been going back to God too many times to ask for reduction in prayers and I am too embarrassed to do it again.

One cannot find a more ridiculous description of a meeting with God than this one in which Muhammad presents Moses as being wiser than God. Twenty years after Muhammad's death, even his most loyal believer Uthman could not stomach the details of the "night journey" when he collated and edited the Qur'an. As described in detail elsewhere in this book, Uthman rejected and burned large chunks of the Qur'anic material. He arranged the remaining verses in an almost reverse chronological order so that people would find it hard to relate them to Muhammad's life. He divided the verses at random between suras rather than at their relevant places, and published the Qur'an in the form of thousands of unassembled pieces of a jigsaw puzzle. Hence, the following verse is probably the only verse that mentions the "night journey" in the Qur'an:

> Glory to him (*God*) who took his servant (*Muhammad*)
> For a Journey by night from the Sacred Mosque (*Ka'ba*)
> To the farthest Mosque (*Masjid al Aqsa*),
> Whose precincts I (*God*) blessed,
> To show him some of Our Signs. (Sura 17, verse 1)

Upon hearing the story of the "night journey," many well respected tribal elders called Muhammad a liar. One of these was al Aswad bin al Muttalib of the Banu Asad, about whom

Muhammad prayed, 'O God, blind him and take away his son.' Then he issued the following verses:

> Announce what you have been ordered
> And turn away from the *mushraykeen* (secular/multi-faith people)
> I (*God*) am enough for those who deride you
> Those who put another god beside God
> In the end they will know.   (Sura 15, verses 94-96)

When misfortune or death came to any of Muhammad's critics, the committed believers would spin a story and spread it around that God, through Gabriel, had punished him for criticizing Muhammad.

The boycott of the Hashimis, and its annulment:
Muhammad responds with more insults for his elders

The leaders of the two largest Meccan clans, Abu Jahl of the Banu Makhzum and Abu Sufyan of the Umayyads, signed a proclamation inscribed on sheepskin vellum and nailed it to the door of the Ka'ba. The proclamation prohibited people from marrying the Hashimis or engaging with them in commercial dealings of any kind including buying or selling of food items. It instructed people to keep the Hashimis away from caravans and markets, and shun them until they stopped supporting Muhammad.

However, the proclamation had little effect because of many reasons. Firstly, the leaders of only two clans had signed it. Secondly, almost all Meccans respected Muhammad's uncles and they could not shun them from public places. Thirdly, it was not possible to avoid intermarriages; even Abu Talib's sister and daughter were married to men of the rival Makhzum. Fourthly, while the boycott targeted the Hashimis, Muhammad's supporters came from many other clans too; for example, Abu Bakr, Umar, and Uthman were not Hashimis and, if needed, they could buy and sell on behalf of the Hashimis.

Some people did try to apply the sanctions. Abu Lahab supported the boycott against his own clan because he wanted his people to oust Abu Talib and make him the chief instead. Khadija's stepbrother had two sons; one had become a believer but the other was not. Under pressure from his clan, he divorced his wife, who was Muhammad's daughter, and Uthman married her. However, the Meccan merchants did not want to miss a business deal and they kept dealing in privacy. The proclamation only emotionally hurt the Hashimis, and Abu Talib responded by lampooning the Quraysh in his following poem:

> The honour of the Quraysh is worthless
> Who wants the protection of cowards?
> I would rather have the protection of a weak camel
> Murmuring and spraying its flock with urine
> Lagging behind the herd and struggling
> To climb a ridge, like a weasel
> Our own brothers refuse to help us
> They flung us aside like a burning coal
> And slander us among the people
> He (*Abu Sufyan*) turned his face away as he passed
> Walking as if he were one of the great men of the world
> He shows sympathy and claims to be our friend
> But hides evil schemes in his heart
> Your boycott is a shameful affair against collective welfare,
> But remember, if we will suffer, you will suffer too.

The Islamists call this boycott "banishment" and trumpet it as a glaring example of "the persecution of Muslims" but the earliest Arab histories show that it was a Meccan custom to isolate all kinds of rioters, and this had happened in the past regardless of what faith one had.[67] Still, the kind secular Meccans kept sending food and clothes to their tribal relatives.[68] Abu Jahl met Hakim bin Hazam with his slave carrying flour intended for his aunt Khadija. He hung on to him and said, 'Are you taking food to the Hashimis? By God, before you and your food move from here, I will shame you in Mecca.' Abu'l Bakhtri, a secular noble came to him and said, 'What is going on between you two?' When told that Hakim was taking food to the Hashimis, he said, 'It is food which belongs to his aunt and she has sent him to get it. Are you trying to prevent him taking her own food to her? Let the man go his way!'

Abu Jahl refused until they came to blows, and Abu'l Bakhtri took a camel's jawbone and knocked him down, wounded him, and trod on him violently while Muhammad's uncle Hamza looked on nearby and did not intervene. Meanwhile Muhammad was exhorting his people night and day openly proclaiming his message without fear of anyone.[69]

Another unbeliever, Hisham bin Amr, whose people highly respected him, would also send camels loaded with food, clothes, and other necessities to the Hashimis.[70] In order not to offend others, he would bring a camel laden with food and clothes by night, take off its helter, give it a whack on the side, and send it towards the Hashimis. Finally, he initiated persuading the Meccans to annul the boycott. He went to Zuhayr bin abi Umayya and said, `Are you content to eat food and wear clothes and marry women while you know of the condition of your maternal uncles? They cannot buy or sell, marry, nor give in marriage. By God, if they were the uncles of Abu'l Hakam (*i.e. Abu Jahl*) and you asked him to do what he has asked you to do he would never agree to it.'

Zuhayr said, `Confound you, Hisham, what can I do? I am only one man. By God if I had another man to back me I would soon annul the boycott.'

Hisham said, `You have found a man – me.'

`Find another,' said Zuhayr.

So Hisham went to Mut'im bin Adiy and said, `Are you content that two clans of the Banu Abdu Manaf should perish while you keep following the Quraysh? You will find that they will soon do the same to you.' Mut'im made the same reply as Zuhayr and demanded a fourth man, so Hisham went to Abu'l Bakhtri who asked for a fifth man, and then to Zama'a bin al Aswad and reminded him of their kinship and duties. Zama'a asked whether others were willing to co-operate in this task and he gave him the names of the others. They all arranged to meet at night and bound themselves to take up the question of the boycott until they had secured its annulment. Zuhayr claimed the right to act and speak first. So on the morrow when the people gathered, Zuhayr dressed up in a long robe and, went round the Ka'ba seven times. Then he came forward and said, `O people of Mecca, are we to eat and clothe ourselves while the Hashimis perish, unable to buy or sell? By God I will not sit down until this evil boycotting document is torn up!'

Abu Jahl, who was at the side of the mosque, exclaimed, `You lie by God. It shall not be torn up.'

Zama'a said, `You are a greater liar; we were not satisfied with the document when it was written.'

Abu'l Bakhtri said, `Zama'a is right. We are not satisfied with what is written and we don't hold by it.'

Mut'im said, `You are both right and anyone who says otherwise is a liar. We take God to witness that we dissociate ourselves from the whole idea and what is written in the document.'

Hisham spoke in the same sense.

Abu Jahl said, `This is a matter which has been decided overnight. It has been discussed somewhere else.'

Abu Talib was sitting at the side of the mosque. When Mut'im went up to the document to tear it to pieces he found that worms had already eaten it except the words `In Your name O God,' which was the customary formula with which Quraysh began their writing.[71]

Muhammad himself admitted that the boycott was no pain at all when he said, `Until the death of Abu Talib, the Quraysh did nothing unpleasant to me.'[72] However, at the end of the boycott, he became even more arrogant and ordered his followers to pray five times a day in public in their different way – not facing the Ka'ba but Syria.

XXX

The following events show that Muhammad did not sympathize even with Abu Talib who had supported him, and stood up to the Quraysh elders for him.

When Abu Talib fell ill and people learned of his grave condition, the Quraysh reminded one another that now that Hamza and Umar had joined Muhammad, and his influence had grown among all the Quraysh clans, they better see Abu Talib and reach some compromise. Utaba and Shayba, sons of Rabi'a, Abu Jahl, Umayya bin Khalf, and Abu Sufyan, with some other notables came to see Abu Talib. Abu Sufyan said to Abu Talib, `You know that we have always respected your standing and now that you are close to death, we are deeply concerned on your account. You know the trouble that exists between us and your nephew, so call him and let us make an agreement that he will leave us alone and we will leave him alone; let him have his religion and we will have ours.'

When Muhammad came, Abu Talib said to him, `Nephew, these nobles want to make a compromise based on give and take. You give something to them and they will give something to you.'

Muhammad answered, `Give me one word, "Yes," and you can rule the Arabs and conquer the Persians. You must say there is no

God but Allah and you must repudiate what you worship beside him.' He insisted that the Quraysh leaders abandon all the totems, and deny the intercession of lessor gods.

Abu Sufyan and the others threw up their hands in frustration and said, `Do you want to make all the gods into one God, Muhammad? That would be an extraordinary deed.' What they meant was that it would involve too much bloodshed to make it possible. Then they departed saying one to another, `This fellow is not going to give you anything you want, so go and continue with the religion of your fathers until God judge between us.'

Abu Talib consoled Muhammad by saying, `Nephew, I don't think that you asked them anything extraordinary,' but in turn Muhammad demanded that Abu Talib should testify to his position as God's messenger.[73] `You say it, uncle, and then I shall be able to save you on the Day of Judgement.

Abu Talib replied, `I would have said what you want, but the Quraysh would think that I am afraid of death and they will taunt my brothers and you, saying that I succumbed to the fear of death. Hence, I say that I die in the religion of your grandfather Abd al Muttalib.'

When Abu Talib was dying, Muhammad again asked him to recite: "There is no God but Allah and Muhammad is his messenger." Abu Talib said, `I must remain in the ways of my fathers.' Abbas looked at him as he was moving his lips, put his ear close to him, and said, `Nephew, by God my brother has said what you wanted him to say,' but Muhammad arrogantly replied, `I did not hear it.'[74] When he saw that Abu Talib had died without Muhammad saying any words of thanks to him, Abbas said, `Muhammad, what good did you bring to Abu Talib who raised you and always supported you against your opponents?' Muhammad haughtily replied, `Abu Talib's feet only are in hell but the fire still affects his brain. If it was not for the divine protection which I have granted to him, he would be all in hellfire.'[75] Thus, he contradicted his own words, `Do not speak ill of the dead.'

Muhammad issued the following verses about the last meeting of the Quraysh nobles with Abu Talib:

The unbelievers are surprised that one of their own warns them
And they say, `It is spell and lies;
To make all the gods into one God would be extraordinary'
And their leaders departed, content with their (*many*) gods

Saying, `We did not see this even in the last religion (*Christianity*)
Is he the only one who receives revelations?
They doubt my revelations
Because they have not yet tasted my torture. (Sura 38, verses 4-8)

The Meccans had argued that the Christian belief in the holy trinity – God, Jesus, and the Holy Spirit – meant that even Christians did not have one God. Muhammad went even further. He declared that Christians too were unbelievers, and issued the following verses:

Those too are surely unbelievers who say that
God is the third of the three
If they will not desist from what they say,
They will face grievous punishment
Jesus, son of Mary, was nothing but a messenger
And there had been many messengers before him
His mother was a righteous woman
The two used to eat their meals together
See how we offer arguments
And then see how they turn their backs.   (Sura 5, verses 73-75)

Muhammad's uncle Abu Lahab had not seen eye to eye with Abu Talib in supporting Muhammad and another nephew, Abu Salama, who had joined Muhammad's group,[76] but he had always been there when the tribe needed him. When Muhammad was born, Abu Lahab had sent his slave woman, Thobia, to breastfeed him.[77] Later Abu Lahab's sons Utaba and Utayba had married Muhammad's daughters Ruqayya and Umm Kalthum.[78]

After Abu Talib's death, Abu Lahab became the chief of the Hashim clan. To honour the memory of his dead brother, and to fulfil his duty as the new Hashimi chief, he came to offer his protection to Muhammad but Muhammad said that because of their concessions to the idol-temples, Abu Talib, Abd al Muttalib, and all the Quraysh in their graves, would remain in the fires of hell. Abu Lahab was so shocked at his ingratitude for his own grandfather and uncle that he withdrew his offer of support.[79] He turned against him and said, `Muhammad makes many promises but all to be fulfilled after our deaths.' He would blow on his hands and say, `Muhammad's promises bring nothing in my hands.'

Muhammad did not like this, and he vindictively taunted him and his wife Umm Jameel in the following Qur'anic verses:

Abu Lahab's hands will wither; he will perish
He will not profit from his wealth and gains
He will roast in flaming fire
His wife shall carry the wood for fuel!
Around her neck, a rope of palm fibre cast! (Sura 111)

Muhammad's aunt heard these verses and was very angry. She came with a stone to hit him but then stopped and retreated after issuing verbal taunts in verse:

We reject the reprobate,
His words we repudiate
His religion we loathe and hate.[80]

Muhammad quickly turned his aunt's hesitation to his advantage and said, 'God had blinded her so she could not see me.'[81] He was very keen to show that he had miraculous powers. His associates had already begun to spread myths that he had "divine protection."

However, the "divine protection" did not work in all cases. Word got around that Muhammad had lost Abu Lahab's protection, and this encouraged some of his neighbours and young louts to do mischief to him, such as throwing a sheep's uterus on him when he was praying, or in his cooking pot. Because he lacked the ability to sense the consequences of his actions, he still expected the Hashimis to protect him and so he would come out of the house carrying the sheep's uterus on a stick and shout, `O sons of Abdu Manaf, what sort of protection is this?'

Once a young lout threw dust on his head. He came home and one of his daughters got up to wash it, weeping as she did so. `Don't weep my girl,' he said, `for God will protect your father. Quraysh never treated me like this while Abu Talib was alive.' In saying this, he conveniently forgot what he had said about Abu Talib shortly after his death: `Abu Talib's feet only are in hell but the fire still affects his brain. If it was not for the divine protection which I have granted to him, he would be all in hellfire.'

XXX

Either shortly before or after Abu Talib's death, depending on which report one follows, Khadija also died. On her death, she was sixty-seven and Muhammad around fifty-one. He now needed a wife to look after his daughters. His relative Khowla suggested that he should marry A'isha, the daughter of his friend Abu Bakr. However, A'isha was only around six years old and could not possibly look after his daughters – much older than she was. Hence, Khowla suggested two marriages at the same time: One with A'isha and the second with a widow Sawda bint Zama'a, both from the Quraysh.

Sawda came to live with Muhammad while A'isha remained in her father's home. When Muhammad was fifty-four and A'isha was nine, she left her parents to live with him. When he died at the age of sixty-three, A'isha was only eighteen but not allowed to remarry because she had been the apostle's wife. Abu Bakr had taught the best of Arab verse and proverbs to his daughters. Hence, A'isha became a major source of knowledge about Muhammad's life after his death.

<u>Muhammad travels to Ta'if
to solicit support from the Thaqif</u>

Muhammad travelled to the town of Ta'if in the mountains, a day's journey southeast of Mecca. His aim was to see if they would accept his claim to apostolate and, being rivals to Mecca, raid Mecca under his leadership. Full of himself, he did not take into account that he had denigrated their temple of Laat, and that the Thaqif had links with the Meccans, many of whom had summer houses in Ta'if because of its cooler climate, ample springs and greenery. To keep his trip totally secret, he went alone.

He met a number of Thaqif chiefs and leaders among whom were three brothers: Abdu Yalalyl, Masud and Habib, sons of Amr bin Auf. One of them had a Quraysh wife of the Banu Jumah. Muhammad sat with them, invited them to accept his apostolate, and asked them to help him against his opponents at home.

The brothers did not like such blatant treason against one's own tribe and one of them said, 'If God has sent you, I would tear up the covering of the Ka'aba.' The other said, 'Could not God have found someone better than you?' The third said, 'By God don't let me ever speak to you for if you are an apostle from God as you say you are, then I should dare not speak to you and if you are abusing God's name, then it is not right that I should speak to you.' In despair, Muhammad left saying, `Seeing that you have acted as you have, keep the matter secret.' He was scared of the Meccans finding out about this and taking further measures against him.

However, the three brothers told everyone and their louts and slaves insulted him and shouted after him until a crowd gathered and compelled him to take refuge in an orchard belonging to two Meccans, Utaba bin Rabi'a and his brother Shayba, who were there at that time. The louts who were following him went back. He made for the shade of a vine and sat there while Utaba and Shayba watched him, feeling sorry for what he had to endure from the local louts. Despite his attempted treason, they felt sympathy for a fellow Meccan.

Muhammad prayed, `O God, I complain to you of my weakness, little resources, and lowliness before men. O Most Merciful, you are the Lord of the weak, and you are my Lord. To whom will you send me? To one afar who will misuse me? Or to an enemy to whom you have given power over me? If you are not angry with me, I care not. I take refuge in the light of your countenance which illumines the darkness and rightly orders the things of this world and the next, lest your anger descend upon me, or your wrath light upon me. There is no power and no might except you.'

When Utaba and Shayba heard this prayer, they were moved with compassion. They called a young Christian slave of theirs called Addas and told him to take a bunch of grapes on a platter and give it to Muhammad to eat. Addas did so, and when Muhammad put his hand in the platter he said "In the name of God" before eating. Addas looked closely into his face and said, `By God, this is not the way the people of this country speak.' Muhammad asked `Then from what country do you come, O Addas, and what is your religion?'

He replied that he was a Christian and came from Nineveh.

Muhammad's knowledge of the Christian scriptures came in hand and he said, `From the town of the righteous man Jonah son of Matta!'

`But how do you know about him?' asked Addas.

`He is my brother; he was a prophet and I am a prophet too,' Muhammad replied to impress him.

Addas bent over him and kissed his head, his hands, and his feet.

The two brothers looked on and one said to the other, `He has already corrupted our slave!' And when Addas came back they said to him, `You rascal, why were you kissing his head, hands, and feet?' He answered that he was the finest man in the country who had told him things that only a prophet could know. They replied, `You rascal, don't let him seduce you from your religion, for it is better than his.'

Muhammad returned from Ta'if without getting anything out of Thaqif. To dispel his despair, he took refuge in imagination and spun a story: When he reached Nakhla, he rose to pray in the middle of the night, and a number of *jinn* passed by. He spun as far as to say that these were seven *jinn* from an area called Nasibeen. The *jinn* listened to him and when he had finished his prayer, they turned back to their people to tell them about having believed and responded to what they had heard. Muhammad even issued "divine verses" about this event:

> And when We (*God*) favoured you,
> Some of the *jinn* listened to you reciting the Qur'an
> When they arrived, they told each other to keep quiet
> And at the end of the recitation,
> They returned to their nation and warned their people
> `O nation, we have heard the book sent after Moses;
> It confirms the earlier books, and guides
> Towards the true religion and the straight path
> O nation, believe in the caller to God
> God will forgive your sins and save you
> From a painful punishment. (Sura 46, verses 29-31)

> Say: It has been revealed to me that a number of the *jinn* listened
> And said, `We have heard a strange Qur'an
> Which guides towards the straight path
> We have believed and we will not make partners to God
> Who is exalted, and has neither a wife nor a son
> And the stupid among us used tell lies about God.
>   (Sura 76, verses 1-4)

When Muhammad left Ta'if, and was close to Mecca, a Meccan passed and he asked him if he would take a message for him and the man said that he would. Muhammad told him to go to Akhnas bin Shariq and say, `Muhammad asks if you will give me protection so that I may convey the message of my Lord?' When the man delivered his message Akhnas replied that an ally could not give protection against a member of the main tribe. When the man told Muhammad of this, he asked him if he would go back and ask Suhayl bin Amr for his protection in the same words. Suhayl sent word that the Banu Amir bin Lu'ayy could not give protection against the Banu Ka'ab – one of the Meccan tribes. He then asked the man if he would go back and make the same application to his tribal relative Mut'im bin Adiy. Mut'im said, 'Yes, tell him to enter,' and the man came back and told this to Muhammad.

The next morning Mut'im girt on his weapons, and he, his sons, and his nephews accompanied Muhammad into Mecca.[82] Mut'im knew that Muhammad was the archenemy of their secularism but he still protected him. When Abu Jahl saw them he asked, 'Is this protection or a call to arms? Have you become a follower of him?' Mut'im said, 'I am only offering protection,' to which Abu Jahl replied, 'We shall protect whomever you protect.' These secular Meccans upheld the gallant values of the Arabs but they would soon pay a heavy price for not being able to see through Muhammad's apparently noble claims.

Muhammad returned to Mecca and dwelt there but the Meccans now more than ever resented his presence because of his attempted treason. One day he went to the Ka'aba when the others were there, and when Abu Jahl saw him he said, 'This is your prophet, O Banu Abdu Manaf,' meaning that a traitor to Mecca was their prophet. Utaba bin Rabi'a, though he was an unbeliever too, replied, 'Why should you brother if we have a prophet or a king?'

Instead of thanking Utaba, Muhammad said, 'O Utaba, you were not angry on God's behalf or his apostle's behalf, but on your own account. As for you, O Abu Jahl, a great blow of fate will come upon you so that you will laugh little and weep much; and as for you, O leaders of Quraysh, a great blow of fate will come upon you so that you will experience what you most abhor and that with force!'

XXX

Muhammad kept seeking allies to be able to attack his own people and offered himself to the tribes of Arabs at the fairs whenever an opportunity came, telling them to believe in him and defend him until God should make victorious the message with which he had charged him, which in plain words meant eliminating all other faiths.

Rabi'a bin Abbad reported that when he was a youngster with his father in Mina, Muhammad used to stop by the Arab encampments and tell them that he was the apostle of God Who had ordered them to worship Him, renounce the rival gods, believe in His apostle and protect him until God made plain His purpose in sending him. An artful and elegant fellow with two locks of hair, wearing an Aden cloak, used to follow Muhammad. When Muhammad had finished his appeal, he used to say, `This fellow wishes only to get you to strip off Laat and Uzz'a from your necks and your allies in exchange for the misleading innovation he has brought. Don't obey him and take no notice of him.' Rabi'a asked his father who the man was who followed Muhammad and contradicted what he said, and he answered that it was his uncle Abdul Uzz'a bin Abdul Muttalib, known as Abu Lahab.

Ibn Shihab al Zuhri reported that he went to the tents of Kinda where there was a sheikh called Mulayh. Muhammad invited them to come to God and offered himself to them, but they declined.

Muhammad bin Abdul Rehmaan reported that Muhammad went to the tents of Kalb to a clan called Banu Abdallah with the same message, adding, `O Banu Abdallah, God has given your father a noble name.' But they would not give heed. Muhammad also went to the Banu Hanifa where he met with the worst reception of all.

Al Zuhri reported that he went to the Banu Amir bin Sa'sa'a and one of them called Bayhara bin Firas said, `By God, if I could take this man from Quraysh I could eat up the Arabs with his guidance.' Then he said to Muhammad, `If we actually give allegiance to you and God gives you victory over your opponents, shall we have the power after you?'

Muhammad replied, `Authority is a matter which God places where He pleases.'

Bayhara answered, `I suppose you want us to fight for you with the Arabs and then if you win, someone else will reap the benefit! Thank you, No!'[83]

Muhammad persuades the tribes of Medina and conspires against their Jewish neighbours

After thirteen years of efforts in Mecca, Muhammad finally ascertained that he could not capture the Ka'ba from the Banu Makhzum and the Umayyads without armed assistance from somewhere far from Mecca. He then began to woo the tribesmen of Medina, then known as Yathrib, who used to come to Mecca for the annual hajj pilgrimage. He had good knowledge of the social and cultural structures of people of Medina because of family history and ties: His mother was from Medina. His father had died there and, when he was six, his mother too had died on the way back from there. His maternal relatives, the Banu Najjar clan, lived in Medina.[84] His great grandfather Hashim, on one of his travels to Syria, had stopped over in Medina, married a woman of the Khazraj tribe and then carried onwards to Syria only to die there. Nine months later the woman had given birth to Hashim's son. When this boy was seven, Hashim's brother Muttalib, who had no son of his own, travelled to Medina, snatched his nephew from his mother and brought him over to Mecca. Because, in the beginning, Muttalib had hidden the fact that he had snatched his nephew, and told people that the he had bought the boy as a slave, people kept calling him Abdul Muttalib, meaning the slave of Muttalib.

The Meccans saw Medina as little more than a caravan stopover inhabited by low class peasants and Jews. It consisted of several loosely connected villages along the eight miles strip of a fertile valley dotted with springs and date palms. Its economy relied on agriculture, dates, date-syrup and wine, oil from the sap, vegetables, charcoal, animal fodder, palm-ropes, roofing material made of palm branches, and trade with Mecca. Those who owned land could make a good living. Medina, like Mecca, suffered from inter-tribal rivalry but while the Meccans competed for control over the Ka'ba, the Medinians fought over issues of land ownership. Hence, each of its villages had a small, fortified stronghold, or fortress, where people could retreat when attacked.

The Quraysh, along with the Medinian tribes Aus and Khazraj, had migrated from Yemen to escape economic hardship in the 5th century. The former had settled in Mecca when no one lived there but the Aus and Khazraj had settled in Medina, already populated by Palestinian Jewish tribes who had spread throughout the Middle East in several waves after their unsuccessful rebellion against the Roman rule in the 2nd century. The Jews had settled in the chain of valley oases from Jordan to northwest Arabia in the towns called Tabuk, Tayma, Khyber, and the southernmost, Yathrib (Medina). Like everyone else, they too used the word "Allah" for God, spoke the regional Hejazi Arabic and were hard to differentiate from the Arabs.

In Medina, the Jewish settlements consisted of three Jewish tribes, Qaynuqa, Nadir, and Qurayza. These were farmers, traders, ironsmiths, and goldsmiths. The other two major tribes, Aus and Khazraj were largely peasants. They had no clear religion as such but they followed the practices of many. They had no holy book; they had idols and a vague code of morality but little concept of paradise and hell, life after death and the Day of Judgement.[85] They were largely peasants, illiterate, and suffered from an inferiority complex vis-à-vis the Jews, whom they called the "people of the book" – the Torah.

Like the Aus and Khazraj, the Jews too were divided on tribal lines and were often as hostile to each other as to anyone else. They were also divided on religious lines between the Jerusalem Talmud and the Babylonian one, depending on which rabbi they followed. However, they had an education system through schools called *bayt al madaris* (houses of education). The other Medinians largely respected them and used to take oaths, such as when they feared infantile deaths due to the spread of diseases, that if their sick child would survive, they would make him a Jew.[86] However, many of them were jealous too of the lands, which the Jews had developed through hard work and commercial and agricultural skills. Thus, the Aus tribe would at times kidnap Qaynuqa Jews for ransom while the Khazraj would do the same to the Nadir and Qurayza Jews. This was because the Aus were allies of the Nadir and Qurayza Jews while the Khazraj were allies of the Qaynuqa Jews. At times, some of the Aus and Khazraj would kill a Jew of their non-allied tribe, for which they paid no blood money.[87]

The Medinian peasants revered and envied the Meccan Quraysh as well for having the multi-faith and income-generating shrine – the Ka'ba. They were regular pilgrims to the Ka'ba. They believed that if they had a prophet and a holy book, they too could be people of "status and wisdom" like the Jews and the Quraysh: They believed that a prophet could ward off disease and earthly depravations, and bring about prosperity.

For the Jews and the higher status Meccans, reading and writing was not something miraculous. The Meccans had a long tradition of hanging the best poetry in the Ka'ba. Therefore, most of them were not willing to believe that Muhammad's poems were "divine revelations." However, the largely illiterate Bedouins and peasants of Medina were attracted to the belief that God had sent the Qur'anic verses to Muhammad via the Angel Gabriel. The belief was not peculiarly related to Muhammad because many contemporary men and women had claimed that they had received their verses from God and large numbers of people had believed them.

Being one of the elite Quraysh, Muhammad had always despised the peasants as low-class people and said, `The home that houses agricultural implements is the home of Satan.'[88] However, having failed to win support of the elite Meccans or any tribe around Mecca, he now courted the Medinian peasants when they arrived on pilgrimage and among whom he found reverence for his "revealed" verses. In winning them over, his uncle Abbas played a key role by negotiating and telling the Medinians that the Hashim clan much revered Muhammad.[89] The Medinian visitors had known Abbas for long because Abbas used to visit Medina for trade and money lending. Hence, he had influence over them, especially because a number of them had been unable to pay him back.[90] Abbas knew that the Medinian peasants had the potential to become a fearsome force, which could be used to raid others, to conquer lands, and hopefully to conquer Mecca for the Hashimis. If the Medinians did that, Abbas told them, he would forgive the loan repayments they owed him. Many years later, after the take-over of Mecca, Muhammad would announce to the Medinians that they no longer owed the money they had borrowed from Abbas.

Abbas planned to support Muhammad covertly by being his secret informer in Mecca.[91] Until the conquest of Mecca, he would stay in Mecca, keep pretending that he was on the side of the secular Meccans, and secretly send information to Muhammad in Medina about the trade, commerce and defence activities of the Umayyads and the Banu Makhzum,[92] particularly about the days when their trade caravans would pass by Medina.

XXX

Six men of the Khazraj tribe met Muhammad and heard his preaching which, as usual, would be full of curses against the unbelievers. Then they convinced each other that he was the prophet whom the Jews were expecting. This was because when the Aus and Khazraj used to raid the Jewish tribes, the latter would sometimes say to them, `A prophet will be sent soon. His day is at hand. We shall follow him and fight you with his help and you will perish as Aad and Iram perished.'

Muhammad's preaching enhanced their jealousy of the Jews as they said to each other, `This is the very prophet of whom the Jews warned us. Don't let them reach to him before us! Let's be the first in swearing allegiance to him before the Jews take up this prophet too' (*i.e. in addition to Moses and other Jewish prophets*).

Then they said to Muhammad, `We have left our people, for no one is so divided by hatred and malice as we are. Perhaps God will unite us through you. So let us go to our people and invite them to this religion of yours, and if God unites us in it, then no man will be mightier than you.'

Thus saying they returned to Medina, and they told their people about Muhammad with such enthusiasm that in every home in Medina people knew about him.

As mentioned above, out of jealousy a belief had spread among the Medinians that the Jews were expecting a prophet who would lead them to rout, kill, and cleanse other people. In fact, one finds that Muhammad later led his Medinians followers, called the "Ansar" (helpers) to rout the Jews from Medina and install himself as the largest landowner on the confiscated Jewish lands. Accordingly, during the negotiations between Muhammad and the Medinians, he kept hinting that under his leadership, he could make them masters of the Jewish agricultural lands and property in Medina and that, with his Qur'an, they would have their own holy book; hence no inferiority complex vis-à-vis their Jewish neighbours or the Meccans. The reported conversations among the Medinians also show that they believed that it was a prophet's task to lead people to war, conquests, and booty of the vanquished. It has since been a typical strategy of Islamic sects that they accuse their prey of having the same designs as they themselves harbour.

The Aus tribe and the Jewish Banu Qurayza had friendly ties and allegiances. Before these six men of the Khazraj came and met Muhammad, some men of the Aus had come to Mecca to seek Quraysh help against the Khazraj, and Muhammad had invited them to follow him. Some of the Aus had agreed but their chief had gotten so furious, because of his friendship with the Jews, that he began to throw pebbles at his men and shouted, `This is not why we came to Mecca.'[93] In the same period, the battle of Bu'ath had taken place between the Aus and Khazraj. Then, as mentioned above, Muhammad and his uncle Abbas offered their plan to the Khazraj tribesmen, when they arrived for the hajj, and, six of them became believers.

In the following year, twelve men of the Khazraj came and swore allegiance to Muhammad. This was called the first Aqaba or "the pledge of women" because it did not impose upon them a duty to wage war. Ubaada bin al Samat reported:

> I was present at the first Aqaba. There were twelve of us and we pledged ourselves to the prophet in the manner of women because this was before the order to war. The undertaking was that we should associate nothing with God; we should not steal, fornicate, or kill our offspring; we should not slander our neighbours; we should not disobey him in what was right; if we fulfilled this, paradise would be ours; if we committed any of those sins, it was for God to punish or forgive as He pleased.[94]

When these twelve left, Muhammad sent with them Mus'ab bin Umayr to read his verses to them and instruct them in his religion. Mus'ab ended up leading the prayers because the Medinians could not bear to see one of their rivals take the lead.

XXX

In the following annual hajj, seventy-three men and two women came from Medina to swear allegiance to Muhammad. To keep it a secret, they met him in the valley of Mina, three miles outside Mecca. The distant location and the attempts to secrecy show that this was not solely about religious causes, as evident in the following reports. Ka'ab bin Malik reported:

> When we had completed the hajj and the night came in which we had agreed to meet the apostle, there was with us Abdallah bin Amr, one of our chiefs and nobles whom we had taken with us. We had concealed our business from those of our people who were *mushraykeen* (secular/multi-faith). We said to him, `You are one of our chiefs and nobles and we want to wean you from your present state lest you become fuel for

the fire in the future.' Then we invited him to accept Islam and told him about our meeting with the apostle at al Aqaba. Thereupon he accepted Islam and came to al Aqaba with us, and became a leader (*naqib*). We slept that night among our people in the caravan and when a third of the night had passed, we went stealing softly like sand grouse to our appointment with the apostle, as far as the gully by al Aqaba. There were seventy-three men with two of our women. We gathered in the gully waiting for the apostle until he came with his uncle Abbas who was at that time a *mushrik* (secular/multi-faith); albeit he wanted to be present at his nephew's business and see that he had a firm guarantee. When he sat down, he was the first to speak and said: `O people of al Khazraj (the Arabs used the term to cover both Khazraj and Aus). You know what position Muhammad holds among us. We have protected him from our own people who think as we do about him. He lives in honour and safety among his people, but he will turn to you and join you. If you think that you can be faithful to what you have promised him and protect him from his opponents, then assume the burden you have undertaken. But if you think that you will betray and abandon him after he has gone out with you, then leave him now for he is safe where he is.'

We replied, `We have heard what you say. You speak, O apostle, and choose for yourself and for your Lord what you wish.'

The apostle spoke and recited the Quran and invited men to God and then said, `I invite your allegiance on the basis that you protect me as you would your women and children.'

Al Baraa'a took his hand and said `By Him Who sent you with the truth we will protect you as we protect our women. We give our allegiance and we are men of war possessing arms which have been passed on from father to son.'

While al Baraa'a was speaking, Abu'l Haytham bin Tayyihan interrupted him and said, `O apostle, we have ties with other men (he meant the Jews) and if we sever them perhaps when we have done that and God will have given you victory, you will return to your people and leave us?'

The apostle smiled and said, `No, blood is blood and blood not to be paid for is blood not paid for. I am of you and you are of me. I will war against them who war against you and be at peace with those at peace with you. Bring out to me twelve leaders that they may take charge of their people's affairs.' And we produced nine from al Khazraj and three from al Aus.

Abdallah bin Abu Bakr reported:

The apostle said to the twelve leaders, `You are the guarantors for your people just as the disciples of Jesus, Son of Mary, were responsible to him, while I am responsible for my people, that is, the Muslims.' They agreed.

Asim bin Umar reported:

To test their faith to the apostle, al Abbas bin Ubaada said, `O men of Khazraj, do you realize to what you are committing yourselves in pledging your support to this man? It is to war against all men – even red and black men. If you think that if you lose your property and your nobles are killed you will give him up, then do so now for it would bring you shame in this world and the next. But if you think that you will be loyal to your undertaking even if you lose your property and your nobles are killed, then take him, for by God it will profit you in this world and the next.'
They said that they would accept the apostle on those conditions. But they asked what they would get in return for their loyalty, and the prophet promised them paradise.[95]

The reports make it obvious that, disguised in religious terms, these negotiations were about making war on the unsuspecting Jews who had been the first to settle in Medina more than three centuries ago. The Aus and Khazraj had migrated from Yemen much later but they now wanted to grab the Jewish agricultural lands. More reports state that the initial questions, which Muhammad asked the Khazraj, included, `Are you friends of the Jews?' to which they replied in the affirmative[96] and then the following dialogue took place:

Uncle Abbas: 'O Ansar (helpers) of Khazraj, Muhammad is a highly respected member of our tribe. We have always supported him against his opponents. Now he wants to live with you. Do you swear that you will support him until death? If you cannot, tell us now before it is too late.'

Baraa'a (*the first leader of the Khazraj*): 'We are raised in the shadow of swords. We are armed warriors and we have learned tactics of war from our elders. We swear allegiance to the messenger and we will protect him.'

Abu'l Haytham (*second leader of the Khazraj*): 'O messenger of God, we have good relations with the Jews. This allegiance to you binds us to break our relations with the Jews. We are afraid that after you win power and authority, you might choose to abandon us and return to your home town.'

Muhammad: 'That will never happen. When you will want blood, I shall want blood. When I shall want blood, you will want blood. When I forgive, you will forgive and when you forgive, I shall forgive. You are mine and I am yours. I shall fight whom you will fight and I shall reconcile with those whom you reconcile with.'[97]

Abbas bin Ubaada: 'O Khazraj, do you understand what you are swearing allegiance to? You are swearing that you will be bound to go to war against blacks and whites. If you are afraid that you will lose property or high-ranking men in battles, then tell us now. If you are willing to risk your property and lives for the sake of greater gain in the end, only then swear allegiance.'

The Khazraj: 'We are willing to risk property and lives in loyalty to the apostle Muhammad.'[98]

The reports quoted above indicate that the ethnic cleansing of the Jews of Medina was in Muhammad's mind before he migrated there. In the quoted dialogue in which the Khazraj swore allegiance to Muhammad, the statements, "This allegiance to you binds us to break relations with the Jews..." and, "When you will want blood, I shall want blood. When I shall want blood, you will want blood ..." clearly indicate this. The Aus and Khazraj were bitter rivals and Muhammad planned to unite them by providing them a common target – the Jews. Hence, they said to Muhammad, `No people are more divided by enmity and malice than we are. Perhaps you will unite us with God's will.'

In this second pledge, called "pledge of men," the oath-takers clasped Muhammad's arm one by one and swore themselves to armed protection and help, as one of them later remembered, `We pledged ourselves to fight in complete obedience to the messenger, in ease and in hardship, and in evil circumstance.'

The irony of the matter is that the Jews of Medina used to inform the locals about how a man named Muhammad had come to the Meccans as a messenger and that the Quraysh had doubted his claims.[99] The Jews had raised the Medinians' curiosity and here, some of the Medinians were bonding with Muhammad to break allegiance with the Jews and to follow him to shed their blood.

The Islamists claim that the subsequent cleansing of the Jews from Medina was their own doing; that the Jews used to plot against Muhammad. The evidence the Islamists put forward relies entirely on the "divine revelations" sent to Muhammad. No factual evidence of such plotting exists but there is enough evidence to show that Muhammad coveted the Jewish lands, which the Jews had developed through centuries of hard work and interest in agriculture. Further events in Medina show that the Jews had no idea what Muhammad had in store for them.

XXX

When the Khazraj were swearing allegiance to Muhammad, a man on the hilltop saw them and shouted at the top of his voice, 'O people of Mina! Wake up! There are *Subaat* (apostates; the plural of *Sabi*) gathered and *Muzamam* (the cursed; derogatory label for Muhammad) is with them. They have gathered to make war on you!'

Muhammad knew this man and he said, `This is the worm of the hill; the son of Azyab.' Then he shouted, `Do you hear O enemy of God, I swear I will kill you.'

Muhammad hastily terminated the session and commanded the Khazraj to return to their camp quickly and separately on their camels. One of them, Abbas bin Ubaada, lost patience and said, `If you order us we will fall on the people of Mina tomorrow with our swords.' Muhammad replied, `You are not allowed yet; but go back to your camp.'[100] They left and slept until the morrow.

The next morning, the Meccans leaders came to the Khazraj camp to investigate, saying that they had heard that the Khazraj had invited Muhammad to come to Medina and pledged to support him in war against Mecca, adding that they neither wanted nor expected to go to war against Khazraj.

Those of the Khazraj who were not part of the conspiracy did not know about it and so they swore that nothing of the kind had happened. Their unsuspecting leader Abdallah bin Ubayy said,

'This is a serious matter; my people are not in the habit of deciding a question without consulting me in this way and I do not know that it has happened.[101] However, when the Medinians had left Mecca, the Meccans investigated the report closely and found that it was true. They went in pursuit and overtook Sa'ad bin Ubaada and Mundhir bin Amr. Both were the leaders of Muhammad's co-conspirators. The later got away but they caught Sa'ad and brought him back to Mecca beating him on the way and dragging him by the hair, for he was a very hairy man. Sa'ad later reported:

> As they held me, a number of Quraysh came up, among them a tall, white, handsome man of pleasant appearance and I thought that if there was any decency among them this man would show it. But when he came up he delivered me a violent blow in the face and after that I despaired of fair treatment. As they were dragging me along, a man took pity on me and said, 'You poor devil, haven't you any right to protection from one of the Quraysh?' 'Yes,' I said, 'I have. I used to guarantee the safety of the merchants of Jubayr, the son of Mut'im bin Adiy, and protect them from those who might have wronged them in my country; also Harith, the son of Harb bin Umayya.'
> He said, 'Very well, then call out the names of these two men and say what tie there is between you.'
> This I did and that man went to them, found them in the mosque beside the Ka'ba, and told them of me and that I was calling for them and mentioning my claim on them. When they heard who I was they acknowledged the truth of my claim. They came, and had me released. The name of the man who hit me was Suhayl bin Amr, brother of Banu Amir bin Lu'ayy.

Among those who had come to investigate in the Khazraj camp was Harith bin Hisham, the grandson of the Makhzum chief Mughira. Harith was wearing a pair of new sandals. When he asked the Khazraj if they had sworn allegiance to Muhammad, a Khazraj man cunningly tried to distract him and said to their elder, 'O Abu Jabir, seeing that you are one of our chiefs, can't you get hold of a pair of sandals such as this young Qurayshi has?' In frustration, Harith threw his sandals at him and said, 'By God you can have them.' Abu Jabir reprimanded his man, 'Gently now, you have angered this young man, so give him back his sandals.' But the man grabbed the sandals and said 'By God I will not, it is a good omen and if it proves to be true, someday I shall snatch his entire property from him.'[102]

This apparently minor but very revealing event and many more events of similar nature demonstrate that many Ansar were bandits and hooligans. When they returned to Medina after swearing allegiance to Muhammad, they started by committing mischief: An old man named Amr had a wooden idol, which he revered and kept clean. His son Mu'adh had sworn allegiance to Muhammad. He, along with other men, would sneak into Amr's house at night, steal his idol, and dump it in into a cesspit. The next morning the old man would find his idol, wash it, perfume it, and bring it back. Then he would say to his idol, `If I knew who did this to you, I would treat him shamefully!' When night came and he was fast asleep, they did the same again and he restored the idol in the morning. This happened several times until one morning he found his idol back in the sewage tied to a dead dog. The old man had no choice but to submit to Muhammad's followers.

XXX

When the Medinians had gone back to Medina, Muhammad told his Meccan followers to move to Medina in small groups to avoid attention but, in a small town, this was impossible. Relatives found out what their kith and kin were planning and tried their best to stop them from leaving. One emigrant was intercepted by his uncle half-way out of Mecca, accompanied by Abu Jahl, and told that his mother was so grieved at his departure that she had vowed not to comb her hair; she would sit under the scorching sun until she sees him again. When they had brought him back, his uncle told the Meccans, `O men of Mecca! Deal with your fools the way we have dealt with ours.'

Umm Salama, who later became Muhammad's fourth wife after her husband's death, tried to leave along with her husband Abdallah and son but her relatives stopped her from leaving. Her in-laws took away her son and so her husband left alone for Medina. Umm Salama reported:

> I was separated from both my husband and my son, and there was nothing I could do but weep. I used to go out every morning and sit in the valley weeping continuously until a year or so had passed when one of my cousins passed, saw my

plight, and took pity on me. He said to his tribesmen, `Why don't you let this poor woman go? You have separated husband, wife, and child.' So they said to me, `You can join your husband if you like;' and then they returned my son to me. So I saddled my camel and took my son and carried him in my arms. Then I set forth making for my husband in Medina. Not a soul was with me. I thought that I could get food from anyone I met on the road. When I was in Tan'im, I met Uthman bin Talha who asked me where I was going and if I was all alone. I told him that except for God and my little boy I was alone. He said that I ought not to be left helpless like that and he took hold of the camel's halter and went along with me. Never have I met an Arab nobler than he was. When we halted, he would make the camel kneel for me and then withdraw; when we reached a stopping-place, he would lead my camel away, unload it, and tie it to a tree. Then he would go away from me and lie down under a tree. When evening came he would bring the camel and saddle it, then go behind me and tell me to ride; and when I was firmly established in the saddle he would come and take the halter and lead it until he brought me to a halt. This he did all the way to Medina. When he saw a village of Banu Amr bin Auf, he said, `Your husband is in this village, so enter it with the blessing of God.' Then he went off on his way back to Mecca.

Events like this make a mockery of the Islamist claims (which base on Qur'anic propaganda such as sura 60 verse 1) that the unbelievers had forced the believers to leave Mecca through torture and persecution. Actually, most often, they had tried to stop them from leaving. Many migrants too could not bear being away from their relatives and they returned to Mecca in disobedience of Muhammad's orders. In reaction, Muhammad issued threats against them couched in religious guise:

> Turn to your Lord (*in repentance*) and surrender to His Will
> Before the penalty comes on you
> After which you shall not be helped
> And follow the best revealed to you from your Lord
> Before the penalty comes on you suddenly
> Without your knowledge
> Lest the soul should say, `Woe is me!

I neglected my duty towards God
And was but among those who mocked!
If only God had guided me,
I should certainly have been among the righteous!'
Or the soul should say when it actually faces the penalty
`If only I had another chance,
I should certainly be among those who do good!'
(*The reply will be*), `No, there came to you my verses
And you rejected them: You were haughty,
And you became one of those who rejected faith!'
On the Day of Judgment you will see
Those who told lies against God, their faces will be turned black
Is the abode of the haughty not in hell? (Sura 39, verses 54-60)

A man named Hisham bin al Aas succumbed to the temptation to return to Mecca. Umar wrote the above-mentioned verses on a piece of parchment and sent them to him. Hisham was returning to Mecca when he received those verses. He could make nothing of them until he said, `O God, make me understand it.' Then he realized that the verses were about the returnees and he was one of them. So he turned back his camel and returned to Medina.

Throughout the year 622, which marks the first year of the Islamic calendar, believers abandoned one home after another. By the autumn hundreds of men, women and children had migrated. These included Umar and Uthman but Ali and Abu Bakr stayed with Muhammad. The leading Meccans tried to make light of it, and Abu Jahl said, `Nobody will cry over their leaving,' but people were very upset. As many grieved over the loss of their kith and kin to Muhammad's designs and schemes, anger focused on him, the cause of all this pain. Amr bin al Aas, one of Muhammad's devotees, was once asked about the worst way in which Quraysh showed their enmity to Muhammad, and he replied as follows:

> I was with them one day when the notables had gathered in the Hajr and they talked about the apostle. They said that they had never known anything like the trouble they had endured from this fellow; he had declared their mode of life foolish, insulted their forefathers, reviled their religion, divided the community, and cursed their gods. What they had borne was past all bearing – or words to that effect. While they were thus discussing him the apostle came towards them and kissed

the black stone, then he passed them as he walked round the temple and they said some injurious things about him. This I could see from his expression. He went on and as he passed them the second and third time, they did the same. He stopped and said, `Will you listen to me O Quraysh? I swear by God I will bring you slaughter.' This word so struck the people that they all stood silent and still. The most rowdy among them spoke to him in the most kind way possible saying, `Depart, O Abu'l Qasim, for by God you are not violent.' The next day when they were speaking about what had happened the day before, the apostle appeared again and they leapt upon him, encircled him, and said, `Are you the one who said so-and-so against our gods and our religion?' The apostle replied, `Yes, I am the one who said that.' And I saw one of them seize his robe. Then Abu Bakr intervened weeping and saying, `Would you kill a man for saying God is my Lord?' And they left him. That is the worst that I ever saw Quraysh do to him. Abu Bakr's daughter told me later, `Abu Bakr returned that day with his hair torn. He was a very hairy man and they dragged him along by his beard.

Muhammad would not allow Abu Bakr and Ali to migrate to Medina before him but he wanted to see all the other believers settle first in Medina, prepare the town's people, and gather in large numbers to receive him on his arrival. Having learned his lessons in the art of propaganda, he wanted a show of strength in numbers on his first entry into Medina – the opposite of the way it had happened in Ta'if where he had gone alone. Medina would be a very different affair.

The Quraysh had been seeing with alarm that Muhammad had broken the rule of tribal loyalty, taken pledge from outsiders, and sent his followers to live with them. He had inflicted deep wounds to hundreds of Meccans by alienating their closest relatives and making them leave the town. Now they feared that Muhammad would bring an outsider army to make war on Mecca or use his Medinian base to rob Meccan caravans as they passed by Medina on route to Syria. This was possible because the total population of Medina was about the same as that of Mecca – around twenty-five thousand. However, they did not have Muhammad's aggressive and presumptuous nature, and though they held meetings to deliberate and find a course of action against a traitor, they could not bring themselves to kill a man who always tried to invoke sympathy by pointing at his being "an orphan" and "a man of God."

They held a meeting to take counsel what they should do about Muhammad, for they were now in fear of him. Those present included Utaba and Shayba, sons of Rabi'a, Abu Sufyan, Tu'ayma bin Adiy, Jubayr bin Mut'im, Harith bin Amir, Nadir bin al Harith, Abu'l Uzz'a abu'l Bakhtri, Zamm'a bin al Aswad, Hakim bin Hazam, Abu Jahl bin Hisham, Nubayh and Munabbih, sons of Hajjaj, and Umayya bin Khalf. The discussion opened with the statement that now that Muhammad had gained adherents outside the tribe, they were no longer safe against a sudden attack and the meeting was to determine the best course to pursue.

One leader proposed that Muhammad should be locked up but another clan leader pointed out that Muhammad's followers could attack the house and free him, which would make the authorities look powerless. Another leader suggested that they should drive him out of Mecca, `Let him go wherever he wants and the harm he has done will disappear. We will then restore our community harmony,' but this plan too could backfire because Muhammad was capable of influencing the Bedouin tribes and lead them to attack Mecca. `Muhammad could use the Bedouin tribes to destroy us, seize power, and do away with us,' said another leader.

Abu Jahl came up with another plan; he asked every tribe, other than the Hashim clan, to select a strong young man from them and form a multi-tribal group. This group was to strike Muhammad with their swords as one so that the responsibility for bloodshed would divide equally among all clans. The Hashims would not be able to retaliate against the entire Quraysh and would have to accept the blood money to which they would all contribute and pay. Having agreed to this decision, they all dispersed.

However, the evidence that such a plot was planned comes again only from Muhammad. He claimed that the angel Gabriel had warned him about the plot. He sent a message to Abu Bakr to meet him outside Mecca that very night and told Ali to lie in his bed and to wrap himself in his green Hadrami mantle, for no harm would befall him. He himself used to sleep in this mantle. To make the story look more miraculous, he stated that a group of assassins waited all night outside his house while he slipped out and they could not see him. This story was reported as follows:

When they were all outside his door, Abu Jahl said to them, `Muhammad alleges that if you follow him you will be kings of the Arabs and the Persians. Then after your deaths, you will be raised to gardens like those of the Jordan. But if you do not follow him, you will be slaughtered, and when you are raised from the dead you will be burned in the fire of hell.'

The apostle came out to them with a handful of dust saying, `I do say that and you are one of them.' God took away their sight so that they could not see him and he began to sprinkle dust on their heads as he recited these verses:

> By the wise Qur'an, you are among the prophets and on a straight path. This has been revealed by the Exalted and Merciful to warn those whose ancestors were not warned and therefore they remain heedless. The majority has believed the truth but these will not believe. We have fixed yokes round their necks right up to their chins, so that their heads are forced upwards. And We have placed a curtain in front of them and a curtain behind them; We have covered them and they cannot see. (Sura 36, verses 1-8).

When he had finished reciting, not one of them was without dust on his head. Then someone came and asked them what they were waiting for there. When they said that they were waiting for Muhammad, he said, `But good heavens Muhammad came out to you, put dust on the head of every single man of you and then went off on his own affairs. Can't you see what has happened to you?' They put up their hands and felt the dust on their heads. Then they began to search (inside the house) and saw Ali on the bed wrapped in the apostle's mantle and said, `By God it is Muhammad sleeping in his mantle.' Thus they remained until the morning when Ali rose from the bed and then they realized that the man had told them the truth.

One cannot find a more ridiculous story than this in which a group of assassins stand outside Muhammad's house all night, chatting, then walk-in to confirm that he was still in bed, then resume their chat, still waiting when – just like Muhammad's numerous assassins described later – they could have simply walked in and killed him.

Nevertheless, to convince his followers that this miracle really happened, Muhammad issued the following verses claiming as usual that God had sent them:

Remember when the unbelievers were scheming
If they should arrest you, kill you, or exile you
They made their schemes and God made His schemes
And God is the best schemer. (Sura 8, verses 30)

Muhammad and Abu Bakr left together through the back-window of Abu Bakr's house and hid in a cave near Mecca for three days fearing that Quraysh would chase them on route to Medina. It is surprising that Muhammad did not notice the discrepancy between his two claims: He claimed to have come out of his house unseen by the besiegers but then he hid in a cave for three days for fear of being seen. It seems that logic was not his main concern.

Abu Bakr's son Abdallah, daughter Asma, and slave Amir brought them news and food every day in the cave. Asma reported that Abu Jahl came and asked her where her father was, and when she replied that she did not know, he slapped her. However, this too seems unlikely because all that Abu Jahl needed was to follow any of the abovementioned three, who supplied news and food to the couple hiding in the cave, and he would have found where Muhammad was hiding.

People spun stories about Muhammad's "escape," and others believed them despite their implausibility. The Quraysh announced a reward of a hundred camels to the one who would bring Muhammad back. A man named Suraaqa bin Malik claimed that, lured by the reward of a hundred camels, he had chased Muhammad and Abu Bakr and caught up with them though his horse kept stumbling and throwing him. When he reached them, his horse's forelegs went into ground and it fell. Then, as it got its legs out of the ground, smoke arose like a sandstorm. Suraaqa knew then that Muhammad was "divinely protected." However, strange enough, this "miracle" did not encourage him to believe in Muhammad and he waited to tell his story until, after thirteen years, Muhammad had won all his victories in the region and Suraaqa had no choice left but to become a believer.

XXX

Muhammad's followers in Medina had had ample time to raise the curiosity of the people of Medina about him. One day, when they eagerly waited for him in the outskirts of Medina, and were about to return in disappointment, a Jew stepped up on the roof of his house. He told them that he could see some men approaching from a distance and added, `It seems this is the prophet you have been waiting for.'[103]

People ran out to greet Muhammad and women sang his praises on the beats of duf – a half-drum made of camel skin stretched over a round wooden frame. Thus encouraged, thinking that he would soon have a jihadi force to be able to supersede the Meccans, Muhammad issued the following verses:

> Permission is given to those who make war
> Because they are wronged
> And God is their most powerful helper
> They have been wrongfully expelled from their homes
> Just because they say, `Our Lord is God'
> If God would not displace one set of people by another
> Monasteries, churches, synagogues, and mosques,
> In which the name of God is said in abundance,
> Would be destroyed
> God will certainly help those who help him
> Verily God is full of Strength, and Exalted in Might.
> (Sura 22, verses 39-40)

> Fight them until no more seduction remains
> And God's religion becomes dominant
> And if they stop then end hostilities except with the cruel.
> (Sura 2, verse 193)

Muhammad begins to split the multi-faith society of Medina: The Covenant of Medina

Muhammad settled in Medina along with around two hundred of his Meccan followers whom he had advised to migrate before him. Some of these lived off the food and shelter offered by their Medinian hosts but some bought their own houses and pieces of farmland. Many, such as Abu Bakr, had brought large sums of money with them, which shows that these were nothing like the "victims of exile," which Islamists portray. Muhammad instituted brotherhood between his fellow emigrants (*muhajirin*) and the helpers (*Ansar*) and said, 'Let each of you take a brother in God.' He himself took Ali by his hand and said, 'This is my brother.' His uncle Hamza became the brother of Muhammad's ex-slave Zayd bin Haritha. To him Hamza gave his last testament before the battle of Uhud.

Then he had his first mosque constructed from mud-bricks, reed, wood, twigs, and palm trunks. It consisted of an open compound inside a mud-brick boundary wall, a palm-thatched cover in the centre for shade, and lean-toes against the walls as sleeping quarters. Other than for prayers, this was a gathering place where meetings took place and decisions made. Using the same material, adjacent to the mosque, they also erected huts for his wives. To summon his followers to prayers and meetings, he first thought of using a trumpet like that of the Jews but this was too obvious an imitation and so he ordered a clapper to be made and beaten when the believers should pray. Meanwhile, a believer told Muhammad that he had found a better way, a loud call to prayer, which had come to him in a dream. Muhammad liked this idea and said, 'God be praised for that!'

It is said that a man's character is revealed when he gains power. In Mecca, the power was in the hands of the secular tribal chiefs and, despite Muhammad's attempts to take power by inviting outsiders to raid Mecca, they had largely tolerated him and his followers for more than a decade. They had exchanged insults, and clashes had taken place but the chiefs had neither killed nor exiled Muhammad or his followers. Now Muhammad would reveal how he would use his newly gained power in Medina, called Yathrib in those days.

Muhammad initiated by drafting a document and inviting the Jews to sign it alongside his followers. This so-called treaty, covenant, or charter, while accepting the existing tribal divisions, also divided the people of Medina between Jews and believers through its clauses that specifically dealt with these two groups:

Clauses about the believers

- This is a document from Muhammad, the prophet. The emigrant Quraysh, the believers of Yathrib, and those who follow them and fight alongside, are a special community, *the Ummah* (nation), to the exclusion of all other men.

- A believer shall not slay a believer for killing an unbeliever, nor shall he help an unbeliever against a believer. Believers are friends of each other to the exclusion of outsiders.
- When believers are fighting in the way of God, no separate peace shall be made. In every raid, a rider must carry another behind him. The believers must avenge the blood of one another shed in the way of God.
- Whosoever shall kill a believer without good reason shall be subject to retaliation unless the next of kin is satisfied with blood money and the believers shall be against him as one man, and they are bound to take action against him. The curse of God and His wrath on the Day of Judgment shall rest on the man that shall aid or shelter an evildoer and neither repentance nor compensation will be accepted from him.
- Believers shall not leave anyone destitute among them by not paying his redemption money or blood money in kindness.
- Whoever is rebellious or seeks to spread injustice, enmity, or sedition amongst the believers, the hand of every man shall be against him even if he were the son of one of them.
- The Quraysh emigrants, according to their several clans, shall pay the blood money for a murder among them, and shall redeem their prisoners. The Banu Auf, according to their present custom shall pay the blood money they paid in heathenism, and redeem their prisoners; the Khazraj tribes of Banu Sa'ida, Banu al Harith, Banu Jusham, and Banu al Najjar likewise; the Aus tribes of Banu Amr bin Auf, Banu al Nabit and Banu al Aus likewise.

Clauses about the Jews

- The Jew who follows us shall have aid and support. He shall not be wronged nor shall his enemies be aided.
- The close friends of the Jews are as the Jews; none of them shall go out to war except with the permission of Muhammad but he shall not be prevented from taking revenge for a wound.
- Among the Jews and their adherents, who shall transgress and do iniquity, he alone and his family shall be punished.
- The Jews shall be responsible for their own expenditure, the believers for theirs but each must help the other against anyone who attacks the people of this document (in which case) the Jews must pay with the believers so long as the war lasts. They

- must seek mutual advice and consultation, and they can protect themselves from treachery by being loyal (to the believers).
- The contracting parties are bound to help one another against any attack on Yathrab. The Jews shall contribute to the cost of war so long as they are fighting alongside the believers. If they are called to make peace and maintain it, they must do so; and if they make a similar demand on the believers, it must be carried out except in the case of a holy war.

Most Medinian tribes contained converts to Judaism. Muhammad gave them a group identity as Jews, which was separate from their tribal identity and added the following clause about these:

- The (convert) Jews of al Aus and their ex-slaves have the same standing as the people of this document and they can protect themselves from treachery by being loyal (to the believers). The (convert) Jews of Bani Auf, Bani al Najjar, Bani al Harith, Bani Sa'ida, Bani Jusham, Bani Tha'alba, Bani Aus, Jaffina, and Bani al Shutayba, are one community with the believers and their ex-slaves except those who behave unjustly and sinfully, in which case they are responsible for the hurt that will come to them and their families. They can protect themselves from treachery by being loyal (to the believers). The Jews have their religion and the believers have theirs.

General Clauses

- (The Meccan) Quraysh and their helpers shall not be given protection. No *mushrik* (secular/multi-faith person) shall protect the property or persons of Quraysh (of Mecca) nor shall he intervene in a matter against a believer.
- Strangers under protection shall be treated on the same footing as their protectors; but no stranger shall be taken under protection save with the consent of his tribe. A stranger under protection shall be as his host doing no harm and committing no crime. A woman shall be given protection only with the consent of her family.
- He who slays a man without warning slays himself and his household, unless it be one who has wronged him, for God will accept that.

- War and Peace shall be made in common. And none but the evil man and the oppressor shall change the conditions of this charter.
- Yathrib shall be a sanctuary for the people of this document.
- If any dispute or controversy likely to cause trouble should arise, it must be referred to God and to Muhammad the apostle of God.
- God approves of this document. This deed will not protect the unjust and the sinner.

Hitherto, people had tribal identities, regardless of their faith. That is why Muhammad's tribe had protected him despite his change of faith but, as can be seen, he divided people into believers, *mushraykeen* (secular/multi-faith) and Jews. The Islamists hail this as "unifying various tribes under one banner of Islam" but they ignore the far more treacherous division, which Muhammad created, by separating people because of their religion. Instead of eliminating tribal identities and unifying people as humans, he added another division to it. Thus, the Covenant of Medina laid the foundation of separation between Muslims and Jews that would last for as long as Islam would last.

The charter spelled out blood-money arrangements and the responsibilities of each tribe in case external forces attacked the town. It determined a mandatory contribution towards a war fund, in exchange for the right to seek protection from murder, loot and plunder.[104] However, it also laid the foundation of allowing the believers to kill the unbelievers with impunity and no revenge would be due.

Among the clauses of the charter was, "If they (the Jews) are called to make peace and maintain it they must do so; and if they make a similar demand on the believers it must be carried out except in the case of a holy war." In other words, "holy wars" would be exempt from efforts to make peace. Muhammad had pre-emptively introduced the concept of "holy wars" and though Medina was not under threat of any attack, and no outside force had attacked it so far, Muhammad invented a threat to justify his ensuing preparations for war. There was neither a friendly intention nor a need behind such a treaty because the Jews and the other Medinian tribes had never fought each other as two distinct communities, and each non-Jewish tribe had some Jewish converts as part of their tribe. If there was a need for a treaty, it was between the Aus and Khazraj, who had fought many battles against each other, but Muhammad arranged for this treaty to segregate the Jews from the believers.

The Jews had no choice but to sign because Muhammad's men had already begun to spread rumours that the Jews had bad intentions about them. For example, for a few months when there was no childbirth among the emigrants, they spread word that the Jews had cast an evil spell upon them.[105] Another anti-Jewish rumour was spread that a Jew of the Banu Zariq tribe had cast an evil spell on Muhammad, which had stopped him from seeing his wives. During the months in which the first mosque of Medina was being built, Abu Umama, the chief of Banu al Najjar, died and Muhammad said, `How unfortunate is the death of Abu Umama! The Jews and the Arab hypocrites are sure to say, "If he were a prophet his companion would not die" but I have no power from God for myself or for my companions to avert death.'

Because the Banu al Najjar were Muhammad's maternal relatives, after the death of Abu Umama, he became their chief in addition to being the "apostle of Allah."

Muhammad preaches from the Torah and beguiles
the Jews into respecting him as a leader

For many years, Muhammad had been praying facing Jerusalem. A niche in one wall of the mosque he built showed the direction of prayers (*qiblah*). He also imitated the Jews in his reciting and praying manners,[106] and in banning pork. The Jews used the attribute *ar-Rehmaan* (the merciful) for God, which also appears as *Rehmaana* in the Babylonian Talmud. Muhammad borrowed this too and instead of the Meccan, *Bayismak Allah* (in the name of God) he started saying *Bismillah-ar-Rehmaan-ar-Raheem*. Although both *Rehmaan* and *Raheem* mean the same, Muhammad had to show that his phrase was different from the Jewish one because all too often people had accused him of copying from the older religions.

At that time, his Qur'an consisted of only a few chapters (*suras*) which did not provide detailed codes of conduct. Hence, Muhammad led the Ansar in consulting the Torah for rules and regulations. This strengthened the Ansar belief in him as the messiah whom the Jews expected but who had eventually come to them. It enhanced their sense of victory over the Jews and lent more credibility to Muhammad as the last of the long list of the earlier prophets.

Among the many commands that Muhammad took from the Torah was one stating that if a man had sex with an animal, both the man and the animal should be killed. Eating the meat of a sexually abused animal was unlawful (*haraam*).[107] Other commands that he borrowed from the local versions of the Torah will be mentioned at relevant places. The Jews welcomed the newcomers, participated in their prayers, and would amicably say, `We are believers too.'[108] For some time, it seemed that Muhammad had denounced the Meccan multi-faith society for nothing because he was now participating in multi-faith prayers with the Jews. But this was only a learning stage. As soon as Muhammad had established a rapport with the Jews and borrowed as much from their religion as he needed, he began to pressurize them to recognize his apostolate and follow him. He cleverly linked his "revelations" to the Jewish faith and, as usual, inserted threats and lures to respectively coerce and motivate them into submitting to him:

> Before this, was the Book of Moses as a guide and a mercy: And this Book confirms it in the Arabic tongue to admonish the unjust, and bring glad tidings to those who do right. (Sura 46: verse 12)

> And who turns away from Abraham's religion but such as debase their souls with folly? We elevated him in this world and he will be in the hereafter in the ranks of the righteous. (Sura 2, verse 130)

The Jews argued that Abraham and all the Jewish prophets had advised their people to abide by Judaism. In response, Muhammad issued the following verses:

> Abraham and Jacob told their sons that God had chosen this religion for them and they should submit to it.
> Were you witnesses when death appeared to Jacob? Behold, he said to his sons: "What will you worship after me?" They said: "We shall worship your God and the God of your fathers, of Abraham, Isma'il and Isaac, the one God. (Sura 2, verses 132-133)

They say: 'Become Jew or Christian if you would be guided.'
Say: 'No! I would rather follow Abraham's true religion, and he joined not partners with God.'
Say: 'We believe in God, and the revelation given to us, and to Abraham, Isma'il, Isaac, Jacob, and the Tribes, and that given to Moses and Jesus, and that given to prophets from their Lord: We make no difference between one and another prophet: And we submit to God.'
So if they (*Jews*) believe as you believe, they are indeed on the right path but if they turn back and breakup, God will suffice you, and He is the All-Hearing, the All-Knowing.
Take the sign of God. And who has a better sign than God.
Say: 'Will you dispute with us about God, seeing that He is our God and your God; that we are responsible for our doings and you for yours; and that we are sincere in Him?' (Sura 2: 135-139)

In his early days in Medina, Muhammad hoped that by invoking the names of the Jewish prophets and by following the Torah, he would bring the Jews to follow him as their new prophet. Hence, at times, he told the Ansar to be kind to the Jews and preached, 'The Torah teaches us not to kill, not to exile, and pay blood money for murder. Why is it that you, the Ansar, follow part of the Torah in paying blood money but do not follow the other parts which tell us not to kill and not to exile?'[109] He also issued the following verses:

The believers, the Jews, the Christians, and the *sabis* (people with no religion), those who believe in God and the Last Day, and do good deeds, shall have their reward with their Lord; on them shall be no fear, nor shall they grieve.   (Sura 2, verse 62).

Do not dispute with the people of the nook except with politeness
Unless it be with those of them who are cruel
But say, 'We believe in the revelation which has come to us
And in that which came down to you
Our God and your God is one and to Him we bow.'
(Sura 29, verse 46)

Say, 'O people of the book! Come to what is common between us:
That we worship none but God
That we associate no partners with him

That we make not gods from among ourselves other than God.'
If then they turn back, say,
`Bear witness that we bow to God's Will.   (Sura 3, verse 64)

Say, `We believe in God, and in what has been revealed to us
And what was revealed to Abraham, Isma'il, Isaac, Jacob,
And the Tribes, and in the books given to Moses, Jesus,
And the prophets, from their Lord
We make no distinction between one and another among them
And we bow to God's will.
          (Sura 2, verse 136, and repeated in Sura 3, verse 84)

He also kept his followers from attacking the Jews, for the time being, by issuing verses such as the following:

Most of the people of the book want to turn you away from belief
Out of jealousy and malice, though the truth is obvious to them
Forgive them and ignore them until God sends orders (*to fight*)
God has power over everything. (Sura 2, verse 109)

The Jews appreciated this because it showed that Muhammad was interested in protecting them from occasional murder and robbery by some of the Ansar. But, as the subsequent events were to show, what he really intended by such preaching from the Torah was to instil the concepts of "murder" and "exile" in his followers' minds as essential and regular elements of his religion. When Muhammad's god spoke too often about murder and exile, it made it easier for his followers to commit both acts.

<u>Muhammad recruits the poor by
sheltering, feeding and training them</u>

Muhammad began to gather the poorest and most deprived nomads around him. He preached goodwill and charity to his well-off followers in order to help feed the poor. These unfortunate were called "people of the shelter" (*ashaab-s-safa*) because they lived under a large shelter made of palm trunks, branches and leaves, next to the mosque. Some of them would gather firewood during the day to exchange it for food. Most had no more than a coarse sheet of cloth with which they covered their bodies. Some Ansar would send them cheese and dates to eat but, at times, they went without food for as long as two days. During longer prayers in the mosque, some would faint and fall due to weakness and malnutrition. The well off would see them lying on the floor and think they were insane.[110]

When the relatively well-off Ansar sent food, Muhammad would distribute it among these poor men. Sometimes, he would allocate the poor to the wealthy to take home and feed them. A rich follower would at times take eighty poor and feed them. To encourage feeding these poorer adherents, Muhammad issued revelations such as:

> If a believer feeds a hungry believer, God will feed him fruits in paradise; if a believer clothes a naked believer, God will clothe him in fine clothes in paradise; if a believer offers water to a thirsty believer, God will offer him special wine in paradise.[111]

For some time it seemed Muhammad was kind to the poor and made the rich look after them. However, having installed himself as the chief of this community of the deprived and their Ansar hosts, he found himself increasingly under pressure to do more for his devotees, such as arranging money to buy wives for them. Buying a wife or slave woman for matrimony was an already existing custom and Muhammad sanctioned it in Sura 4, verses 24-25 of the Qur'an.

The economic pressures grew and he found himself unable to fulfil the growing needs of his poorer followers. However, rather than find ways and means to engage them in economically productive activities, he began training them into religion, fasting, five-times-a-day prayers, and learning his "divine verses" by heart. Consequently, a large number of men became dependent on charitable provisions, which he obtained from his Ansar hosts. The poor had little choice but to adore Muhammad, attributing **supernatural powers and miracles to his person.** The level of reverence these adherents showed for him can be inferred from the following description given by Urwa bin al Zubayr to the Quraysh:

> When Muhammad performs his ablutions, his devotees compete and jostle around to secure the water that has touched his body. When his hair fall, they pick it up and preserve it as a holy relic. When he spits, people fall on each other to pick the spittle, which they consider to have medicinal properties.[112]

Muhammad encouraged such adoration by claiming that he had miraculous powers. For example, once he lost one of his camels and could not find it. A critic named Zayd bin al Lusayt remarked, `Muhammad claims that he receives revelations from the heavens but he does not know where his camel is!' When Muhammad found his camel, he claimed that God had informed him that his camel was at a certain place.[113]

As narrated above, Muhammad's hundreds of devotees depended on him for their daily provisions. Consequently, they had no choice left but to do anything he asked of them. The following pages describe how these men succumbed to conducting robberies, ransom-taking, and secret assassinations.

The testimonies to robberies and assassinations

Scores of recorded testimonies show that hundreds of poor and needy men became Muhammad's secret assassins and bandits. Among these is the testimony of Ibn abu Hadrad who could not afford to pay dowry to obtain a wife, and he sought Muhammad's help. Muhammad asked him to wait. Ibn abu Hadrad waited for some days until the nomadic Banu Jusham tribe encamped in al Ghaba. Muhammad summoned Ibn abu Hadrad and two other men and told them to kidnap the chief of the Banu Jusham and bring him to Medina. He gave them an old thin she-camel which, as reported, was so weak that it could not get up until men pushed it from behind, and said, `Make the best of it and ride it in turns.' The reason for giving such a weak camel, as will be shown, was that Muhammad wanted them to return on the camels looted from the tribe.

Ibn abu Hadrad and his two men set forth with bows and swords until they arrived near the settlement in the evening as the sun was setting. He hid at one end of the camp and ordered his companions to hide at the other end, and told them that when they heard him shout *Allah o Akbar* (God is great) as he ran to the camp, they were to do the same and run towards him from the opposite side.

They intended to take the tribe by surprise late in the night but the tribe had a shepherd who had gone out with the cattle and was so late in returning that their chief got worried, hung his sword round his neck, and said that he was going on the track of him, for some harm must have befallen him.

As the chief passed by Ibn abu Hadrad, and came in range, he shot him in the heart with an arrow, and he died without uttering a word. Ibn abu Hadrad leapt upon him, cut off his head, and ran in the direction of the camp shouting *Allah o Akbar* and his two companions did likewise. Shouting out to one another in the darkness, the tribe believed that a large number of bandits had attacked them, and they fled with their wives, children, and such of their property as they could easily lay their hands on.

The three bandits drove off a number of camels and brought them to Muhammad. They showed him the severed head of the chief, and he rewarded Ibn abu Hadrad with some of the looted camels to help him with the dowry required to buy a wife.[114]

The Islamists justify the above quoted banditry by stating that Muhammad sent these men to attack the Banu Jusham because the tribe was gathering people to attack him. In evidence, one finds that although Muhammad did tell his men that the tribe was gathering people to attack them, the details of the event make a mockery of this justification. On the one hand, the Islamists state that the tribe was gathering a large force to attack the Muslims, and on the other hand, they state that three men on a weak and thin camel were able to force the tribe to flee while they drove off a number of their camels. When one scrutinizes the details, only one explanation seems to fit the events: Muhammad's men raided a weak and unarmed tribe, who got scared when their chief was murdered, and so they fled, leaving their cattle and camels behind. Because the looters had swords, bows and arrows, and they rode the looted camels, it was not safe to chase them on foot.

One finds the Islamists repeatedly covering up for numerous acts of plain banditry by stating that Muhammad feared an attack and hence raided first. They ignore the facts that Muhammad's men were based in Medina when they conducted these early raids on weak nomadic tribes who had little arms and resources to attack a town. Even the heavily armed Quraysh did not succeed in entering Medina when they later tried to attack it.

Among the several testimonies recorded by Muslim historians, is the testimony of Jundab bin Makith Juhni, which reads as follows:

> The prophet sent us, led by Ghalib al Kalbi, on a night cavalry raid on the Banu al Mulawwah tribe who were in al Kadid. When we reached the place called Qudayd, we met al Harith

al Laythi and seized him. He pleaded that he was going to the prophet to be a believer but we bound him tightly, left him in charge of a young slave and told him to cut off his head if he tried to escape. We went on until we came to the valley of al Kadid at sunset. My companions sent me to spy on the target tribe. So I left them and went on until I came to a hill overlooking the tribe. As I was lying low on the hilltop a man came out from his tent and said to his wife, `I see something black on the hilltop; perhaps the dogs have dragged one of your garments up there.' She checked her clothes and told him that nothing was missing. He then shot two arrows at me but I did not move. He shouted at his wife, `If it was a spy of some gang he would have moved, for both my arrows have hit him; in the morning go and get the arrows back. Do not let the dogs chew them.' Then he went inside his tent. We gave the tribe time until their cattle returned in the evening and they milked them and went to sleep. We waited until it was close to dawn. We wanted to attack close to dawn because otherwise it would be hard to escape in darkness. Close to dawn, we attacked the tribe. Our war cry was "Slay! Slay!" The tribesmen cried out to one another for aid but we killed some and drove off their cattle. We were quick to ride back until we passed by al Harith and the slave and carried them along with us. The tribe tried to chase us but could not cross on foot a stream in the way and so they stood looking at us as we drove off their cattle to the prophet. Whilst driving the cattle to the prophet, one of our camel riders sang:

Muhammad will not allow that these camels
Should disappear in the darkness of night
And not reach his grazing fields
Full of fresh and juicy grass.[115]

In analysing this testimony, one might argue that Muhammad had nothing to do with the booty his men were taking but then one is faced with overwhelming evidence that proves that loot and booty had become his primary source of sustaining his growing number of followers. For example, the earliest Islamic histories sate that when Muhammad sent Abd al Rehmaan bin Awf to raid Domat'l Jindal, he gave him instructions not to cheat on the booty.[116] As to whether one can trust the testimony of Abd al

Rehmaan bin Awf, it is sufficient to point out that Muhammad's two daughters and Abd al Rehmaan bin Awf's daughter were married to Uthman who was Muhammad's closest associate and the third caliph in the series of Muslim rulers. Muslim historians regard Abd al Rehmaan bin Awf's veracity beyond doubt because he was the head of the consultative body (shura) which nominated Uthman as the third caliph. Moreover, scores of reports from Muhammad's closest associates and evidence from the Qur'an reveal that booty had become the major source of sustenance for the believers, along with the slave trade.

The slave trade

Among the events showing the intermittent enslavement and sale of men, women and children by Muhammad and his followers is the well-recorded event whereby Muhammad's slave turned foster son Zayd bin Haritha returned from a raid with many captives of various classes, both well off and poor. These were sold and, because families were separated in the process, when Muhammad came to see the captives, he found that they were crying. He asked why they were crying and when he was told they were crying because families had been split in the process of selling them as individual slaves, he said, `Do not separate mothers from children but sell them together.'[117] Some reports suggest that Muhammad did not stop this practice of separating families during the sale[118] while another report states that he forbade separating mothers from children and, on one occasion, he commanded that two slave brothers should be sold together.[119]

Contrary to the Islamists' claim that Muhammad abolished slavery, not a single verse in the Qur'an bans slavery per se. The narrations only show that Muhammad's view of slavery depended on who the slave was and what position he or she held in his scheme of things. During his lifetime, Muhammad possessed a total of sixty-three slaves, men and women – not all at one time.[120] He often did not allow the freeing of slaves unless the slave had paid back his/her price to the owner. This process of freeing a slave based on a contract stating that the slave would earn and pay back his/her price was known as *mukataybut*.[121] Kind unbelievers too used to free their slaves.[122]

Muhammad's wife A'isha once bought a slave woman called Burayra and freed her on condition that all the money and property she would make, she would bequeath it to A'isha.[123] A'isha made this investment for she saw in the slave woman the ability to make money.

Muhammad's another wife Maymuna too owned a slave called Suleiman ibn Yasser who became an erudite narrator of *hadeeth* (orally transmitted narrations) in the hope that he would be freed but she demanded a large sum in price, which he was unable to pay.[124]

Once, a man in Medina, on his deathbed, freed his slave. Muhammad quickly arrested the slave, sold him to Naeem bin Abdallah for eight hundred dirhams, and kept the money for himself. He then declared, 'A slave remains a slave so long as one dirham of his price remains due upon him; if someone kills a slave, he should pay his/her price to the owner and, in case of a slave under *mukataybut*, the killer should pay the remaining price.'[125] He also declared, 'A slave who marries without the permission of his owner is to be charged with fornication and duly punished.'[126]

However, Muhammad knew the potential of slaves to be good fighters for him. Hence, in order to encourage the slaves to join in jihad, he declared, 'If a believer frees a male believer slave, God will spare him the tortures of hell.' To win slaves against their unbeliever owners, Muhammad declared to unbeliever slave owners, 'If you will kill your slave, we shall kill you, if you will sever their noses or ears, we shall do the same to you, and if you will castrate your slaves, we shall castrate you.'[127]

In short, the slave ownership rights of believers were protected – except when the slave could be better used as a free man – but the slaves of unbeliever owners were lured to leave their masters and become jihadis.

When his poorer followers could not pay dowries to buy wives, Muhammad issued another statement, 'If a believer frees a female slave, the owner will be saved from hell.'[128] Freed female slaves could be taken as wives with lesser dowry or none. The Qur'an states:

> …You can marry two, or three, or four, but if there is a doubt of inequality, then have one wife or take slave women. That will be more suitable to prevent you from doing injustice (among wives).
>
> (Sura 4, verse 3)

Note that in order to be fair to one's wife, Muhammad prescribes taking more women only as "slaves." When his own wives demanded that he should not take more wives, Muhammad promised that if he were attracted to more women, he would take them only as slaves. This will be described later.

According to *Shari'a* (Islamic Law), even after marriage, a slave woman cannot enjoy the status of a free woman. For example, a slave-wife can be divorced with two warnings instead of three. During the divorce process, she is allowed to remain in the master-husband's house only until she has had two menstrual periods rather than the prescribed three, for free women.[129] Children from slave-wives cannot get a share of inheritance equal to that of those born of free wives.[130] Bearing a child for the master does not much improve her situation, as the following oral tradition (*hadeeth*) states:

> Slave women, from whom you have had children, may be sold: This matter has been disputed among the companions of the prophet. Although most consider it unfair, the respected scholar Hazrat Jabber said, "During the life time of the prophet we used to sell those slave women who were mothers of our children." Caliph Umar once said, "How can you sell a woman who has delivered your child and you have become one flesh," but Caliph Ali, Jabber and other companions considered it allowed (*halaal*) to sell slave mothers of our children. Caliph Ali once said, 'I and Umar used to consider it unfair to sell those slave women who had delivered our children but now I know that this is allowed in Shari'a.'[131]

Muhammad preaches to the people of Medina

The first hundred or so verses of the Sura "The Cow" describe how Muhammad created hatred and anger in the hearts of his men against those he wanted to raid, plunder, and enslave if they refused to submit to him. These he called the "unbelievers," or "hypocrites." In these verses, he also replied to his critics in the form of threats, warnings, and taunts. Some of these verses are as follows:

> As to those who reject faith, it is the same whether you warn them or do not warn them; they will not believe. God has set a

seal on their hearts and on their hearing; on their eyes is a veil; great is the penalty they incur.

Some of them say, 'We believe in God and the Last Day,' but they do not believe. They try to deceive God and the believers but they only deceive themselves, and they do not realise it. In their hearts is a disease, and God has increased their disease, and grievous is the penalty they incur because they are false.

When it is said to them, 'Do not make mischief on the earth,' they say, 'Why, we only want to make peace!' Surely, they are the ones who make mischief, but they do not realise it.

When it is said to them, 'Believe as the others believe,' they say, 'Should we believe as the fools believe?' Surely, they are the fools but they do not know.

When they meet those who believe, they say, 'We believe,' but when they are alone with their evil ones, they say, 'We are really with you: We were only joking.' God will throw back their mockery on them, and give them space in their trespasses so they will wander like blind ones. These have bartered guidance for error but their trade is profitless and they have lost true direction.

They are like those who kindled a fire; when it lighted all around them, God took away their sight and left them in utter darkness. So they could not see. Deaf, dumb, and blind, they will not return to the path. Or they are like those with a rain-laden cloud in the sky: In it are zones of darkness, and thunder and lightning: They press their fingers in their ears to keep out the stunning thunder-clap while they are in terror of death. But God is ever around the rejecters of faith! The lightning all but snatches away their sight; every time the light helps them see, they walk therein, and when the darkness grows on them, they stand still. And if God willed, He could take away their faculty of hearing and seeing, for God has power over all things.

O people! Praise your Lord Who created you and those who came before you to give you the chance to learn righteousness. He made the earth your couch, the heavens your canopy, sent down rain from the heavens and brought forth fruits for your sustenance. Do not set rivals to God when you know the truth. And if you are in doubt about what We (*God*) have revealed from time to time to Our servant (*Muhammad*), then produce a Sura like this and call your witnesses or helpers besides God, if you are true. But if you cannot – and surely you cannot – then fear the fire whose fuel is men and stones, prepared for those who reject faith. (Sura 2, verses 6-24)

This kind of preaching did not really mean that it was up to God to punish the unbelievers. As the subsequent events showed, the preaching was a pretext to develop a case and unleash murder, war, destruction and confiscation of the lands and properties of others.

Muhammad preaches to the Jews of Medina

Muhammad continued to show to the Jews and Christians that he was well versed in their scriptures and accepted them as true but, in turn, he wanted them to follow him as the new prophet in addition to Moses and Jesus. Presenting himself as God, he apparently addressed the Jews and Christians but mostly he recited these verses to his largely illiterate followers and brainwashed them into believing that the Jews and Christians were inherently "ungrateful nations:"

> Children of Israel! Remember the favour which I (*God*) conferred upon you, and I preferred you to all other people. So prepare for the Day of Judgement when one soul shall not benefit another, intercession shall not be accepted, compensation shall not be taken, nor shall anyone be helped.
> And remember, We (*God*) delivered you from the people of Pharaoh: They set you hard labour and punishments, slaughtered your sons and let your women-folk live; therein was a tremendous trial from your Lord.
> And remember We divided the sea for you and saved you and drowned Pharaoh's people within your very sight.
> And remember We appointed forty nights for Moses, and in his absence you took the calf for worship, and you did grievous wrong. Even then, We forgave you; there was a chance for you to be grateful.
> And remember We gave Moses the scripture and the criterion between right and wrong: There was a chance for you to be rightly guided.
> And remember Moses said to his people, `O my people! You have indeed wronged yourselves by your worship of the calf: So turn in repentance to your Maker, and slay yourselves; that

will be better for you in the sight of your Maker.' Then He (*God*) turned towards you in forgiveness, for He is Forgiving, most Merciful.

And remember you said, `O Moses! We shall never believe in you until we see God manifestly,' but you were dazed with thunder and lightning as you looked on. Then We raised you up after your death: You had the chance to be grateful.

And We gave you the shade of clouds and sent down to you Manna and quails, saying, `Eat of the good things We have provided for you.' But they rebelled; to Us they did no harm, but they harmed their own souls.

And remember We said, `Enter this town, and eat of the plenty therein as you wish; but enter the gate with humility, in posture and in words, and We shall forgive you your faults and increase the lot of those who do good.' But the transgressors changed the word which had been given to them; so We sent on them a plague from heaven, but they transgressed repeatedly.

And remember Moses prayed for water for his people; We said, `Strike the rock with your staff,' and from there gushed forth twelve springs. Each group knew its own place for water. So eat and drink of the sustenance provided by God, and do neither evil nor mischief on the earth.

And remember you said, `O Moses! We cannot live with one kind of food always; so beseech your Lord to produce for us what the earth grows, its herbs, and cucumbers, its garlic, lentils, and onions.' He said, `Will you exchange the better for the worse? Go down to any town, and you shall find what ye want!' They were covered with humiliation and misery; they drew on themselves the wrath of God because they went on rejecting the signs of God and slaying His messengers without just cause, they rebelled and went on transgressing.

(Sura 2, verses 47-61)

However noble these verses may seem, they created hatred in the hearts of Muhammad's men against the Jews and Christian.

XXX

Muhammad had declared that he was the last apostle but, like his followers, the Jews too believed in the end of apostolate; they believed that the days of prophecy had ended twelve centuries before with the Babylonian exile. Likewise, the Christians believed that there could be no more messiahs after Jesus but Muhammad wanted them to believe in him as the next apostle after Moses and Jesus. While telling his followers not to accept anyone other than him as a prophet, he was not willing to give the same right to the Jews and Christians. Demanding against their will, Muhammad wrote the following letter to the Jews of Khyber:

> In the name of God the compassionate the merciful
> From Muhammad the apostle of God, friend and brother of Moses who confirms what Moses brought.
> God says to you, `O people of the book, you will find in your scriptures written, "Muhammad is the apostle of God," and those with him are severe against the unbelievers but merciful among themselves. You see them bowing, falling prostrating, seeking bounty and acceptance from God. The mark of their prostrations is on their foreheads. That is their description in the Torah and in the Gospel... God has promised forgiveness and a great reward to those who believe and do well. I command you by God, by what He sent to you, by the manna and quails He gave as food to your earlier tribes, and by His drying up the sea for your fathers when He delivered them from Pharaoh's slavery, that you tell me: Do you not find in your scriptures that you should believe in Muhammad? If you do not find it in your scripture then there is no compulsion upon you. The right path has become plainly distinguished from error. So I call you to God and His prophet.[132]

However, when many Jewish leaders told him that there was nothing about him in their scriptures, Muhammad changed his own stance (If you do not find it in your scripture then there is no compulsion upon you), called them "evildoers" and issued the following threats:

> We gave the scripture to Moses and sent apostles after him
> And we gave clear signs to Jesus, supported by the holy spirit
> But whenever an apostle brought to you
> Something against your inclination, you resorted to arrogance
> Rejecting some apostles and killing some. (Sura 2, verse 87)

> We have sent you (*Muhammad*) with clear signs
> And none but the evildoers disbelieve in them
> Is it not that whenever they make a covenant,
> A party of them ignores it?
> No, most of them do not believe
> Whenever an apostle of God came to confirm their scriptures
> A group of the people of the book ignored their book
> As if they did not know about it   (Sura 2, verses 99-102)

In Mecca, Muhammad had made his Qur'anic verses out of his arguments with the Quraysh unbelievers. Now he began to do the same in Medina and wrote many of his verses out of his arguments with the Jews, as if the unbelievers were actually helping him write his Qur'an though he claimed that God sent the verses to him.

Mahmud bin Sayhan, Nu'maan bin Ada, Bahri, Uzayr, and Salaam came to him and said, `Is it true, Muhammad, that what you have brought is from God? For our part we cannot see that your verses are as well arranged as the Torah is.'

He answered, `You know quite well that it is from God; you will find it written in the Torah which you have.'

Rabi Finhaas, Abdallah bin Suriy'a, Ibn Saluba, Kinana bin al Rabi'a, Ka'ab bin al Asad, Shamwil and Jabal were there and one of them said, `Muhammad, did neither men nor *jinn* tell you this?'

He said, `You know well that it is from God and that I am the apostle of God.' They said, `When God sends an apostle He does for him what he wishes, so bring down a book to us from heaven that we may read it and know what it is, otherwise we can produce verses like those you have.' Muhammad said, `If men and *jinn* came together to produce verses like these, they will not be able to do it.'

Based on these conversations, Muhammad issued the following "verses from God:"

> By God, you people know that it is from God, and it is written in the Torah that I am the messenger of God. If all the humans and *jinn* join their efforts, even then they would not be able to produce a book like mine.   (Sura 17, verse 88).

Two men, Rifa'a and Suwayd, had friends who had become believers. To appease the believers, the two would say that they too were believers but at times, they objected to the believers' excessive zeal, and raised questions about things such as the lack of practicality in their five-a-day prayers, which kept them from engaging in fulltime work. Muhammad issued the following verses about them:

> O believers, choose not as friends among Jews or unbelievers
> Who have chosen your religion to make a jest and game of it
> And fear God if you are believers.
> When you call others to prayers,
> They make fun of it because they are unwise.
> (Sura 5, verses 57-58)

Some men came to Muhammad and said, 'Tell us when the last day will be if you are a prophet as you say.' Muhammad issued the following verses:

> They ask you about the hour when it will come to pass
> Say, only my Lord knows of it.
> None but He will reveal it at its proper time.
> It will be heavy in the heavens and the earth
> Suddenly it will come upon you
> They ask you as though you know about it
> Say Only God knows about it, but most men do not know
> (Sura 7, verse 187)

A number of men came to Muhammad and asked him, 'God created creation, but who created God?' Muhammad was so angry that his colour changed but later he issued the following verses:

> Say, God is one; God is independent
> He was born of none and He gave birth to none.
> No one is of him. He is content to be one. (Sura 112)

When he recited this to them they said, 'Describe His shape to us, Muhammad; his forearm and his upper arm, what are they like?' Muhammad was even angrier than before and rushed at them but later he issued the following verses:

They do not think about God in the way they should;
The whole earth will be in His grasp on the day of resurrection
And the heavens folded up in His right hand
He is Pure and Exalted, above what they associate with Him
(Sura 39, verse 67)

Abu Hurayra reported that Muhammad said to his followers, 'Men question their prophet to such an extent that one would almost say, "Now God created creation, but who created God?" And if they say that, say, "God is one. He was born of none and He gave birth to none." Then spit three times to the left (because Satan stays on your left) and say I take refuge in God from Satan the damned.'[133]

Secret assassinations of critics in Medina

Finally, Muhammad had had enough. He was worried that questions and discussions about his verses would reduce the number of his followers, as people will find out the truth about him.

A very old man named Abu Afak of the Banu Amr bin Awf tribe was fearless enough to speak the truth. He was upset at his fellow townsmen turning into bandits who regularly prayed to God but were unable to differentiate between moral and immoral. He said:

I have lived long but never seen a people,
More keen in keeping their word,
And eager in hospitality
Than the Ansar, the offspring of Qayla –
The maternal ancestress of Aus and Khazraj
The Ansar would overthrow mountains rather than submit
But their guest has bewitched them
He has come to live among us and divided us
Through his preaching, he says in one breath
"Allowed" and "forbidden" for same sort of things
Mixing moral with immoral
But if it is power and might you want, Medinians
Why not follow a ruler of your own?

Abu Afak had made the most correct diagnosis of Muhammad's sociopathic behaviour: In his lust for power, Muhammad had failed to distinguish right from wrong. This judgement was the most serious threat to Muhammad's claims because if people would begin to think that God could not sanction robberies and murders, Muhammad would lose credibility as God's messenger.

Abu Afak's revelations extremely offended Muhammad and he said to his devotees, `Who will avenge me on this rascal?' One of his most zealous devotees, Salim bin Umayr, assassinated Abu Afak in the darkness of night, and one of Muhammad's poets, named Umama bin Muzayriya, boasted:

> You (Abu Afak) dared to charge God's religion
> And Muhammad of lies.
> Hence a sincere believer gave you a plunge
> In the darkness of late night saying,
> 'Take this Abu Afak – a gift to your old age.'
> Whether it was a ghost or man who slew you
> I would not say who it was.

The phrase, "whether it was a ghost or man" needs explanation: Muhammad's devotees had spread word that ghosts called *"jinn"* protected Muhammad and killed for him. This propaganda enhanced the fear that was common among the superstitious. It was one aspect of the psychological control that inspired awe, respect, and fear among the ill-informed, illiterate, and superstitious people who followed prophets and mystics in Arabia. Even in the 21st century, the "pirs" or so-called "holy men," in many countries, still control the minds of millions through similar means as Muhammad used; inspiring awe, respect, fear, and adoration in the subjects' minds by claiming that *"jinn"* serve them. The phenomenon is not particular to Muhammad and has its own psychological and social dynamics.

A woman named Asma bint Marwan was deeply grieved at poor Abu Afak's murder. She knew that it was not ghosts or *"jinn"* but one of Muhammad's devotees who had assassinated Abu Afak. In her grief, she addressed her townsmen as follows:

> By the common ancestor of the Medinian tribes,
> You are obeying an alien in killing your own chiefs
> Foolish men of Khazraj, will you be cuckolds?

And allow this stranger to take over your nest?
You put your hopes in him
Like hungry men waiting for a cook's broth
Is there no man of honour to rebel against this vile group?
And dash the hopes of the profit seeker?

When Muhammad heard what Asma had said, he said to his men, 'Who will rid me of Marwan's daughter?' That same night, one of his assassins, Umayr bin Adiy al Khaatmi, who was from the tribe of Asma's husband, sneaked into Asma's house, found her asleep with her baby in her arms, and plunged his sword through her chest.

In the morning, he came to Muhammad and told him what he had done. Muhammad blessed him, 'O Umayr! You have helped God and His messenger.' However, Umayr was afraid of retaliation from Asma's five sons and he told this to Muhammad. Muhammad knew that according to the Arab tribal code, it was very unlikely that a tribe would kill one of their own men to avenge the murder of a woman. Hence, he replied, 'Not even two goats will butt their heads for her.' Still, to protect his assassin, Muhammad sent a message to the Banu Khaatma, 'I have killed the daughter of Marwan, O sons of Khaatma! Now stand against me if you can; do not keep me waiting.' The threat worked and, fearful of Muhammad's assassins, the men of the Banu Khaatma came and swore allegiance to him. Muhammad's official poet Hassan bin Thabit celebrated this victory over a defenceless woman as follows:

Your tribes, Banu Wa'il, Banu Waqif and Banu Khaatma
Are inferior to the Khazraj – the Ansar
In her grief, when she called upon her tribe to commit idiocy,
Death befell her – as it was hovering over her head
She challenged Muhammad – a man of glorious origins,
Noble in his demeanour and manners
Hence, before midnight he dyed her in her own blood
And was still not a sinner.[134]

The last verse "and was still not a sinner" needs explanation: Because Muhammad had made lawful the secret killings of those who tried to reveal the truth behind his apostolate, his assassins were not sinners even after a murder. This is what poor Abu Afak had meant when he had said that Muhammad had made moral what used to be immoral. In addition, the criterion for "nobleness" had changed; a noble in Muhammad's religion was one who would kill his critics.

This criterion for nobleness has lasted among Muslims to the modern times: In British India the Muslims hailed Ghazi Alam Deen for murdering the author of the book, "A Colourful Prophet;" The Iranian Ayatollahs issued death sentence against Salman Rushdie for writing the "Satanic Verses." In Holland, a believer killed Theo Van Gogh for making a film about Islam. In Pakistan, Governor Salman Taseer's bodyguard killed him for seeking to change the Law of the Prophet's Sanctity that was being used to kill innocent persons. Muhammad's ghosts haunt his critics even in the 21st century.

Another man who saw what evils Muhammad had added into the Hanafi faith was a monk by the name of Abu Amir. He was an ascetic and wore a coarse hair garment. Hence, he was called "the monk." When Abu Amir saw his people joining Muhammad, he migrated to Mecca along with a group of virtuous people who were too weak to resist the aggressive followers of Muhammad. Before he left for Mecca, Abu Amir came to see Muhammad and asked him about the religion he had brought.

`The Hanifiya, the religion of Abraham,' said Muhammad.
`That is what I follow,' said the monk.
`You do not,' Muhammad snapped.
`But I do! You, Muhammad, have introduced into the Hanifiya things which do not belong to it.'
`I have not. I have brought it pure and white.'
`May God let the liar die a lonely, homeless, fugitive!'
`Well and good. May God so reward him!'

When Muhammad heard that the monk had migrated, he said, `Do not call him a monk; call him a sinner.' Later, when Muhammad took over Mecca, Abu Amir fled to Ta'if. When the people of Ta'if too surrendered, he migrated to Syria and died in exile.[135]

XXX

During Muhammad's raid on Tabuk (described later), many held back and a man named Julas bin Suwayd bin Samat Julas said, `If this man is a true prophet then we are worse than donkeys.' However, his stepson Umayr bin Sa'ad reported these words to Muhammad. Julas was so scared that he rushed to Muhammad and swore that he had not said it. Muhammad issued the following verses:

> They swear by God that they did not say
> When they did actually say words of unbelief
> And they disbelieved after they had submitted (*to the apostle*)
> They planned but could not carry out and had nothing to avenge
> Though God and His apostle had enriched them with booty
> If they repent, it will be better for them
> And if they turn back, God will afflict them
> With a painful punishment in this world and the next
> In this world, they will have no friend or helper. (Sura 9, verse 74)

Julas repented and saved his life but his brother Harith bin Suwayd bin Samat fled and went to Mecca.[136] Muhammad ordered Umar to kill him if he could get hold of him. Harith sent to his brother Julas asking for forgiveness so that he could return to his people but Muhammad issued the following verses about him:

> Those who believe and then turn to disbelief
> And then they go to the extremes of disbelief
> Their repentance will never be accepted
> These are the depraved.   (Sura 3, verse 90)

One report suggests that Harith later came to Medina where some of Muhammad's men found him and murdered him.[137]

At the said assassinations, triggered by the spies who reported to Muhammad, Nabtal bin Harith remarked, `Muhammad is all ears; if anyone tells him anything, he believes it.' Again, Muhammad's spies informed him about the remarks and he said, `If you want to see Satan, look at Nabtal bin Harith.'[138] Then he issued death threats hidden in his following "divine revelations:"

> Among them are those who annoy the prophet
> By saying that the prophet is all ears
> Say, he has good ears to benefit you
> He believes in God and trusts the believers
> He is merciful to those who believe in him
> As for those who annoy the prophet,
> There is a grievous punishment. (Sura 9 verse 61)

On another occasion, Muhammad called his assassin Abdallah bin Unays and said that he had heard that Khalid bin Sufyan bin Nubayh of al Hudhayl tribe was gathering people to attack him, and hence he should kill him. Abdallah asked Muhammad to describe Khalid so that he could recognize him, and he said, `When you will see him he will remind you of Satan. A sure sign is that when you will see him you will feel a shudder.' Abdallah's testimony is as follows:

> I went in search until I found Khalid with a number of women in a howdah seeking a resting place. It was the time for afternoon prayer and when I saw Khalid, I felt a shuddering as the prophet had said. I feared that something would prevent my prayers and so I prayed as I walked towards him with my head bowed. When I approached Khalid, he asked who I was and I answered, `An Arab who has heard of your gathering a force against this fellow and has come to help you.' He said, `Yes, I am doing so.' I walked a short distance with him, struck him with my sword, killed him, and ran off leaving his women bending over him. When I returned to the prophet and he saw me, he said, `Is the job done?' I said, `I have killed him, O prophet,' and he said, `You are right.' Then he took me into his house and gave me a stick telling me to keep it. When I went out with it, people asked me what I was doing with a stick. I told them that the prophet had given it to me and told me to keep it, and they said, `Why do you not go back to the prophet and ask him why?' So I did so, and the prophet said, `This stick will be a sign between you and me on the resurrection day. There are few men who will be carrying such sticks then.'

Abdallah bequeathed that upon his death, the stick should be placed in his winding sheet and so it was buried with him. He also boasted about his assassination of Khalid as follows:[139]

> I left that son of a cow or that of a camel
> In a state where all around him
> His women mourned and tore their dresses in grief
> My sparkling Indian sword had swallowed him
> Before cutting his head, I told him,
> `I am the son of a rich and generous man

And I follow the straight religion of Muhammad
So take this plunge from a noble man.
When the prophet decides to kill an unbeliever
I fall upon him with my tongue and my hands.'[140]

Note in Abdallah's report the deceptive phrase "I have come to help you," before he killed an unsuspecting man, and his boasting about the cowardly and deceptive manner in which he killed. Note also that Muhammad "blessed" him with a special status in paradise.

Abdallah's victim did not suspect him because the noble Arabs had the gallant tradition of challenging their opponents before attacking them. This tradition had kept the Quraysh from secretly killing Muhammad though it would have been very easy for them because of their wealth and influence. However, such moral considerations had no place in Muhammad's schemes. Deception became a regular part of the assassinations, raids, and campaigns, which he and his men conducted. These will be described in this work as chronologically as possible.

Secret assassinations of several men and women created an atmosphere of fear in Medina and more and more people began to revere and obey Muhammad. A large number of people submitted to him to get rid of the fear of murder hanging over their heads.[141] When the Aus tribal chief Sa'ad bin Mu'adh became a believer, his whole tribe submitted to Muhammad.[142]

Muhammad develops a pretext for maligning the Jews and breaking with them

It had been eighteen months since Muhammad had migrated to Medina. Many Jews prayed with him facing Jerusalem,[143] and respected him as a community leader but only one Jew had become a believer[144] (some reports suggest three Jews had converted) and Muhammad was not happy with this. He was now certain that the Jews would not submit to him *en masse* as the apostle of God and he decided to launch the next stage in his scheme of conquering the region. He began by ordering the believers to shun the Jews and break the friendships and ties of mutual protection and alliance that had continued from before Muhammad's arrival in Medina. Accordingly, he invented an "order from God" as follows:

O believers! Do not make friends those outside your ranks
They will not fail to corrupt you; they only desire your ruin
Rank hatred has already appeared from their mouths
What their hearts conceal is far worse.
We have made plain to you the signs, if you have wisdom.
You love them but they do not love you
Though you believe in the whole of the Book
When they meet you, they say, "We believe,"
But when they are alone, they bite the tips of their fingers in rage
Say, `Perish in you rage; God knows all the secrets of the hearts.'
(Sura 3, verses 118-119)

The Jews had trusted Muhammad's pretensions of using the Torah as the guide, and brought some of their cases to him for judgement. He, on the other hand, was waiting for an opportunity to malign them and invent excuses to seize their lands.

One day the Jewish rabbis gathered in their school to consider the case of a married man who had committed adultery with a married woman. They said, `Send them to Muhammad and ask him what the law about them is and leave the penalty to him. If he prescribes *tajbih* (scourging with a rope of palm fibre, blackening of their faces, and mounting them on two donkeys with their faces to the donkey's tail) then follow him. If he prescribes stoning for them, beware lest he deprives you of the mercy that you hold.'

The Jews hoped that he would be as lenient to the couple as he had hitherto been to his own followers: For example, people had once brought a believer to him on charges of fornication. Muhammad had judged that he be given a hundred lashes. When told that the man was small, weak, and might not withstand a hundred whips, Muhammad had said, "Take a bunch of hundred sticks and hit him once." This was very lenient.

The Jews brought the couple to Muhammad and explained their position. Instead of passing a judgement, he walked to meet the rabbis in the school and called on them to bring out their learned men. Abu Yasir, Wahb bin Yehuda and Abdallah bin Suriy'a were with them. Muhammad questioned them and then asked Abdallah bin Suriy'a, the youngest of them, whether the Torah did not prescribe stoning for adulterers. He said, `Yes,' but other rabbis disagreed. Muhammad asked for a Torah. A rabbi sat there reading it and Abdallah bin Salam struck his hand, saying, `This is the verse of stoning which he refuses to read to you.'

Muhammad said, `Woe to you Jews! What has induced you to abandon the judgment of God which you hold in your hands?'

They answered, `The sentence of stoning used to be carried out until a man of royal birth and noble origin committed adultery and the king refused to allow him to be stoned. Later another man committed adultery and the king wanted him to be stoned but they said, "No, not until you stone so-and-so." And when they said that to him they agreed to settle the matter by *tajbih* and they did away with all mention of stoning.'

Muhammad said, `I am the first to revive the order of God and His book and to practice it.' He had the fate of a Jewish couple in his hands and he wanted to make full use of this opportunity.

He went back to his mosque and commanded that the two should be stoned against the will of their people. Ibn Abbas, the son of Muhammad's uncle Abbas, reported that Muhammad ordered them to be stoned, and they were stoned at the door of his mosque.[145] When the Jew felt the first stone, he crouched over the woman to protect her from the stones until he was killed, and then the woman was killed.

Abdallah, the son of Umar, said, `I was among those who stoned them.' Muhammad personally supervised the stoning[146] and it did not soften his heart when he saw the man trying to save the woman from stones by covering her with his body.

This gruesome murder of the couple horrified the Jews especially because they had sent them to Muhammad in the expectation that after passing the judgement, he would send them back to them. Instead, he had had them murdered in the most brutal manner. Abdallah bin Suriy'a said that Muhammad could not be a prophet because he did not ask for God's guidance and trusted an old barbaric custom that the Jews had long abandoned. When Muhammad heard about this, he seized the chance and tried to gain political advantage by quickly blaming all Jews, as a nation, for not obeying the orders from God. He branded them as "hypocrites" who tempered with the Torah, and accused them of hiding its verses that prescribed stoning to death for adultery. He gathered his men and declared:

> O believers! Do not befriend the Jews and those who fiddle with religion: They first told you they were believers but now they are unbelievers. Actually, they entered our group hiding disbelief in their hearts and have now left with their disbelief,

and God is aware of what they were hiding (i.e. the verse about stoning).[147]

Intriguingly, the "death by stoning penalty for adultery," which Muhammad claimed was part of "God's Law," he later revoked when his own wife A'isha was accused of adultery. Hence, it is not found in the Qur'an but still many Islamists impose it in many countries, insisting that "oral traditions" carry more weight than the Qur'anic verses.

Muhammad issued many verses as follows to fully exploit the situation and create hatred for the Jews in the hearts of his men:

> O apostle, do not be upset about those
> Who compete against one another in unbelief
> Who say with their mouths, 'We believe,'
> But their hearts do not believe.
> The Jews who listen to lies,
> And listen for those who do not come to see you
> Who send others and stay behind themselves
> And give orders to change the judgement from its context
> They change words from their places, saying,
> 'If this is given to you receive it (*i.e. lighter punishment*),
> And if it is not given to you beware of it.'
> When God intends to destroy a people,
> He does not grant you power over them (*to convert them*)
> God does not intend to purify the hearts of these people.
> They will face grief in this world and grievous torture in the next.
> (Sura 5, verse 41)

> See how they make you to judge for them
> When they have the Torah with God's orders in it
> Then they turn away for they are not believers. (Sura 5, verse 43)

Muhammad kept thinking how he could separate his men further from the Jews, and one day whilst leading the midday prayers, he suddenly stopped and walked all the way back to the other side of the mosque. In doing so, he had to walk through the queues of the worshippers, leaving them surprised if not dumbfounded. When he had reached behind them, he announced that God had changed the *qiblah* (direction of prayers); while in the past, his followers and the Jews had both been praying facing north to Jerusalem, they were now to face south – towards Mecca. Because the Jews would not face Mecca in prayers, his followers would pray without the Jews.[148]

The good-natured among the Medinians did not want segregation and disharmony among neighbours. When they asked him why he had changed the direction of prayers, he replied in his cryptic way that this was done in order to separate those not rightly guided by God and, in the long run, this change would "bear fruit" – the fruit being the Jewish lands:

> We appointed the *qiblah*, which you formerly observed
> Only that we might know who would follow the messenger,
> And who would turn back upon their heels.
> All, except those correctly guided by God,
> Will be upset by the change of the direction of prayers.
> It is not God's purpose to make your faith fruitless.
> (Sura 2, verse 143)

He branded those who were upset at this change as "hypocrites." He also branded anyone who wanted to keep the old friendships with the Jews as "hypocrite," and instructed the "faithful" to stay away from both the Jews and the "hypocrites."[149]

The following verses of the Qur'an testify that Muhammad had always wanted to face Mecca in prayers: Facing Jerusalem in the first sixteen months at Medina was only a ruse to encourage the Jews to accept Muhammad's claims. With a sufficiently large fellowship, Muhammad did not need to have the Jews alongside.

> Indeed I (*God*) see that you (*Muhammad*)
> Repeatedly look towards the sky
> Surely, I (*God*) will change your *qiblah* to the direction you like
> So turn your face to the Sacred House (*the Ka'ba*)
> And wherever you are, turn your face towards it.
> And those who have been given the book (*the Jews*)
> Most surely know that it is the truth from their Lord;
> And God is not unaware of what they do. (Sura 2, verse 144)

He had lost hope that the Jews would follow him as the living replacement of Moses. Hence, he added:

> Even if you (*Muhammad*) were to bring to them (*Jews*) all the signs,
> They would not follow your *qiblah*
> Nor are you going to follow their *qiblah*
> Nor indeed will they follow each other's *qiblah*
> If you, after the knowledge has reached you,
> Were to follow their desires, you will indeed be in the wrong.
> The people of the book know this as they know their own sons
> But some of them conceal the truth which they know.
> (Sura 2, verses 145-146)

In order to rebuild community harmony and friendship, the prominent leaders of the Jews named, Rifa'a bin Qays, Qardam bin Amr, Rafay bin abu Rafay, Ka'ab bin Ashraf, Hajjaj bin Amr, Rabi'a bin al Rabi'a and his brother Kinana, the sons of Abu'l Huqayq, came to Muhammad and pleaded, `Muhammad! What is it that has made you change the direction of prayers? You claimed to be part of the nation of Abraham. You followed Abraham's religion, and we were with you. Please return to your religion and the old direction of prayers and we shall follow you and believe in your truth.' But this did not fit in with Muhammad's plans of takeovers of their lands, and so he replied that God had sent to him the following verses:

> The foolish people will say, `What has made them turn back
> From the *qiblah* they formerly observed?'
> Say to them, `East and west belongs to God;
> He shows the right path to those he chooses.' (Sura 2, verses 142)

<u>Muhammad trains his men in religion and robbery
to raid the Meccan caravans and weaker tribes</u>

Since their arrival in Medina, Muhammad and his followers had begun to spread word that they were afraid of the Meccans coming to Medina to kill him. Using this invented threat as a pretext, they had been gathering swords, spears, bows and arrows. They placed guards in their areas at night.

The peaceful way to live would have been to work as hard as the Jews did in trade, agriculture, irrigation, and the iron-smith and gold-smith businesses but that did not fit in with Muhammad's larger plan of conquering Mecca and the whole of Arabia as a starting point to marching towards the Byzantine and Persian empires.[150] Farming would make his followers settle down rather than be regular jihadis. Hence, when once Ali showed interest in irrigation and plantations, Muhammad derided him by calling him "the father of dust" (*Abu Turaab*) and warned him, `What have you been up to, *Abu Turaab*? Shall I tell you of the two most wretched creatures? Uhaymir of Thamood who slaughtered God's camel, and one who shall strike you here, Ali,' and he put his hand to the side of his head, `until your beard is soaked from blood,' and he took hold of his beard.[151]

To keep his followers from farming, he derided it by declaring, `When you will begin to sell agricultural produce in advance, chase bulls, like to do farming, and abandon jihad, God will inflict you with humiliation which He will not remove unless you return to your religion.'[152]

In his mosque, Muhammad preached to his followers to build forces, develop fighting skills, and procure arms especially bows and arrows.[153] He declared that those who did not participate in jihad either by intention or by deed were hypocrites.[154] Those who did not want to participate in the impending bloodshed disgusted him.

The trade caravans of the Quraysh were at great risk because Medina lies on route from Mecca to Syria, and Muhammad's men could attack them from Medina. Muhammad began to send spies with instructions to develop friendly contacts with the caravans and to return with insider reports.

When Muhammad had come to Medina, he was fifty-three years of age and it was thirteen years after he had made his first claim to being God's apostle. At the beginning of his twelfth month in Medina, he began to send out raiding parties and himself rode to as far as Waddan, looking for Quraysh. There he found a weak tribe called the Banu Damra bin Bakr whose leader Makhshi bin Amr al Damri submitted to him and he returned without making war. Then he sent his relative Ubayda bin al Harith bin al Muttalib with sixty or eighty riders from the emigrants, not a single Ansar among them. They went as far as Hejaz where they encountered a large number of Quraysh but no fighting took place except that Sa'ad bin abi Waqqas shot an arrow on that day. Muhammad's two spies, al Miqdad bin Amr and Utaba bin Ghazwan, were travelling with the Meccans in order to assess their strength and what merchandise they carried. Ikrima bin Abu Jahl was in command of the Meccans. When the two spies saw the troops of Ubayda, they fled the caravan, joined the believers, and returned with them to Medina. Abu Bakr heard of this encounter and composed the following verses:

> You see that neither admonition nor a prophet's call
> Can save some of Lu'ayy (*a Quraysh sub-tribe*) from unbelief
> A truthful prophet came to them and they gave him the lie,
> And said, 'You shall not live among us.'
> When we called them to the truth, they turned their backs,
> They howled like bitches driven back panting to their dens.

In March 623, seven months after the *hijra* (migration), Muhammad's uncle Hamza tried to raid a Meccan caravan led by Abu Jahl at the seashore in the territory of Juhayna. Hamza had thirty riders from the emigrants; none of the helpers took part. Abu Jahl led around two hundred riders from Mecca. The local tribal chief Majdi bin Amr al Juhani intervened because Bedouin chieftains received negotiated payments to protect caravans travelling through their territory. The believers left with nothing and Hamza composed the following verses about this encounter:

> When we saw each other, they halted and hobbled the camels,
> And we did the same, an arrow-shot distant
> We said to them, 'God's rope is our victorious defence,
> You have no rope but error.' Abu Jahl warred there unjustly,
> And was disappointed, for God frustrated his schemes.
> We were but thirty riders, while they were two hundred and one. Therefore, O Lu'ayy, obey not your deceivers,
> Return to Islam and the easy path,
> For I fear that punishment will be poured upon you
> And you will cry out in remorse and sorrow.

Abu Jahl answered him in verse, saying:

> I am amazed at the causes of anger and folly,
> And at those who stir up trouble by lying polemic,
> Who abandon our fathers' ways – those noble, powerful men.
> They come to us with lies to confuse our minds,
> But their lies cannot confuse the intelligent.
> We said to them, 'O our people, strive not with your folk
> Controversy is the utmost folly

For if you do, your weeping women will cry out
Wailing in calamity and bereavement.
If you give up what you are doing,
We are your cousins, trustworthy and virtuous.'
They said to us, `We find Muhammad
One whom our cultured and intelligent accept,'
When they were obstinately contentious
And all their deeds were evil,
Majdi (*the Bedouin chief*) held us back from them
Because of an oath binding on us, which we cannot discard,
A firm tie, which cannot be severed.
But for Ibn Amr (*the Bedouin chief*) I should have left some of them
Food for the ever-present vultures, un-avenged
But he had sworn an oath, which made
Our hands recoil from our swords.
If time spares me, I will come at them again,
With keen, new polished swords,
In the hands of warriors from Lu'ayy, son of Ghalib,
Generous in times of dearth and want.

All around Medina, there were many smaller and militarily weaker Bedouin tribes. Muhammad began sending emissaries to these tribes with messages not to provide food and water to the Meccan caravans. Then he bound them with cleverly drafted treaties that put them at risk of loot and plunder if they refused to obey him. For example, the treaty he made with the Banu Damra tribe, who lived around eighty miles from Medina states:

From Muhammad the messenger of God
To the people of the Banu Damra
Your lives and property will be safe
You will be supported against invaders
On condition that you fight for God's dues (*deen*)
And come to help when the messenger calls you.[155]

Muhammad would send jihadis to intimidate those tribes that refused to obey his orders. Before a raid, his spies[156] would determine the best time to attack, which was usually the time when the tribesmen would take their camels and cattle to pasture or water, and left the tribe unprotected. His favourite poet Hassan bin Thabit once described such a raid in the following verses:

We rode straight into your homes
There we stopped and made our horses urinate
Then we picked your women and children
Loaded them on our fast and sturdy horses
And galloped back home
The unbelievers were living in comfort in their homes
But now their faces are the faces of slaves
Our master is the prophet for all lands
He reads to us his book of illumination
And we affirm him.[157]

Another poet issued the following threats to those who would not obey Muhammad's orders:

The true prophet came to them but they rejected him.
When we invited them to truth, they retreated
And hid in their holes, moaned, and breathed heavily
If they will not give up their stray path
We shall carry out our promise:
Soon an attack will end the purity of their women
And bring unsparing vultures to their corpses.[158]

<u>Physical cleanliness and moral depravation:
How were the jihadis disciplined?</u>

Muhammad used personal control and fear to obtain obedience and loyalty. When he would send a gang of jihadis, he instructed them to kill those who disobeyed the leader. If a less than obedient man was injured, he was to be left where he lay and, in case he survived, he was not to have a share in the booty. The one who tried to abandon the gang, which was called "giving up belief," was to be killed.[159] To alleviate the guilt some of his men might feel over the acts of banditry and murder, he declared, `When you kill in the way of God, you are doing a noble act and hence the booty and slaves that you take is not a bad thing. If your intention is to spread God's religion, then all that you do is in God's name.'

A jihadi once complained that during the raids, some of them had killed women and children. Muhammad replied, `Women and children are with the enemy. It does not matter.' However, he soon realized that women and children could be sold as slaves and he amended his "divine message" to state, 'Kill the adult men and let the young live.'[160]

Because Muhammad conducted the disciplinary training in the mosque, he made it compulsory for his men to attend the mosque five times a day. His men were terrified if they forgot to attend the prayers with the others.[161] If someone had prayed alone, even in the mosque, he would order him to pray again with the group.[162] He threatened those who could not come to the mosque, by saying, 'I will gather firewood and burn your homes.'[163] Only slaves, women, children and the sick were excused from praying in the mosque but they had to pray in their homes.

Abdallah bin Amr bin al Aas reported that when Muhammad came to Medina, the fever of Medina smote his companions until they were extremely ill to such a degree that they could only pray sitting. The fever had not affected Muhammad. One day he came out to them when they were praying sitting and he said, 'Do you know that praying while sitting is only half as valuable as standing and praying?' His followers painfully struggled to their feet despite their weakness and sickness.

During sermons, Muhammad spoke in a loud voice, his eyes would turn red with anger and excitement, and he would warn his followers about imaginary enemies that were about to attack them. If someone would dare speak during his sermons, he would reprimand them in severe words such as, 'One who speaks during a sermon is like a donkey laden with books, and one who tells the former to shut up, loses God's acceptance of one's prayers.'[164]

Muhammad was concerned that someone pointing at errors and contradictions in the contents of his sermons could make him lose respect among the believers when he wanted unconditional obedience from them. One day, he ordered the expulsion of many men from the mosque whose intelligence he had found threatening to his authority. He saw some men of Banu al Najjar talking with lowered voice among themselves, and he ordered that they should be ejected. His devotee Abu Ayub got up and went to Amr bin Qays, one of the al Najjar, who was the custodian of their gods during the pagan era, took hold of his foot and dragged him outside the mosque, Amr saying meanwhile 'Would you drag me out of the date-barn of the Banu Tha'alba?' Then Abu Ayub went for Rafi' bin Wadi'a, another of the Banu al Najjar, gripped him by his robe, slapped his face, and dragged him forcibly out of the mosque, saying, `Faugh! You dirty hypocrite! Keep out of the apostle's mosque, you hypocrite!'

Another of Muhammad's bouncers, Umara bin Hazm, went for Zayd bin Amr who had a long beard, seized him by the beard, and dragged him violently out of the mosque. Then clenching his fists he punched him in the chest and knocked him down, Zayd crying meanwhile, `You have torn my skin off!' Umara answered, `God get rid of you, you hypocrite, God has a worse punishment than that in store for you, so don't come near the apostle's mosque again!'

A third bouncer Abu Muhammad went for Qays bin Amr who was a young man and pushed him in the back of the neck until he ejected him from the mosque.

A fourth bouncer, Abdallah, hearing the order to clear the mosque, went for al Harith bin Amr, a man with long hair, and taking a good grip of it he dragged him violently the whole way along the floor until he threw him out. Al Harith kept saying `You are very rough, Abdallah,' and he replied, `Serves you right, you enemy of God, for what God has sent down about you, don't come near the apostle's mosque again, for you are unclean.'

A fifth thug of Banu Amr bin Auf went for his brother Zuwayy bin al Harith and put him out violently, saying, `Faugh! You are doing Satan's work for him!'

Muhammad branded the ejected men as hypocrites and ordered that these should not come near the mosque.[165]

Some men could not always come to the mosque or could not stay long because of the routine activities of life but Muhammad insisted that they should come and stay for as long as he wanted them to. This led those, who were busy in essential chores, to make excuses such as, `My stomach was upset and I needed to go out.' Muhammad then made a "divine law" to prevent his followers from leaving the mosque. The law stated, `If you are in doubt that there is something in your stomach, do not leave the mosque unless you hear the wind coming out or really feel that it is coming out.' Some others made excuses such as, `Because I had touched my private parts, I had to go out to wash myself.' For these he issued another "divine law" stating, `If you touch your penis during prayers, you do not need an ablution.'

Later in history, Muslim scholars, who were not able to understand the context of the abovementioned laws, made them an immutable part of Islamic guidance. Because these scholars presented sex as a filthy act, they could not understand the law which stated, 'If you touch your penis during prayers, you do not need an ablution,' and so they inferred that there must have been a mistake, and they re-wrote a contradictory law, 'If you touch your penis in the mosque, you need another ablution.' Among these laws, which governed the most private and trivial aspects of the lives of Muhammad's followers, was one that stated, 'When you wake from sleep, you need an ablution.' When asked why, Muhammad replied, 'Eyes are like a lid on your anus; when eyes close, the lid opens.'[166]

One "hadeeth" (oral tradition) states that one should take a bath after copulation and cleanse oneself of the filth of intercourse.[167] Until one does so, one should not touch food, pray or read the Qur'an. Also, during their menstruation periods, women are not allowed to pray or touch the Qur'an, and men are forbidden to have sexual intercourse with them.[168]

These laws, such as, "Whilst urinating, do not touch your penis with your right hand," and, "Do not use your right hand for wiping after defecation because the right hand is used for eating your meals,"[169] actually reveal the wretched physical conditions in which Muhammad's poorer followers lived. He had to teach them the most elementary aspects of hygiene when he recruited, fed, clothed, trained, and let them loose among the self-sustaining sedentary or nomadic tribes to bring booty.

Extensive training in rituals, fixed manners of sitting, standing, prostrating, and performing ablutions show that Muhammad wanted to condition his men into obeying orders the way army commanders do. He would taunt them if they failed to do so, such as his following commands show: "Do not sit like a camel.[170] Do not place your hands on the ground the way beasts and dogs sit; to sit in such a way that your hands and bum touch the ground first, is to follow Satan."[171]

Muhammad banned humour and jokes related to religion in order to instil reverential behaviour among people.[172] He would tell them what they could wear and which types of clothes were forbidden. If one wore clothes that he did not like, he would taunt them, 'Has your mother told you to wear coloured clothes?'[173]

The effect of these fourteen hundred year old commands continues and one is amazed to see, in the 21st century, the Saudi and Gulf Arabs, *en masse*, wearing only white or a few shades of grey, like a uniform. Exceptions among these are rare.

In present day mosques and madrasahs, millions of pupils suffer the humiliation of learning under duress, for years, about how to conduct the petty and private aspects of living. With modern sanitary facilities, there is hardly any need to concentrate on methods of cleaning oneself with water, earth, or sand alone but these cleaning methods remain in Islamic textbooks because the mullahs insist that these are the "divine ways" of the "Holy Prophet." They construe any suggestion to removing them from Islamic books as blasphemous, and do not see that the primitive socio-physical conditions, which required the use of these methods, no longer exist.

Even in the 21st century, word goes around in the worldwide Muslim communities that serious thinking takes away a man's faith and, therefore, not recommended. Consequently, their cultural focus is not on finding objective solutions to eradicating poverty, hunger and disease but on using all legal and illegal means possible to amass wealth for their families and praying to God to solve their massive social problems through divine intervention.

Muhammad would often forget what he had taught and, to the perplexity of his followers, perform his own prayers in a different way. When his followers would point to this, he would make excuses, `I am only human. I forgot.'[174] He would often issue a "divine revelation," then forget it and issue a different one. For example, he forbade his followers from executing punishments in the mosque but when they once tied a man to a pillar in the mosque, on charges of idolatry, he ignored it.[175] He allowed women to wear gold but also forbade it.[176] On certain occasions, he forbade the use of expensive cloth for wrapping corpses but on other occasions said, `Wrap your dead in expensive clothes because, in the graves, they meet each other and proudly show their dresses.'[177] When he heard that Negus, the Christian king of Abyssinia who had been kind to believers, had died, he arranged funeral prayers for him[178] but then he also ordered not to offer funeral prayers for unbelievers.[179] At times, he forbade people from visiting graves but, at other times, he recommended it.[180]

In his prayers, Muhammad added taunts at the frugal and the pacifist: "O God, I seek your protection from stinginess and cowardice."[181] This prayer appears honourable but its meaning in his context was, "If you seek God's pleasure, spend on my war efforts and keep fighting to bring booty." One needs to remember that one-fifth (*khums*) of each booty went to Muhammad.

To create antipathy in the hearts of his men against those whom they were going to raid, he included, in prayers, curses for the would-be victims alongside blessings for those who followed him.[182]

Muhammad wanted his followers to plead to God to bless him and his family in the same way as He had blessed Prophet Abraham and his family.[183] There is a glaring contradiction here: Muhammad claimed that God had sent him as His last, final, and most beloved prophet to bless the believers, but instead he commanded the believers to plead to God to bless him. More than a billion Muslims now carry out his command of praying five times a day, and each prayer includes a petition to God to bless Prophet Muhammad and his family (*darud-shareef*) as much as He had blessed Prophet Abraham and his family.

Following these commands, millions in the poverty-stricken Muslim countries devote their lives in practising these rituals, which ultimately harden their minds and hearts. Cynical preachers instruct Muslims to follow the rituals in minute details, and waste years of their younger generations on training them in how to sit, stand, prostrate, and perform ablutions and rituals in the prescribed manners, with penalties and taunts for the non-conformist. However, a deeper analysis makes it more plausible that Muhammad's aim in enforcing these strictly choreographed rituals, and five-times-a-day prayers, was to distract his followers from thinking about the real moral issues such as if murder, robbery and pillage of others was moral or immoral. By focusing their attention on such petty acts as ablutions and defecations, Muhammad kept them from seriously thinking that robbery and rape were morally much worse than, for example, being absent from the five daily prayers, not washing in the prescribed manner, or not fasting.

The raid on the Mustalaq tribe and the kidnapping of its chief's daughter

The Mustalaq tribe lived at a distance of around nine miles from Medina, and their chief was Harith bin abi Drar.

In their customary way, Muhammad and his men raided this tribe at a time when most men of the tribe were away, pasturing their camels. There were only ten tribesmen in the camp and they caught them in surprise.[184] After killing these ten, the believers took six hundred captives, two thousand camels, and around four thousand goats,[185] which they transported to Medina. Muhammad temporarily distributed the captive women and children among his men for safekeeping, and handed over Juwayriya, the daughter of the tribal chief Harith, to Thabit bin Qays.

Juwayriya requested Thabit to free her in exchange for some money, to which he agreed but Juwayriya had no money and so she began to beg for money to buy her freedom. She came to Muhammad and begged for some money. At that time, A'isha was sitting with him. A'isha later stated, `Juwayriya was very pretty. When I saw her going towards the apostle I thought she will definitely influence his heart as much as she has impressed me, and so I felt jealous.'[186] A'isha was right in suspecting that Juwayriya's beauty would affect Muhammad because when he saw her, he said to her, `Will you accept that I pay your entire price to Thabit and marry you?' Juwayriya accepted the offer and found refuge in Muhammad's home.

Juwayriya's father returned home and found that Muhammad and his men had kidnapped his daughter, along with the women and children of his tribe. He understood the greed behind such a brazen act and so he gathered the leftover camels, which he and his men had taken to pasture, and began his journey to Medina to offer these as the price to buy his daughter's freedom.[187]

Before entering Medina, Harith hid two camels in a cave, hoping to use them later for travelling back with his daughter. However, Muhammad's spies at the border of Medina informed Muhammad that Harith had hidden two camels in a cave. When Harith offered his camels to Muhammad and pleaded for the release of his daughter, Muhammad said, `Are these all the camels you have?' Harith replied in affirmative. Muhammad said, `And what about the two camels you have hidden in a cave outside Medina?' Harith was so shocked by Muhammad's knowledge and so disappointed at not being able to travel back that he had no choice but to request to be taken in as a tax-paying believer. The other men of the Mustalaq tribe followed their chief as they saw that they had no option but to become subjects. The captives of the tribe were then released and their lands were returned because, without the lands, the tribe could not earn enough to be able to pay the taxes. Then Muhammad appointed Walid bin Aqaba to collect taxes from them and "honoured" Harith by raising the status of his daughter to a regular wife. He even paid the dowry money to

Juwayriya's father though, in the first place, he had looted it from the latter's tribe. The booty of the vanquished, ransom money and slaves were traditionally considered as the legitimate property of the raiders. One report states that Muhammad took the ransom and then married Juwayriya,[188] which means that he paid the dowry from her ransom.

Chronologically, this raid took place after the Battle of Badr. Its events show Muhammad's way of subjugating people to his rule, a process Islamists euphemise as "Islam" ("surrender" in Arabic).

The issue of adultery

Intermittent raids on weaker tribes had enabled Muhammad's men to acquire hundreds of slave women. They kept some and sold some to those who found it cheaper than paying dowry to marry a free woman. In addition, some slave-owners allowed others to have sex with their slave women for money. Traditionally, an owner had the right to use his slave for sex. This did not classify as adultery but if the slave had sex with someone else without his master's permission, the master could punish the slave. Muhammad issued many contradictory commands about this. On one occasion he said, `Apply the laws of Shari'a on your slaves as well,' but on another occasion he declared, `If a slave women commits adultery, beat her, if she does it a second time, beat her, third time, beat her, fourth time, sell her for whatever price you may get even if it be a rope.'[189]

Once, some slave women complained to Muhammad that their owners made money by allowing others to have sex with them. They demanded from him to instruct their owners to allow them to earn wages and buy their freedom. As stated earlier, under the custom of "mukataybut," slaves could buy their freedom by working and paying their market price to their masters.[190] Because taking captives and selling them as slaves was a source of income and a major incentive in jihad, Muhammad did not ban slavery but he consoled both the slave women and the owners by issuing the following verses:

> Those who cannot afford (*to pay dowry*) to marry,
> Should avoid sexual gratification by stealth
> Until God blesses them with wealth
> Those of your slaves who want contractual freedom
> (*That is, who can earn and pay their price*)

> Free them if you know they are truthful
> And give them something from God's provision
> And do not force your slave women to prostitution
> When worldly gain is your intention
> But if someone compels the women
> God, after the compulsion, is Kind and Merciful.
> (Sura 24, verse 33)

In other words, there was no "divine order" requiring men to free their slaves. Consequently, another serious problem arose. When men obtained younger slave women through raids and booty, many would lose interest in their wives but they still expected them to remain chaste. At times, some of these men would accuse their wives of having committed adultery and demand their executions[191] knowing that Muhammad had set the precedent when he had ordered the stoning of the aforementioned Jewish couple.

At first, Muhammad did order the execution of some women[192] including one who was pregnant. He told one of his men to provide shelter for her until the delivery of the child. After she had delivered the child, he ordered that her clothes be tied over her and then she be stoned to death. A second report suggests that the pregnant woman was given respite until the child was able to eat solid food, and then she was killed.

Muhammad soon realized that the precedent of stoning would be hard to follow on all occasions: In a society where sexual intercourse with slave women was common and there was little penalty for these women, death penalty for others placed the slaves at an advantage. Hence, when once a man demanded the stoning of his wife, Muhammad showed reluctance to do so. He asked the man's wife to admit or refute the charge.[193] From then on, when women would deny the charge of adultery, he would often set them free.

Another man once accused his wife of having committed adultery with a short grey-eyed man. Muhammad ordered the accuser to wait until the delivery of the child and said, 'If the child is grey-eyed and short, then come to me.'[194]

Another man complained that his wife had delivered a black child though he was not black. Muhammad said to the accuser, 'What colour are your camels?' The man said that his camels were red. Muhammad asked if there was a khaki camel among them.

The man said, `Yes.' Muhammad said, `How did this happen?' The man replied that some old link in the lineage could have caused it. Muhammad said, `Could this not be the case with your child?' The man still refused to accept that the black child was his own but Muhammad refused to charge the mother with adultery. He then devised rules to avoid a death sentence when a case of adultery was brought to him, and commanded: "As long as there is a way out, do not inflict dire penalties." If an accused woman would claim coercion into the sexual act, or state that sexual intercourse was forced upon her when asleep, there would be no dire penalty.[195]

On one occasion, when Muhammad and his followers were engaged in the battle of Badr (described later), some women of Medina seduced a halfwit named Ma'iz bin Malik, who had been left in the town. When Muhammad returned from the battle, Ma'iz told him that he had committed adultery. Muhammad did not want to hear this because it involved the wives of those who had just returned home from the battle, and so he turned his face away. Ma'iz approached him again and said the same thing. Muhammad tried his best to shut him up and said, `Are you drunk?' Ma'iz denied. Muhammad said, `Are you mad?' Again, Ma'iz denied. Muhammad then said, `Perhaps you just kissed or slept with them or just pressed their hands.' Ma'iz said, `No, I did the full act.' Muhammad again gave him a chance to save his life, `Do you know what adultery means?' Ma'iz said, `Yes. I know it is unlawful and a man is allowed to do this act only with his wife.' Muhammad said, `Are you certain that you penetrated the women the way a rope falls in a well or a needle is dipped in a bottle?' Ma'iz said, `Yes.' Greatly upset, Muhammad said, `Why are you telling me all this?' Ma'iz said, `So that you could purify me of the sins that I have committed.' The man left Muhammad no choice but to order that he be stoned to death.[196] The names of the women in question were not revealed.

Muhammad did not want adultery charges brought to his attention immediately after the jihadis had returned from a raid. He knew that many wives were not faithful to their husbands. Hence, upon return from the raids, he would not allow men to make a surprise return to their homes. He commanded to them, `Before you go home, let your wives know that you are in town so that they may make themselves presentable.'[197] As a further measure, he tried to reduce the numbers of his men's wives in order to reduce the chances of adultery occurring among them. For example, when Ghilan bin Salma submitted to Islam, he had ten wives and Muhammad ordered him to divorce six of them.[198]

When some of Muhammad's companions accused his youngest wife A'isha of having committed adultery (described later), he wanted to punish the accusers. He replaced the death penalty for adultery with a hundred lashes and added further safeguards by demanding that there should be four credible male witnesses to the act of intercourse, or self-admission of guilt be verbally repeated four times in front of the *qazi* (judge). In the absence of this evidence, those who laid the blame were to receive eighty lashes.[199] He issued this as a "divine order" as follows:

> Those who accuse chaste women of adultery
> And are unable to produce four witnesses
> Then give them eighty lashes and never accept their testimony
> These are evildoers. But if they repent and reform
> Then God is Kind and Merciful.
> About men who accuse their wives of adultery
> And there is no witness other than the plaintiff husband
> Then he should swear four times that he is telling the truth
> And swear a fifth time that if he were a liar
> May Allah's curse fall upon him
> And she (*the accused wife*) may prove her innocence
> By swearing four times that her husband is a liar
> Then swear a fifth time that if her husband was truthful
> May Allah's curse fall upon her.   (Sura 24, verses 3-9).

These later provisions in the "adultery law" were to discourage men from bringing adultery cases to Muhammad because no sane man and woman would commit adultery in full view of four credible male witnesses. Nevertheless, a man once produced four witnesses against his wife but, because the wife refused to admit guilt, Muhammad simply ordered the separation of the couple.

With advancing age and with some pointing fingers at his own wife, Muhammad had reversed his attitude towards adultery. Thus, when another man charged his wife of adultery, Muhammad asked him simply to divorce her. The man said he was afraid that he would be unhappy without her and Muhammad said, `In that case enjoy her company.'[200] This flexibility proves beyond doubt that, contrary to the Islamist propagandist claims, Muhammad's laws were not sent by God but shaped by his circumstantial needs and disposition.

The transmutation between religious and banditry-related terms

Modern Muslims define "zakat" as charity money but, as will be described, zakat originated as a forced tax which Muhammad's jihadis collected from weaker tribes. They collected the taxes from the homes and water wells[201] of the vanquished tribes and invited their stronger men to come to Medina and join Muhammad's forces. They told them that they would have shares in booty if they participated in jihad (banditry in this context). If they refused to participate, they were to pay the unbeliever tax (*jizya*). If they refused to pay *jizya*, the jihadis would challenge and attack them. This explains that when Muhammad used the term, "God's dues" (*deen Allah*), he meant the money, goods and property which people were supposed to hand over to him in God's name. However, the word "deen," other than its customary meaning, "due tax," now also means, "religion," which shows the transmutation, over time, from its older meaning.

Muhammad trained the jihadis to stay hungry for long periods to enable them to travel long distances without much food in order to raid the tribes and Meccan caravans. Staying hungry during the day is now practised as fasting during the whole month of Ramadan, and considered a purely religious act.

Muhammad usually conducted surprise raids when the tribesmen were away and it was easy to take women and children as captives. He would not attack during the day but wait until sunset and preferably raid in strong stormy conditions. Raids on unsuspecting tribes were called "sarria," as against "razzia" which was traditionally a Bedouin raid on a caravan. Rules and regulations were formed for the distribution of booty: It was divided among the jihadis after taking out one-fifth (*khums*) for Muhammad. Those who stole from it were warned of grievous punishments on the Day of Judgement.[202] A horseman would get double the share of a foot-warrior. Favoured jihadis would get a bonus on top of their regular share. This bonus was called "nafl"[203] but, in modern Islamic terminology, "nafl" is known as the bonus prayers, which Muslims offer to God in addition to their regular prayers.

The same has happened with the term "Islam:" The word "Islam" literally means "surrendering" or "submitting." When the jihadis used to raid the tribes and order them to surrender, in Arabic they would shout, "isl'm" or "sal'lim" (surrender or submit). In Arabic, the one who surrenders is called "ma sal'lim," the shortened form of which is "Muslim." They called the process of making people to surrender and extort taxes from them as "Islam," meaning, "surrendering." Later on, people began to associate this process of "surrendering to Muhammad" with the accepting of a new religion and a new way of life. Likewise, much later in history, scholars euphemized the term "Muslim" as meaning, "the one who has submitted to God." One needs to remember that Muhammad often equated himself with God and spoke as if God was speaking.

During his life, Muhammad allowed "temporary marriages" (*mut'a*) twice, but also banned them twice. He allowed them until the raid on Khyber, then banned them, and then allowed again before the raid on Autas to motivate the jihadis by allowing them to copulate with captive women. Then he ordered those who had "temporary wives" to abandon them.[204] His own temporary marriages are reported in Islamic reference books.[205] During the raid on Autas many women, whose husbands were away, were taken captives. The jihadis hesitated from copulating with these women because, being more interested in money, they wanted the husbands of these women to return with ransom money and seek their release.[206] When they sought Muhammad's advice, he brought in a "divine revelation" which stated:

All married women are forbidden to you except those captives whom you possess. (Sura 4, verse 24)

Because he usually allowed these "temporary marriages" during the banditry raids and banned afterwards, though these occurred in other times as well, one cannot escape the inference that he used rape or copulation with captive women to motivate the jihadis, though he euphemised it as a religious act. The above quoted Qur'anic verse and the religious term "mut'a" permitted the jihadis to copulate even with married captive women.[207]

Because Muhammad's men intermittently committed acts of banditry, and prayed to God five times a day, the terms pertaining to these two sets of activities interacted in their diction. A bandit terminology evolved, which transformed into religious terms, or *vice versa*. This process was inevitable because Muhammad strictly occupied his followers both with extensive prayers and with banditry raids. Because he presented both sets of activities as equally righteous, the moral distinction between the two disappeared. Trying to determine if religious terms came first and transmuted into banditry-related terms or *vice versa* is like a "chicken first or egg first" situation. However, one may claim with certainty that, much later in history, good-natured Muslim scholars gradually euphemized almost all banditry-related terms as prayers and rituals in their attempts to hide the banditry side (jihad) of Islam and offer it as a "noble religion."

The first raid on a Meccan trade caravan, taking booty and prisoners for ransom

The believers wanted to hurt and weaken the Meccans by raiding and robing their trade caravans and so they embarked on expeditions in search of the caravans. In the beginning, the Medinian Ansar were not asked to join, and these raids were markedly unsuccessful. For example, in the previously mentioned raid led by Hamza, he had returned with nothing. A month later, they tried again with double the force to raid a caravan led by Abu Sufyan but failed again. Muhammad himself led several expeditions in search of the Quraysh caravans but returned without being able to attack them. He was still observing and experimenting in order to develop his techniques.

In January 624, Muhammad dispatched Abdallah bin Jahsh, with eight emigrants and none of the Ansar, towards Mecca. He wrote for him a letter and ordered him not to look at it until he had journeyed for two days, and to do what the letter stated but not to put pressure on any of his companions. When Abdallah had travelled for two days, he opened the letter and found written, "Travel to Nakhla, mid-way between Mecca and Ta'if. Stay there, spy on the Quraysh and keep us informed of their activities."[208] Having read the letter Abdallah said, `To hear is to obey.' Then he said to his companions, `The apostle has commanded me to go to Nakhla to lie in wait there for Quraysh so as to bring him news of them. He has forbidden me to put pressure on any of you, so if anyone wishes for martyrdom come forward, and he who does not, may go back; as for me I am going on as the prophet has ordered.' None of his companions went back.

They journeyed along the Hejaz until at al Furu'a, two of his men, Utaba bin Ghazwan and Sa'ad bin abi Waqqas lost the camel they were riding in turns, and they stayed behind to search for it. Abdallah and the rest of them carried on to Nakhla until they found a small caravan of the Meccan Quraysh carrying dry raisins, leather, and other merchandise. Among them were Uthman bin Abdallah and his brother Noufal, who were the grandsons of the Makhzum chief al Mughira, Amr bin al Hadrami, who was the son of an ally of Harb bin Umayya, and al Hakam bin Kaysan, who was the ex-slave of Hisham bin al Mughira. When the Meccans saw the raiders, they were afraid of them because they had camped near them but when they saw that one of them had shaved his head, they felt safe and said, `They are just pilgrims, you have nothing to fear from them.'

The raiders took council among themselves, for this was the last day of the sacred months, and they said, `If you leave them alone tonight they will get into the sacred area and will be safe from you; and if you kill them, you will kill them in the sacred month.' So they were hesitant to attack them but then they encouraged each other, and decided to kill as many as they could and take what they had. One of the raiders named Waqid bin Abdallah shot Amr bin al Hadrami with an arrow and killed him, while Uthman and al Hakam surrendered. Noufal escaped and rode to Mecca. Abdallah and his companions took the caravan and the two prisoners and came to Medina with them. Abdallah said to his companions, `A fifth of the booty belongs to the apostle.' So he set apart for Muhammad a fifth of the caravan, and divided the rest among his companions.[209]

When Noufal returned with a Meccan force, they found Utaba bin Ghazwan and Sa'ad bin abi Waqqas, whom the raiders had left behind because they had lost their camel. They arrested these two and took them to Mecca.

In the pre-Islamic period, killing was prohibited in and around the Ka'ba, and fighting was stopped during the sacred months. Even prisoners on death row had respite until the end of the sacred months. For example, the Meccans had delayed the execution of a man named Khubayb, who had killed a Meccan, until the end of the sacred months.[210] Hence, the news of the raid appalled the Quraysh and the Jews: The raid had taken place in the sacred months, even though it was the last day, without provocation, and prisoners had been taken for ransom in the manner of ordinary bandits.

At first, Muhammad said to the raiders, 'I did not order you to fight in the sacred month,' and he held the caravan and the two prisoners in suspense and refused to take anything from them.

In Mecca, the Quraysh said, 'Muhammad and his companions have violated the sacred month, shed blood therein, taken booty, and captured men.' Muhammad's supporters still living in Mecca taunted the Quraysh and argued that they had done it after the sacred months though Muhammad had admitted that it had been done within the sacred month. When Muhammad heard about the condemnation, he changed his stance and justified his men's banditry as follows:

> Killing is compulsory though it disgusts you
> What you find disgusting may turn out to be good for you
> And what you like may turn out to be bad for you
> God knows it and you do not know
> They say, 'How can you kill in the sacred months?'
> Say, 'Killing in sacred months is bad,
> But even worse is stopping people from God's way
> And disbelieving, and barring people from visiting the Ka'ba
> And exiling its inhabitants is even worse a sin in God's eyes
> And sedition is a greater sin than murder.
> (Sura 2, verses 216-217)

This was Muhammad's customary recourse to exaggeration and propaganda. No one had expelled him from Mecca. All Muslim histories state that he had left Mecca after obtaining promises from the Ansar of Medina that they would fight under his command. Besides, his men had perpetrated both sedition and murder but the secular Meccans had taken no revenge from his supporters in Mecca (see their names in the next section, "The battle of Badr") who taunted them and justified the raid by saying that the believers had robbed and killed before the beginning of the sacred months.[211] Unlike him, the Meccans had not launched secret killings of their critics.

Instead of examining his conscience, Muhammad ordered his poets, Hassan bin Thabit, Ka'ab bin Malik, and Abdallah bin Rawaha to lampoon the Quraysh. Abu Bakr was an expert in the lineage, ancestry, and kinship ties of the Quraysh. Muhammad told

Hassan bin Thabit to go to Abu Bakr and learn about the weakest points of the Quraysh in order to be able to hurt them incisively through satire.[212] In doing so, he conveniently forgot that when his elders had said that his "revelations" were just poetry, he had replied, `To have a rotting belly filled with pus is better than being a poet.' Either Abu Bakr or Abdallah wrote a satire about the raid as follows:

> Though you defame us for killing him,
> More dangerous to faith is the sinner who envies
> Our lances drank the blood of Ibn al Hadrami
> In Nakhla when Waqid lit the flame of war,
> Uthman bin Abdallah is with us – a prisoner,
> Tied with a leather band streaming with blood.

The Quraysh sent message to Muhammad to return Uthman and al Hakam, and he said, `We will not return them until Sa'ad and Utaba are returned. If you kill them, we will kill your two friends.' The Meccans gave in and released the two men.

When Abdallah and his fellow raiders were relieved of their anxiety, they were anxious for reward, and said, `Can we hope that it will count as a jihad for which we shall be given the reward of combatants?' Muhammad took one-fifth of the booty, distributed the rest among them, and gave the bandits moral support with his "God-sent revelations" stating that God himself had ordained the raid:

> Those who believe, migrate, and fight in God's way, and those who shelter and protect them, are true believers. These receive forgiveness and provisions (*booty*). (Sura 8, verse 74)

> If God had not ordained it beforehand,
> You would be heavily punished for what you took (*the booty*)
> But now what you looted is allowed (*halaal*)
> So take it, enjoy, and keep your duty to God
> God is Forgiving, Merciful. (Sura 8, verses 68-69)

<u>The Battle of Badr</u>

Muhammad received information from his Hashimi tribesmen that Abu Sufyan was returning from Damascus with a large trade caravan of more than two thousand camels, with the money and merchandise belonging to numerous Meccan investors. It would make an easy target because only thirty or forty (some reports suggest seventy) armed guards escorted it. Muhammad incited his followers to raid this caravan, and said, `This caravan has commodities of various kinds; if you raid it, God might grant you booty from it.'[213]

Urwa bin al Zubayr and other scholars report on the authority of Ibn Abbas that when Muhammad heard about Abu Sufyan coming from Syria, he summoned his men and said, `This is the Quraysh caravan containing their property. Go out to attack it, perhaps God will give it to you as a prey.' The people answered his summons, some eagerly others reluctantly because they had not thought that he would go to war with the Meccans.

When Abu Sufyan got near to the Hejaz, he kept seeking news and questioning every rider in his anxiety, until he got news from some riders that Muhammad had called out his companions against him and his caravan. He took alarm at that and hired Damdam bin Amr al Ghifari and sent him to Mecca, ordering him to call out Meccans in defence of their property, and to tell them that Muhammad was lying in wait for it with his companions. So Damdam left for Mecca at full speed.

The following event suggests that Muhammad's uncle Abbas had sent message to him stating that Abu Sufyan's caravan contained merchandise belonging to almost every rich investor of Mecca. The Hashimis in Mecca were secretly aware of Muhammad's plan to raid Abu Sufyan's caravan and, therefore, three days before Damdam arrived, Muhammad's aunt Aatika, the sister of Abbas, saw a dream, which frightened her. She sent to her brother Abbas saying, `Brother, last night I saw a dream which frightened me and I am afraid that evil and misfortune will come upon your people, so treat what I tell you in confidence.' He asked what she had seen, and she said, `I saw a rider coming upon a camel who halted in the valley. Then he cried at the top of his voice, "Come forth, O people, do not leave your men to face a disaster that will come in three days." I saw the people flock to him, and then he went into the mosque with the people following him. While they were round him, his camel mounted to the top of the Ka'ba. Then he called out again, using the same words. Then his camel mounted to the top of Abu Qubays, and he cried out again. Then he seized a rock and loosened it, and it began to fall, until at the bottom of the mountain it split into pieces. There was not a house or a dwelling in Mecca that did not receive a piece of it.'

Abbas knew that Muhammad's impending raid would affect almost every major household in Mecca, as the dream foretold. Hence he said, `By God, this is indeed a vision, and you had better keep quiet about it and not tell anyone.' Then he went out and met al Walid bin Utaba, who was a friend of his, and told him about Aatika's dream and asked him to keep it to himself. Al Walid told his father and the story of the dream spread in Mecca until Quraysh were talking about it in their public meetings.

In the following report note Abbas's admission to telling lies in order to keep the Quraysh from knowing about the impending raid. Abbas reported:

> I got up early to go round the temple, while Abu Jahl was sitting with a number of Quraysh talking about Aatika's dream. When he saw me he said, `Come to us when you have finished going round the Ka'aba.' When I had finished I went and sat with them, and he said, `O Sons of Abdul Muttalib, since when have you had a prophetess among you?'
> `And what do you mean by that?' I said.
> `That vision, which Aatika saw,' he answered.
> I said, `And what did she see?'
> He said, `Are you not satisfied that your men should play the prophet that your women too should do so? Aatika has alleged that in her vision someone said, "Come forth to war in three days." We shall keep an eye on you these three days, and if what she says is true, then it will be so; but if the three days pass and nothing happens, we will write you down as the greatest liars of the people of the Ka'aba among the Arabs.'
> I contradicted it and denied that she had seen anything. Then we separated. When night came every single woman of Banu Abdul Muttalib came to me and said, `Have you allowed this evil rascal to first attack your men and then go on to insult your women while you listened? Have you no shame that you should listen to such things?' I said, `By God, nothing much passed between us but I swear by God that I will confront him, and if he repeats what he said, I will rid you of him.'
> On the third day after Aatika's dream, I was still enraged. I went into the mosque and as I was walking towards Abu Jahl to confront him so that he should repeat some of what he had said and I could attack him, for he was a thin man with sharp features, sharp tongue, and sharp sight, lo, he came out towards

the door of the mosque hurriedly. I said to myself, `What is the matter with him, curse him, is all this for fear that I will insult him?' But lo, he had heard something which I did not hear, the voice of Damdam crying out in the bottom of the valley, as he stood upon his camel, having cut its nose, turned its saddle round, and rent his shirt, while he was shouting, `O Quraysh, the transport camels, the transport camels! Muhammad and his companions are lying in wait for your money and merchandise that is with Abu Sufyan. I do not think that you will overtake it. Help! Help!'
This diverted him and me from our affair.

The Meccans prepared quickly, saying, `Do Muhammad and his companions think this is going to be like the caravan of Ibn Hadrami? By God, they will soon know that it is not so.' Every man of them either went himself or sent someone in his place. All went; not one of their nobles remained behind except Abu Lahab. In his place, he sent al Aas bin Hisham bin al Mughira who owed him four thousand dirhams, which he could not pay. So he hired him on the condition that he should be cleared of his debt. Al Aas went on his behalf and Abu Lahab stayed behind.

Umayya bin Khalf had decided to stay at home because he was a stately old man, corpulent and heavy. Uqba bin Abu Mu'ayt came to him as he was sitting in the mosque with his companions. Uqba carried a censer burning with scented wood. He put it in front of Umayya and taunted him, `Perfume yourself with that, for you are like a women!'

`God curse you and what you have brought,' Umayya said, and then got ready and went out with the rest.

When the Quraysh had finished their preparations and decided to start, they remembered the quarrel there was between them and Banu Bakr of Kinana and were afraid that in their absence, the Banu Bakr would attack them in the rear.

The cause of the war between Quraysh and Banu Bakr was a young lad of one of Quraysh tribes who had gone out in search of his lost camel in Dajanan. He was a youngster with flowing locks on his head, wearing a robe, a good-looking clean youth. He passed by Amir bin Yazid who was the chief of Banu Bakr at that time. When he saw him, he liked him and asked him who he was. When he had told him and gone away, Amir called his tribesmen and asked them if there was any blood outstanding with Quraysh, and when they said there was, he said, 'Any man who kills this youngster in revenge for one of our tribe will have exacted the blood due to him.' So one of them followed him and killed him in revenge for the blood Quraysh had shed.

When Quraysh had discussed the matter, Amir had said, 'You owed us blood so what do you want? If you wish, pay us the blood money you owe us, and we will pay you the blood money we owe. If you want only blood, man for man, then ignore your claims and we will ignore ours;' and since this lad was of no great importance to this clan of Quraysh, they said, 'All right, man for man,' and ignored his death and sought no compensation for it.

Now while the lad's brother Mikraz was travelling in Marr al Zahraan he saw Amir on a camel, and as soon as he saw him, Amir went up to him and made his camel kneel beside him. Amir was still wearing his sword when Mikraz brought his sword down on him and killed him. Then he twirled his sword about in his belly, and brought it back to Mecca and hung it overnight among the curtains of the Ka'ba. When morning came, Quraysh saw Amir's sword hanging among the curtains of the Ka'ba and recognized it. They said, 'This is Amir's sword; Mikraz has attacked and killed him.' Now they waited for Amir's tribe to take revenge.

While this vendetta was going on, the issue of Muhammad kept them occupied until when Quraysh decided to go to Badr they remembered the vendetta with Banu Bakr and were afraid of them.

Mikraz said the following verses about his killing Amir:

When I saw that it was Amir
I remembered the lifeless corpse of my dear brother
I said to myself, 'It is Amir, fear not my soul
And look to what you do.'
I was certain that as soon as I plunge my sword into him
It would be the end of him.
I swooped down on him, on a brave, experienced man,
With a sharp sword, and when we came to grips,
I did not show myself a son of ignoble parents.
I fulfilled my vengeance, forgetting not revenge,
Which only weaklings forgo.

When Quraysh remembered their quarrel with Banu Bakr and it almost deterred them from going, Suraaqa bin Malik, a chief of the Banu Kinana said, 'I guarantee that the Kinana will not attack you in the rear,' so they went off speedily.

The Meccans had summoned men from various tribes and raised a cavalry nearly one thousand strong which fast marched to Badr under Abu Jahl's command. Again, Muhammad's Meccan spies informed him of the dispatch of the Meccan force.

XXX

Muhammad set out for Badr in the month of Ramadan. His companions had seventy camels on which they rode in turns: Muhammad with Ali, Hamza with Zayd bin Haritha, Abu Kabsha with Muhammad's slave, Anasa, and Abu Bakr, Umar, and Abdul Rehmaan bin Auf shared one camel. They carried three flags; Mus'ab bin Umayr had one, Ali carried a black flag and led the emigrants, and the third was with one of the Ansar.

On their way to Badr, they met a nomad who did not know Muhammad by face. Muhammad asked him about the Quraysh caravan, but found that he had no news. Muhammad's companions did not like the way the nomad spoke to him and they said to him, 'Salute Allah's messenger.' He said, 'Have you got him with you?' and when they said that they had, he said, 'If you are Allah's messenger, then tell me what is in the belly of my she-camel here.' Salama bin Salama did not like this and he taunted him, 'Don't question Allah's apostle; I will tell you what it is: You fornicated with your camel and she has in her belly a little goat from you!' Muhammad said, 'Enough! You have spoken obscenely to the man.' Then he turned away from Salama and sent a man to scout for news about Abu Sufyan's caravan.

Muhammad bypassed the locations of the clans of Banu Ghifar because he believed they would inform the Quraysh about his location. News came to him that the Meccans had set out to defend their caravan. He told the people about this and asked for their advice. Abu Bakr and then Umar got up and spoke well. Then al Miqdad got up and said, 'O apostle of Allah, go where Allah tells you for we are with you. We will not say as the Israelites said to Moses, "You and your Lord go and fight and we will stay at home," but you and your Lord go and fight, and we will fight with you. By God, if you were to take us to the farthest point of Yemen, we would fight resolutely with you against its defenders until you conquered it.'

Al Miqdad had heard the story of the Israelites from Muhammad himself in his Qur'anic verses as follows:

Remember Moses said to his people, 'O my people!
Call in remembrance the favour of Allah upon you,
When He produced prophets among you, made you kings,
And gave you what He had not given to any other nation.
O people! Enter the holy land, which Allah has assigned to you,
And turn not back shamefully,
For then you will be overthrown, to your own ruin.'
They said, 'O Moses! In this land are very strong people
Never shall we enter it until they leave it
If they leave, then shall we enter.'
Among their God-fearing men were two blessed men
They said, 'Assault them at their gate
When once you are in, victory will be yours;
Trust God if you have faith.'
They said, 'O Moses! While they are there,
We shall never be able to enter, to the end of time.
You and your Lord go and fight while we sit here and watch.'
He said, 'Lord! I have power only over myself and my brother
So separate us from these rebellious people!'
God said, 'Therefore the land will be out of their reach
For forty years they will wander through the land
Do not grieve over these rebellious people.' (Sura 5, verses 20-26)

Muhammad thanked al Miqdad and blessed him. Then he said, 'Give me advice, O Men,' by which he meant the Ansar. This is because they formed the majority, and because when they had paid homage to him in Aqaba they had stipulated that they were not responsible for his safety outside their territory, and that when he was there they would protect him as they did their wives and children. So he was afraid that the Ansar would not feel obliged to fight for him unless he was attacked in Medina, and that they would not feel it incumbent upon them to go with him against an enemy outside their territory. When he spoke these words Sa'ad bin Mu'adh said, 'It seems as if you mean us.' When he said that he did, Sa'ad said, 'We believe in you, we declare your truth, and we have given you our word and agreement to hear and obey. So go where you wish, we are with you; and by God, if you were to ask us to cross this sea and you plunged into it, we would plunge into it with you;

not a man would stay behind. We are not against the idea of meeting your enemy tomorrow. We are experienced in war, trustworthy in combat. It may well be that God will let us show you something which will bring you joy, so take us along with God's blessing.'

Muhammad was delighted at Sa'ad's words and he said, `Forward in good heart, for God has promised me one of the two parties; either the caravan or the army and by God, it is as though I see the enemy lying fallen on the ground.'

They stopped near Badr. He and one of his companions rode on until he stopped by an old man of the Bedouin and said to him, `Have you heard anything about Quraysh and about Muhammad and his companions?' The old man said, `I won't tell you until you tell me which group you belong to.' Muhammad said, `If you tell us we will tell you.' The old man said, `Tit for tat?' `Yes,' Muhammad replied. The old man said, `I have heard that Muhammad and his companions went out on such-and-such day. If that is true, today they should be here where we are, and I heard that Quraysh went out on such-and-such day, and if this is true, today they are in such-and-such place.' When he had finished he said, `Which group are you with?' Muhammad lied to him and said, `We are from Ma.' Then he left him, while the old man was saying, `What does "from Ma" mean? Is it from the water of Iraq?'

This time, the number of Medinians in the raiding party exceeded that of the emigrants. They had come out of Medina for the two-day ride to Badr because they knew that Meccan spring caravans stopped there. Badr was a major watering spot for men and camels with its several wells and hollowed out cisterns that stored the water of winter flash floods.

In the modern Islamic texts, the Islamists claim that Muhammad fought this battle to spread Islam but all the narrations of the event, quoted by Muhammad's companions, and even the Qur'anic verses about Badr, clearly show that he and his men wanted to rob the caravan. The evidence comes straight from their own records whereby Muhammad said to his followers, `Be happy for God has promised one of the two to you; either the caravan or the army,'[214] and, after the battle was over, he confirmed this in his "divine revelations:"

> And when God promised
> That one of the two groups will fall to you
> And you wanted to take the unarmed caravan

But God wanted to triumph His word
And cut the backbone of the unbelievers. (Sura 8, verse 7)

Muhammad always took precautions to keep his preparations for raids secret. When he planned a route, he would use vague language and named places other than those that he was to raid.[215] This strategy, called "toriah," involved giving either wrong information to his followers or scant information on a "need to know" basis. For example, when he was planning to migrate to Medina, he did not inform even his best friend Abu Bakr that he was to leave until the last day[216] and, when he was planning to raid the Banu Lehan tribe, he told his followers that they were to prepare to travel to Syria.[217] Had the secret been out, the Banu Lehan could have prepared and defended them better. Whilst travelling to Badr, he kept his routes to himself. He used spies to bring news of the position of the caravan and the Meccan army. He did not pass through those tribes who could possibly inform the Meccans about his routes and the number of his men, and, when he sought information from people on route, he would not tell them who he and his men were.[218]

Muhammad had initially motivated his followers by telling them that the aim of the Badr raid was to rob the caravan, but finally led them to fight the Meccan warriors.[219] The booty of Meccan weapons was more important to him, for his future raids, than the merchandise with the caravan.

He encamped near Badr where his militia arrested two men who were fetching water from the wells. These said that they were fetching water for the Meccan army but Muhammad's men believed that they were lying and they tortured them to extract "the truth" about the caravan. When Muhammad was certain that the two were not lying, he inquired them about the numbers of the Meccan army. The men could not guess. He said, `How many camels are slaughtered in the Meccan camp each day for food?' The men said, `Some days nine, some days ten.' From this figure, he estimated that the Meccan force would be between nine hundred and a thousand. He also found out the names of the Meccan chiefs who were with the army and told his men, `These chiefs comprise the heart of Mecca.'

XXX

Abu Sufyan made a stopover in an oasis, found some camel dung, and poked at it with a stick. From the date seeds that he found in the dung, he concluded that these camels must have come from Medina and hence could belong to Muhammad's spies. He quickly made a detour and led his caravan far from Badr by doubling back and travelling along the Red Sea. He then sent another fast rider to intercept Abu Jahl with the message, `You came out to protect your caravan. God has kept it safe, so turn back.' However, Abu Jahl knew that if they went back, word would spread among the Bedouin that Muhammad had grown strong enough to force the Quraysh to change their routes. The Bedouin would start negotiating with Muhammad, and that would lead to the end of Meccan prestige in Arabia. Accordingly, he declared, `We will spend three days in Badr; we will slaughter camels, give food to eat and wine to drink to all people so that the Bedouin may hear of our strength and continue to respect us.'

In the Meccan force, Hakim bin Hazam and Utaba bin Rabi'a argued that while the caravan had escaped safely, there was little point in going to fight.[220] Abu Jahl sneered, `Your lungs are inflated with fear.' Another leader pointed out that they would be fighting their relatives and said, `By God, even if you defeat Muhammad in this battle, how will you look one another in the face without loathing when you will see someone who has killed your nephew or your kinsman? Let us turn back.' Again, Abu Jahl responded with scorn, `You say this only because your son is Muhammad's follower. Don't try to protect him.' Then he called the brother of a man killed in the Nakhla raid to come forward and remind them of his brother's murder. By the time the grieving brother had finished, many were riled up for vengeance. Despite this, around three hundred men rode back to mecca. Most of the rest went along with Abu Jahl but only to stand by and watch. They still felt for their relatives on the other side and did not realize the extent to which these had been brainwashed by Muhammad into hating them as unbelievers. The real fighting force of the Meccans were thus reduced to less than half, that is, if those who had come to provide supportive services such as camel feeding and cooking the daily meals for the ten-day journey, is taken into account.

On his part, Muhammad too could have gone back to Medina. There was no need to fight but he was eager to fulfil his promises of bringing God's curse on those who had refused to accept his status as God's messenger and, for that, he was not going to wait for the Day of Judgement. Because they had to travel only around two days from Medina, his men arrived at Badr first and dug in on the higher ground. They stood guard at the water well that was on the higher ground, and blocked the other wells and cisterns. When the Meccans arrived, they found that the only usable well was in enemy's hands. Many Meccans died when they tried to get water from this well.[221]

The Meccan chiefs considered it below their dignity to engage in individual combats with the lower class peasants. Hence, in the one-to-one contests, the chiefs refused to enter into combat with the Ansar peasants.[222] On the other hand, the Ansar were keen on attacking the Meccan chiefs in order to rob them of their better clothes, shoes and armour, and to secure the reputation of having killed a man of status and prestige.

Abu Jahl had once slapped a shepherd boy, who was now on Muhammad's side, looking for Abu Jahl. He found Abu Jahl riding a horse but it had been raining all night and the ground was too soggy for the horse to move fast. He struck at Abu Jahl's leg with his sword and it came flying off. Another report suggests that two Medinian shepherd boys surrounded him and one of them severed his leg with his sword. Abu Jahl was in grief at two things; firstly, his tribal relatives in Medina had tried to rob the caravan and, secondly, his Meccan relatives were not fighting as one force, and so his last words were, `My own relatives arranged for my murder; where is the pride in it? I wish I had been killed by a man of honour and not by low class peasants.' When he fell and lay dying on the ground, one of the Ansar lads placed his foot on his neck. Abu Jahl struggled to raise his head and said, `You shepherd! Watch your feet.' The shepherd cut his head off and presented it to Muhammad who thanked God for enabling him to fulfil his prophecy about his childhood rival: [223]

> If he will not desist, we shall drag him by his forelocks
> The wrongful liar's forelocks. (Sura 96, verses 15-16)

The Islamists assert that Muhammad was victorious because God sent a thousand angels to fight on his side. They claim this because Muhammad encouraged his men by saying that angels had come to fight alongside them. The fact was that these "angels" were none other than Muhammad's secret agents and sympathizers within the Meccan army itself, as detailed below, who betrayed the Umayyads and the Banu Makhzum at the last hour. Accordingly, the following factors led to the defeat of the Meccan army:

- The Meccans had travelled ten days to reach Badr. They had logistical issues and they had to keep around a hundred camels in reserve as food to be able to travel back. Most men in their force were not supposed to fight but to look after the camels, horses, food, and other supplies. On the other hand, Muhammad's men were not far from Medina. They had travelled only two days to reach Badr and they were not worried about supplies for the short return journey.
- The Meccans did not fight as one group but each clan stood as a separate unit with no unified command. Those who had no share in the caravan, and those who did not want to fight, merely stood by and watched. The Umayyads and Banu Makhzum were largely the only clans that fought and died in the battle.
- The Banu Zahra and Banu Adiy clans, along with many of the Hashimis, defected and left[224] while the Meccan leader Umayr bin Wahb, a secret convert, did not fight. He had been torturing his people to coerce them to accept Muhammad as God's messenger.[225]
- Muhammad had told his men not to attack his secret agents among the Meccans. These included his uncle Abbas; his first cousins Aqeel and Talib (the sons of Abu Talib and brothers of Ali); his son-in-law Abu'l Aas; and Hakim bin Hazam, the nephew of Khadija. These were obviously not keen on fighting against Muhammad.[226] All five pretended to surrender and were ostensibly taken as prisoners but later released and sent back to Mecca. This shows that these had just pretended to be with the other Meccans.

There is enough evidence to show that most of those mentioned above were participants in Muhammad's bid to rule Arabia:[227] Abbas used to inform him about Meccan arrangements and Abu'l Aas secretly visited him in Medina.[228] All these played their role in dividing the Meccan alliance and this explains Abu Jahl's last words, 'My own relatives arranged for my murder – where is the pride in it?'

Muhammad had ordered his men not to kill a Meccan noble Abu'l Bakhtri, who had protected and supported him during his years in Mecca. However, one of the Ansar killed Abu'l Bakhtri whilst the latter was trying to save one of his friends.[229]

Another reason for the Medinian victory was the lack of common ethics among them: For example, the Meccans had always protected their Medinian believer friends on their visits to Mecca. In fact, the believers were free to enter, stay in or leave Mecca as they wished. The Meccan chief Umayya bin Khalf had protected the believer Sa'ad bin Mu'adh on his pilgrimage to Mecca[230] but the ungrateful Sa'ad did nothing to save him[231] though the two had been lifelong friends. During the battle, Umayya found his second believer friend Abd al Rehmaan bin Awf picking up shields from corpses as his booty. Umayya pleaded to Abd al Rehmaan to arrest him and his son, save their lives, and promised a handsome reward. Abd al Rehmaan agreed to this and took them as prisoners. However, Umayya had once owned Bilal as slave, and punished him for following Muhammad, until Abu Bakr had bought him off. Bilal now wanted to kill Umayya. When he saw Umayya and his son under the protection of Abd al Rehmaan, he goaded the Ansar not to spare Umayya, and shouted, `This man is the chief of unbelievers and if you spare him, he will kill me.' The Ansar gathered around the father and son like vultures. Umayya tried to protect his son but one of the Ansar hit the son's foot with his sword. Umayya screamed and Abd al Rehmaan shouted, `I can do nothing now. Save yourself!'

When the Ansar had slaughtered Umayya and his son, Abd al Rehmaan expressed grief not at the murder of his friend and his son but at losing his booty and said, `May God curse Bilal; he made me lose my ransom as well as my booty.'[232]

After the battle, Muhammad over-saw the dumping of the corpses in a ditch. They could not carry the badly mutilated bodies and so they covered them with earth where they lay. Muhammad surveyed the field as much in sadness as in pride and said, `Here the Quraysh have thrown their dearest flesh and blood to you.'

Then he stood by the ditch and addressed the dead:

O the people of the ditch!
You were the worst people of my tribe (*Quraysh*)
You rejected me but others affirmed my apostolate
You exiled me but others gave me shelter

You came to fight with me but others helped me
Do you not see that my Lord has fulfilled his promise to me?
Did your Lord fulfil his promise to you?[233]

Men asked him why he had addressed the dead and he replied, `The dead heard what I said.' He then ordered the execution of three prisoners of war, namely Tayyuma bin Adiy, Nadir bin Harris, and Uqba bin Abu Mu'ayt. His men tied them and beheaded them.[234]

Many relatives had fought on opposing sides: Abu Bakr had fought his son and during the fight shouted, `You evil man, where is my money that I left with you?'[235] Umar had killed his uncle, and Huzayfa had fought his father Utaba bin Rabi'a.[236] Huzayfa felt sorry when they roughly dumped his father's corpse in the ditch. Muhammad questioned his grief for his "unbeliever" father and Huzayfa made an excuse to pacify Muhammad, `I am not sad at his death. I am sad because my father was a very kind man and I hoped someday he would become a believer.'[237]

Forty-four Meccans had died in the battle. Some were executed though they had surrendered. However, the believers kept around seventy prisoners who were rich enough to pay ransom for their release.

On Muhammad's side, fifteen believers had died in the battle, some by their own mistakes. One fell of a high rock in his excitement and broke his neck. Another's horse panicked, threw him down, and fatally kicked in his head. A third swung his sword so hard that it missed the enemy and cut his own leg. He bled to death. Muhammad had encouraged one of his men to fight without body armour and he had died of injuries, which the armour could have prevented.[238]

As the remaining Meccans departed, the believers roamed the battlefield picking chainmail and swords and harnessing the abandoned horses and camels. The question of distribution of the booty caused great unrest. Those who had collected booty on the battlefield did not want to give a share to those who had been chasing the Meccans and strayed far from where the booty was. Those who had been protecting Muhammad and could not participate in the loot, wanted an even larger share. When the quarrel over the booty turned nasty, Muhammad took the matter in his own hands and decided that all participants should get an equal share.[239] As usual, he claimed that God had sent this decision to him:

> People ask you to issue an order about the booty
> Tell them that the booty belongs to God and the messenger
> So fear God and resolve your differences. (Sura 8, verse 1)

Muhammad himself took an ornate double-edged sword and a precious camel that belonged to Abu Jahl, but even larger than the booty was the ransom they would obtain for the captives.

They returned to Medina, and when the townsmen congratulated them on the victory, a young fighter named Salama said, 'We do not deserve congratulations because we fought against bald old men who were as easy to slaughter as tied-up camels.' Muhammad smiled and said, 'But those were the chiefs of Mecca.'

When they brought the captives to Medina, Muhammad's wife Sawda taunted a prisoner, who was her relative, saying, 'How come you surrendered? Could you not die with honour?' Muhammad reprimanded her, 'Sawda why are you encouraging rebellion against God and His messenger?' Sawda apologized and said, 'O messenger of God, I could not control myself when I saw his hands tied to his neck.' Sawda's words reflect the callousness of primitive Arabia but the mind-set still prevails among Muslim mothers who encourage their sons to play with their and others' lives in conducting jihad.

Many prisoners were relatives of their captives. Mus'ab bin Umayr found his stepbrother Abu Aziz bin Umayr in the custody of a peasant and, to help his brother, he said to the peasant, 'Do not kill him because his mother is very rich and she will pay a large ransom for him.'[240]

When they discussed the fate of the prisoners, Umar demanded the execution of all, each to be killed by his kin[241] to avoid issues of inter-tribal revenge. However, Muhammad needed his tribal relatives, uncle Abbas in particular, to go back to Mecca and help in the conquest of Mecca. He therefore decided it was better to get four thousand dirhams in ransom for each prisoner.

The Meccans paid ransom for some captives but some Meccans seized some Medinians, when the latter went on pilgrimage to Mecca, and exchanged them for their captive relatives. Abbas and Muhammad's son-in-law, Abu'l Aas, pretended to pay a ransom, which he later returned to them.[242]

After his release and return to Mecca, Abu'l Aas told his wife Zaynab, Muhammad's daughter, that Muhammad wanted her to come to Medina. When Zaynab was leaving Mecca, a man named Habbar bin al Aswad and his friend, Huwayrith bin Nuqaydh, tried to stop her. Muhammad heard about this and he dispatched a party of secret assassins with instructions to burn Habbar and his accomplice to death. Later, he changed his orders to a simple murder.[243]

Muhammad reflected upon the battle of Badr in his following "divine revelations:"

> When He caused drowsiness to fall on you and calm you
> And sent upon you rain from the sky
> To assuage all satanic scruples from your hearts
> And fortify your hearts and steady your feet
> When your Lord sent the angels to support you,
> And strengthen those who believe;
> I will cast terror into the hearts of unbelievers
> Therefore, strike off their heads and their every finger.
> (Sura 8, verses 11-12)

> O Believers! When you confront the unbelievers
> Do not turn your backs to them
> And the one who turns his back to them
> Except as a tactics in fight
> Or to return to the security of his comrades
> Will face the wrath of God
> And will be thrown in hellfire.
> It is not you who killed them but God killed them
> It is not you who stoned them but God threw the stones
> So that He may reward the believers with abundance.
> (Sura 8, verses 15-17)

> Remember when you were a minority
> And felt insecure with other people
> And God gave you land and power
> And fine food and things of life
> So that you may be grateful.   (Sura 8, verse 26)

> Did you see how the angels killed the unbelievers?
> Smiting their faces and their backs,
> And saying, 'Taste the penalty of the blazing fire.'
> (Sura 8, verse 50)

The Islamists claim that the above quoted verses are God's words; a serious study of these verses shows that these could easily be called blasphemous because they present God as a murderer, robber, and tormenter.

One of those killed at Badr was Khunays bin Huzayfa, the son-in-law of Umar – Muhammad's closest associate. Khunays was married to Hifza – Umar's daughter. When the turmoil of the battle was over, Muhammad married Hifza to please Umar and to take off him the burden of looking after a widowed daughter.

Muhammad provokes more hatred against the Jews

The booty from Badr was swords, spears, horses, camels, and the ransom for the captives. For his men, Muhammad now needed regular supplies of food, meat, milk, fruit and dates for which he required more agricultural lands. In the scattered settlements of Medina, the Jewish tribes – the first settlers of Medina – had largely developed these lands.

To motivate his followers to attack the Jews, Muhammad and his men spread rumours that the Jews had hidden treasures of gold and silver. In addition, many Ansar did not want to pay back the money they owed to the Jews. Muhammad greatly pleased them by declaring, 'To charge interest on money is the same as marrying your own mother.'[244]

In addition to this commonplace slander, Muhammad added pleas to God against Jews and Christians in his regular prayers: 'O God! Kill the Jews and Christians because they have turned the graves of their prophets into places of worship.' Then he equated this "sin" with idolatry, which he had earlier declared to be the greatest sin in God's eyes. A'isha later explained these allegations to mean that the Jews and Christians used to make tombs over the graves of their saints and hence these two religions were evil.[245] Reference to Christians was stipulated to disguise the true targets of the ensuing attacks, confuse the Jews, and catch them unaware. The lack of evidence in Muhammad's allegations did not matter to his greedy followers. No one could dare ask him where the graves of the Jewish and Christian prophets were, and where Muhammad had seen these graves turned into objects of worship. Questions that would cast doubt on his unconditionally assumed veracity always led to the doubter being branded either an unbeliever or a hypocrite and, as described earlier, placed under fear of assassination. Muhammad reinforced his message through his claim that God had sent to him the following verses:

> O you who believe!
> Take not the Jews and Christians as your friends
> They are but friends to each other
> And he amongst you who befriends them is one of them.
> God does not guide unjust people
> Those in whose hearts is a disease (*the cowards*)
> Eagerly rush towards them, saying,
> 'We fear a change of fortune would bring disaster upon us.'
> God will give victory or an order according to His will
> Then they will repent at what they concealed in their hearts
> And those who believe will say,
> 'Are these the men who swore by God that they were with you?' Their deeds will be in vain and they will fall into nothing but ruin.
> O believers! If any of you turns back from his faith,
> Soon God will bring forth people who will love Him
> And He will love them
> They will be soft with believers but strict with unbelievers,
> They will fight in the way of God,
> And pay no attention to the criticism of others.
> (Sura 5, verse 51-54)

When Muhammad forbade eating animals that had either died of natural causes or slaughtered in the name of idols, men asked him if they could sell the fat and skin of such animals. They used the fat of these animals in leather processing and there was no harm in it but Muhammad disallowed it and said, 'May God destroy the Jews because they sell animal fat.' This was another of his ways to keep instilling hatred against the Jews and to keep people away from economically productive activity so that they would be available for jihad raids. Because of his economically unwise commands, and taking a large number of people out of productive work, there was a shortage of commodities.

Consequently, prices went up in Medina. When people asked Muhammad to fix the prices of commodities, he replied, `God raises the prices, creates poverty or prosperity, and provides food.'[246]

The Jewish friends of the Ansar observed how the latter were losing their long-term productive habits and resources to the pursuit of quick booty. They sensed that these trends would make the Ansar needy and desperate, and so they advised them to be cautious with their resources. The Jewish leaders, Qardam bin Qays, Osama bin Habib, Na'fay bin Amr, Huyayy bin Akhtab and Rifa'a bin Zayd bin al Taboot used to visit the Ansar and caution them, `Don't be in a hurry to contribute to the war fund; don't waste your resources or otherwise you will be at risk of destitution. It is not wise to waste because no one knows what the future might bring.' Muhammad's informers reported this to him and he issued the following "divine revelations:"

> The stingy are advising others to be stingy
> And hide the wealth which God has given to them
> We have prepared gruesome torture for these unbelievers,
> And those who spend to show-off to other people
> But have no faith in God and the Last Day
> And their companion is Satan – the worst companion
> It would not have hurt if they had spent in God's way
> Out of what God has given them. (Sura 4, verses 37-39)

In plain words, Muhammad believed that he had rights over the wealth and property of others; God had given it to them so that they could hand it over to His messenger. If they would not contribute towards his schemes, he would take it by force.

The Jewish leaders came to see him. Rifa'a said, `Muhammad please pay attention to what we say until we are able to explain and make you understand what we really mean.' Muhammad refused to listen, found faults in their manner of speaking, and told his followers that he had received "revelations" about the Jews:

> Have you seen those who were given part of the Book (*Torah*)?
> They purchase humiliation and want to lead you astray
> God knows well who your enemies are
> Some Jews deviate from the subject of conversation
> They say, `We heard and we disobey,' and then they say

> 'Listen to us and be kind to us,' without listening to me,
> With their tongues, they slander our religion
> Had they said, 'We hear and we obey
> Now hear us and pay attention to us,'
> It would have been good for them
> But God has cursed them because of their disbelief
> And very few of them believe.
> O people of the book (*the Jews*)! Believe in what we sent
> Before we mutilate your faces and twist them backwards
> Or curse you the way we cursed the people of Sabbath
> And (*thus*) fulfil God's will. (Sura 4, verses 44-47)

This reference to the mutilation of bodies and twisting heads backwards shows that, after causing the mutilation of his Meccan relatives' corpses at Badr, Muhammad had become apathetic to it. On the one hand, he maligned the Jews, on the other he and his followers continually pestered and bullied them for monetary contributions and loans. In frustration, one of the Jews said, 'If Muhammad is a prophet, why does he not receive money from God? Are God's hands tied?' When Muhammad heard this, he issued his "divine revelations" as follows:

> The Jews say, 'God's hands are tied!'
> No. Their hands shall be tied
> And they shall be cursed for what they say.
> God's hands are free and he spends the way he likes
> When God sends his verses to me and I read to them
> It only enhances rebellion and unbelief among many
> We have cast among them enmity and hatred
> Till the day of resurrection. (Sura 5, verse 64)

The Jews did not want to give up Judaism.[247] Like most settled and working people, they were mainly averse to robbery and shedding blood and some of them explained this to Muhammad by saying, 'Muhammad, if your angel Gabriel had not repeatedly brought to you orders of bloodshed and torture, we would definitely have followed you.' Muhammad replied with his "revelations:"

> Tell those who foster enmity against Gabriel
> 'Gabriel brings God's orders, guidance,
> And good news for the believers.'

> Tell the enemies of God, of His angels,
> Of his apostles, and Gabriel and Michael,
> `Surely God is the enemy of the unbelievers.'
> We sent upon you clear guidance
> None rejected it but the sinful
> And they followed Satan's teachings,
> Which Satan brought as sorcery
> In the days of Prophet Solomon. (Sura 2, verse 97-102)

Muhammad kept adding to his list of the Jewish sins; he accused them of practising sorcery and hiding the verses in the Torah that allegedly confirmed his apostolate. He cursed them for disobeying Moses and God, for rephrasing the scriptures, and ridiculed them as those whom God had turned into apes and swine as punishment.

> Shall I tell you about those from these people (*Jews*)
> Upon whom God sent his curses and showed his fury
> He transformed them into apes and swine,
> And worshippers of sorcerers
> They dwell in evil and stray away from the right path.
> (Sura 5, verse 60)

Muhammad prepared a full propaganda campaign against the Jews. Accusing them of breaking their covenant with God,[248] he pre-emptively charged them with causing their own expulsion from their homes when, in fact, he himself was planning to do so, as the later events showed. Accusing them of being responsible for bringing about their eventual deaths, he brought the following "revelations:"

> And We (*God*) made a covenant with the children of Israel: You shall not serve any but God and you shall do good to your parents, to the near of kin, to the orphans and to the needy. You shall speak to men good words, keep up prayers, and pay the taxes. Then you turned back except a few of you and now you backslide.
> And We (*God*) made a covenant with you: You shall not shed your own blood and you shall not expel yourselves out of your towns. Then you promised, and you testified. Yet you slay yourself and expel some of you out of your homes by

supporting one another in sin and enmity. If they are taken as captives, you ransom them while their very expulsion was unlawful. Do you believe in part of the Book and disbelieve in the other? What then is the reward of these acts but humiliation? You shall face the most grievous punishment, and God is not at all oblivious of what you do.

These people (*Jews*) buy the life of this world at the price of the hereafter; their penalty shall not be lightened nor shall they be helped. (Sura 2, verses 83-86)

One sign of Muhammad's purely malicious nature was that before perpetrating a gross crime against humanity, he used to accuse his would-be victims of doing the same.

In order to create more excuses, Abu Bakr went to a Jewish school and found Rabi Finhaas teaching his pupils. He stood in front of him and challenged him, `Finhaas, fear God and surrender to Islam because Muhammad is God's messenger and you know that your scriptures prophesise his advent.'

Finhaas said to Abu Bakr, `We do not need you but you need us all the time. We do not seek money from you but you seek money from us. If your God were as great as your master Muhammad says, you would not need money from us. Muhammad has banned usury but he always offers us interest and seeks loans. If he is a messenger, why does he seek loans from us?'

Abu Bakr slapped Finhaas in the face, and shouted, `Were it not for the treaty between us, I would cut off your head, you enemy of God.'[249] Rabi Finhaas immediately went to see Muhammad and complained about Abu Bakr. Muhammad asked Abu Bakr what had compelled him to slap the Rabi, and Abu Bakr lied, `The enemy of God spoke blasphemy. He alleged that God was poor and that they were rich, and I was so angry that I hit his face.'

Abu Bakr's words reflect Muhammad's regularly expressed claim: He considered himself God's sole representative and challenging him meant a challenge to God. His equation of himself with God is visible in the Qur'anic verses where the issuer of the verses frequently alternates between the person of Muhammad and God.

Rabi Finhaas denied that he had said those words but, instead of reprimanding Abu Bakr, Muhammad added more lies to the Rabi's statement. He levelled more charges against the Jews as a nation and enhanced his verdict by issuing the following "divine revelations:"

> God has heard those who say, `God is poor but we are rich.'
> I (*God*) take account of what they say,
> And their killing the prophets (*Jesus*) unjustly,
> And I will say, `Taste the torture of burning;
> You brought this upon yourself through your deeds.
> And God is not cruel to His servants (*the believers*).'
> These people say that God has ordered them
> Not to believe in any of His messengers
> Unless he brings such a sacrifice as fire consumes
> Say, `Indeed, there came to you messengers before me
> With clear arguments and with that which you say;
> Why then did you kill them, if you are truthful?'
> (Sura 3, verses 181-183)

In the quoted verses, Muhammad accused the Jews, collectively, of "killing the prophets" when in fact the Jews of Medina had not killed any prophet. Levelling false allegations against prospective victims has been a hallmark of the Muslim provocateurs since Muhammad made a habit of it.

Muhammad himself went to a Jewish school where there were a number of Jews and called them to accept his apostolate. Nu'maan bin Amr and Harith bin Zayd said to him, `What is your religion, Muhammad?' He said, `The religion of Abraham.' The Jews said, `But Abraham was a Jew.' Muhammad replied, `Then let the Torah judge between us.'

The Jews did not know how Torah could judge in this claim. Muhammad threatened them with hellfire, and the Jews uttered their belief that people will be in hell for a short time and then they will be forgiven. Because some Christians believed that Abraham was Christian, Muhammad issued the following verses pointing to the mistake that both Jews and Christians made:

> O people of the book!
> Why do you argue about Abraham (*being a Jew or a Christian*),
> When the Torah and the Bible were not sent until after him?
> Have you no understanding? (Sura 3, verses 65)

And in the very next verses he made the same mistake of which he had accused the Jews and Christians:

> Abraham was neither a Jew nor a Christian
> But surely a Muslim Hanif. (Sura 3, verses 67)

However, logic was never one of Muhammad's main concerns. Once, Christians from Najran and the local Jews assembled before him, and Abu Rafi'a asked him, `Do you want us, Muhammad, to worship you as the Christians worship Jesus?' Muhammad replied, `God forbid that I should order you to worship any but God; I want you to become Muslims (Sura 3, verses 79-80).' This in fact meant worshipping Muhammad because Jews and Christians already worshipped God.

Secret assassinations of the Jewish leaders begin

In order to mentally prepare his followers to raid their Jewish neighbours, Muhammad regularly hinted at whatever wealth the Jews had, hiding his intentions by saying that it did not belong to its owners but to "God:" One needs to keep in mind that Muhammad considered himself the only manifestation of God on earth:

> And let not those who hoard up
> What God has bestowed upon them of His bounty
> Think that it will benefit them.
> Nay, it is worse for them.
> The wealth, which they hoard, will be tied to their necks
> Like a twisted collar, on the Day of Judgment.
> God's is the heritage of the heavens and the earth,
> And God knows of what you do. (Sura 3, verse 180)

A Jewish leader, Ka'ab bin Ashraf, had friendly relations with some chiefs of Mecca who were killed at Badr. Mourning their deaths, Ka'ab wrote a eulogy in which he remembered them as follows:

> For such battles, tear and rain flow in torrents
> The flower of the Quraysh perished around the wells of Badr
> The nobles who used to shelter the poor
> And feed the destitute in times of famine.

In response, Muhammad's poet Hassan bin Thabit wrote a satire in which he coarsely taunted Ka'ab as follows:

> Weep on like a pup following a little bitch
> God has cooled the heart of our prophet
> And humiliated those who fought him.

Ka'ab replied by saying that one should not be cursed for grieving over one's friends' deaths. Again, the believers posed as victims of Ka'ab's poetry, invented excuses that he had been insulting chaste believer women in his poetry, and hatched a plan for his secret murder. The act of murder was made all the more treacherous by that the men sent to assassinate him were his two foster brothers and three trusted friends whose hearts had been hardened by Muhammad's "divine" hate-mongering against the Jews. These five men could enter Ka'ab's house because of their relationship and friendship with him. To ensure that they would not succumb to their memories of old friendship and fraternity with Ka'ab, Muhammad walked with them mid-way and strengthened their resolve with prayers, `Go in God's protection; O God! Help them.'

It was full moon and the five men invited Ka'ab to come out for a walk to which he unsuspectingly agreed. As they strolled, the men passed comments on the perfume Ka'ab was wearing and then one of them asked if he could smell the oil Ka'ab had applied to his hair. As Ka'ab bowed to let him smell his hair, they attacked him with swords. However, in the confusion of who was to do what, some of them injured each other as well.

When they returned to Muhammad and gave him the "good news" of the assassination, he applied his spittle on their wounds saying that this would heal them.[250]

Muhammad's poets celebrated the murder of Ka'ab by lauding the assassins as "lions." The assassination created fear and terror among the Jews, which was sustained by Muhammad's command, `Kill any Jew whom you can.'

Following the said command, a man named Muhaysa killed his Jewish employer called Ibn Sanina. Muhaysa's elder brother Huaysa reprimanded him and said, `You ungrateful enemy of God! You killed your patron who fattened you with his money.' Muhaysa replied, `By God! His murder was commanded to me by such a great person who, if he orders me to slay you, I would not hesitate a moment.' The elder brother was shocked to hear this. In disbelief he asked, `If Muhammad orders you to kill me, will you really do so?' Muhaysa boasted, `I will do so with great pleasure.' Huaysa was so terrified that he went to Muhammad and became a believer in him.[251]

XXX

When Muhammad had come to Medina, Abdallah bin Ubayy of the clan of Banu Hubla was the most respected leader of the town; none of his own people contested his authority, and Aus and Khazraj had never rallied to one man before him as they did to him.[252] He was about to be crowned as the king of Medina but he had relinquished his status in favour of Muhammad's authority. Upon his arrival, Muhammad had no proper clothes and Abdallah had given him his best clothes to wear. Believing in Muhammad's story of persecution and exile, Abdallah had allowed his people to follow Muhammad and when the Quraysh had sent him threats to either expel Muhammad from Medina or face dire consequences, he had ignored the threats and allowed him to stay.[253]

However, after seeing the real face of Muhammad, Abdallah began to criticize the raids on Meccan caravans. These raids were putting Medina's trade with Mecca at risk and gradually decimating a large part of Medina's economy. Abdallah also refused to break his lifelong friendship with the Jews. For these reasons, Muhammad branded him a "hypocrite."

Usama bin Zayd bin Haritha reported that Muhammad once rode to Sa'ad bin Ubaada to visit him during his illness. He mounted on an ass with a saddle surmounted by a cloth of Fadak with a bridle of palm fibre. Usama was a child and so Muhammad gave him a seat behind him. He passed by Abdallah bin Ubayy as he was sitting in the shade of his fort with some of his men. When Muhammad saw him, he got off the animal and sat with them reciting his verses to them. He admonished and warned Abdallah while the latter uttered not a word. Finally, when Muhammad had finished speaking Abdallah said, `There would be nothing finer than what you say if it were true. But sit in your own house and if anyone comes, talk to him about it and don't annoy those who do not come to you, and don't come into a man's gathering with talk which he does not like.'

Abdallah bin Rawaha was one of the believers who were sitting with him at that time and he said to Muhammad, `No, do come to us with it and come into our gatherings and quarters and houses. For by God we love it, God has honoured us with it and guided us to it.' When Abdallah saw that his own people were opposing him, he grieved and, later, wrote the following verses:

> When your friend is your opponent,
> You will always be disgraced
> And your adversaries will overthrow you.
> Can the falcon mount without its wings?
> If its feathers are clipped, it falls to the ground.[254]

Muhammad got up and went into the house of Sa'ad bin Ubaada, his face showing the anger raised by Abdallah. Sa'ad asked him why he looked so angry and he told him what Abdallah had said. Sa'ad said, `Don't be hard on him; for God sent you to us as we were making a special headdress to crown him, and by God he thinks that you have robbed him of a kingdom.'

The expulsion of the Banu Qaynuqa and confiscation of their lands

Accusing their prey of insulting "chaste Muslim women" has been the most common tactics of Muhammadan provocateurs over the centuries: The Pakistani Islamists claim that Muhammad bin Qasim invaded Sindh because the Hindus had abducted a Muslim woman from an Arab ship. The said tactics were successfully used in Afghanistan against the Afghan progressives and Russians who, the Islamists propagated, "wanted Muslims to marry their sisters and mothers." When the Americans landed in Afghanistan in 2001, similar allegations were levelled against them. Examples of how this Islamic politics of incitement works in the 21st century abound in the bulk emails, websites, and propaganda posters which Islamists post to millions across the world. As to how the chastity of women became a mob gathering and instigating strategy in Islam, its historical background can be seen in the following event.

Muhammad assembled the Jews in the market of the Qaynuqa tribe and threatened them, `Convert to Islam or you will be decimated just like the chiefs of Mecca have been at Badr.' The ill-fated Jews remained defiant and said, `Don't deceive yourself

Muhammad. You have killed a number of inexperienced Quraysh who did not know how to fight. But if you fight us you will learn that you have met your equals.'[255] Muhammad went back and issued the following verses:

> Say to the unbelievers, 'Soon you will be defeated
> And gathered into hell, a wretched resting place
> You saw the example of the two parties, which fought
> One fought in the way of God and the others were unbelievers
> Seeing twice their number with their own eyes
> God strengthens with his help whom he will
> In that is a warning for those who have eyes.
> (Sura 3, verses 12-13)

Subsequently, some believers instigated a quarrel in a Jewish goldsmith's shop and, using the trivial excuse that the goldsmith had lifted the hijab of a believer woman, killed him. The Jews killed the murderer of the goldsmith and this gave Muhammad the excuse he was looking for. He resolved that the Qaynuqa should have come to him when their man was murdered and, by taking revenge from a believer, they had violated the Treaty of Medina. He ordered murder of all their men, enslavement of their women and children, and confiscation of their property. Then he laid siege of the tribe.[256] The Qaynuqa held for fifteen days. When they ran out of water, they came out of their fortress and threw themselves at Muhammad's mercy.

Among the so-labelled "hypocrites" was the aforementioned Abdallah bin Ubayy who refused to tolerate the massacre of Banu Qaynuqa. He stood in front of Muhammad and, despite his wrath, shouted, 'Muhammad, I will not leave you until you agree to be kind to my friends. These seven hundred Jews have been with me through the thick and thin of life. How can you slaughter them all in one day? For God's sake, fear the turn of events.'[257]

As Muhammad turned away, Abdallah grabbed him by the collar and they struggled for a while. The believers came to intervene but Muhammad raised his hand to hold them off. He could not yet ignore Abdallah because he was the leader of those Medinians who had been feeding and clothing him and his emigrant followers since their arrival in Medina. Finally, he allowed the seven hundred or so men, women and children to go into exile. What they left behind, land, palm groves, houses, and cattle, was divided among the emigrants. Muhammad took a fifth of this property. He had fulfilled another part of his scheme.

> They played their tricks and God played His tricks
> And God is the best trickster. (Sura 8, verse 30)

The penalty of banishment of a whole tribe was an entirely new tradition in Arabia. Muhammad had falsely claimed that the Quraysh had banished him from Mecca and now he was banishing others from their homelands.

Abdallah bin Ubayy had put his own life at risk to save his neighbours but, because the majority of his men had been lured by the booty and abandoned him to join Muhammad, he was militarily too weak to save the Jews from exile and, later, from mass murder. Three days later, when the Medinians saw the Qaynuqa leaving town, women and children on camels while men on foot, they understood that Muhammad was now the new king.

There were many reasons for which Abdallah's men had joined Muhammad. Those who worked to earn had to pay taxes to Muhammad's jihadis. By becoming a jihadi, they would not need to work hard on a daily basis and pay taxes but receive shares from the booty. Hence, many had found it easier to loot and plunder in the guise of pleasing God. In a community if even a few people resort to unremitting violence and worst atrocities, they can control the entire population through fear and intimidation. After seeing how Muhammad had taken over Medina and disrupted community relations between the Jews and the other tribes, Abdallah had regretted giving him shelter. Subsequently, he had unsuccessfully tried to convince his people to stop favouring Muhammad and his followers so that they could be discouraged from staying in Medina. This had happened as follows.

During the earlier described raid on the Mustalaq tribe, a fight had broken out between the Medinians and the Meccan emigrants at which Abdallah had addressed his Medinian men as follows:

> We have made a mistake in sheltering and fattening these greedy Quraysh; the old idiom fits in our situation: "You fattened your dog too much and, one day, it devoured you." You made room for these emigrants in your town, gave them shelter, protection, property, and houses but look what they are doing now. If you stop now, they will have no choice but

to move to another place. When we will return to Medina, the honourable ones must expel the meaner from there.

Muhammad's spy Zayd bin Arqum informed him about this and Umar stood up to kill Abdallah but Muhammad stopped him and said, 'If you kill him, word will get around that Muhammad kills his companions and those who give him shelter.' He then used his tacit and deceitful methods. He touched the ear of Zayd saying, 'These ears heard what God has confirmed as true.' Then he indirectly addressed Abdallah by issuing a whole set of verses titled, "The Hypocrites:"

> When the hypocrites come to you (*Muhammad*), they say,
> "We bear witness that you are indeed the messenger of God."
> God knows that you are indeed His messenger,
> And God bears witness that the hypocrites are indeed liars
> They have made their oaths a cover-up
> To obstruct men from the path of God
> Truly evil are their deeds
> That is because they believed, then they rejected faith
> Therefore, a seal has been set on their hearts
> And they do not understand.
> When you look at them, their appearance pleases you
> And when they speak, you listen to them
> (*But*) They are like pieces of propped up timber.
> They think that every cry is against them
> They are the enemies; so beware of them.
> The curse of God be on them! How deluded they are!
> And when it is said to them,
> "Come, the messenger of God will pray for your forgiveness,"
> They turn aside their heads,
> And you see them turning away their faces in arrogance.
> It is equal to them whether you pray for their forgiveness or not
> God will not forgive them
> Truly, God guides not rebellious transgressors.
> They say, "Spend nothing on those who are with God's messenger
> So that they may leave (*and quit Medina*)."
> To God belong the treasures of the heavens and the earth
> But the hypocrites do not understand.
> They say, "When we will return to Medina,
> The more honourable will expel the meaner from there."

Honour belongs to God, His messenger, and to the believers
But the hypocrites do not know. (Sura 63, verses 1-8).

Because this chapter mentioned what Abdallah had said, when he heard it, he knew that it was about him. He also knew that Muhammad's "divine revelations" about "grievous punishment from God" usually heralded a secret assassination. The knowledge that his own men had become Muhammad's spies disheartened him so much that he apologized to Muhammad and thus saved his life.[258]

Some years later, Muhammad said to Umar, `If I had ordered Abdallah killed when you had advised it, the chiefs of Medina would have shook with fury. But now, if I order them to kill him, they would do it with their own hands.'

XXX

After the deaths of Utaba and Abu Jahl at Badr, the Umayyad leader Abu Sufyan had become the new chief of Mecca. He tried to unite the Meccans by stopping internecine revenge killings, and settling tribal disputes.[259] He also vowed to avenge those killed at Badr, and rode secretly to Medina with two hundred men on camels. He knew that two hundred men on camels were not enough to defeat Muhammad's men. He had hoped that the Jews of Medina would join him but he was not sure. Hence, having camped with his men and camels at a certain place outside Medina, he went alone to see Huyayy bin Akhtab, the chief of the Banu Nadir, and knocked at his door. Huyayy, who had seen the cleansing of the Qaynuqa tribe, was so scared of Muhammad and his men that he did not open the door.[260]

Abu Sufyan then went to see Salaam bin Mishkam, the chief of the Banu Qurayza. Salaam treated Abu Sufyan as a guest but refused to participate in an attack on the believers because he had signed the Treaty of Medina, which barred the Jews from helping the Meccans. Abu Sufyan had no choice but to consider his oath fulfilled with a relatively minor gesture; his men killed one or two Ansar whom they found hanging around their camp, and burned a few crops[261] before returning to Mecca.

By refusing to join forces with Abu Sufyan against Muhammad, the remaining two Jewish tribes of Medina placed their lives at Muhammad's mercy. The entire Jewish generations born in the Middle East during the next fourteen centuries would pay the heaviest price for this grave error of judgement, as Muhammad would leave the "Godly" example of the ethnic cleansing of Jews for the coming generations of Muslims to follow.

If the Jews of Medina had joined forces with Abu Sufyan, and succeeded in silencing Muhammad, Middle East would have probably remained a multi-faith continent. Jewish, Zoroastrian, Christian, and pagan communities would still co-exist in the continent as they did before Arab rulers began to imitate Muhammad in wiping out every other religion from the Middle East.

Muhammad keeps inciting anti-Jewish sentiments
and steps up raids on Meccan caravans

The confidence of the Ansar was enhanced by their victory in Badr and by the token revenge that the Meccans took for their seventy dead and seventy prisoners. Now that the Ansar had killed many of the noblest Quraysh, obtained ransom for prisoners, and confiscated parts of the Jewish lands, they began to strut in pride and deride other religions. It reflected in their following poems:

If it were not for our Lord, we would have become Jews
Though Judaism is a weak religion.
If it were not for our Lord, we would have become Christians
And be like the monks who live in mount Jalil.
But now we have our own distinct and strong religion.[262]

Victoriously, Muhammad declared, `I shall cleanse Arabia of Jews and Christians. Only believers will live here.'[263] He enhanced his denunciation of the Jews and kept showing that Jewish knowledge and practices were false. A man once came to him and asked, `I have a slave woman and because I do not want to have a child from her, I do "uzl" (ejaculating outside vagina). The Jews tell me that this is like a minor murder.' Muhammad replied, `The Jews lie. You can do uzl.' But then he realized that a woman might still get pregnant, and this would make him lose credibility among others. He quickly added, `If God wants the birth, you will not be able to stop it.' In refuting the alleged Jewish belief, Muhammad conveniently forgot that during his early days in Medina, he had been telling his followers, 'To ejaculate outside the vagina is the same as to bury someone alive.'

Another man said to Muhammad, 'The Jews say that if you penetrate into the vagina from the backside you will get a child with squint-eyes.' Muhammad replied, 'Your women are your fields into which you can enter the way you like. (Sura 2, verse 223).'[264] He would not let go even minor things in which he found a Jewish link, such as his command, 'Do not pray with your hands on your hips. Only Jews pray with their hands on their hips.'[265]

XXX

The Quraysh re-routed their caravans towards the longer and expensive path, away from Medina, through the barren steppes of Najd and southern Iraq, but it did not help. With practice in fasting and help from the intimidated tribes on route, Muhammad's jihadis were now able to reach Najd. He dispatched a group led by his slave turned foster-son, Zayd bin Haritha, who successfully looted a caravan carrying silver, and brought the booty to him.[266] The leader of the caravan was, again, Abu Sufyan. The merchants and guards could not save the goods but they succeeded in fleeing with no loss of life. Muhammad's official bard Hassan bin Thabit mocked the Quraysh and tauntingly advised them to abandon their trade with Syria:

> Abandon the streams of Syria
> Sharp swords bar you from Syria
> Swords, like the frightening teeth
> Of thorn-fed pregnant she-camels.

<u>Abu Sufyan wins at Uhud, spares Muhammad's life and Muhammad glorifies death in jihad</u>

The Meccan trade, cut off from the bazaars of Syria and Iraq, was gradually dying. The pilgrim trade too had diminished because of the fears of bandit raids. The Meccans had no option but to prepare for war in order to be able to re-open their previous trade routes, re-build their prestige, and increase the number of pilgrims to Mecca.

Abu Sufyan gathered around three thousand men, largely supplied by his Bedouin allies, and around two hundred horsemen. In the following spring, he set out for the ten-day march towards Medina. When his army had set up camp in the barley fields beneath Mount Uhud three miles from Medina, he sent a messenger to the Aus and Khazraj with the message: "We do not need to fight you; leave us to deal with our cousin Muhammad and we will leave you be." The Medinians paid no heed to the message because they were now effectively under Muhammad's rule.

In Medina, Muhammad sought advice from his *shura* – the advisory council – which still included Abdallah bin Ubayy. Abdallah said, `By God, whenever we have gone out of Medina to meet an enemy, we have suffered heavy losses but when an enemy has entered Medina, we have inflicted heavy losses on them. Let the Meccans stay where they are for it is the worst place to stay without access to fresh water. If they enter Medina, men will fight them face to face and women and boys will throw stones on them from rooftops. They will be forced to retreat.' Muhammad was of the same opinion but his headstrong followers said, `O apostle of God, lead us forth to meet our enemies lest they think we are too weak and cowardly to fight them.' Upon their insistence, Muhammad decided to march towards Uhud with a thousand men but as soon as they were out of Medina, Abdallah declared that he would go no further. He was treaty-bound to defend Medina but going further would be to turn from defence to offence. He said, `Muhammad has obeyed unwise men and not listened to me. I don't see why we should lose our lives in this ill-chosen place,' and he left with his three hundred men.

Muhammad asked his companions whether anyone could take them near the Quraysh by a road that would not pass by them. Abu Khaythama undertook to do so, and he took him through the property of Banu Haritha until he came out in the territory of Mirba' bin Qayi who was a blind man. He had heard about Muhammad's methods of gradual take-over by dividing the community on religious grounds, and leading one group to raid the other, and he detested him for that. When he perceived the approach of Muhammad's men, he got up and threw dust in their faces saying, `You may be the apostle of God, but I won't let you through my garden!' He took a handful of dust and said, `By God, Muhammad, if I could be sure that I should not hit someone else I would throw it in your face.' Sa'ad bin Zayd rushed at him and hit him on the head with his bow so that he split it open. Muhammad said, `Do not kill him, for this man is blind of heart as much as blind of sight,' but it was too late.

The cleverly chosen path enabled Muhammad to position his men with Mount Uhud on their back and the jagged ancient lava flows of the *harra* on both sides. The Meccan cavalry could not pass these and, therefore, could only attack through the barley fields in the front. In difficult circumstances, Muhammad's men could climb up the mount and take refuge in its caves. He also posted fifty archers on the hill with strict orders not to leave their posts either in victory or defeat and defend them with their arrows from Meccan cavalry. Thus, he believed that he had protected the rear of his army. Contrary to the advice he had given to an ill-fated man at the battle of Badr, he covered himself with two layers of body armour.[267]

The battle began at daybreak. Each side had brought their women along for encouragement, fetching water, and tending to the wounded. Women happily joined battles because it was against the Arab custom to attack women, and they knew that they were safe in both victory and defeat. On the Meccan side, Abu Sufyan's wife Hind bin Utaba led fifteen widows and daughters of men killed at Badr. They had come to encourage and watch their men taking revenge.

In the beginning, the believers fought well. Their archers, positioned on the foot of the hilltop, repulsed every charge of the Meccan cavalry, and maimed many horses by shooting arrows at them. The Meccans broke ranks and fled, which gave the impression that they had been defeated. It was at this point that the archers' gave in to greed. One of them later reported, `I saw the women tucking up their skirts and running to pick booty. Someone shouted, "Plunder! Plunder!" Nobody listened to the commander shouting that Muhammad's orders were to hold fast. The archers left their posts and ran onto the battlefield.' Relying on their experience in Badr whereby those who did not hasten to strip the corpses of clothes, shoes, and arms, obtained little share in the booty, the believers hastened to strip the bodies of the fallen men too early into the battle. This gave the opportunity to the Meccan archers, led by Khalid bin Walid, to hit a large number of believers with arrows shot from the hilltop. The believers had no knowledge that Khalid had moved onto the hilltop with his best archers.

Abu Sufyan's cavalry commander saw his chance. He rallied his riders to wheel around and come at the believers from their now unprotected rear. The infantry charged after him and the battle turned. As they cut down one believer after another, the survivors ran for the slopes of Mount Uhud but the Meccans had dug ditches in the battlefield overnight. The believers did not know this and many fell in these ditches.

Some believers mistakenly killed some of their own side. Their panic heightened when a stone hurled at Muhammad injured him and he fell into a ditch. Ali and Talha pulled him out.[268] He staggered up a hilltop where a rider attacked him but he stuck a spear in his neck.[269] While Muhammad's helmet had saved his life, the force of the stone had smashed its metal faceguard deep into his cheek, split his upper lip, broken his nose, and gashed his forehead, which bled profusely. He was furious to see his men in flight.

At the battle of Badr, Muhammad's uncle Hamza had slain the Meccan chief Utaba. Now Utaba's daughter, Hind, Abu Sufyan's wife, had brought her Ethiopian slave named Wahshi to find Hamza and spear him in revenge.[270]

Hamza was a fierce fighter who taunted every enemy fighter he came across that day. In particular, he came across a man whose mother was a female circumciser in Mecca. Hamza knew him and as he whirled his sword over his head, he yelled, `Come get me, you son of a clitoris-cutter!' However, the son of the clitoris-cutter was Hamza's last kill. Wahshi later reported, `I balanced my javelin until I was satisfied and then I hurled it at Hamza. It struck him in the lower belly with such force that it came out between his legs. He staggered towards me and fell. I waited until he was dead. Then I went to his corpse and recovered my javelin.

A rumour spread that Muhammad was dead. The Meccans eased their counter-attack because Abu Sufyan had made it clear that their quarrel was only with Muhammad. As the Meccan women searched the barley fields for booty, gathering up swords, daggers, chainmail, bridles, saddles – anything of value – the believers retreated further up the slopes of Mount Uhud, stoning the few Meccans who still tried to chase them.

Close to nightfall Abu Sufyan rode beneath the hill and shouted, `In God's name, is Muhammad really dead?' One report states that Muhammad was hiding in a cave with Ali and Umar, and Abu Sufyan challenged him by shouting, `O enemy of God! Come out and fight.' Muhammad kept quiet. Ali found this insulting and sought permission to leave the cave and face Abu

Sufyan but Muhammad said, `Stay back. This is not the day to fight.' Abu Sufyan repeated, `Is Muhammad alive or dead?' Umar shouted, `He is alive and he is listening to you.' Abu Sufyan shouted back, `Some of your dead have been mutilated. I neither commanded this nor forbade it and I am neither happy nor upset about it. Wars go by turns. This is our day for what had been your day.'

Another report suggests that Abu Sufyan found Muhammad hiding behind a rock on Mount Uhud and was in a position to kill him. Instead, he apologized that some of his men had mutilated the corpses of those killed, including that of Hamza, and then ordered his army to break camp and set off back to Mecca.[271]

The Islamists quote this event as evidence that God protected Muhammad but one need considering that in tribal Arabia, killing Muhammad would have sparked a major conflict between the Hashimis and the Umayyads. Many Hashimis were still Abu Sufyan's allies, some hypocritically though, and were part of the Meccan elite, which would have further split if Abu Sufyan had killed Muhammad. On his part, the ungracious Muhammad tried to turn his defeat into victory by using his favourite technique of secretly sending an assassin to kill Abu Sufyan in Mecca. This will be described later.

When the Meccans had departed, Muhammad saw the mutilated body of his uncle, and was greatly distressed. However, to show that he was too strong to be moved by the state of the corpse, he said, `I would have left this corpse to be eaten by beasts and vultures but I am afraid that people will start following my example.' To show his followers that "the dead are in fact alive in the heavens," and thus encourage them to participate in future battles, he addressed the corpse, `Hamza! It is because of you that I am in pain but never again will such pain afflict me. I have never found myself in a more infuriating situation. If God gives me the opportunity, I will mutilate thirty bodies of the Quraysh in revenge.'[272] However, despite this promise, when Muhammad took over Mecca some years later, he did not execute even Wahshi. This was because Wahshi was a very skilful spearman and Muhammad used him to assassinate Musaylima Kazaab, another prophet who had dared to rival him.[273]

The believers buried their dead in a hurry. They did not wash the corpses and did not offer funeral prayers.[274] Back in Medina, when Muhammad could not bear the moaning and wailing of women crying over their killed men, he banned mourning. He gave his blood-stained sword to his daughter Fatima for washing. Ali, Fatima's husband, also did the same.[275]

An ally named Quzman, though he was not a believer, had killed nine Meccans in the battle but he was lying wounded in his house. The believers said to him, 'Cheer up, O Quzman; you have done gallantly today and your sufferings have been for God's sake.' He said, 'Why should I cheer up? I fought only to protect my people.' When the pain of his wounds became unbearable, he took an arrow from his quiver, cut a vein in his hand, and killed himself. Hearing about his suicide, the ever-ungrateful Muhammad said, 'He belongs to the people of hell.'[276]

Another young believer Yazid bin Haatib was terminally injured. When men gathered by his deathbed and said to him, 'O son of Haatib! There is good news; you are going to go to the gardens of paradise,' his old father sneered, 'Hump! By God, it is the garden of thorns. You deceived my poor boy and lured him to his death.'[277]

About the humiliation at Uhud, a man called Mu'attib bin Qusyahr remarked, 'If Muhammad had divine powers we would not be slaughtered in Uhud.'[278] Muhammad's informers reported this to him. He branded Mu'attib and his friends as "hypocrites" and issued his "revelations," stating that the believers had invited the defeat by not obeying his orders in their lust for booty, by turning back and running away, and by doubting the power of God:

> God did indeed fulfil His promise to you
> With His permission you were about to annihilate your enemy
> But you flinched and doubted and disobeyed the order,
> When He brought you in sight of what you covet (*the booty*).
> Among you are some who yearn for this world
> And some who desire the hereafter.
> Then He diverted you from your foes in order to test you
> But He forgave you for He is full of grace to those who believe.
> You were climbing up the high ground,
> Without even casting a side glance at any one,
> And the messenger in your rear was calling you back
> That is why God gave you one distress after another
> As punishment, to teach you not to worry about
> That which you lost (*the booty*) and that which befell you

For God is well aware of all that you do.
After the distress, God sent peace upon you
Some of you were calm but others too anxious about their lives;
In their ignorance, they turned cynical about God
And said, `Do we have power over anything?'
Say, `All power belongs to God.'
They conceal within their souls and would not reveal to you
And say, `If we had God's support we would not be slain.'
Say, `Had you remained in your houses,
Those for whom death was ordained
Would surely have gone to places where they would be slain.'
God wanted to test you and see what was in your hearts
And purge it; God knows what is in your hearts.
Those who turned back on the day of the battle
Satan alone caused them to backslide,
Because of their misdeeds (*the haste in taking booty*).
But God has forgiven them.
O Believers! Be not like those who disbelieve
And say of their brethren when they travel to fight,
`Had they stayed with us, they would not have been slain;'
Thus, God makes this to be an intense regret in their hearts;
God gives life and causes death and God sees what you do
If you are killed in the way of God, your sins will be forgiven,
Which is better than what you gain in this world;
Whether you die or you are killed, you return to God.
(Sura 3, verses 152-158)

Because Muhammad had not listened to Abdallah's advice against a forward attack, the latter and his friends had not participated in the battle. The events of the battle had shown that Abdallah was right; it had been foolish to engage the Meccan army in open ground, and Muhammad had come close to getting himself killed or made captive – saved only because of Abu Sufyan's grace. To keep his followers from doubting his status as God's messenger and appreciating Abdallah's wisdom, Muhammad launched a propaganda campaign. He laid the blame of defeat on Abdallah and confirmed him as a "hypocrite." Accordingly, when Abdallah went to the Friday prayers and stood to speak, the believers forced him to leave. Some men advised him to seek pardon but he said, `I do not need Muhammad's forgiveness.'[279] He said that he was right about the mistake of a forward attack and if men had stayed in Medina, they would not be slain. In response, Muhammad sent to him death threats disguised in the following "revelations," which he addressed to his followers:

> When a misfortune befell you (*the believers*),
> Though you had certainly afflicted (*the unbelievers*)
> With twice as much (*in the previous battles and raids*),
> You began to say, `Where did this (*setback*) come from?'
> Say, `It is your own doing.' God has power over all things.
> And what befell you on the day when the two armies met
> Was with God's approval
> So that He could know the believers and the hypocrites.
> When it was said to them, `Come, fight in God's way.'
> They said, `If we knew how to fight,
> We would certainly have followed you.'
> They were on that day much nearer to unbelief than to belief.
> They say with their mouths what is not in their hearts,
> And God best knows what they conceal.
> Those who stayed at home said of those who fought,
> `If they had listened to us they would not have been killed,'
> Say to them, `Then avert death from yourselves
> If you speak the truth.' (Sura 3, verses 165-168)

Muhammad gathered his followers and delivered a sermon describing "the life of the slain in the heavens," aimed at encouraging his men to continue to fight. In his customary fashion, he turned the situation of slaughter and pain upside down by portraying death in waging war as an achievement people should long for:

> About brothers who died in Uhud, God has kept their souls with green birds who fly over the streams of paradise. They eat the fruits from the trees of paradise and dwell in the shadow of the heavens lit by golden torches. When they tasted the fragrant drinks and foods, and enjoyed the comforts of their bedding, they said, 'If our brothers down on earth knew how luxurious lives we have here, they would not neglect their duties in jihad and not shy away from the battlefield.' Upon hearing this, God said, 'I shall pass on your message to believers on earth.' Hence, God has sent to me the following revelations:[280]

> Do not think of those slain in the way of God as dead
> They are alive with their Lord who feeds them.
> Compared to those left behind who have not yet joined them
> The dead are very happy; they are neither afraid nor sad.
> (Sura 3, verses 169-170)

A simpleton Jew, named Mukhayr, believing that he was treaty-bound to join Muhammad in the battle, was killed in Uhud. Upon his return, Muhammad took ownership of Mukhayr's oasis and property and said, `Mukhayr was the best Jew.'[281]

Muhammad quickly recovered from the humiliation of Uhud, ordered the execution of two prisoners of war, Mu'awiya bin Mughira and Abu Uzz'a al Ajmi, and dispatched a spy by the name of Mu'abd from his allied Khuza'a tribe. Mu'abd's mission was to gather news if the Meccan army intended to regroup and return to attack, and to deceive their leaders about Muhammad's strength and intentions.[282] For spying, Muhammad usually used unbelievers or those whose conversion to Islam was not known. The Khuza'a tribe were his confidants and spies but, being unbelievers, they were not suspected by the Quraysh. Hence, they could obtain information about Meccan plans.[283]

Mu'abd met Abu Sufyan and misinformed him that the believers were well motivated, had regrouped and gained strength, and would be hard to beat if re-attacked. If Abu Sufyan intended to re-attack, the false news discouraged him from doing so.

A Meccan warrior, Abdallah bin Jahsh, had been killed in the battle and his wife, Zaynab bint Khuzayma al Halaliya, was now in the believer's hands. Muhammad married her but she died in about two months. This event and many similar ones show that despite enmity between men, women could be looked after in the enemy's home. Likewise, later, Muhammad married Abu Sufyan's daughter though the two men were still each other's rivals.

Uhud was not his only defeat. Muhammad sent Abdallah bin Abd al Asad to raid the Banu Asad tribe. Abdallah was defeated and killed. Muhammad asked his widow Umm Salama to marry him. She refused and said that she was old, of a jealous nature, and had many children. Muhammad sent his reply saying, `As for you being old, I am older than you; as for you having a jealous nature, God will cast jealousy out of your heart; as for the children, they belong to God and His messenger.'[284] Umm Salama had no choice but to marry him.

The expulsion of the Banu Nadir and confiscation of their lands

As explained earlier, Muhammad's men could not sustain themselves without regular booty. Many had taken loans to prepare for war. They hoped to pay back by selling the booty but the defeat at Uhud had dashed their hopes, and their morale was at its lowest. They needed to conduct new raids and bring booty.

Four months after the battle of Uhud, Muhammad dispatched Abu'l Auja al Salami with forty jihadis towards Najd to raid the Banu Sulaym tribe but the tribe defeated and killed all of them except one named Amr bin Umayya al Damri.[285] The man of the Banu Sulaym who captured Amr had once taken oath that he would release a captive to honour his mother. Hence, he set Amr free.

On his way back to Muhammad, Amr found two men of the Banu Amir tribe sleeping under a tree. Frustrated at his group's defeat, he mistook them as belonging to the Banu Sulaym and killed them.

The Banu Amir had a treaty with Muhammad, which stipulated that if any of the two parties would kill a member of the other, the killer's side would pay blood money. Accordingly, they demanded payment from Muhammad. This increased Muhammad's financial burden and, although he agreed to pay the blood money, he did not want to pay it from his own pocket. He quickly hatched a scheme: He planned that he would ask the Banu Nadir Jews to pay the blood money on grounds that the Treaty of Medina, which he had made them to sign, bound them to help the believers. Because the Banu Nadir had nothing to do with Amr's two murders, Muhammad guessed that they would refuse to pay this sum. This would provide him with an excuse to label them as those who broke the treaty, and confiscate their lands. However, contrary to his expectations, when he went to the Banu Nadir, with Abu Bakr and Umar by his side, and asked them to pay the said blood money, the intimidated Jews agreed. They asked them to take a seat while they gathered the money.

Muhammad did not want to lose this opportunity to confiscate their lands, worth a lot more than the blood money. He quickly worked out another scheme: Instead of waiting, he went back to his mosque and invented a "revelation" stating that God had informed him that the Banu Nadir were planning to kill him by throwing a stone on him from the top of the wall by which he was sitting.[286] He had become so confident about his schemes that he did not even bother that he had left Abu Bakr and Umar with the Banu Nadir without telling them about the "danger." He then gathered his men and began planning to besiege the tribe. Within an hour, he sent the Nadir a message: "Leave my town because you have committed treason by plotting against me." Medina was no longer the town of those who had first inhabited it but his town, henceforth to be called "Medina-tul-Nabi" (the town of the prophet).

Banu Nadir went to Abdallah bin Ubayy for support, and told him that they faced a massacre or expulsion. Abdallah had little power to stop Muhammad but he tried to help them and said, `Do not worry; if you are expelled, we shall migrate with you, and if you are attacked, we shall come to your help.' As usual, Muhammad's informers told him about this meeting. He did not like this[287] and he issued more "divine revelations" against Abdallah and his men:

> Have you not seen these hypocrites?
> They say to their unbeliever brethren from among the Jews:
> `If you are expelled, we shall migrate with you,
> And we will never obey anyone's orders about you
> And if you are attacked, we will certainly come to help you.'
> And God testifies that they are most surely liars.
> For indeed if the Jews are expelled, they will not go with them,
> And if the Jews are killed they will not help them,
> And indeed if they help, they will turn back and flee,
> And then they will not be helped.
> You (*believers*) cast more terror in their hearts than does God;
> This is because they are a people who do not understand.
> They will not fight against you as one group
> Except in fortified towns, or from behind walls
> The disunity between them is severe:
> You may think that they are one group,
> But their hearts are disunited;
> That is because they are a people who have no sense.
> They are like Satan who leads men to reject faith
> And when the men turn unbelievers, Satan says to them,
> `I am not a party to you because I fear God
> Who is certainly the Lord of the worlds.' (Sura 59, verses 11-16)

This was a taunt at Abdallah and his men because, after promising support, they had not been able to stop the earlier expulsion of the Qaynuqa Jews. The quoted verses show that Muhammad knew that the Jews too lacked unity. They lived as separate tribes so that one tribe would not come to help the other. Hence, he marched with his men and besieged the Nadir who locked themselves up in their homes. Upon seeing that they would not come out of their homes, he ordered his followers to cut down and burn their palm groves. In Arabia, it is very hard to grow trees, especially date palms. Each tree had required generations of careful tending and work so that to destroy these was to destroy a whole history and economy. The Jews pleaded, `Muhammad, you used to prohibit sedition and condemned those who instigated sedition. Why are you cutting and burning our trees?' Many of Muhammad's followers were drunk on date wine and so unruly that he banned the consumption of alcohol.

Finally, upon the persistent pleas of the Medinian friends of the Nadir, Muhammad condescended not to kill them. He allowed them to go into exile with as little of their moveable property as they could carry on one camel for every three persons. Some of them migrated north toward the oasis of Khyber while the others went further on toward Syria and Palestine.[288]

Instead of his usual one-fifth share in the loot, Muhammad took over the entire Banu Nadir property for himself and distributed little among his followers. He justified it by saying that because the jihadis did not have to fight this time, they could not demand a share. To ward off any objections from people, that he was trying to be the richest man among them, he issued the following "revelations:"

> That which God took from them (*the Jews*)
> And bestowed on His messenger,
> For this property, you did not fight or use your horses or camels
> God confiscates for His messenger whatever He wants
> This property is for God and for His messenger,
> And for his relatives, orphans, the needy, and the travellers,
> So that it may not be something taken by the rich among you
> And whatever the messenger gives to you, accept it,
> And stay away from whatever he forbids to you,
> And fear God for He is strict in punishment. (Sura 59, verses 6-7)

The term used for such property as had fallen to the exclusive use of Muhammad was "fay." He spent the "fay" income on the upkeep of his wives, slaves, horses and arms.[289] He then rationalized the plunder of the Nadir by presenting their banishment as the fulfilment of "God's schemes:"

> God caused the expulsion of the people of the book (*the Jews*)
> From their homes, as soon as we stormed them.
> You never thought they would get out of their homes,
> And they thought their fortresses will defend them from God.
> But God came upon them through those they never expected
> And cast terror in their hearts – so much so that
> They demolished their homes with their own hands
> And the hands of the believers.
> Therefore, take a lesson, O you who have eyes!
> And had it not been that God had decreed for them exile,
> He would certainly have punished them in this world,
> And in the hereafter they shall have chastisement of the fire.
> That is because they resisted God and His messenger
> And if anyone resists God, verily God is severe in punishment.
> Whether you cut down the tender palm-trees
> Or you left them standing on their roots,
> It was by leave of God so that He might cover with shame,
> The rebellious transgressors. (Sura 59, verses 2-5)

These verses, and thousands more, show that at least at certain times Muhammad believed that he was God; God's actions had become synonymous with Muhammad's actions.

The verses, "Their homes were destroyed by theirs' and believers' hands" refer to the events whereby some Jews had taken out the doors of their homes to take with them, while Muhammad's men – the believers – plundered the leftover property.

Only two Jews of the Banu Nadir succumbed to Islam and their property was returned to them. The character of one of them, Yamin bin Umayr, can be judged by the quoted report that he sent a hired assassin to murder his cousin by the name of Amr bin Jahsh.[290]

Muhammad's official bards celebrated the expulsion as follows:

> I can sacrifice my family on the great person of Muhammad
> Whose deeds are eternal; he has banished the Jews to alien lands

They sleep under trees of fire (*in the desert heat*)
And live in the land of small bushes.
When Ka'ab was murdered, he tried to run like a wild camel
The Jewish women had not mourned enough at Ka'ab's death,
When the messenger humiliated them and made them to bow.
They lived in nice places
But now their camels are tired of travelling
And they have no choice but to keep riding to alien lands
Three men to a camel – the Banu Nadir follow the Qaynuqa
They have betrayed their homes and their palm trees.

However, a conscientious poet expressed grief at the expulsion of the Banu Nadir. His verses tell us about their social characteristics:

The homes of the Banu Nadir had courtyards to play games
But their dwellers are there no more – they are gone.
Do you remember the noble women who lived in these houses?
Wide-eyed, attractive, patient and mature women
When a beggar came to their door,
They would treat him with a smile
And give him what he wanted,
Fearless of a reprimand for being generous.
Do not call me an ally of the Jews; I am not
But they deserve appreciation for their good deeds;
When you were hungry and thirsty in times of famine,
They used to slaughter animals for you
They were honourable and chivalrous in battlefield
And always welcomed those who sought common weal
But the lust for power has made you fanatical.[291]

The battle of the Allies (*Ahzaab*), and war by deceit

Some leaders of the exiled Banu Nadir, including Huyayy bin Akhtab, Salaam bin Abu'l Huqayq, Abu Rafi'a and al Rabi along with some others of Banu Wa'il met the Quraysh in Mecca and told them about how Muhammad had exiled their tribe and usurped their lands and properties. The Islamists assert that the Jews invited the Quraysh to join them in an attack on Muhammad but this seems unlikely because the Jewish tribes had no joint forces and none of their tribes took part in the subsequent battle of the Allies, also known as the battle of the Ditch. In fact, there is no record showing that the Jews collectively participated in any battle as Quraysh allies. Most probably, they went to the Quraysh to share their grief and see if these, being powerful and influential, could get them their lands back. Some of the Quraysh said to them, `You, O Jews, are the first scripture people and know the nature of our dispute with Muhammad. Is our religion the best or is his?' They replied that their religion was surely better than his, they had not invaded other peoples' lands, and hence they had a better claim to be in the right.[292] Because people regularly travelled between Mecca and Medina, Muhammad heard about this and issued the following "revelations:"

> Have you not seen those who were given a part of the Book? They believe in sorcery and evil, and say to the unbelievers that they are better guided to the right path than the believers are! They are men whom God has cursed. And those whom God has cursed will find no one to help. Do they still have a share in (*their*) properties? If they had, they would not give a farthing to their fellow men. Are they jealous of those whom God has given His bounty? We (*God*) had already given the people of Abraham (*the Jews*) the Book and Wisdom, and conferred upon them a great kingdom, but some of them believed, and some of them turned their faces from him: And enough is hell for a burning fire. Those who reject our verses, we shall soon cast them into the fire. When their skins are fully roasted, we shall change them for fresh skins so that they may taste the punishment. (Sura 4, verses 51-56).

These verses show how furious Muhammad was when his relatives' religion was elevated above his, and that after usurping lands and properties, he was now taunting their previous owners of being jealous of what "God had given to him."

By using these usurped resources and properties, Muhammad resumed his raids, and led expeditions to the Banu Maharab, the Banu Tha'alba, and the Ghatfan tribes.[293] To stop these raids, the Meccans began to form an allied force which included the Ghatfan and some other tribes such as the Banu Fazara, Banu Mura, and the Ashja'.

Muhammad had ample time to prepare. First, he ordered the early spring crops in the fields around Medina to be harvested to deprive the approaching army of fodder for their horses and camels. His Persian follower Salman Farsi told him about a clever strategy to defend Medina, which he had seen in practice in Persia. Upon his advice, the people of Medina began to dig a three and a half mile long trench on the northern side of the town; hills and oases naturally protected the other three sides. Men, women and children set digging a dry moat studded with sharply pointed stakes to impale the horse of any rider trying to leap across. With ten people assigned to dig sixty feet, it took them six days to cover the entire northern entrance to Medina. They heaped the excavated stones and earth into a high defensive berm behind it. Salman Farsi reported:

> I was digging with a pick in the trench where a rock gave me much trouble. The apostle saw me hacking and saw how difficult the place was. He dropped down into the trench, took the pick from my hand and gave such a blow that lightning showed beneath the pick. This happened a second and a third time. I said, "What is the meaning of this light beneath your pick as you strike?" He said, "Did you really see that, Salman? The first means that God will make us conquer the Yaman; the second Syria and the west; and the third the east. Keep conquering and to the resurrection day you will not conquer a city whose keys God had not given beforehand to Muhammad."[294]

Many reports of similar nature show that particularly since the Ansar had shown willingness to fight for him and booty, Muhammad had wanted to carry on conquering. Accordingly, he would continue to raid others' territories even after taking Mecca. He had always wanted to show to his tribe that they could achieve hegemony under his leadership. Eventually, he would succeed in establishing the rule of the Quraysh over everyone else in the region. The Quraysh sub-tribes would call themselves "Muslims" but they would continue to fight each other even more than before. Later, they would massacre each other in the name of Islam, Khilafa, and "peace."

When Muhammad's men had fully dug the trench, the Quraysh came with their men and encamped between al Juruf and Zughaba with ten thousand of their men and their allies from Banu Fazara, Banu Mura, Banu Kinana and the people of Ashja' and Tihama. Ghatfan too came with their followers from Najd and halted at

Dhanab Naqma towards the direction of Uhud. Abu Sufyan led the Quraysh while Uyayna bin Hisn led the Ghatfan.

Muhammad pitched his camp with three thousand men behind the trench, and gave orders that women and children, who had participated in the digging of the trench, be taken up into the forts. When the Meccans and their allies saw the trench, they exclaimed, `This is a dishonourable trick; a shabby trick borrowed from Persia, which the Arabs have never employed! What kind of cowards hide behind mounds of earth erected by women and children?'

Huyayy bin Akhtab of the exiled Nadir tribe went out to Ka'ab bin Asad of the Qurayza – the last remaining Jewish tribe in Medina. When Ka'ab saw him, he shut the door of his fort in his face and refused to meet him. Huyayy had travelled for many days and he was tired and hungry. He accused Ka'ab of shutting him out because he was too stingy to let him eat his corn. This so enraged Ka'ab that he opened his door while saying that Huyayy was a man of ill omen and that he himself was in treaty with Muhammad and did not intend to go back on his word because he had always found him loyal and faithful. Huyayy boasted, `Good heavens, Ka'ab, I have brought you immortal fame and a great army. I have come with Quraysh with their leaders and chiefs whom I have halted where the torrent-beds of Ruma meet, and Ghatfan with their leaders and chiefs whom I have halted in Dhanab Naqma towards Uhud. They have made a firm agreement and promised me that they will not depart until they have made an end of Muhammad.' Ka'ab said, `By God, you have brought me immortal shame and an empty cloud which has shed its water while it thunders and lightens with nothing in it. Woe to you Huyayy, leave me as I am for I have always found Muhammad loyal and faithful.' Huyayy kept on persuading Ka'ab but at last he gave way. He believed in Ka'ab's trust in Muhammad and promised that if Quraysh and Ghatfan returned without having killed Muhammad, he would enter Ka'ab's fort with him and await his fate.[295]

When Muhammad heard of this, he sent Sa'ad bin Mu'adh, the chief of Aus, and Sa'ad bin Ubaada, chief of Khazraj, together with Abdallah bin Rawaha, whose deceitful nature would be made evident later in his dealings with the Khyber Jews, and told them to go and see if it was true that Huyayy was residing in Ka'ab's house. `If it is true give me an enigmatic message which I can understand, and do not affect the people's morale; and if they are loyal to the treaty, speak out openly before the people as this will raise their morale.'

Sa'ad bin Mu'adh and Abdallah bin Rawaha wanted to usurp the Qurayza property. Hence, when they met Ka'ab and Huyayy, Sa'ad began to revile them and they reviled him back. Sa'ad bin Ubaada said to him, `Stop insulting them, for the dispute between us is too serious for recrimination.' Then the two Sa'ads returned and Sa'ad bin Mu'adh lied to Muhammad by saying, `The situation is even more deplorable than we had heard; they spoke disparagingly of you, saying, "Who is the apostle of God? We have no agreement or treaty with Muhammad." This was exactly what Muhammad wanted to hear because he had plans to cleanse Medina of the remaining Jews. Hence, he shouted, "Allah Akbar. Be happy O believers!"

The Meccans remained camped nearly a month without fighting except for some shooting with arrows, and the siege. Although the Meccans and their allies could not cross the trench, the believers felt threatened by their greater numbers. From behind the berm, they could see hundreds of cooking fires burning by night, and by day, they faced the menace of enemy arrows. Fear was everywhere until the believers imagined vain things. Rumours, that the Jews too were planning to attack them, further enhanced their fear. Disaffection was rife among them to the point that the aforementioned sceptic Mu'attib bin Qusyahr said, `Muhammad promises that we will conquer Persia and Rome, and rob the treasures of Chosroe and Caesar but our state is such that we cannot go to urinate without fear of death.'[296]

Because Muhammad knew that the rumours about the Jews were his own invention and hence baseless, when some men sought his permission to return to their homes in the town on the pretext that these were not safe from the Jews, he issued taunts in the form of "divine revelations:"

> The hypocrites, and those in whose hearts is a disease, say,
> `God and His prophet promised us nothing but a delusion.
> We cannot withstand the enemy. Let us go back!'
> And a group of them seek the prophet's permission to leave;
> Saying that their homes are not safe, though their homes are safe;
> Actually, they want to desert and escape the battle.
> If the enemy had entered and they were invited to treason,
> They would have committed it with little hesitation.

> They had already sworn unto God that they would not flee
> And an oath to God must be abided by.
> Say, `You will not profit if you run from death and killing,
> Because you will dwell in comfort for only a little while.
> Who can save you from God if He intends to harm you,
> Or intends to be kind to you?'
> They will not find any friend or helper other than God
> God knows those among you who hinder others,
> And those who say to their brethren, `Come back to us;'
> And they come not to fight but a little,
> These men are misers in giving their support
> In times of fear of battle, they stare at you
> And their eyeballs rotate in their sockets
> Like the eyes of those in their death throes
> But when the time of fear is gone, their tongues rattle fast
> They talk much in their greed for wealth from the booty
> They are unbelievers and God has made their deeds fruitless.
> They would rather be in the desert with the desert Arabs,
> Asking for news about you, and if they were among you
> They would not fight but a little. (Sura 33: 12-20)

Behind the scenes, negotiations went on with enticements to switch sides. Spies acting as double agents, and emissaries slipped back and forth between the various Medinian villages, oases, and the besieging camps. When conditions pressed hard, Muhammad sent a messenger to Uyayna bin Hisn and al Harith bin `Auf al Murra, who were leaders of Ghatfan, and offered them a third of the dates of Medina for their return journey rations so that they would go back with their followers and leave him and his men alone. Then he sent for the two Sa'ads, told them of it, and asked their advice. They said, `Is it a thing you want us to do, or something God has ordered you to do which we must carry out? Or is it something you are doing for us?' He said, `It is something I am doing for your sake. By God, I would not do it were it not that I have seen the Arabs have shot at you from one bow (i.e. united), and gathered against you from every side and I want to break their offensive against you!'

Sa'ad bin Mu'adh said, `When we and these people were *mushraykeen* and idolaters, they never hoped to eat a single date of ours except as guests or by purchase. Now, after God has honoured and guided us and made us famous through you, are we to give them our property in humility? We certainly will not. We will give them nothing but the sword until God decides between us.' Muhammad said, `You shall have it so.' Sa'ad took the peace treaty, which Muhammad was proposing to the Ghatfan and was yet to be signed, and erased what was written, saying, `Let them do their worst against us!' However, the historian Tibri states that the Ghatfan indeed took the dates upon which they broke their alliance with the Quraysh and went back to Najd, showing that they had joined the Quraysh only for booty and, hence, they had no religious issues with Muhammad.

The siege continued without any actual fighting, but some horsemen of Quraysh, among whom were Ikrima bin Abu Jahl and Hubayra bin Abu Wahb, both of Makhzum tribe, Abdallah bin Mughira and Amr bin Lu'ayy, donned their armour and went forth on horseback to the stations of Banu Kinana, saying, `Prepare for fighting and then you will know who are true knights today.' They galloped forward, made for a narrow part of the trench, beat their horses, and jumped to the other side. Ali and some other men came to challenge them but realized that they, being tribal relatives, knew each other. Ali invited Amr to either become a believer or fight with him. Amr refused to do either of the two and said, `You are like my nephew and I do not want to kill you.' Ali replied, `But I do want to kill you.' Ali sought Muhammad's permission to fight Amr and Muhammad refused it twice because he did not want Amr, being his relative, to be killed by Ali. Then Amr challenged them again and said, `Where is your paradise of which you say your martyrs will enter? Can't you send a man to fight me?' At this, Muhammad allowed Ali to fight. Amr aimed at Ali with his sword but it stuck in his shield. This gave Ali the chance to hit in the vein at the base of his neck and he fell down. With Amr, two more men were killed. One was struck with an arrow and he died later in Mecca. The other, Abdallah bin Mughira, fell in the trench and the believers stoned him. He shouted, `O Arabs! Death is better than this,' so Ali went down in the trench and killed him. The other horsemen escaped.

Muhammad had taken into account that the Jews and the Meccans might join forces and he used a cunning manipulator called Naeem bin Mas'ud to create mistrust between the two communities. Naeem had become a believer but the Meccans and the Jews did not know about his conversion and both trusted him as a friend.

Muhammad said to Naeem, 'War means deceit; if you can, go and deceive the Jews and the *mushraykeen* into mistrusting each other.'

Naeem went to the Jewish Banu Qurayza and said, 'I have always been your true friend. Do you trust me?' They replied that they had no doubts about his friendship. He then said, 'You see, your situation is different from that of the Meccans. They are outsiders while you belong to Medina. If they win, they will loot and plunder this town, which will affect you as well. On the other hand, if they lose, they will escape to Mecca and leave you to deal with the believers against whom you cannot defend yourselves. Therefore, if the Quraysh invite you to join them, you should demand that you will participate only if they leave some of their chiefs in your custody as a guarantee that they will not leave until they have routed the believers.'

After deceiving the Jews, Naeem went to the Quraysh and lied to them, saying that he had discovered that the Jews were bargaining with Muhammad for permission to let their exiled tribes return to Medina. 'In exchange for this,' he said, 'the Jews have promised to Muhammad that they will arrest the chiefs of the Quraysh and hand them over to him for beheading. After the beheadings of your chiefs, they plan to join Muhammad in attacking you.' To ensure the Quraysh that he was telling the truth, Naeem said to them, 'Send a messenger to the Jews and ask them to join you in the battle – you will find for yourselves that what I have told you is true.'

The Quraysh sent Ikrima bin Abu Jahl to the Jews with the message, 'Our horses and camels are dying. We cannot wait any longer and we are going to attack tomorrow. We want you to join us in the attack.' As expected, the Jews replied, 'We cannot participate in the attack unless you keep some of your chiefs in our custody because we are afraid that you might push us into battle and then abandon us to be decimated by Muhammad.'

When the Quraysh heard this, they believed that Naeem was right about the Jews[297] and the mistrust grew. They could not continue their siege in cold weather and stormy conditions. Strong winds would extinguish their fires and they could not cook meals. They lifted their siege and rode back to Mecca.

Muhammad commented on this as follows:

So that God could reward the truthful for their truth
And punish or ignore the hypocrites – as He wills

For God is Forgiving, Merciful;
He repulsed the unbelievers (*the Meccans*) in their rage
They gained nothing (*from this expedition*)
And God sufficed the believers in killing
God is Strong and Mighty.
(Sura 33, verses 24-25)

The events of the Ahzaab show how Muhammad taught and allowed "war of deceit" (*harb al khid'aa*) to his followers[298] and how he succeeded. These also show that the Meccan tribes and the Jewish tribes did not fight as one but each pursued their narrow short-term self-interests. The mistrust between the Jews and the Quraysh defies the Islamist assertion that the Jews and the unbelievers were in league against Muhammad for which reason he mercilessly massacred the Qurayza tribe, as described below.

The massacre of the Banu Qurayza, confiscation of their lands, and enslavement of their women and children

Muhammad and his men had been in a state of battle readiness for a month, besieged by the Meccans, but the Meccans had returned without a fight. After this month-long ordeal, there was no booty to distribute and the believers were greatly disappointed. They were desperate and willing to plunder. Muhammad found this situation a great opportunity to eliminate the Banu Qurayza[299] whose oases and property he had been coveting for long. The evidence showing that he coveted the bits of fertile lands in and around Medina comes from the raiding parties he had been sending. For example, he had sent Ali to raid the Banu Abdallah bin Sa'ad tribe in the oases of Fadak; then he had sent Bashir bin Sa'ad to the Banu Murra tribe again in the same oases; subsequently, he had sent him again in the direction of Khyber[300] to test the strength of the Jews who farmed there.

As usual, Muhammad invented a "divine order" saying that Gabriel had come to him wearing a silken headdress (*a'mama*) and riding a pony with a message from God, which said, "Do not disarm yet; I am proceeding with angels to create terror in the hearts of the Banu Qurayza. Proceed towards them."[301] Again, some Medinians were shocked at the idea of murdering and robbing their neighbours and friends. Muhammad quickly branded these as "hypocrites," and his poet Hassan bin Thabit taunted them:

Do you love the Jews and their religion?
The hearts of the Jews of Hejaz are donkeys' hearts.[302]

Because donkey is a beast of burden, "donkey's heart" was a taunt at all those people who engaged in hard work, such and tilling and farming, to make a living. Bandits who lived off booty and murder were applauded as "lion-hearted."

Muhammad led his men to the Banu Qurayza, who locked themselves in their fortress. Standing outside, he shouted at them, `O brothers of monkeys! Has God not humiliated you? Has He not sent His curse upon you?' This accorded with Muhammad's "divine revelations" quoted earlier as follows:

> Shall I tell you about those from these people (*Jews*)
> Upon whom God sent his curses and showed his fury
> He transformed them into apes and swine,
> And worshippers of sorcerers
> They dwell in evil and stray away from the right path.
> (Sura 5, verse 60)

> And surely you know about those who violated the Sabbath
> And we commanded them to become humiliated monkeys.
> (Sura 2, verse 65)

From the safety of their fortress, the terrified Jews addressed Muhammad by the endearing term, "Abu'l Qasim" (the father of Qasim), and pleaded for kindness but Muhammad lodged his men by the well and deprived them of water. Without water, he knew, they would not be able to remain in their fortress for long.

The siege lasted twenty-five days during which time the Jews discussed amongst themselves what their options were. Their leader, Ka'ab bin Asad, presented three options to them: The first option, submitting to Muhammad as the messenger, was rejected. The second option, which Ka'ab put forward, was to kill their own women and children, because Muhammad would otherwise enslave and sell them, and then die in a fight. They rejected this too because none had the courage to kill their women and children. Ka'ab then put forward the third option, `On Saturday,' he said, `they will not expect us to attack them. Let us attack them on a Saturday and get the maximum advantage of surprise.' But the Jews refused to tarnish the sanctity of Saturday.

In disappointment, Ka'ab sneered, 'None of you was ever resolute, even for a night.'[303]

On the twenty-fifth day, the exhausted, thirsty and hungry Jews asked Muhammad to send Abu Lababa from their allied tribe, the Aus, to advise and help them reach a decision. When Abu Lababa arrived, the terrified women and children gathered around him and burst into tears beseeching his help. They pointed out that they had worked side by side with everyone else to dig the trench though the trench was at the northern entrance to the oasis, and their village was eight miles away at the southern end. They had not worked against Muhammad. Abu Lababa had many happy memories with these families. To see them as hungry, thirsty, and in fear for their lives saddened him but he could do nothing to save them. The Jews asked him if they should obey Muhammad's command and come out of their fortress. Abu Lababa wanted to tell them that they would be slaughtered but he was too scared of Muhammad's agents watching him, and so while he said, 'Yes,' he also moved his hand across his neck to symbolize and indicate the impending slaughter.

Because Abu Lababa had indicated to the Jews that they faced slaughter, when he came out of the fortress, he was so scared of Muhammad's reaction to his gesture that he tied himself up with a pillar in the mosque and begged his forgiveness. Muhammad granted it but only after six days had passed, during which time Abu Lababa remained tied to the pillar.

A few Jews succumbed and converted to Islam. One secretly escaped through the siege. The remaining came out of the fortress and were locked up in a farmhouse. The Aus tribe pleaded with Muhammad not to slaughter their allies and friends but he left the decision with the Aus chief Sa'ad bin Mu'adh. Sa'ad had been severely injured by a Meccan arrow during the battle of Ahzaab. Muhammad had very cleverly lodged him in his house on the pretext of tending to his wounds. Being his guest, Sa'ad could not but agree to Muhammad's will. He conveniently forgot his life-long alliance[304] with the Banu Qurayza, and decided that the men should be beheaded, their properties distributed among the believers, and the women and children enslaved. Muhammad endorsed this by saying, 'Your decision is the same as God sent to me from the heavens.'[305]

The only plausible explanation for killing these men, in the context of Muhammad's future actions, is that he had plans to raid the Jewish farmlands in Khyber and he did not want to exile the Qurayza men to Khyber only to fight them there. It was militarily wiser to finish them off while they were in his hands.

Accordingly, Muhammad went to the central market of Medina where people were busy buying and selling. He had several trenches dug in the market and he asked his followers to bring the Qurayza men for slaughter. The believers beheaded them in separate morning and afternoon shifts, resting from their labours in the heat of the midday. Because the Qurayza had been allies of the Aus tribe who were rivals of the Khazraj tribe, the Khazraj men were happily beheading the Qurayza one by one while the Aus watched the slaughter of their friends in dismay. Muhammad noticed the sadness on their faces and decided to be more sadistic than usual. He stopped the Khazraj men from beheading and ordered the Aus tribesmen to behead the remaining captives. By that time, only twelve captives remained but he wanted many more of the Aus to participate in the slaughter. He therefore ordered two Aus tribesmen to kill one and said, `I want one of you to injure and the second to finish the job.' He then named the men one by one saying, `You injure and you kill.' Thus, he devised the gruesome method by which twenty-four Aus men had the blood of their friends on their hands – for no sane reason. One by one, the believers beheaded around seven hundred men and dumped their bodies in the trenches dug for the purpose. Some eyewitness accounts had it that four hundred bodies were buried in these trenches, others as many as nine hundred.

Because Muhammad had ordered the beheading of only adult males, his followers asked him to show them a way to ensure that one was an adult. He told them to check if one had grown pubic hair or not. The one with signs of having grown pubic hair was deemed to have reached adulthood. Only these were beheaded.[306]

Huyayy bin Akhtab, the aforementioned Nadir chief, had torn his dress to ward off the believers from removing and snatching it. Before his beheading, he tried to console his men by telling them that God had written this fate for his chosen people and therefore they should not grieve over their deaths. One of Muhammad's poets taunted him as follows:

> You tried your best to be honourable
> And left no stone unturned
> But God abandons those who abandon Him.

A believer named Thabit bin Qays pleaded with Muhammad to spare his old friend Zubayr bin Bata Qarzi, who had done Thabit many favours during his life. Muhammad granted the exemption but Zubayr was so shocked at the beheading of his close friends and relatives that he had lost the will to live. In bewilderment he said, `Let me go where my friends have gone,' and was beheaded. Abu Bakr taunted Zubayr by saying, `He will meet his friends in hell where he will stay with them for eternity.'[307] Abu Bakr, the first caliph of Islam, and father of A'isha, is among the most highly revered figures in Islamic propagandist literature, but the event quoted here shows that he was callous enough to taunt an old man who was beheaded for no sane reason.

One woman too was executed because she had killed one of the believers besieging her tribe. Although she had killed in defence of her people, she was executed because an unbeliever was not allowed to kill a believer in any circumstances.

Among the Qurayza women, Muhammad liked Rayhana and took her as his slave. He did offer her the option to be his wife but she refused because Muhammad's wives had to remain indoors. She preferred to remain a slave[308] so that she could go out of the house, visit her tribe's women, and sometimes stay with them.

Because his men had been under siege and in a state of battle readiness for a month, and then they had besieged the Jews for another twenty-five days, Muhammad decided to please them by giving shares in this booty. Everything the Qurayza owned – houses, date orchards, cattle, camels, and personal property – was divided among the believers. He kept only one-fifth for himself. This time, horsemen were given three times the share of a foot warrior rather than the customary double. Some captive women and children were distributed among his men while others were sold as slaves. Muhammad sent Sa'ad ibn Zayd to the Najd slave market with his share of the captive women and children. Sa'ad sold these in Najd and bought horses and arms in exchange.[309]

Then Muhammad sat in his mosque and gloated over this massacre of innocent men, by issuing his "divine verses" as follows:

> And God brought the people of the book (*the Jews*)
> Out of their fortresses, and cast terror in their hearts
> Some you slaughtered and some you enslaved

And he made you heirs of their lands, houses and wealth;
Lands in which you had never trodden.
And God has power over everything. (Sura 33, verses 26-27)

The following verses of a believer, boasting "victory" over the Jews, provide information about how the Jews lived, what their professions were, and what the believers did to them:

In Yathrib (Medina) they had built fortresses in the oases
And they housed fine cattle in them.
They used camels for watering, which they had trained
Saying, `Go back,' and `Move forward.'
They lived an easy life with fruits and juices.
We came upon them with our arms
On our white war-loving camels and horses.
When we halted on the sides of the mountain,
They were terrified by the sudden arrival of our horses
And our sudden raid from the rear as well.
They fled swiftly in terror
As we came on them like lions from the bushes.
We made captives of their leading men
And divided their women and children among us.
We took their houses and became the owners.
The rightly guided messenger brought us the truth;
We testified: "You speak the truth, O God's messenger
You were sent with the illumination of a powerful religion."[310]

One can see in these verses the recurrent motif that religion and robbery had become one. These verses also explain the meaning of the word "truth" (*sadaaqa*) as understood by Muhammad and his men. The more the lands Muhammad conquered, the more people of the region believed in his "truth" and called him "truthful" (*saadiq*).

A man named Abu Sufyan bin Harith predicted that the confiscation of the Jewish lands would ruin the agriculture of the area because Muhammad's men did not like farming and knew very little about it. In his words:

If palm trees were camels, they would say:
Let's move from here, the place is not fit for us now.[311]

Muhammad sends an assassin to Mecca to kill Abu Sufyan

Through conquests and confiscations, Muhammad had acquired a position of influence and domination among the tribes in and around Medina. But the Quraysh, being the custodians of Ka'ba, were still the most influential in Arabia and Muhammad knew that if he attacked Mecca, he would be defeated. To soften his target, he sent Amr bin Umayya, a violent thug whom the Meccans had expelled, to assassinate Abu Sufyan. However, when Amr entered Mecca, along with a helper, despite precautions, a man recognized him and shouted at the top of his voice, 'Amr bin Umayya is here!'

The Meccans rushed towards Amr and his helper, saying, 'By God, Amr has never brought anything but evil.' The two thugs escaped and hid in a cave where they stayed a couple of days until the pursuit died down. Then they went to al Tamim, and while Amr took the way to al Safra, his companion travelled to Medina and told Muhammad what had happened.

Amr continued on foot until he looked down on the valley of Dajanan. He went into a cave with his bow and arrows, and while he was there, in came a one-eyed shepherd of the Banu al Dil tribe with his sheep. When he asked who he was, Amr lied, telling him that he was one of the Banu Bakr, a tribe friendly to the Meccans. The shepherd lay down to relax and sang:

I would not be a Muslim as long as I live
Nor heed to their religion give.[312]

The verses filled Amr with rage and when the shepherd was asleep and snoring, he killed him by piercing his sound eye with the end of his bow and forcing it out of the back of his neck. Then he travelled to Rakuba and al Naqi where he met two Meccans whom the Quraysh had sent to spy on Muhammad. Amr recognized them and called on them to surrender. When they refused, he killed one while the other surrendered and Amr brought him to Muhammad.[313] Because Amr had bound his prisoner's thumbs with his bowstring, using it as handcuffs, when Muhammad saw him he laughed heartily. Amr told him what had happened and he blessed him.

Whilst trying to assassinate Abu Sufyan, Muhammad also made a political manoeuvre. He knew that Abu Sufyan's daughter

Umm Habiba had migrated to Abyssinia with her Christian husband who had died. Muhammad sent a messenger to the king of Abyssinia asking him to send Umm Habiba to him for marriage. The king paid four hundred dirhams to Umm Habiba and sent her to Medina.[314] The marriage enabled Muhammad to develop relations with Abu Sufyan and the Umayyads and, later, win many of them to his side. Some reports suggest that Muhammad married Umm Habiba one year after the Truce of Hudaybiya.

The Truce of Hudaybiya

Muhammad decided to take Mecca through a relatively long-term political strategy. With his few thousand men, he could raid and plunder weaker tribes and the sedentary agriculturalist Jews but leading his largely alien jihadis to raid his own relatives in his hometown was beyond his proudly tribal nature. Except in time of need when he had to incite them in a battle, he had never allowed men from other tribes, even his devotees such as his Medinian poet Hassan bin Thabit, to insult the Quraysh[315] though he himself insulted and slandered those Quraysh who opposed him. When he would find that a certain tribe was even distantly related to him, he would stop his largely booty-seeking men from attacking them.[316]

Raiding holy Mecca would jeopardize his claim of being God's messenger. Hence, he sent messages to many Medinian tribes to travel to Mecca with him on a hajj pilgrimage, and around seven hundred came along. Some reports suggest these were fourteen hundred. Travelling in conspicuously peaceful array, they carried no bows, swords or spears, just the traditional daggers that were as much part of a traveller's equipment as the goatskin bags for carrying water. For sacrifice at the Ka'ba, they took seventy specially fatted camels each adorned for sacrifice with woven garlands and necklaces. Muhammad knew that attacking pilgrims was the last thing the Meccans would do – even if these were their worst enemies.

The Meccans sent out a cavalry squadron led by Khalid bin Walid, the commander whose marksmen had killed scores of Medinians in Uhud, to bar the route into the town. Muhammad sought the services of an expert traveller who changed their route and led them overnight on a rough and rugged path among canyons until they encamped at Hudaybiya, a few miles north of Mecca, where a large acacia tree stood by a winter pool. By the time the Meccan cavalry found where they were, they had lit fires, washed, and wore pilgrim sheets – *ahram*. The squadron commanders sent riders back into the town to ask what he should do and Abu Sufyan called an emergency meeting of the Meccan elders. Some of them wanted to let Muhammad perform the hajj while others mistrusted his intentions. One chieftain said, `How can we turn away those who have come to honour the House of God?' The only way to break the impasse was through negotiations. Over the next few days, envoys rode back and forth between Mecca and Hudaybiya trying to persuade Muhammad to turn back.

On Muhammad's side, some of his men, especially the violent Umar who had said, `The blood of a *mushrik* (secular/multi-faith person) is like the blood of a dog,'[317] wanted to fight for entry to Mecca. Instead, Muhammad told him to go to Mecca as his envoy and negotiate with the Quraysh. Omar backed out saying that none of his Banu Adiy tribe lived in Mecca to protect him; and because of his rough treatment of many Meccans, they would surely kill him. Muhammad knew that Omar was keen to raid Mecca because he had no tribal relatives in there to worry about. He then sent Uthman to negotiate and tell the Meccans that he had not come to fight his own people. Because Uthman and Abu Sufyan were both Umayyads, he expected a positive outcome. The Umayyads treated Uthman well and invited him to go around the Ka'aba but Uthman said that he would not perform hajj until they allowed Muhammad to do so.

While Uthman was in Mecca, a rumour spread that the Quraysh had killed him.[318] Muhammad was concerned and he for a moment he suspected that the Meccans might take a chance and attack them. He then sat under the acacia tree and started to take oaths from his followers promising that they would fight until death. As his men took oaths, no "divine revelation" came to inform him that the news of Uthman's murder was false. Finally, a man named Jud ibn Qays, who had not taken the oath to fight, informed Muhammad that the news was false.

The Quraysh then sent Suhayl bin Amru to Muhammad for negotiations, and a treaty known as the Truce of Hudaybiya was agreed and signed. It stipulated that there would be no war between Mecca and Medina for ten years, Muhammad would stop his raids on Meccan caravans, and people of all religions would be free to come for pilgrimage to Mecca. In the meantime, any tribe wishing to ally themselves with either party was free to do so. If a Meccan would leave to join the believers, the believers would send him back but if one of the believers would leave and come to the Meccans, the Meccans would not send him back. Each side would refrain from expressing enmity towards the other, and people would be free to practice whatever religion they had. Muhammad would not enter Mecca that year but the next year the Quraysh would vacate Mecca for three days so that his believers could perform hajj.

During the negations, tactically and temporarily, Muhammad abandoned his claim to apostolate, as the following records of the negotiations show:

> Muhammad told Ali to write the treaty of reconciliation beginning with: In the name of God, the most Gracious and Merciful (*Bismillah ar Rehmaan ar Raheem*).
> The Quraysh negotiator said, 'I do not know this phrase; you must write: In the name of God (*Bayismak God hum*).'
> Muhammad said to Ali, 'Write as he says.'
> Then Muhammad said to Ali, 'Write: This is the treaty of armistice between Muhammad, God's messenger, and Suhayl bin Amru.'
> The Quraysh negotiator said, 'If we admitted that you were the messenger of God, there would be no quarrel between us. How can we sign a treaty which states that you are the messenger of God? Just write that you are Muhammad the son of Abdallah.'
> Muhammad said to Ali, 'Write: Muhammad bin Abdallah.'[319]

During the negotiations, to appease the unbeliever Quraysh, Muhammad even sacrificed a camel – decorated with a silver ring around its nose – in the name of Abu Jahl whom he had been cursing since childhood.[320] Typical of his habit of not giving something from his own pocket, the camel had once belonged to Abu Jahl, and Muhammad had taken it after his killing at Badr.

As to why Muhammad agreed to abandon his claim to apostolate, though temporarily, one needs to recall his previous treaties with the Jews, praying with them facing Jerusalem, consulting the Torah, and subsequently, his gradual takeover of their lands. Likewise, in time, he would break the Truce of Hudaybiya too and gradually take over Mecca. Muhammad had learned to start with treaties of friendship and gradually conquer.

Another reason for Muhammad's tactical acceptance of this seemingly humiliating treaty was that in Mecca many Quraysh, particularly the Hashimis, were secretly on his side. While his staunchest opponents from Banu Makhzum and Banu Umayya had been killed in Badr, those who supported him were still living in Mecca. He hoped that with more conquests, the number of his supporters – those who believed in his "truth" – would grow and, in time, he would be welcomed in Mecca as the "messenger of God."

The Truce of Hudaybiya confused many of Muhammad's followers: He had been telling them that believers must decimate the unbelievers and they would gain a lot of booty from the battles, but now he had made this "humiliating" compromise with the unbelievers. When the baffled Umar confronted Muhammad about it, the following dialogue took place:

Umar: Are you not the messenger of God?
Muhammad: Why not. I am.
Umar: Are we not believers?
Muhammad: Why not. We are.
Umar: Are the Meccans not unbelievers?
Muhammad: Why not. They are.
Umar: Then why are we allowing them to humiliate us?[321]

Muhammad was not in the habit of revealing his long-term plans even to his closest associates. He actually wanted to centralize the power of the Arabs under his leadership, to be able to march towards the Byzantine and Persian empires.[322] He had hoped that the gathering of the Medinians would make his relatives succumb to let them enter Mecca for hajj; he would show-off by sacrificing seventy camels, play the role of the magnanimous chief of all Arabs, and hatch some new schemes to take-over Mecca, but this had not happened.

Muhammad needed to clarify to the booty-seekers among his followers why he could not attack Mecca at that time, and so he used his customary trick. He knew that using the "orders from God" excuse was the best way to quieten his followers and so he issued the following "divine revelations:"

> God was well pleased with the believers
> When you swore allegiance to me under the tree,
> And He knew what was in your hearts,

> So He sent down peace and rewarded us with a near victory
> And much booty that you will capture. God is ever Mighty, Wise.
> God has promised you much booty that you will capture,
> And has given you some of it before.
> On this one, He held back the hands of men from you,
> That it may be a sign for the believers
> And that He may guide you to a right path
> And to other booties which you have not yet been able to take
> God will arrange them; He has power over all things.
> And if the unbelievers had fought with you,
> They would certainly turn back,
> Then they would not find any protector or a helper.
> Such has been the course of God that has indeed run before,
> And you shall not find a change in God's course.
> And He it is Who held back their hands from you
> And your hands from them in Mecca
> After He had given you victory over them
> And God sees what you do.
> The unbelievers turned us away from the Sacred Mosque
> And stopped the offering from reaching its destined place;
> Were it not for the believing men and women (*living in Mecca*),
> Whom, not having known, you might have mowed down,
> And thus, something hateful might have afflicted you
> They would have suffered great difficulties
> And you could face problems you did not know about
> If we could separate the believers from unbelievers in Mecca
> We would inflict horrible punishment on the unbelievers.
> (Sura 48, verses 18-25)

The last verses contradict the Islamist propaganda that the "unbeliever" Meccans oppressed Muslims and that was why Muhammad had fought against them. One needs to remember that these verses come from the Qur'an itself.

The Truce of Hudaybiya, available in many Islamic history books, is a testimony to the fact that the fight between Muhammad and the so-called unbelievers was not about monotheism. As will be shown, Muhammad had used religion to exploit the Ansar to rob and fight for him but in future, only the Quraysh would rule the Muslim world for nearly two centuries. The Sunni caliphs, the major Shi'a imams, Umayyads, Marwanids, Abbasids, and

Alawites, were all Quraysh. Within fifty years, the Umayyads would decimate the Ansar just as the Ansar had decimated the local Jews. The Quraysh were masters of cunning and deceit in which Muhammad had excelled. He often equated himself with God and, accordingly, he had declared:

> They played their tricks and God played His tricks
> And God is the best trickster. (Sura 8, verses 29-30)

XXX

Muhammad and his men returned to Medina. Most were deeply disappointed at not being able to take booty. Many felt that those who had not participated in the expedition were actually better off because they had not incurred the expenses of travel. Many had not joined him in this journey because they feared that the Meccans would kill him and his men. These were now afraid that Muhammad would punish them and so they made excuses. Muhammad warned them, and raised the spirits of those who had gone with him to Mecca, by issuing the following "divine revelations":

> The desert dwellers who stayed back will say to you:
> `Our properties and families kept us from going (*with you*);'
> They will ask for forgiveness.
> They say with their tongues what is not in their hearts.
> Say to them: Who can stop God if He intends to harm you?
> Or if He intends to do you good; God is aware of your deeds.
> No! You believed that the messenger and the believers
> Would never return to their families,
> And that seemed pleasing to your hearts;
> And you thought an evil thought and you are doomed to perish.
> And whoever does not believe in God and His messenger,
> Then surely, We (*God*) have prepared burning fire for these.
> When you set forth for the next booty,
> Those who stayed behind will say,
> `Allow us to follow you.'
> They will want to change God's will
> Say, `By no means shall you follow us.'
> They say, `You envy us;' (*because they had saved the travel expenses*)
> They have a limited understanding of things.

Say to the desert dwellers who stayed behind
You shall soon be invited to fight against a powerful people
You will fight against them until they submit;
Then if you obey, God will grant you lots of booty
And if you turn back as you turned back before,
He will punish you with a painful punishment.
(Sura 48, verses 11-16)

This invitation to fight and "lots of booty" was a reference to Muhammad's next plan: The pillage of the Jews of Khyber. By telling his men to taunt the "desert dwellers," he wanted to raise their curiosity and increase the number of his jihadis.

Accordingly, after his return to Medina, Muhammad waited only three months before raiding Khyber. His raid on Khyber reveals the falsehood of the Islamists' justification of the slaughter of the Jews as "the Jewish conspiracies against Islam:" This is because Muhammad raided Khyber after he had signed the peace treaty with the largely weakened Meccans and there was no threat to him from any side. Moreover, since his first major battle – the battle of Badr – each time he had amassed his jihadis on pretext of fighting the Quraysh, he had led them to rob and decimate the weak and unsuspecting Jews.

The massacre and enslavement of the Khyber Jews

Khyber, eight miles from the last settlement of Medina, was the richest of the northern Hejaz oases. Its vast date-palm plantations were divided among seven Jewish tribes, each with its own fortified stronghold. These had been living there for more than a millennium. Over the centuries, they had developed irrigation and agriculture, and turned part of the desert into farmlands and oases[323] in which they grew dates and vegetables and pastured cattle, horses and camels.

When Muhammad had banished the Banu Qaynuqa and Banu Nadir from Medina, they had migrated to Khyber. When he had massacred the Banu Qurayza, the few remaining Jews too had escaped to Khyber. Abu Rafay Salaam bin Abu'l Huqayq had taken over as their new leader. At the time of the massacre of the Banu Qurayza, Abu Rafay was in Khyber and so he had escaped death. Now Muhammad spread word that Abu Rafay would warn the Khyber Jews by telling them about the horrible massacre of the

Banu Qurayza, and the Khyber Jews might prepare to attack. On this false pretext, and to terrify his target people, Muhammad used his customary method and sent five secret assassins of the Khazraj tribe to murder Abu Rafay. The Khazraj competed against the Aus in excelling in serving Muhammad. Because it was the Aus men who had earlier assassinated Ka'ab bin Ashraf (a Khazraj ally), the Khazraj now wanted to prove that they were no less keen on secret assassinations than their Aus rivals had been.

Five Khazraj men, led by Abdallah bin Atiq, travelled to Khyber and reached Abu Rafay's house. When they knocked at the door, Abu Rafay's wife answered and asked who they were. They replied that they were hungry travellers and wanted food. She opened the door, led them to Abu Rafay's room, and left to bring food. As soon as she went out, the five locked the door from inside. When she heard the door being locked, she realized her mistake and began to scream and shout but, before the neighbours could reach to help, the five men had murdered Abu Rafay and escaped. One of the assassins even returned to confirm that Abu Rafay was dead, and he joined the crowd of spectators that had gathered there.

When the assassins returned to Muhammad, a quarrel broke out as each claimed that his plunge had killed Abu Rafay. Muhammad examined the five swords and decided in favour of the man whose sword was smeared with undigested food along with the blood from Abu Rafay's stomach.[324]

After Abu Rafay, Yusayr bin Rizam became the chief. He began a tour of his allied tribes to gather support in defending Khyber. Muhammad's spies informed him about this and he chose Abdallah bin Rawaha, a deceitful man who pretended to be a friend of the Jews, to negotiate terms of surrender with the Jews. Abdallah would attend their meetings, gain their trust, and then report to Muhammad. In the final negotiations, Muhammad sent Abdallah with thirty emissaries and invited Yusayr to pay homage to him. In return, he assured Yusayr that he would accept him as the ruler of Khyber.

Being hardworking agriculturists, artisans, and traders, the Jews had not developed enough military resources and skills to fight. In addition, their allies had betrayed them in the past and therefore, Yusayr believed that submitting to Muhammad and getting a guarantee of peace for the remaining Jews was his best option. He thus embarked upon the journey to Medina with his thirty delegates and Muhammad's thirty emissaries. However, halfway into the journey, Abdallah bin Rawaha drew his sword out and murdered Yusayr while, at the same time, as planned, his men attacked the unsuspecting Jewish delegates and murdered all of them.[325]

After Yusayr, the Khyber Jews appointed Kinana bin al Rabi'a as their new chief. Kinana knew that his people were doomed because Muhammad was planning to conquer the entire region and he had sent a letter to the Banu Fazara tribe, stating, `If you do not come to help the Jews, we will give you a share in the Khyber properties after our conquest.' In reaction, Kinana pledged to pay half of Khyber's agricultural produce to his neighbouring tribes in exchange for help in defence but none came to support. Muhammad also sent message to the Ghatfan, Khyber's Bedouin allies, stating that he would give them a share in Khyber's dates for not intervening, and the Ghatfan agreed. In its nature, the situation was not much different from that of a pack of wolves surrounding their prey.

As an established practice, the Arabs did not fight in the month of Muharram. To gain the maximum advantage of surprise, Muhammad decided to attack in this month.[326] His favourite time for raid was early morning. He arrived near Khyber with his jihadis and stayed the night in the outskirts. Early morning, when they saw the settlement from a distance, he raised his hands and recited the following prayers:

> O Lord of the heavens and their reflections
> O Lord of the lands and their cultivations
> O Lord of the devils and their perversions
> O Lord of the winds and their propulsions
> We beg for the welfare of this town and its people
> And protection from the evil of this town and its people.[327]

Prayers were Muhammad's customary ruse in which he usually proclaimed the opposite of what he actually did. On occasion after occasion, he had wreaked havoc upon the weak and vulnerable but presented himself as the Jesus-like victim who sought to bless the world. His collective prayers and pretentious implorations to God would continue for so long that, at times, his closest associates had been compelled to ask him to cut them short.[328]

Dawn was breaking and farmers were walking towards their fields with spades and baskets in their hands. When they saw the jihadis, they dropped their tools and began to run back to their homes shouting and screaming, `Muhammad and his warriors are here.' Seeing them flee in panic, Muhammad said, `God is Great! Khyber is already desolate. When we descend upon a people, their screams are horrible because they have been forewarned about us.'

The Jews locked themselves insides their fortress-homes and the siege began. Because the cattle and goats of the besieged were grazing outside in the fields, Muhammad's men had ample supply of food.[329] He decided to stay put and storm the fortresses one by one.

When the second fortress fell, some of the jihadis came to Muhammad and asked him to give them something from the booty. He wanted them to keep fighting and not run away with a share and so he raised his hands and prayed, `O God! You know about these men but I have nothing to give them. Please grant these men victory over the largest fortress and make it full of wealth and grain.' The men were thus motivated to continue, and they succeeded in breaking into the fortress of Sa'ab bin Ma'az, which contained the largest stores of provisions. During the raid, they raised the slogan, "Hit O victorious ones, hit."[330]

On the tenth day of the siege, the people inside three of the fortresses pleaded for permission to go into exile. Muhammad allowed them to leave on condition that they would leave all their property behind. When the owners of the oasis of Fadak heard about the reprieve, they too agreed to go into exile and leave their property behind. Muhammad took the entire Fadak property for himself declaring that Fadak had fallen in the category of "fay," which meant that because the jihadis did not have to fight for it, they could not have a share in it.[331]

One by one, the believers captured all the fortresses. It had taken them twenty days; they had lost only fifteen men, and killed ninety-three Jews.[332] Many women had participated in the raid to tend to the injured, and these took shares from the booty.[333]

When the one-to-one dual between a Jewish man named Yasser and the believer Zubayr bin al Awwam was about to begin, Zubayr's mother requested Muhammad not to send her son into the dual, fearing that he would be killed. Muhammad said to her, `No, your son will kill the Jew.'

Among the captured was the Khyber chief Kinana bin Rabi'a. Muhammad believed that the he had a treasure hidden somewhere and he wanted to know its location but Kinana would not tell. Muhammad ordered the aforementioned Zubayr to torture him. Kinana was tied to the floor, Zubayr sat on him, and burned his chest bit by bit with flint stones until Kinana was nearly dead but still would not tell.[334] Disappointed, Muhammad had him killed.[335] Later, a small treasure was found hidden in a camel hide.

One of Muhammad's poets named Ibn al Qaiyum praised this victory in the following poem for which Muhammad granted him many animals and chicken from the booty:

> From the messenger's side, a great militia
> Of broad-shouldered and strong-boned men
> Raided the fortress with shining swords and spears
> They stormed and terrified its people to tears
> The fortress inhabitants saw the night's darkness
> Though it was midday sun with full brightness
> The warriors left nothing in there except hen
> To scream each morning within their den
> The fortresses were besieged by the Banu Ashal, the Banu Najjar
> The men from the Banu Salma and the Banu Ghifar
> The Meccan emigrants wore iron helmets with glee
> Helmets that had on them written, `We do not flee'
> The Jews fell in the sand and the dust of mêlée
> They opened their eyes wide to be able to see
> Muhammad's victory and our glee.[336]

Now that he had enough food resources, Muhammad forbade the believers from eating the meat of donkeys, ponies, and wild birds.[337] These were added to the list of forbidden (*haraam*) items.

<u>Saffiya – The best of the booty: Regulating the distribution of captured women and booty</u>

When they took the second fortress, Bilal found two women in there, and he brought them to Muhammad in such a coarse manner that he trampled over the corpses of their slain relatives.[338] One woman kept crying while the other was speechless with horror, mute, as if in a coma. This silent one was Saffiya, the pretty, seventeen-year-old daughter of Huyayy bin Akhtab whom Muhammad had had beheaded during the massacre of the Qurayza. She was in Khyber because she had been married to the Khyber chief Kinana bin Rabi'a, whom, only a day or two ago, Muhammad had had tortured and killed. The jihadis had also killed Saffiya's uncles and brothers. Although her real name was Zaynab, since her capture, the jihadis called her "Saffiya" meaning "the best of the booty," a term that traditionally referred to the booty that was to be reserved for the leader of the bandits.[339]

After a while, Bilal appeared again and when the crying woman saw him, she began to shriek and throw dust in her hair. Muhammad sneered and said, `Take this *shaitana* (she-devil) away from me.' Then he covered Saffiya, who sat silently, with his cloak and, to show her that he was a merciful man, scolded Bilal, `Bilal, has God plucked mercy from you heart that you let these women see the corpses of their men?'[340] Afterwards, when they were distributing the captured women as slaves, Wahiya Kalbi asked Muhammad to grant him a slave girl. Muhammad paid little attention, brushed him aside, and said, `Take anyone you like.' Wahiya picked Saffiya and took her home.

Sometime later, other jihadis came to Muhammad and objected, saying that Saffiya was the daughter of a chief and had grown up enjoying a high status. She was the prettiest of all the captured women and should therefore come to him.[341] Because Muhammad had unwittingly given Wahiya the choice and was now going to repeal his decision, he compensated Wahiya by giving him seven slave girls and took Saffiya for himself.[342] After a few days, he married her in a tent and his attendant women did the bride's makeup. During the night, as the newlyweds slept in the tent, a jihadi named Abu Ayub stood on guard with a sword in his hand. In the morning, Muhammad came out of the tent and asked him why he had stood guard all night. Abu Ayub replied, `O messenger of God, you have recently killed her father, husband, uncles and brothers, and decimated her tribe. I was afraid she might take revenge on you.'[343] Muhammad blessed Abu Ayub with prayers.

One is bound to wonder how Saffiya felt being with the man who had had her father, husband, uncles and brothers killed. It is known from reports that Saffiya used to say, `I was my father's favourite, and also my uncle Yasser's. When they saw me with other children, they used to pick me up.'[344]

The Islamists sanitize this affair by asserting that Saffiya embraced Islam but they pay no attention to the coercive circumstances in which she had had no choice. As for the other women who were distributed, they justify this by stating that because their men folk had either been killed in the battles or enslaved, they had to be looked after. The factual reports show that what the Islamists call "battles," were little more than bandit raids. Because of these raids and plunder of tribal settlements, a large number of displaced women desperately searched for men who could provide them with food and shelter. For example, once, a woman came to Muhammad when he was sitting with his companions and begged, `O messenger of God, I offer myself to you.' He scrutinized her body, looked at the upper half and then the lower half, lowered his head and kept quiet. The desperate woman kept waiting for an answer. When no answer came, a man stood and said, `O messenger of God, if you do not need this woman, give her to me.' Muhammad asked the man if he had something to give to the woman as dowry. The man had nothing except the sheet wrapped around his loins. He offered to give the sheet of cloth to the woman at which Muhammad said, `What use is this to her? If she wears it, you will be naked. If you wear it, she will be naked.' Finally, he asked the man, `Can you recite some verses of the Qur'an?' The man recited some verses and Muhammad said, `I make you the owner of this woman.'[345]

Until the conquest of Khyber, the jihadis took the liberty of having sex with captured women (euphemised as "temporary marriage" or "mut'a") but this used to lead to disputes among them about the permanent ownership of these women. The jihadis did not even care if these women were pregnant. The abovementioned event whereby Wahiya Kalbi hurriedly took Saffiya for himself before Muhammad had the chance to choose her for himself, made Muhammad realize the need to regulate the distribution of these women. Subsequently, he issued a "divine law" stating that believers could copulate with enslaved women only after one month of their capture and, in case the woman was pregnant, they should wait until the delivery of the child.[346] Later he qualified this "law" with a clause: "If the woman is not visibly pregnant, then wait until she has had her menstruation periods."[347] The one month restraining period allowed sufficient time to settle the disputes regarding ownership of captive women and, in case of pregnant women, to know if the child's father was alive.

The making of an "eternal and divine law" about the treatment and distribution of enslaved women leaves no doubt in the veracity of the assertion that Muhammad intended to continue the tradition of attacking others and enslaving their women. Sexual motivation was so much on his mind that when he saw the corpse of one of his jihadis, he turned his face away and when asked why he had turned his face away, he replied, `I saw two wide-eyed "hoors" (pretty women) sitting in intimacy by his side in paradise.' This was his typical diversionary tactics: By referring to pretty women allotted in paradise to the so-called martyrs, Muhammad wanted his men to ignore that they could die in the battles. Subsequently, he delivered the following sermon, which throws light on the disputes that had arisen among the jihadis regarding the distribution of captured women and booty:[348]

> O Believers in God and the Day of Judgement, it is not lawful for you to irrigate someone else's crop with your water, that is, to have sex with women who are pregnant with someone else's child. It is not lawful to copulate with captive pregnant women until they have delivered the child.
>
> It is not lawful to sell booty before it is properly distributed. It is not lawful to take an animal from the booty, ride it, and return it in a weaker state. It is not lawful to take clothes from the booty and return them in a used condition.[349]

Muhammad's slave, Mid'am, was helping him disembark his camel when someone shot an arrow at them. The arrow hit and killed Mid'am. People said, `Mid'am is a martyr and will go to paradise because he saved Muhammad's life,' but Muhammad sneered and said, `Never. I swear by God that Mid'am is under a blanket of fire in hell because he was dishonest with the booty.' Muhammad's associate Abu Hurayra explained Mid'am's "dishonesty" as follows: Mid'am had once told Muhammad that he had taken two shoelaces from the booty, and Muhammad had said, `You will be tied with laces of fire in hell.'[350] He condemned the slave to hell for taking two shoestrings though the slave had died in serving him. As for himself, Muhammad took over a fifth of the property and distributed the rest among those who had participated in the raid.

The settlement of the Khyber lands

From the aforementioned cleansing of the Jews of Medina, the takeover of their lands, and the consequent ruin of agriculture in these lands, Muhammad correctly guessed that the same would happen in Khyber. His men did not have the skills required in farming and raising cattle, and he did not want them to learn these because he needed them for further battles. Hence, when he offered the escaping Khyber Jews the chance to cultivate their lands on condition that they could keep half of the produce, they agreed to it.[351] However, he stipulated the condition that he would retain the prerogative to expel them whenever he would want.[352] This started a process of gradual cleansing of the Jews: As more and more believers were available to cultivate the lands, they expelled more and more Jews until, during the reign of Caliph Umar, they had expelled almost all Jews from Medina and its surrounding areas.[353]

The aforementioned thug Abdallah bin Rawaha, who had helped Muhammad by deceiving and murdering the Khyber chief Yusayr bin Rizam and his thirty delegates, received his reward: Muhammad appointed him as the collector of taxes for Khyber.[354] The taxes included agricultural produce and livestock. These lands became the major source of funding for Muhammad's family, associates, the ruling elite, treasury, entertaining guests, and the endless jihad.[355]

With Khyber secured, Muhammad marched on to the smaller Jewish dominated oases of Tayma, halfway between Medina and the ancient city of Petra in what is now southern Jordan. The tribes there offered no resistance and he turned them into his serfs.

XXX

Before the news of the conquest of Khyber could possibly reach Mecca, a believer Hajjaj bin al Laat Salmi sought Muhammad's permission to go to Mecca, deceive the Quraysh, and collect some funds for trade. Muhammad allowed him to do so. When he reached Mecca, some Quraysh men said to him, `Give us news of Muhammad; we have heard that the butcher is in Khyber; do you think he will be able to conquer the most fertile and prosperous town of Hejaz?' Hajjaj pleased them by saying that the Jews had defeated and arrested Muhammad in Khyber and they now planned to behead him in Mecca. He then added that the Jews were selling the property of the defeated believers at throwaway prices, and it was the best time to invest in this property. He was able to beguile some of the Quraysh into giving him investment funds on an equity share basis.

Hajjaj took the money and quickly left but, on his way out, he informed Abbas that his nephew had become the master of the best lands of Hejaz and married, as he said, "the princess of Khyber," meaning Saffiya. Abbas was so happy that he performed special prayers in the Ka'ba and then broke the news to Quraysh, also telling them that Hajjaj had lied to them. The duped Quraysh were furious but unable to retrieve their money as Hajjaj had already left Mecca.[356]

Muhammad's wives quarrel and conspire in jealousy: A'isha is accused of adultery

As Muhammad was taking more wives and slave women, his wives were getting jealous of each other. Because there was little they could do against him, some of them intrigued and conspired against each other. Muhammad once married the daughter of the leader of a major clan to seal an alliance with the clan. A'isha volunteered to prepare the bride for wedding and, under the guise of sisterly advice, told her that he would value her more if she first resisted him on the nuptial night by saying, "I seek God's protection from you." The bride did not know that this phrase was used to seek annulment of a marriage. Hence, when she uttered the phrase, Muhammad said, `You have sought the right protection,' and left the room. Next morning, he divorced her and sent her back to her parents.

The jealousy between the wives showed in full in the "Afak affair," narrated as follows. In her own words, A'isha reported:

> When the apostle intended to go on an expedition he cast lots between his wives to see which of them should accompany him. He did this on the raid on Banu Mustalaq and the lot fell on me, so the apostle took me out. When the camel was being saddled for me I used to sit in my howdah; then the men who saddled it for me would come and take hold of the lower part of the howdah, lift it up, and put it on the camel's back and fasten it with a rope. Then they would take hold of the camel's head and walk with it. On this occasion, when the apostle finished

his raid, he started back and halted when he was near Medina and passed a part of the night there.

In the morning, when the caravan began its journey, A'isha's minders thought she was in her carriage but actually, she was not. The next day, A'isha arrived with a young warrior, Safwan bin al Mu'attal al Salami, and many began to wonder why the two had stayed behind. A'isha said that she had gone far in the desert, looking for a secluded place to relieve her of a call of nature. When she came back, she realized that she had lost her necklace. She went back to find her necklace without telling anyone and the caravan began the journey without her. It would have been a matter of at most an hour for a healthy teenage girl to catch up with the caravan on foot but instead, as A'isha reported:

> I returned to the place and there was not a soul there. The men had gone. So I wrapped myself in my smock and then lay down where I was, knowing that if I were missed they would come back for me, and by Allah I had but just lain down when Safwan bin Mu'attal al Sulami passed me; he had fallen behind the main body for some purpose and had not spent the night with the troops. He saw my form, came, and stood over me. He used to see me before the veil was prescribed for us, so when he saw me he exclaimed in astonishment "Za'ina (a woman carried in a howdah)" while I was wrapped in my garments. He asked me what had kept me behind, but I did not speak to him. Then he brought up his camel and told me to ride it while he kept behind. So I rode it and he took the camel's head going forward quickly in search of the army, and by Allah we did not overtake them and I was not missed until the morning. The men had halted and when they were resting, we came, and the liars spread their reports and the army was much disturbed. But by Allah I knew nothing about it.

Safwan's job was to walk behind the caravan to look for things that had fallen on the ground and bring them back to the caravan. When he found A'isha sitting alone, he brought her to the caravan. However, the excuses held little water because in looking for lost items, Safwan did not need to stay so far behind and out of sight of the caravan as to take a day to reach it.

Muhammad's close relatives and associates, including Hamna bint Jahsh – the sister of his wife Zaynab – his poet Hassan bin Thabit, and a close relative of Abu Bakr whose name was Mistah bin Uthatha, spread word that A'isha and Safwan had stayed behind on purpose. Otherwise, why had she lain down to wait when she could have easily caught up with the caravan on foot?[357] Abu Bakr used to make an allowance to Mistah because he was of his kin and needy. He said, `Never will I give anything to Mistah again, nor will I ever help him in any way after what he said about A'isha and brought evil on us.' However, someone later told Abu Bakr that God said, "And let not those who possess dignity and ease among you swear not to give to kinsmen and the poor and those who emigrate for God's sake. Let them forgive and show forbearance. Do you not wish that God should forgive you? And Abu Bakr said, `Yes, by Allah, I want God to forgive me,' so he continued the allowance that he used to give to Mistah, saying, `I will never withdraw it from him.'

A'isha reported:

Then we came to Medina and immediately I became very ill and so heard nothing of the matter. The story had reached the apostle and my parents, yet they told me nothing of it though I missed the apostle's usual kindness to me. When I was ill, he used to show compassion and kindness to me, but in this illness he did not and I missed his attentions. When he came in to see me when my mother was nursing me, all he said was, `How are they?' I was pained and asked him to let me be taken to my mother so that she could nurse me. `Do what you like,' he said, and so I was taken to my mother, knowing nothing of what had happened until I recovered from my illness some twenty days later. Now we were an Arab people: we did not have private toilets which foreigners have in their houses; we loathe and detest them. Our practice was to go out into the open spaces of Medina. The women used to go out every night, and one night I went out with Umm Mistah bint Abu Ruhm bin al Muttalib. Her mother was the daughter of Sakhr bin Amir of the Tayyum tribe, an aunt of Abu Bakr. As she was walking with me she stumbled over her gown and exclaimed, `May Mistah stumble.' I said, `That is a bad thing to say about one of the emigrants who fought at Badr.' She replied, `Haven't you heard the news, O daughter of Abu Bakr?' And when I said that I had not heard she went on to tell me of what the liars had said, and when I showed my astonishment she told me that all this really had happened. By Allah, I was unable to do what I had gone to do and went back. I could not stop crying until I thought that the weeping would burst my liver. I said to my mother, 'God forgive you! Men have spoken ill of me and you have known of it and have not told me a thing about it.' She replied 'My little daughter, don't let the matter weigh on you. Seldom is there a beautiful woman married to a man who loves her but her rival wives gossip about her and men do the same.'

The greatest offenders were Abdullah bin Ubayy among the Khazraj, and Mistah and Hamna bint Jahsh, for the reason that her sister Zaynab was one of the apostle's wives and only she could rival me in his favours. As for Zaynab, Allah protected her by her religion and she spoke nothing but good. But Hamna spread the report far and wide insulting me for the sake of her sister, and I suffered much from that.

The apostle had stood in the mosque and addressed the men, though I knew nothing about it. After praising God, he had said, 'Some men are tormenting me by spreading rumours about my family. By Allah, I know only good of them. And these men say these things of a man (i.e. Safwan) of whom I know naught but good, and when he comes to my house, I am always with him.'

When the apostle made this speech Usayd bin Hudayr of the Aus stood up and said, 'If they are of Aus let us rid you of them; and if they are of the Khazraj give us your orders, for they ought to have their heads cut off.' Then Sa'd bin Ubaada got up – before that he had been thought a pious man – and said, 'By Allah, you lie. They shall not be beheaded. You would not have said this had you not known that they were of Khazraj. Had they been your own people you would not have said it.' Usayd answered, 'Liar yourself! You are a hypocrite arguing on behalf of the hypocrites.'

Feelings ran so high that there was almost fighting between these two clans of Aus and Khazraj. The apostle left and came in to see me. He called Ali and Usama bin Zayd and asked their advice. Usama spoke highly of me and said 'They are your family and we and you know only good of them, and this is a lie and a falsehood.' As for Ali he said, 'Women are plentiful, and you can easily change one for another. Ask her slave girl, for she will tell you the truth.' So the apostle called Burayra to ask her, and Ali got up and gave her a violent beating, saying, `Tell the apostle the truth,' to which she replied, `I know only good of her. The only fault I have to find with A'isha is that when I am kneading dough and tell her to watch it she neglects it and falls asleep and the sheep come and eat it!'

Then the apostle came to see me. My parents and a woman of the Ansar were with me and both of us were weeping. He sat down and after praising God he said, `A'isha, you know what people say about you. Fear God and if you have done wrong as men say then repent towards God, for He accepts repentance from His slaves.' As he said this my tears ceased and I could not feel them. I waited for my parents to answer the apostle but they said nothing. By Allah I thought myself too insignificant for God to send down concerning me a Qur'an which could be read in the mosques and used in prayer, but I was hoping that the apostle would see something in a dream by which God would clear away the lie from me, because He knew my innocence, or that there would be some communication. As for a Qur'an coming down about me by Allah I thought far too little of myself for that. When I saw that my parents would not speak I asked them why, and they replied that they did not know what to answer, and by Allah I do not know a household which suffered as did the family of Abu Bakr in those days. When they remained silent my weeping broke out afresh and then I said, `Never will I repent towards God of what you mention. By Allah, I know that if I were to confess what men say of me, God knowing that I am innocent of it, I should admit what did not happen; and if I denied what they said you would not believe me.' Then I racked my brains for the name of Jacob and could not remember it, so I said, `I will say what the father of Joseph said: "My duty is to show patience and God's aid is to be asked against what you describe." (Sura 12, verse 18)[358]

Meanwhile, Hassan bin Thabit wrote a poem in which he inserted a line of satire about Safwan – the accused young man – as follows:

The vagabond immigrants have become powerful and numerous
And the Son of Furay'a (Safwan) has become unique in the land

He has achieved a distinction (*by sleeping with the prophet's wife*).
As for Quraysh, I will never make peace with them
Until they leave error for righteousness
And abandon Laat and Uzz'a
And all bow down to the One, The Eternal,
And testify that what the apostle said to them is true,
And faithfully fulfill the solemn oath with God.

When Safwan heard what Hassan was saying about him, he came with a sword and wounded him, saying:

Here is the edge of my sword for you!
When you lampoon a man like me,
You don't get a poem in return!

Thabit bin Qays leapt upon Safwan, tied his hands to his neck, and took him to the quarters of Banu Harith bin Khazraj. Abdullah bin Rawaha met him and asked what had happened, and he said, `Do I surprise you? He smote Hassan with the sword and by Allah he must have killed him.' Abdullah asked if Muhammad knew about what he had done, and when he said that he did not, he told him that he had shown much daring in arresting a Qurayshi and that he must free him. He did so. Then they went to Muhammad and told him of the affair and he summoned Hassan and Safwan. Safwan said, `He insulted and satirized me and rage so overcame me that I smote him.' Muhammad said to Hassan, `Do you look with an evil eye on my people because God has guided them to Islam? Be charitable about what has befallen you,' meaning that Safwan was his Quraysh tribesman, and an insult to Safwan was an insult to the prophet's tribe, and Hassan apologized. However, because Hassan had received the wound in defending Muhammad's honour, he gave him in compensation a property and a house belonging to Abu Talha bin Sahl, which he had given as alms to him. He also gave him a Coptic slave girl named Sirin, who was the sister of Muhammad's slave girl Maria, and she gave him a son. On the other hand, subsequently, Safwan was killed at a battle.[359]

To stop people from gossiping and to warn his wives of dire consequences of lewdness, Muhammad issued the following verses:

> Wives of the prophet!
> Those of you who clearly commit a lewd act
> Shall be doubly punished; this is easy enough for God.
> But those of you who obey God and His messenger
> And do good works, shall be doubly rewarded;
> For them there is a rich provision.
> Wives of the prophet! You are not like other women
> If you fear God, do not be soft in your speech to other men
> Lest the lecherous men should lust for you
> Be formal in what you say, stay in your homes,
> And do not display your finery
> As was done previously in ignorance.
> Attend to your prayers, give alms,
> And obey God and His messenger.
> Women of my house, God seeks to remove impurity from you
> And give you a thorough cleaning. (Sura 33, verses 30-33)

Muhammad was in a quandary; if he divorced and punished A'isha, people would say, `God's messenger has been deceived by a young girl.' If he took her back, they would see him as too weak to implement God's law on his wife. Only God could resolve this issue.

After about a month of separation from A'isha, when talk of the affair had died down, Muhammad went to see her and issued a "divine revelation," as A'isha reported:

> By God, the apostle had not moved from where he was sitting when there came over him from God what used to come over him and he was wrapped in his garment and a leather cushion was put under his head. As for me, when I saw this I felt no fear or alarm, for I knew that I was innocent and that God would not treat me unjustly. As for my parents, as soon as the apostle recovered I thought that they would die from fear that confirmation would come from God of what men had said. Then the apostle recovered and sat up and there fell from him as it were drops of water on a winter day, and he began to wipe the sweat from his brow, saying, `Good news, A'isha! God has sent down (word) about your innocence.' I said, `Praise be to God,' and he went out to the men and addressed them and recited to them what God had sent down concerning me. Then he gave orders about Mistah bin Uthatha and Hassan bin

Thabit and Hamna bint Jahsh who were the most explicit in their slander and they were flogged eighty stripes.

The "revelations" which Muhammad issued were as follows:

> We have sent down a sura with clear instructions for you to remember. About the woman and man guilty of adultery or fornication flog each of them with a hundred stripes: Let not compassion move you in their case, as prescribed by God, if you believe in God and the Last Day, and let a party of believers witness this punishment.
> An adulterous man marries none but an adulterous woman or a *mushrik*. And an adulterous woman marries none but an adulterous man or a *mushrik*: To the believers such a thing is forbidden. And those who charge a chaste woman and produce not four witnesses, flog them with eighty stripes and reject their evidence ever after, for such men are wicked transgressors, unless they repent thereafter and mend (their conduct), for Allah is Oft- Forgiving, Most Merciful. (Sura 2, verses 1-5)

In the long term, these verses served as a curse for raped women because many Islamic clerics refused to register cases of rape if four men had not witnessed the rape. To add insult to injury, when a woman insisted that she had been raped, the clerics would punish her with eighty lashes for accusing a man without producing four witnesses. Because rapes are not generally committed in front of four witnesses, Muhammad's attempt to help A'isha served as a permanent license to rapists in many Islamic countries for more than a thousand years.

After issuing these "divine revelations," Muhammad retaliated by declaring that his sister-in-law Hamna bint Jahsh, his poet Hassan, and his follower Mistah bin Athatha had been falsely accusing A'isha of adultery and hence they should be flogged. About this flogging, a poet said the following:

> Hassan, Hamna, and Mistah tasted what they deserved
> For falsely slandering their prophet's wife
> They angered the Lord of the glorious throne and were chastised.
> They hurt God's apostle and saw a public and lasting disgrace.

Lashes rained upon them like raindrops
Falling from the highest clouds.

However, eighty lashes for each of these did not placate A'isha who, for the rest of her life, hated Ali and Hassan though the latter composed verses in which he extolled her purity and cursed himself as follows:[360]

Chaste, keeping to her house, above suspicion,
A noble woman of the ever glorious Lu'ayy bin Ghalib,
Pure, God having purified her nature
And cleansed her from all evil and falsehood.
If I said what you allege, let my hands be paralysed.
How could I say it,
With my lifelong affection for the family of the apostle
Who brings splendour to all gatherings,
His rank so high that the highest leap would fall short of it?
What was said will not hold but words that slander me will.

Years later, still haunted by the event, though Safwan had died at a battle, A'isha used to say, `Questions were asked about Safwan bin Mu'attal and they found that he was impotent; he never touched women. He was killed as a martyr after this.' She remained Ali's enemy forever and, twenty years after Muhammad's death, led an army against him at the battle of The Camel – described later.

The "divine revelations" about A'isha's innocence also included warnings for "scandal mongers" as follows:

Those who brought forward the Afak event are a group among you. Do not consider it as an evil for you but a good thing: To every one among them will come the punishment of the sin that he committed, and for those who played a major role, there will grievous punishment.
Why did not the believers – men and women – when they heard of the affair, think the best and say, `This (allegation) is an obvious lie?' Why did they not bring four witnesses to prove it? Because they did not bring witnesses, in the sight of God, they stand as liars! Were it not for the grace and mercy of God on you, in this world and the next, a grievous penalty would have befallen you for gullibly propagating this affair.

You propagated with your tongues and poured out of your mouths rumours of which you had no knowledge. And you thought it was a minor affair, but it was very serious for God.
And when you heard it, why did you not say, `It is not right for us to speak about it. Glory to God, this is a huge slander!'
God admonishes you to never repeat such things if you are believers. He makes the signs plain to you. God is full of knowledge and wisdom.
Those who love to spread profanity among the believers will have a grievous penalty in this life and in the hereafter.
God knows, and you do not know.
O believer! Do not follow Satan's example. If one will follow Satan, one will command what is shameful and wrong.
And were it not for the grace and mercy of God on you, not one of you would ever have been pure. God purifies whom He pleases and God hears and knows. (Sura 24, verses 11-21)

Those who level false allegations against innocent women will be cursed in this world and the hereafter and shall receive grievous punishment. On that day, their tongues, hands, and feet shall testify against them. Evil women are for evil men and pure women are for pure men. These pure people are free from the allegations levelled against them, and God blesses them with prosperity. (Sura 24, verses 23-26)

<u>Muhammad marries the wife of his foster son and abolishes the tradition of treating foster children as one's own</u>

Muhammad's first wife Khadija had gifted him a slave boy named Zayd bin Haritha. According to a pre-Islamic custom, people could adopt and foster children, and treat them as their own. Muhammad too had adopted Zayd as his son.

Zaynab was Muhammad's young cousin from a high-status house of the Quraysh. Her family had left Mecca and moved to Medina. Muhammad decided that she and Zayd would make a suitable couple but to other people, the daughter of a free and high-status family marrying an ex-slave was unthinkable. This was because the Arabs jealously guarded their genealogical heritage: The so-perceived "superior" tribes still do not marry in the so-perceived "inferior" tribes – let alone a slave or former slave. Hence, Zaynab and her family refused to accept this marriage and

Muhammad issued threats in the form of the following verses of the Qur'an:

> It is not right for believing men and women,
> When God and His messenger have decided on a matter,
> To exercise their won authority in their affairs.
> He who disobeys God and his messenger
> Is indeed on a clearly wrong path. (Sura 33, verse 36)

These verses were enough to scare Zaynab's family and she saw no option other than marrying Zayd. The Islamists hail this event as Muhammad's achievement in breaking class barriers but what followed this marriage pours cold water on their claims.

Once, Muhammad went to Zayd's home when the latter was not in. He saw Zaynab changing clothes, and came out of the house saying, `I praise God who affects our hearts.' Zaynab heard this and narrated the whole event to Zayd. Zayd rushed to Muhammad and said, `Master, if you like Zaynab, I am happy to divorce her for you.'[361] One needs to recall that on his "night journey," Muhammad had told about his meeting a woman named Zaynab in "Paradise" as follows:

> Never have I seen a man more like myself. This was my father Abraham. He took me to Paradise and there I saw a pretty woman with dark red lips and I asked her to whom she belonged, for she pleased me much when I saw her, and she told me that she belonged to Zayd bin Haritha.

Were it not for the fact that Muhammad himself narrated this whole story in his Qur'anic verses, one might be inclined to state that the event never happened; that it is below the dignity of a prophet to cast lustful eyes on his adopted son's wife. However, not only does the Qur'an testify that Muhammad liked Zaynab but also that he hid his desire, for a while, out of fear that people would ridicule him for it. The following verses very clearly state the abovementioned facts:

> And when you (*Muhammad*) said to him (*Zayd*)
> To whom God had shown a favour (*i.e. marriage to Zaynab*)
> And to whom you had shown a favour:
> `Keep your wife to yourself and fear God;'

> You were concealing in your heart
> That which God was going to reveal
> And you feared people (*of scandalizing this*)
> When God had a greater right to be feared.
> Hence, when Zayd had finished with her (*Zaynab*)
> God gave her to you as your wife
> So that believers should have no qualms
> About the wives of their adopted sons
> When the sons have finished with them.
> And God's commands have to be acted upon. (Sura 33, verse 37)

Because in those days the Arabs treated an adopted son as a natural son, this marriage required new Muhammadan legislation, which ended the great Arab tradition of treating foster children as natural. With the new law in place, adopted children could no longer inherit from their foster parents.[362]

As expected, people scandalized this marriage and blamed Muhammad for doing what was hitherto unacceptable in Arabia. He justified his doing by bringing in verses saying that God had wanted him to marry Zaynab:

> There is no barrier in the prophet's way
> For doing what God has sanctioned to him.
> Such was the way of God with those who went before him.
> God's decrees are preordained and unstoppable.
> As for those who deliver God's message,
> And fear God and fear none besides Him
> Sufficient is God's reckoning.
> Muhammad is not the father of any man among you
> He is God's messenger and the attester of prophets.
> And God is aware of all things. (Sura 33, verses 38-40)

When A'isha heard about the revelations allowing Muhammad to marry Zaynab, she made her feelings obvious to him, `Truly, God quickly sends down what you want Him to send,' she said, perhaps still angry that God had waited around a month before sending revelations about her innocence. What she really meant to say was, "You invented a command from God as soon as you wanted to marry Zaynab but when it was a matter of life and death for me, you let me suffer for a whole month."

XXX

The Islamists justify Muhammad in having many wives – whom they call the "Mothers of believers" (*Umhat'l Momayneen*) – by insisting that these contributed to the spreading of Islam by propagating Shari'a among women, and by being the teachers and reformers of women.[363] They claim that Muhammad showed by example how a man could live peacefully and happily with his many wives. However, the Qur'an and the earliest biographies of Muhammad reveal that his wives used to quarrel so much that he threatened to divorce them all, and he warned them that if they would not behave, God would double their punishment.

A'isha once said, `I was never jealous of any of the prophet's wives except for Khadija though she had died before the prophet married me.' This was because Muhammad often missed Khadija despite several marriages. A'isha would tease Muhammad by saying, `How come you miss that toothless old woman when God has given you much younger and better wives?' Muhammad would snub her and say, `Surely God has not given me better wives – He granted me Khadija's children and withheld those of other women.' His other wives would have done their utmost to have children from him – especially A'isha but she could only watch with envy Muhammad doting on his and Khadija's grandsons – Hassan and Hussein – the sons of Ali and Fatima.

In Medina, at one time, Muhammad had ten wives living with him.[364] These were A'isha, Sawda, Hifza, Zaynab bint Khuzayma, Zaynab bint Jahsh, Umm Salama, Umm Habiba, Maymuna, Saffiya and Juwayriya. Of his slave women, only two are well known: He took Rayhana as slave after the men of her Banu Qurayza tribe had been massacred. The second was Maria Qubtiya (*Maria – the Copt*).

Maria and her sister Sirin were Coptic Christians whom Cyrus, the ruler of Egypt, had sent to Muhammad as a gift. Arab historians have used the name "Maquqas" for Cyrus. Muhammad had sent him a letter warning him that it was time the Egyptians believed in him as the apostle of Allah. Cyrus had tried to avoid this threat by subtly appeasing Muhammad, and replied as follows:

To Muhammad bin Abdallah
From the Great Copt – Maquqas
Salam alayk (peace be upon you)

I have read and understood your letter. I knew that the time for the advent of a prophet had come but I believed that this prophet would appear in Syria. I have honoured your messenger and I am sending you gifts. I am sending two respectable Coptic girls for you, a pony, and some fine clothes.[365]

Muhammad kept Maria for himself and gave Sirin to Hassan bin Thabit whom he wished to honour[366] for reasons mentioned earlier and for lampooning the unbelievers.

Maria bore Muhammad a son called Ibrahim (Abraham) but he died in infancy in suspicious circumstances related to the jealousy between Muhammad's wives. The jealousy manifested itself to such an extent that, close to his death, Muhammad doubted that some of his wives were conspiring to poison him. This will be described later.

XXX

Since the produce from the confiscated Jewish lands and the taxes from the tribes around Medina had begun to pour in,[367] Muhammad's wives and daughter Fatima had been demanding finer clothes, jewellery, and slaves for domestic work. They were not happy with the allocation of funds.[368] However, Muhammad wanted to use the funds for further conquests and so, in retaliation, he banned his family members from wearing gold: Fatima's husband, Ali, once gave her a gold necklace. When Muhammad saw her wearing it, he said, `Do you want to wear a necklace of fire in hell?' Fatima quickly sold the necklace and bought a slave with the money.[369]

Once the wives quarrelled so much that Muhammad had to threaten them with the following "divine verses:"

> O prophet! Say to your wives, if you desire the luxuries of this life,
> Come then, I will provide and set you free in a fair manner.
> (Sura 33, verse 28)

The wives realized that if divorced they would lose their status in the community and, because they were not allowed to remarry, they would not have enough means. Hence, they succumbed, temporarily though, to live within the limitations set for them.

Muhammad was able to curb their materialistic desires to some extent but then they began to demand more time from him. Each wife had allotted days when he would spend the night with her. Some wives had no day at all, such as Sawda who, being too old, had sacrificed her day in favour of A'isha. When the wives quarrelled too much about the time he spent with one or the other, Muhammad told them that God had allowed him to spend time with whomever of them he liked, through the following "divine revelations:"

> You may defer any of them (*the wives*), as you wish
> And take to you any of them, as you wish.
> And you may desire any of those
> Whom you had separated from.
> There is no sin in doing so. It is most proper
> So that they may be appeased and not stay in grief
> And happy with what you give them. (Sura 33, verse 51)

The wives then demanded that he should not take more wives, and he compromised by agreeing to take more women only as slaves:

> It is not lawful for you to take more women after this
> Or to change your present wives for other women
> Even though their beauty may attract you
> Except those you take as slave women
> God keeps an eye on all things. (Sura 33, verse 52)

Muhammad once found Saffiya crying and asked why she was crying. Saffiya told him that his other wives treated her as inferior because of her Jewish background. He said to her, `Tell them that they are not better than you because while their husband is a prophet, you in addition had Moses as your great-grandfather and Aaron as your great uncle.'[370]

On another occasion when he was planning to travel with his wives, Saffiya's camel was found sick. There were suspicions that the camel had been made sick so that she could not join the trip. He asked Zaynab to give one of her many camels to Saffiya. Zaynab said, `I do not want a Jewess to ride my camels.' Muhammad was so angry that he did not see Zaynab for two months.[371]

Saffiya was a good cook. She once sent a pot of her best cooking to Muhammad when he was in A'isha's hut. A'isha snatched the pot from the servant and threw it to the ground where it broke into pieces. While A'isha was shouting at Muhammad, her father Abu Bakr came in. He grabbed A'isha to hit her but Muhammad intervened and Abu Bakr left the house in fury.[372]

Once, Muhammad went to Hifza's hut at a time when she was not there. He had his slave woman Maria with him. When Hifza returned, she found the two in her bed and was furious. She reprimanded him and he swore that he would never again sleep with Maria but on condition that Hifza would not reveal his secret. However, he could not resist the temptation, broke his promise, and spent some time in Maria's hut.[373] He justified his breaking of the promise by issuing a "divine order:"

> O prophet! Why do you forbid (*to yourself*)
> That which God has made lawful for you?
> You seek to please your wives
> But God is Forgiving, Merciful.
> God has made lawful for you to break your oaths
> And God is your Protector. (Sura 66, verses 1-2)

Either in retaliation for his breaking his oath or for other reasons, Hifza revealed his aforementioned secret to A'isha.[374] The two began to gossip against Muhammad and Maria, and told the secret to other wives too, who demanded from him to swear that he would never sleep with Maria again.[375] The rift between him and his wives grew and their relations became tense. To scare his wives, he issued the following "divine revelations" stating that God would grant him new and better wives:

> The prophet had a secret with one of his wives
> But she revealed it to the others
> And God informed the prophet that the secret was out.
> (*When questioned by the other wives*)
> The prophet admitted parts of the secret
> And denied the other parts.
> Then the prophet confronted her
> She asked, 'Who has told you that the secret is out?'
> The prophet said, 'I was told by the One who knows everything.'
> O the two wives (*A'isha and Hifza*) of the prophet,
> If you seek forgiveness from God, it will calm your hearts
> But if you will aid each other against the prophet,

God is his Protector
Gabriel, the virtuous believers and angels will come to help him.
And should the prophet decide to divorce you
God will grant him better wives in your place:
Submissive, obedient, faithful, penitent, adoring, and fasting,
Widows as well as virgins.   (Sura 66, verses 3 to 5)

God has given the example of the wives of Noah and Lot
These were married to pious men but they committed dishonesty
The pious men could not avert God's curse upon them
And these women were dispatched to hell with the others
                    (Sura 66, verse 10)

He decided that he would not see his wives for a month and began spending more time with Maria. A'isha later reported, `The prophet separated from his wives. Then he declared it unlawful. Then he declared it was lawful[376] and separated from us for a month.'[377]

Umar once explained the reasons of the insolence of the wives of Muhammad towards him as follows:

The Quraysh used to dominate their women and keep them in check but when we settled in Medina, we found that the women of the Ansar peasants dominated their men and were unruly. Our women began to imitate the Ansar women.
I once reprimanded my wife and she snapped back, at which I said to her, `How dare you answer me back?' She retorted, `Even the apostle's wives shout at him and do not speak to him for days, who are you? Ask your daughter how she speaks to Muhammad.'
I was shocked to hear this. I went to see my daughter and said to her, `Hifza! Is it true that you do not speak to the prophet for days? Have you no fear of God? Do you not know that the prophet's displeasure is the same as God's displeasure? By God the prophet has spared you because he respects my friendship or otherwise he would have divorced you long ago.'
I then went to Umm Salama and said the same to her but she retorted, `Umar, do not interfere in the personal affairs of the prophet and his wives.' I kept quiet.
After a few days, my neighbour banged at my door and shouted for me. I hurried outside thinking there had been an

invasion or something, and asked `What's the matter? Have the Sassanid attacked Medina?' `No. It's worse than that,' said my neighbour, `The prophet has divorced his wives.'

I went to see Hifza. She was sitting alone and crying. I said to her, `Did I not tell you to hold your tongue?'

I then went to the prophet's Mosque and asked his servant to inform him that I wanted to see him but the prophet would not see anyone. I then sent a message to the prophet, `I have not come to seek your forgiveness for Hifza but if you say, I shall strike her head off.'

At this, the prophet called me in. He was lying on a straw mat and there were straw marks on his body. I began to cry. He asked me why I was crying. I said, `I am crying because you, the prophet, are lying in humility on straw while the kings of Rome and Persia are enjoying all the luxuries.' He said, `Let them have this world and we shall receive the hereafter.'

I then asked if he had divorced his wives and he said, `No.'

Then he came out to meet his associates and told them that his month of abstinence was over.' [378]

Muhammad prepares to form an alliance with the "unbeliever" Meccans

The Arabs now knew Muhammad as the richest man of Arabia and the master of the most fertile lands in and around of Medina. Most Meccans were impressed and many had begun to realize that if they followed his methods of conquests (which they called his "truth" or his "religion"), they too could become as resourceful as he was. Around Mecca, there were many targets they could attack and plunder if they had as ferocious fighters as Muhammad had. The other alternative for the Meccans was to submit to Muhammad's leadership and use his Ansar men to fight for them but Abu Sufyan, the chief of Mecca and Muhammad's father-in-law, was not yet willing to do so.

Eight months after the conquest of Khyber, in February 629, Muhammad set out with two thousand men on the promised pilgrimage to Mecca. Abu Sufyan abided by the Truce of Hudaybiya and allowed him in. Accordingly, those Quraysh who did not like him withdrew from the Ka'ba precinct for three days and gave full access to Muhammad and his men. This proves beyond doubt that, contrary to the Islamist propaganda, the

Quraysh elders were not particularly hostile to Muhammad's religion; all they wanted from him was to refrain from insulting their elders and robbing their trade caravans.

During the pilgrimage, Muhammad's spy, uncle Abbas, got him married to Maymuna bint al Harith al Halaliya, the sister of Abbas's wife Lababat'l Kubra.[379] Maymuna was the aunt of one of Mecca's top warriors, Khalid bin Walid, who had played a major role in defeating Muhammad in Uhud and killing many believers. Muhammad had admired Khalid's battle skills and wanted him to come to his side. Seeing better future with Muhammad, Khalid later submitted to him and received the epithet *Saif Allah* – the sword of God.

Being victorious and wealthy had lessened Muhammad's hatred and vengefulness for his unbeliever relatives and he invited them all to his wedding feast. Many attended but some refused.[380] After three days, he returned to Medina and sent one of his slaves, Abu Rafay, to bring Maymuna to Medina.

Power and wealth had given Muhammad the credibility that he had so desperately sought from his tribe. His visit to Mecca marked the end of hostilities with the unbeliever Meccans and many came to Medina to join him. From then on, he gradually marginalized those of his Medinian followers who were too literal about the distinction between believer and unbeliever and hence aggressive towards his unbeliever relatives. He began to make room for more Meccans to join him and to prepare for taking leading positions in a future empire. On his part, Abu Sufyan too allowed his daughter Umm Habiba to travel to Medina and live with Muhammad as his ninth wife.

Among Muhammad's new allies were his first cousin J'afar bin abu Talib and the aforementioned Khalid bin Walid. These now wanted to follow his methods of conquests and he sent them, along with Abdallah bin Rawaha (the deceitful Medinian whom he had used to murder Yusayr and his thirty delegates) and other men to raid the Byzantines. However, the Byzantines were not easy to defeat. They killed J'afar and Abdallah at the battle of Mo'ta while Khalid bin Walid took to flight. When the people of Medina shouted abuses at Khalid, calling him a fugitive, Muhammad defended him by saying, 'They are not fugitives – soon they will regroup and re-attack.' His tribal favouritism for Quraysh against the Medinian peasants showed when, while supporting Khalid despite his running away from the battlefield, he said about Abdullah's death, `I see Abdallah sitting in paradise on a broken seat.' When asked why this was so, he replied, `He had hesitated in attacking the enemy.'[381] When the Medinian peasant women mourned and screamed at the deaths of their men at Mo'ta, Muhammad said, `Tell them to be quiet and if they refuse, fill their mouths with ash.'

Muhammad then sent Ka'ab bin Umayr al Ghifari to raid Dhatu'l Atlah in Syria where the Byzantines killed him and his men.[382] To compensate for the losses at the hands of the stronger Byzantines, Muhammad sent his men to a weak tribe whose chief was Ibn Zafla. Qutba bin Qatada, who led this cowardly raid, described it as follows:

> I shoved my spear so hard into Ibn Zafla's body, it broke inside
> Ibn Zafla bent down like a branch of a berry tree
> Then we gathered and herded the women of his tribe
> The way ostriches are collected and flocked.

Another nomadic tribe, the Banu Ghanam, was saved by their mystic woman who warned her tribe to run away from the believers: She said, `I warn you of this proud nation which looks askance at its victims, rides horses in file after file, and devises methods of shedding blood.' The tribe listened to her and escaped with their belongings.[383]

Then Muhammad sent Zayd bin Haritha to raid Wadi al Qura, where he met stiff resistance from the Banu Fazara tribe who killed many of his men. Zayd was injured and brought back from the battlefield on horseback.

When his wounds healed, Zayd swore that he would take dire revenge on the Banu Fazara. Muhammad helped him by sending more jihadis with him and Zayd was thus able to wreak havoc among the Banu Fazara and massacre a large number of them.[384] Umm Qirna, the oldest woman of the raided tribe, and her daughter were taken prisoners. Umm Qirna held a position of honour among her people and the Arabs used to say, `Had you been more influential than Umm Qirna you could do no more.' But Zayd ordered a jihadi named Qays bin Musahhar to kill her by tying her legs with ropes to two camels and driving them in opposite directions until they split her in two parts.[385] One has to remember that Zayd was Muhammad's foster son, married to Zaynab who later became Muhammad's wife.

Qays later boasted about his "bravery" as follows:

> I knew I would avenge in my lifetime.
> When I saw him (*Mas'ada*), I rode my steed over him repeatedly
> And impaled him on my lance of the best make.

Then they brought Umm Qirna's daughter and the son of the killed man, Mas'ada, to Muhammad. A jihadi named Salama bin Amr bin al Akwa asked Muhammad to give him Umm Qirna's daughter and he gave her to him. Salama gave her to his uncle Hazn bin abu Wahb by whom she bore a son.

Muhammad launches a propaganda campaign in order to popularize the Hashimis

While Muhammad wanted his Quraysh relatives to be preachers, governors, and founders of an empire, his Medinian jihadis still saw them largely as "unbelievers" who had rejected "the messenger" and deserved to be killed. He could not peacefully enter Mecca unless his Medinian jihadis learnt to respect the Quraysh. Sensing that he was now more in love with his unbeliever relatives than with his Medinian jihadis, his official poets Hassan bin Thabit and others began to write poems hailing the Hashimi Quraysh. While previously, they had presented Muhammad as "God's messenger," they now presented the entire Hashimi clan as "God's representatives on earth," whom "God had given the pure and holy book." Hassan began to write as follows:

> The Hashimis have bright faces – the faces of chiefs
> These include (*cousin*) J'afar and his brother Ali
> On top is the sovereign Ahmed (*Muhammad's former name*)
> And (*uncle*) Hamza, and (*uncle*) Abbas, and (*cousin*) Aqeel
> The Hashimis are the source of eternal bliss
> With them, the ordeal of battles becomes easy
> They are God's representatives on earth
> God sends them instructions and revelations
> And has given them the pure and holy book

Another poet, Ka'ab bin Malik wrote:

> In honour and nobility, the Hashimis are superior to all people
> Their wisdom dispels the ignorance of the ignorant
> They do not stand for perversions and folly
> Their orators present the decisive and absolute truth
> Their faces are bright and their generosity knows no bounds
> Their hands keep giving when others make excuses of famine.[386]

A new stage had begun in Muhammad's campaign, aimed at convincing his followers that only the Quraysh and their sub-tribe, the Hashimis, deserved to rule. After being the main force behind Muhammad's successes, the Medinian Ansar would still have to accept a subservient position to the Quraysh. Thus, the seed of enmity between the Ansar and the Quraysh germinated. This enmity would lead to the destruction and rebuilding of the Holy Ka'ba itself, but long after Muhammad's death. This will be described later.

<u>Muhammad finds his excuse and takes Mecca</u>

The defeat at Mo'ta taught Muhammad to ignore the Byzantines for a while and seek weaker targets around Mecca. Two months after this defeat, he found his excuse when his unbeliever allies and informers, the Khuza'a tribe, who lived near Mecca, killed a merchant and looted his goods. The merchant belonged to a tribe allied to the Umayyads and so the latter arranged a retaliatory raid on the Khuza'a and killed one man. The Khuza'a chief named Budayl bin Waraqa came to Medina and told this to Muhammad who quickly jumped to the conclusion that the Umayyads had violated the Truce of Hudaybiya by attacking his allied tribe. Though the Khuza'a had been the first to rob and kill, the Umayyad revenge attack was enough justification for Muhammad to take Mecca – a prospect that greatly worried the Umayyads. Abu Sufyan asked Budayl if he had been to complain to Muhammad and Budayl denied it but Abu Sufyan found out that he was lying. He rushed to Medina and lodged at the home of his daughter, Umm Habiba, Muhammad's wife, who insulted him by wrapping the carpet on which he was about to sit. `Is the carpet not worthy of me,' he asked, `or am I not worthy of the carpet?' `This is the apostle's carpet,' Umm Habiba replied, `and you are an unclean unbeliever.' `By God,' Abu Sufyan said, `since you left my house, you have become worse.'

Abu Sufyan pleaded with Muhammad not to abandon the Truce of Hudaybiya but Muhammad kept quiet. Disappointed, Abu Sufyan returned to Mecca.[387]

In January 630, Muhammad began his preparation to take Mecca but kept the direction of the travel a secret. However, many had guessed that he was planning to take Mecca. His uncle Abbas and two cousins left Mecca and came to join his ten thousand followers on their way. Their main aim was to assure safe conduct for the Meccans and help Muhammad enter Mecca without a fight.

Muhammad encamped outside Mecca and Abbas went out to bring Abu Sufyan and arrange a peaceful entry into Mecca. He rode Muhammad's distinctive white horse so that on his return journey, the believers would not attack them. Abbas reported:

> I rode Muhammad's white horse and went out until I came to the arak trees, thinking that I might find someone who could go to Mecca and tell them where the apostle was so that they could come out and ask for safety before he entered the town by assault.
> As I was going along with this intent, suddenly, I heard the voice of Abu Sufyan, Hakim bin Hazam and Budayl talking together. Abu Sufyan was saying, 'I have never seen so many (cooking) fires and such a camp before.' Budayl was saying, 'These, by God, are the fires of Khuza'a which war has kindled.' Abu Sufyan was saying, 'Khuza'a are too poor and few to have fires and camps like these.' I recognized his voice and called to him and he recognized my voice. I told him that the apostle was here with his army and expressed concern for him and for Quraysh: 'If he takes you he will behead you, so ride on the back of this mule so that I can take you to him and ask for you his protection.' So he rode behind me and his two companions returned.
> Whenever we passed a Muslim fire we were challenged, and when they saw the apostle's mule with me riding it they said it was the prophet's uncle riding his mule until I passed by Umar's fire. He challenged me, got up, and came to me, and when he saw Abu Sufyan on the back of the beast he cried, 'Abu Sufyan, the enemy of God! Thanks to God who has delivered you without agreement or word!' Then he ran

towards the apostle and I made the mule gallop, and the mule won by the distance a beast will outrun a man. I dismounted and went in to the apostle and Umar came in saying the same words and adding, 'Let me strike off his head.' I told the apostle that I had promised him my protection; then I sat by him and took hold of his head and said, 'By God, none shall talk to him this night without my being present,' and when Umar continued to remonstrate I said, 'Gently, Umar! If he had been one of the Banu Adiy bin Ka'ab you would not have said this; but you know that he is one of the Banu Abdu Manaf.' He replied, `Gently, Abbas! For by God your Islam, the day you accepted it, was dearer to me than the Islam of my father would have been had he become a Muslim. One thing I surely know is that your Islam was dearer to the apostle than my father's would have been.'

The apostle told me to take Abu Sufyan away to my quarters and bring him back in the morning. Abu Sufyan stayed the night with me and I took him in to see the apostle early in the morning. When he saw him he said, 'Isn't it time that you should recognize that there is no god but God?' He answered, 'You are dearer to me than father and mother. How great are your clemency, honour, and kindness! By God, I thought that had there been another god with God he would have continued to help me. He who overcame me with God's help was he whom I had driven away with all my might.'

The apostle playfully jabbed him in the chest and said, `Indeed you did. Woe to you, Abu Sufyan, isn't it time that you recognize that I am God's apostle?' He answered, 'As to that I still have some doubt.' I said to him, 'Submit and testify that there is no god but God and that Muhammad is the apostle of God before you lose your head,' so he did so. I pointed out to the apostle that Abu Sufyan was a man who liked to have some cause for pride and asked him to do something for him. He said, he who enters Abu Sufyan's house is safe, and he who locks his door is safe, and he who enters the mosque is safe.'

When Abu Sufyan got up to go back to Mecca, the apostle told me to detain him in the narrow part of the valley at the hilltop so that God's armies would pass by and he would see them; so I went and detained him where the prophet had ordered.

The squadrons passed him with their standards, and he asked who they were. When I said Sulaym he would say, 'What have

I to do with Sulaym?' And so with Muzayna, until all had passed, he asking the same question and making the same response to the reply. Finally, the apostle passed with his greenish-black squadron in which were Muhajirin and Ansar whose eyes alone were visible because of their armour. He said, 'Good heavens, Abbas, who are these?' and when I told him, he said that none could withstand them. 'By God, Abbas, the power of your brother's son has become great.'

It was only under threat of murder that Abu Sufyan had uttered that Muhammad was the messenger of God.[388] He then rushed to Mecca, where he went straight to the Ka'ba and announced, `O Quraysh, Muhammad has come with such forces as you are unable to resist. Anyone who enters my house will be safe.'

Hind, Abu Sufyan's wife, could not tolerate this. She grabbed his beard and shouted to the people, `Kill this fat greasy bladder of lard. A fine leader he is for you.' Abu Sufyan fought her off and appealed again to all of Mecca, `Woe unto you, Quraysh! Do not let her instigate you for you cannot resist the forces that have come.' People shouted back, `God slay you, what good is your house to us?' He added, `And he who enters the Ka'ba precinct, and he who stays at home and bolts his door and withholds from fighting against Muhammad will be safe.' Thereupon the people dispersed to their houses and the Ka'ba.

Before entering Mecca, Muhammad took oaths from the leaders and supervisors of his Medinian fighters that they would neither kill nor fight the Quraysh unless the Quraysh attacked first. This oath baffled the Medinians because they believed, as usual, that they had come to rob and kill "the unbelievers;" that the Meccans were "unbelievers" and the Ka'ba was the "unbelievers' shrine." It had not sunk in their minds that this time they were going to deal with Muhammad's tribesmen and to respect Mecca. Accordingly, one of the Medinian leaders named Sa'ad bin Ubaada raised the slogan:

Today is the day of raid
Today the Ka'ba will be fair game
Today is a day of war; sanctuary is no more.

One of the Muhajirin heard him and told Muhammad who ordered Ali to take the flag from Sa'ad's hand, and lead entry into

Mecca from the right side.[389] He ordered Zubayr bin al Awwam to command the left wing, and he ordered Khalid to enter from al Lit, the lower part of Mecca commanding the right wing with Aslam, Sulaym, Ghifar, Muzayna, Juhayna, and other tribes. Abu Ubayda bin al Jarrah advanced in front of Muhammad and entered from Adhakhir until he halted on a hilltop above Mecca where his tent was pitched.

Safwan bin Umayya was a very influential Meccan chief who had a large collection of armour. He, Ikrima bin Abu Jahl, and Suhayl bin Amr collected some men to fight. Another man named Himas bin Qays began to sharpen his sword. His wife asked him why he was doing so. When he told her it was for Muhammad and his men, she said that she did not think that it would do them any harm. He answered that he hoped to give her one of them as a slave and said:

I have no excuse if today they advance.
Here is my weapon, a long-bladed lance,
A two-edged sword in their faces will dance![390]

Then he went out with Safwan, Suhayl, and Ikrima and a skirmish followed in which they killed three men of Khalid's cavalry who had taken a road of their own apart from Khalid. One of them, called Khunays, whose father's name was Abu Sakhr, fought until he was slain, saying, `I fight today in defence of Abu Sakhr.' Then all of Khalid's men arrived and in the subsequent skirmish, one of Khalid's horsemen was killed while the Meccans lost about twelve or thirteen men before they took to flight. Himas ran off, went into his house, and told his wife to bolt the door. When she asked what had become of his former words, he said that if she had witnessed how Safwan and Ikrima fled when the believers met them with their swords, cut through arms and skulls, and only confused cries could be heard, she would not have blamed him.

Abdallah, the son of Abu Bakr, reported that Muhammad entered Mecca riding a horse and wearing a turban made of a piece of red Yamani cloth. To show his gratitude at how God had honoured him with victory, he lowered his head so low that his beard almost touched the middle of the saddle of his horse.

Abu Bakr's old father Abu Quhafa had never left Mecca. Because his sight had almost gone, he told his youngest daughter to take him up to Mount Abu Qubays so that he could see Muhammad's men entering Mecca. When they got there, he asked her what she could see and she told him `a mass of black.' `Those are the horses,' he said. Then she told him that she could see a man running up and down in front of them and he said that the man was transmitting the orders to the cavalry. Then she said, `By God, the black mass has spread.' He said, `In that case the cavalry have been released, so bring me quickly to my house.' She took him down the mount but the cavalry encountered them before they could get to their house and a believer tore the girl's silver necklace from her neck.

When Muhammad came and entered the mosque, Abu Bakr brought his father to him. On seeing him Muhammad said, `Why did you not leave the old man in his house so that I could go to him there?' Abu Bakr replied that it was more fitting that he should come to him than vice versa. He made him sit before him, stroked his chest and asked him to accept the belief and he did so. Then Abu Bakr got up and taking his sister's hand said, `I ask in the name of God for my sister's necklace.' None answered him, and he said, `Sister, regard your necklace as taken by God for there is not much honesty among people nowadays.'

The aforementioned Safwan bin Umayya went out to Juda to board a ship and escape to the Yaman. Umayr bin Wahb told Muhammad that Safwan, who was influential among his people, had fled from him and asked him to grant him immunity. Muhammad was always keen to have brave and skilled men in his forces, and he agreed to do so. Umayr asked him for a sign to prove it, and he gave him the turban he was wearing when he had entered Mecca. Umayr took it and overtook Safwan just as he was about to embark. He begged him not to waste his life and produced the token of his safety. Safwan replied, `I go in fear of my life because of him.' Umayr answered, `He is your cousin and too clement and too honourable to kill you.' So he went back with him to Muhammad and told him that Umayr had said that he had promised him immunity. Muhammad said that that was true. Safwan asked for two months in which to make up his mind, and he gave him four months. This was very generous compared to the secret assassinations and massacres of those who were not his relatives and had refused to submit to him.

The murders of the critics and apostates in Mecca

After entering Mecca, Muhammad allowed almost all of Quraysh to join his alliance without asking them to believe that he was the messenger. These were influential and powerful members of the local community and Muhammad needed them to gather jihadis for further conquests and rule the Arabs. However, he refused to let his critics live. To make people fear him, and thus respect him more, he named ten individuals and ordered that these should be killed even if they were found hiding behind the curtains of the Ka'ba.

The first, Abdallah bin Khatal of Banu Tayyum, also known as Ibn Khatal, was guilty of apostasy. The second and third were his two slave women, Fartana and Qareeba, who faced death for singing parodies of Muhammad. Ibn Khatal took refuge in the Ka'ba under the traditional belief that his life was safe in the Sacred House but he was murdered within the Ka'ba. Fartana begged forgiveness and saved herself but Qareeba was executed.[391]

The fourth, Huwayrith bin Nuqaydh, used to insult Muhammad in Mecca, and had attempted to dislodge his daughter from her camel when she were migrating to Medina. Ali found him and killed him.

The fifth, Miqyas bin Hubaba, was executed because he had killed a believer who had murdered his brother and, in Muhammadan law, an unbeliever could not take revenge from a believer.[392] This allowed the believers to kill the unbelievers with impunity and takeover their properties. The law continued to serve Arab conquerors for fourteen centuries in numerous Middle Eastern countries and in India. Muslim instigators in Muslim-dominated countries still use this law to kill or expel non-Muslims and takeover their properties. One of his own tribesmen named Numayla executed Miqyas, and his sister eulogized him as follows:

> By my life, Numayla shamed his own tribe
> And distressed our guests when he slew Miqyas
> Who has seen a man like Miqyas;
> Who provided food for young mothers in hard times?

The sixth was a slave woman Sara who had somehow "hurt" Muhammad during his early Meccan years. However, when she begged forgiveness, he pardoned her.

The seventh, Abdallah bin Sa'ad bin abi S'rah, was an apostate. He had become a believer and Muhammad had employed him to write down his "divine revelations" but he had escaped to Mecca and made fun of the "revelations" saying that he could utter better verses.[393] There are reports stating that one of Muhammad's scribes used to add words to the dictation of the "divine revelations." After the dictation, Muhammad used to ask his scribes to read to him what they had written. When this scribe would read back, Muhammad could not tell that the scribe had added to his words. This had made Abdallah bin Sa'ad doubt Muhammad's claim that God sent him verses through the Angel Gabriel. It also explains why similar verses appear many times in the Qur'an.

When Abdallah heard about his death sentence, he rushed to seek the protection of his cousin, who was none other than Muhammad's son-in-law Uthman. Abdallah knew that Muhammad would not deny Uthman's request. Uthman brought him to Muhammad who was sitting with his devotees, and repeatedly requested amnesty for Abdallah. Muhammad kept quiet for a very long time but, upon Uthman's persistence, he finally said, `Alright.'

When the two had gone, Muhammad vented his anger at his Ansar devotees and said, `I kept quiet for a long time in the hope that one of you would get up and strike off his head but you just sat there and did nothing.' One of the Ansar said, `O messenger of God, we were waiting for you to wink at us.' Muhammad replied, `It is below the dignity of the messenger to wink.'

The eighth was Ikrima, Abu Jahl's son, but when his wife submitted to Muhammad and begged forgiveness for him, he forgave him. Ikrima had escaped to Yaman. His wife went to Yaman, brought him back, and Muhammad appointed him to a senior administrative post in Mecca.

The last two men were Umm Hani's brothers-in-law from Banu Makhzum: Umm Hani was Abu Talib's daughter, Ali's sister, and Muhammad's first cousin. The two condemned men, named Harith bin ibn Hisham and Zubayr bin abu Umayya, took refuge in her house. Ali barged in with a sword determined to kill them but she locked them in a room, rushed to Muhammad, and pleaded with him to stop Ali. Muhammad had grown up with Ali and Umm Hani in their house, and he could not ignore her pleas. Hence, he said, `We give protection to those you give protection and we give safety to those you protect. Ali must not kill them.'[394]

Umm Hani's husband, Hubayra, was a poet from the Banu Makhzum who, along with the Umayyads, had been the chief custodians of the Ka'ba. Because the Hashimis and their allies had now taken over, many of these two tribes had to escape. These had correctly seen Muhammad's claims to apostolate as the Hashimi conspiracy to seize control of the Ka'ba, partly made obvious by the accolades of Muhammad's bards in praise of the Hashimis, and in uncle Abbas's conduct who sat all through this time as Muhammad's secret agent in Mecca. The strategy had succeeded. Umm Hani joined her victorious Hashimi relatives and became a believer while Hubayra escaped to Najran. Grieving for his separated wife, he wrote the following verses in which he used her first name "Hind:"

> Does Hind miss me? Does she ask about me?
> Or is it that distance changes people's hearts?
> On a high and inaccessible fort in Najran,
> As I spend my nights in loneliness
> I imagine that my wife has returned to me
> She reproaches me all night and I suffer in agony.
> She took the wrong path (*Islam*) and blamed me
> Claiming that if I follow my tribe, I would be killed,
> However, only her absence is killing me.
> I protect my escaped tribe when the rest are under spear points
> I loathe the jealous and their deeds,
> God will provide food for my people and me
> Words spoken without truth are like an arrow without a head
> So, if you have decided to follow Muhammad,
> And the ties of kinship draw you to your kin,
> And make you abandon kindness for people and me,
> Then stay far away in those dry and dusty rocks [*of Mecca*].[395]

One needs to note in these verses that Hubayra was a monotheist who trusted in God alone and understood the jealousy that was the major motivation behind Muhammad's wars. Muhammad would classify as unbelievers and persecute, despite their belief in one God, those who refused to support him through money or physical participation in the plunder of others.

Banu Makhzum never regained control of the Ka'ba but, around fifteen years after Muhammad's death, the Umayyads seized the power back. Then followed the Umayyad imperial dynasty (661-750 AD) for nearly a century until the Abbasids, who were the Hashimi descendants of Abbas, rebelled, massacred the Umayyads, and ruled the Arab Islamic empire for five centuries (750-1258 AD). This has been summarized in Appendix I.

Modern Muslim beliefs about the conquest of Mecca include the following event written in most Islamic history books:

> Ibn Ishaq heard from Abdallah bin Abu Bakr, who heard it from Ali, the grandson of Muhammad's uncle Abbas that when Muhammad entered Mecca on the day of the conquest, it contained three hundred and sixty idols which Satan had strengthened with lead. Muhammad stood by them with a stick in his hand, saying, 'The truth has come and falsehood has passed away; verily falsehood is sure to pass away.' (Sura 17, verse 81) Then he pointed at them with his stick and they collapsed on their backs one after the other. Then he ordered that all the idols should be collected, burned with fire, and broken up.

Those who believe in common sense more than in devils and miracles would see that Satan did not need to strengthen idols with lead, and idols do not fall when one points a stick at them. What really happened is as follows.

Having rid himself of his Meccan critics, Muhammad set out to decide which idols to destroy and which to keep. Inside the Ka'ba, he broke a wooden pigeon with his own hands but kissed the black stone. The Quraysh had decorated its walls with multi-faith murals, one showing Abraham and the angels, and the other showing Jesus and Mary. Ibn Ishaq states that Muhammad allowed the mural of Jesus and Mary to remain on the wall but his editor Ibn Hisham adopts a later tradition, which states that he had all the pictures obliterated.[396]

Celebrating the victory, Hassan bin Thabit taunted the secular Meccan chiefs as "female slaves" in his following verses:

The swords of the Ansar
Turned the Meccan chiefs into humiliated slaves
In disgrace, those who had been chiefs so far
Matched their female slaves.[397]

Then Muhammad stood at the door of the Ka'ba and delivered a speech stating that God had fulfilled his promise in helping him and making his enemies flee. He annulled the existing tribal claims of blood money, property and privileges in the governance of Mecca, but kept in post the existing custodians of Ka'ba and those who provided water to the pilgrims because they were experienced in doing so. Fearful that offended people would kill others and then find excuses by saying that they did it unintentionally, he ordered that the blood money for the unintentionally slain would be most severe: a hundred camels, forty of which should be pregnant. To humiliate the unbelieving chiefs of Quraysh, he said, 'God has taken from you the pride of paganism and veneration of ancestors. Man came from Adam and Adam sprang from dust.' Then he read to them his "revelations:"

> O people! We (*God*) created you from male and female and made nations and tribes so that you may identify and introduce yourself one to another but in God's sight, the superior is the one who has power from God. The folks say that they believe. Tell them (*O Muhammad*), "You do not really believe but you have only submitted (*become Muslims*) and faith has not yet entered into your hearts. If you obey God and His apostle, God will not lessen your rewards. Believers are those who have faith in God and His apostle, who do not doubt, and who use their money and lives in fighting in the way of God. These are the truthful."
> Say to them, "Do you tell God that you have faith? God knows everything that is in the sky and on earth."
> They impress on you (*Muhammad*) as a favour that they have submitted. Say to them, "Count not your submission as a favour upon me but God has conferred a favour upon you by guiding you to the faith, if you are true." (Sura 49, verses 13-17)

These verses make it clear that in Muhammad's eye only those were believers who "do not doubt him and who use their money and lives in fighting." According to this definition, the believers present at Mecca numbered ten thousand. Around a thousand each were of Banu Sulaym and Muzayna, around four hundred each of Banu Ghifar and Banu Aslam and the rest of them were from the Ansar, Quraysh, and their allies from Tamim, Qays, and Asad.

People gathered to swear allegiance to Muhammad as he sat waiting for them on al Safa while Umar stood below him imposing conditions on the people who paid homage, promising to obey Muhammad. When they had finished with men, they dealt with the women. Among the Quraysh women who came was Abu Safyan's wife Hind bin Utaba who had had Muhammad's uncle Hamza killed in Uhud and mutilated his body. Though she hid her face in a veil out of pride, she was not afraid that Muhammad would punish her because Abu Sufyan sat next to him and he could hardly grieve his new ally and father-in-law. Muhammad had not even killed her slave Wahshi, who had killed Hamza, but found new targets for him.

Muhammad said to Hind, "Do you promise not to associate partners with God," and Hind said, 'By God, you did not ask this of the men but we will carry it out.'

He said, 'And you shall not steal.' She said, 'By God, I used to take a little of Abu Sufyan's money and I do not know whether that is lawful for me or not.' Abu Sufyan told her that as far as the past was concerned it was lawful. Muhammad now realized who she was and said, 'Then you are Hind bin Utaba?' and she said 'I am; forgive me what is past and God will forgive you.'

He said, 'And do not commit adultery.' She answered, 'Does a free woman commit adultery, O apostle of God?'

He said, 'And you shall not kill your children.' She said, 'I brought them up when they were little and you killed them on the day of Badr when they were grown up, so you are the one who knows about killing children!' This was grossly insolent but Umar laughed whole-heartedly at her reply.

Muhammad said, 'You shall not invent slanderous tales.' She said, 'By God, slander is disgraceful, but it is sometimes better to ignore it.'

He said, 'You shall not disobey me in carrying out orders to do good deeds.' She said, 'We should not have sat all this time if we wanted to disobey you in such orders.'

This dialogue shows that Hind hardly respected Muhammad as God's messenger but, being his mother-in-law, Muhammad said to Umar, 'Accept her pledge,' and he asked God's forgiveness for her while Umar accepted homage on his behalf.

Hind's son Mu'awiya would become one of Muhammad's scribes and, just nineteen years after his death, would take revenge from the Hashimis by snatching the entire Arab empire. He would cause the murders of Muhammad's son-in-law Ali and grandson Hassn, and establish the Umayyad dynasty in Damascus. Then his son, Yazid, would have Muhammad's grandson Hussein slaughtered. Thus, Hind's son and grandson would complete her revenge.

Muhammad did not touch women's hands when taking pledge; a vessel containing water was placed in front of him and when he laid the conditions upon women and they accepted them he plunged his hand into the vessel and then withdrew it and the women did the same. Then he would say, 'Go, I have accepted your homage.'

Then Muhammad sat in the mosque. Ali came with the key of the Ka'ba in his hand and asked him to grant his family the right of guarding the Ka'ba and providing water to the pilgrims, but he called for Uthman bin Talha, the existing guardian of Ka'ba, and said, 'Here is your key; today is a day of good faith.' It was very wise of Muhammad to begin his rule in Mecca in alliance with as much of the previous rulers rather than against them. He always began as an ally until he had understood the strengths and weaknesses of those he planned to annihilate. One needs to remember that he had started in Medina as an ally of Abdallah bin Ubayy and the Jews.

The Islamists hail this as Muhammad's magnanimity towards "his enemies" but they do not see that Muhammad had perpetual war on his mind and he needed Ali to fight more battles for him. That is why he had not allowed him to become a farmer in Medina and he could not allow him to look after the Ka'ba. It was militarily wise to let the unbelieving Quraysh look after the Ka'ba at that moment, thus freeing his jihadis, his real powerbase, to continue expanding his empire.

A few days later, Muhammad's allies, the Khuza'a, murdered a man who had come to Mecca from outside. Many had seen that Muhammad had ordered the execution of Ibn Khatal in the Ka'ba and begun to believe that Mecca was no longer sacred. If word got around, outsiders would not travel to Mecca and this would destroy the pilgrim based trade. Muhammad found it necessary to warn people that Mecca was still a safe city, and only "the messenger" had temporarily taken the liberty to kill in there. Accordingly, he delivered the following sermon:

God made Mecca holy the day He created heaven and earth, and it is the holy of holies until the resurrection day. It is not lawful for anyone who believes in God and the last day to shed blood therein, nor to cut down trees therein. It was not lawful for anyone before me and it is not lawful for anyone after me. Indeed, it is not lawful for me except at this time because of anger against its people. Now it has regained its former holiness. Let those present here now tell those that are not here. If anyone should say, "The apostle killed men in Mecca," say God permitted His apostle to do so but He does not permit you. Refrain from killing, you men of Khuza'a, even if there were profit in it, for there has been too much killing. Since you have killed a man, I will pay his blood money. If anyone is killed after my sojourn here, his relatives will have a choice: they will have his killer's life or the blood-money.[398]

The Islamists hail the conquest of Mecca as a victory in which little blood spilled, Muhammad forgave his enemies, and the Meccans accepted Islam. However, the earliest histories reveal that he entered Mecca as an ally of the largely unbeliever Meccans. This alliance was a tactical manoeuvre similar in nature to his earlier cooperation with the Jews but with very different outcomes as follows:

- After signing the Treaty of Medina with the Jews, Muhammad gathered followers and gradually annihilated the Jews as a cultural group because they had refused to give up Judaic code of ethics ("Do not kill and steal") and, hence, did not join him in the plunder of the weaker tribes around Medina.

- The opposite happened in Mecca: When Muhammad entered Mecca, his Quraysh relatives gradually joined him in the pillage of the weaker tribes, which lived around Mecca, in a spate of raids and battles described in the following pages.

The Raids on the tribes settled around Mecca

As he had done in and around Medina, Muhammad demanded jizya tax from the Zoroastrians of Hujar, and began sending armed men to the tribes settled around Mecca. The Islamists state that these jihadis went to preach "Islam" to the tribes but the events reported in the earliest histories tell a different story. For example, Muhammad sent a group of armed men, led by Khalid bin Walid, towards the Banu Jadhima tribe: Some time back, a man named Khalid bin Hisham had killed Khalid's uncle, al Fakih bin al Mughira, because of a property dispute in the territory of this tribe. The Quraysh had investigated and declared that the Banu Jadhima neither had planned the assault nor knew about it until afterwards. Even so, the Banu Jadhima had paid blood money and compensation for the stolen property and the Quraysh had agreed not to go to war with them. Nevertheless, Khalid bore grudge against the tribe and though the slayer of his uncle too had been killed in the said dispute, this had not cooled his desire for revenge.

When Khalid reached the Banu Jadhima, he ordered them to lay down their arms and submit to Islam. The tribesmen did as told though one of their men, whose name was Jahdam, tried to warn them, `What are you doing? Do you not know Khalid bin Walid? He will order people to surrender, arrest them, and then slaughter them. I swear by God, I will not lay down my arms.' Jahdam's tribesmen warned him and said, `Do you want to fight to be slaughtered?' The tribesmen restrained Jahdam and took away his arms. Then they surrendered and embraced Islam. When all this was done, Khalid ordered his men to tie the tribesmen up. After they were all tied up, he began to behead them just as Jahdam had forewarned. Abu Huzayfa and Umar's son Abdallah, a kind man, the opposite of his merciless father, tried to stop Khalid but he told them to shut up. Jahdam cried out and said to his tribesmen, `Alas! You lost the time to fight. I warned you that this would happen.'

Among those to die was a young man whose hands had been tied to his neck. He requested as his last wish to go near the women of his tribe who stood mourning and crying. He stood by a young woman and said to her, `Hubaysha! My life will soon end. I wish you the best and I wanted to tell you that I have always loved you. I used to watch you in the darkness of nights and in the heat of the day but I never revealed the secret that no one has ever had such a place in my heart as you have. I was not sure if you too loved me and I kept saying to you, "Please answer me before your family elder marries you away." Hubaysha replied, `I have always prayed for your life and always welcomed you.'

After the young man was beheaded, Hubaysha fell on his dead body and kissed it many times.

A survivor of the Banu Jadhima massacre stated:

God will take revenge for the evil they did to us
They looted and divided our property among themselves
Their spears came at us again and again
Were it not for Muhammad's religion
Their cavalry would have been driven off.

The last two phrases mean that the tribe believed that by submitting to Muhammad's religion, Khalid would spare their lives: If they had not accepted this religion, they would have fought and driven Khalid's cavalry off.

Modern Muslim textbooks present Khalid bin Walid, instead of Abdallah bin Umar, as a hero who played a major role in spreading Islam. Millions of young Muslims aspire to emulate Khalid but the events quoted above show that he was a tribal brute who shocked even his associates and they complained to Muhammad about this. Muhammad was well aware that Khalid hated the Banu Jadhima because, as mentioned earlier, his uncle had been killed in their territory. Still, Muhammad had sent him to raid them. Perhaps he wanted him to be merciless but, upon hearing about the slaughter, he showed that he was upset. He raised his hands and prayed to God, 'O God I am not responsible for what Khalid did.' Then he asked, 'Did no one try to stop the massacre?' He was told that Abu Huzayfa and Umar's son Abdallah had tried but Khalid had told them to shut up. Then Muhammad sent Ali to Banu Jadhima to return the looted property and to pay them blood money but he did not punish Khalid because he needed him to conquer more territory. Accordingly, he dispatched him to dismantle the Temple of Uzz'a in Nakhla.[399]

The custodians of Uzz'a, the Banu Shayban branch of the Banu Sulaym, were allies of the Hashimis but they used to receive donations and animals for sacrifice at Nakhla and Muhammad wanted these donations to come to him. When the guardian of Uzz'a heard of Khalid's coming, he climbed the mountain on which Uzz'a stood, hung his sword on Uzz'a, and prayed:

O Uzz'a, make an annihilating attack on Khalid,
Throw aside your veil and gird up your train
O Uzz'a, if you do not kill this man Khalid
Then bear a swift punishment or become a Christian.

These verses show that being non-violent or non-defensive was associated with being a Christian.

Khalid destroyed the temple and returned to Muhammad for further instructions.

The battle of Hunayn

One would expect that after capturing Mecca and the Ka'ba, Muhammad would stop all battles but the opposite happened. He began a process of taxing and militarily subjugating the tribes around Mecca, and started with those who worshipped at the Temple of Laat in Ta'if, though these also visited Mecca to worship at the Ka'ba. The large Hawazin tribe decided not to surrender. Their chief Malik bin Awf al Nasri gathered his sub-tribes – Thaqif, Nasr, Jusham, Sa'ad bin Bakr and Banu Hilaal. Other sub-tribes of Hawazin, namely Qays, Aylan, Ka'ab and Kalab stayed away from the battle.

Among the Banu Jusham was Durayd bin al Simma, a very old man who could not fight but offered his valuable advice and knowledge of war. When Malik bin Awf marched towards Mecca with his men, their cattle, wives and children, and halted at Autas, Durayd inquired why Malik had brought all the cattle and the women and children. Malik explained that his purpose in putting them behind his men was to motivate them to fight hard in their defence. Durayd was dismayed and said, `You sheep-tender! Do you suppose that anything will stop a man who wants to run away? If it goes ill, you will be disgraced along with your family and property. You have done no good by sending forward people on foot to meet the cavalry. But now that you have brought them, send them up to the high and inaccessible part of land and meet the wrongdoer *Subaat* (apostates, meaning Muslims, who had abandoned their forefathers' religion) on horseback. If it goes well those behind can join you, and if the battle goes against you, you will have saved your families and stock.'

Malik answered, `I will not do it. You are old and so are your senses. O Hawazin! Obey me or I will lean on my sword until it comes out from my back.' Then he said to his men, `As soon as you see the enemy, throw away your scabbards and attack them as one man.'

When Malik sent spies to Muhammad's allied forces, they were identified and made to run for their lives. On the other hand,

Muhammad's spy, Abdallah bin Abu Hadrad, was able to join the Hawazin, stay with them, and obtain strategic information. Because Muhammad's spies, like everyone else, had come from an unbeliever background, they knew the unbeliever ways of greeting and interacting and were safe from recognition. On the other hand, when the unbelievers went to spy on the believers, they were easily identified because of their lack of knowledge of Muslim prayers, phrases, and rituals.

Muhammad, being the expert user of hypocrites, knew well about the damage that spies could cause and, therefore, he was very intolerant of any suspicious character in his crowd. While he usually succeeded in using his network of spies to his advantage, he deprived his target people of any advantages of spying on him. A large part of the Qur'an consists of curses sent upon the "hypocrites." In cursing these, Muhammad conveniently forgot those who were his secret agents and informers including his uncle Abbas, Naeem bin Mas'ud (who had deceived both the Quraysh and the Jews at Ahzaab), Abdallah bin Rawaha (who had betrayed his Jewish friends and had thirty of them murdered), the abovementioned Abdallah bin abu Hadrad, and the entire Khuza'a tribe.

Muhammad went to see the influential unbeliever Meccan Safwan bin Umayya who had a large collection of armour and said, `Lend us these arms so that we may fight our enemy tomorrow.' Safwan asked, `Muhammad! Are you demanding my armour to confiscate it?' Muhammad said, `No, they are a loan and we will return them to you.'

Safwan lent a hundred coats of mail together with a large quantity of arms. Then Muhammad marched with two thousand Meccans and ten thousand of his Ansar and local men to fight the Hawazin. The tribes on Muhammad's side included the Banu Sulaym, who were relatives of the Hawazin but sought to plunder them. Muhammad's poet, Abbas bin Mirdas, mentioned this in the poem he recited on the night of the attack:

> A ghost has smitten Sulaym – the brothers of Hawazin
> Smitten in the midst of their tents, for ghosts have many forms
> Alas for the mothers when the cavalries of brother tribes
> Confront each other to strengthen brotherly ties (*ironical*).
> You will not return your cousins without a fight (*ironical*),
> Though it is a flagrant disgrace and a shame,

As long as there is milk in the captured camels.
It is a shame so huge it could cover the mountains
It is worse than eating the penis of a wild ass.
Hawazin are a good tribe but they have the Yemeni disease:
If they are not treacherous, they are deceitful
When we crush them, they become kind
Take to Hawazin for the last time, a plain advice from me;
God's messenger will attack you in the morning
With an army extending all over the steppe;
Among them your brothers Sulaym who will not let you go
And the believers, God's slaves, and the Ghassan
On his right are the Banu Asad,
And the confident Banu 'Abs and Dhubyan.
The earth quakes in fear of them.

When Muhammad and his allies reached Autas, they found that the Hawazin had hidden themselves in the byways, side-tracks, and narrow places of the valley. They were fully prepared and they attacked ferociously. Muhammad's allies broke rank and fled, none heeding the other. He withdrew to a safer place and shouted, 'Where are you going, men? Come to me. I am God's messenger.' To his unbeliever allies he shouted, 'I am Muhammad the son of Abdallah.' But his men ran except for a number of Muhajirin and Ansar, and men of his family.

When Muhammad's unbeliever allies saw his men fleeing, some of them expressed their doubts: The half-hearted Abu Sufyan taunted, 'This flight of the believers will not stop before they reach the sea!' This shows that although Abu Sufyan had saved his life by converting, he was not really with the believers. Jabala bin al H'nbal added, 'Muhammad's sorcery will be undone today.' Safwan bin Umayya who had lent all his armour to Muhammad and risked losing it in case of a defeat, got angry, and said, 'Shut up, may God smash your mouth! I would rather be ruled by a man of the Quraysh than by a man of the Hawazin.' These unbelievers had accepted Muhammad's leadership only because he belonged to their tribe.

Frequent pleas to God by "unbelievers" as quoted in the earliest books, coupled with contextual analysis, prove that the Arabs generally believed in God and therefore monotheism was not an issue in Muhammad's wars; that the "unbelievers" were simply those who did not see Muhammad fit to be a prophet; and that most Muhammadan battles were in fact tribal wars. The Islamists, however, ignore the recorded facts and present all Muhammadan wars as wars between Muslims and non-Muslims aimed at spreading monotheism against "polytheism" and "evil."

Muhammad shouted, `O Abbas! Cry loudly, "O Ansar! O comrades of the Acacia Tree!" The Ansar answered, `Here we are.' The Medinian devotees were steadfast in the fight. Muhammad looked down at the mêlée and said, `Now the oven is hot.' A believing woman, Umm Sulaym, who was with him said, `O messenger of God, order the execution of the deserters – they deserve to be killed like those who fight against you.'[400]

A poet of the Abu Salama tribe described the believers' flight and regrouping as follows:

> But for God and His messenger you would have fled
> When fear overwhelmed the cowards
> When our opponents met us on the slope
> While the horses galloped at full stretch,
> Some fled clutching their garments,
> Others knocked sideways by hooves and chests.
> God glorified us and made our religion victorious
> God destroyed them and made them flee
> And humiliated them in the worship of Satan.[401]

Ali and one of the Ansar challenged a man who sat on his camel with the Hawazin flag. Ali came on him from behind and hamstrung his camel and it fell upon its rump. The Ansari leapt upon him and struck him with his sword, which sent his foot flying, and he fell.

The Ansar went on fighting and when those who had run away returned, they found only prisoners. Some of Muhammad's men had been stripping the corpses for clothes and shoes. Squabbles broke out about who had slain whom and hence could take the belongings of his victim. Muhammad ordered that only the killer had the right to take the property of his victim. A man had looted the belongings of a man whom Abu Qatada had killed. After Muhammad's abovementioned order, Abu Qatada claimed his booty back, which he later sold and, with the proceeds, bought a piece of oasis.

Meccan women, who had accompanied their men, sang:

God's cavalry have beaten al Laat's cavalry
And God best deserves to hold fast.

Among the Hawazin, the Thaqif were the most steadfast, and seventy of them died beneath their flag. Among these was Uthman bin Abdallah. When the news of his death reached Muhammad, he said, `God cursed him because he used to hate the Quraysh.'[402] In saying this, Muhammad conveniently forgot that, since his migration to Medina, he had been posing as the victim of Quraysh persecution and using the Ansar peasants and bandits to rob them and fight against them. The Quraysh had allowed him into Mecca and accepted him as their leader only because he had enough jihadis to be able to establish the Quraysh domination in the region.

A Christian slave was killed and when one of the Ansar stripped him of his clothes, he found that the slave was uncircumcised. He called out at the top of his voice, `Look! O Arabs! God knows that the Thaqif are uncircumcised.' Because being uncircumcised was a disgrace among the Arabs, Mughira bin Shu'ba told him to shut up for he was afraid that this rumour would spread out and all Meccans would be taunted as, "the uncircumcised ones." Then Mughira began to uncover other corpses and showed that they were circumcised.[403]

This event shows that circumcision was common among Arabs before Islam, and the belief that it is an Islamic tradition is incorrect. However, in the coming centuries, the imperialist Arabs imposed many of their cultural traditions upon people in the conquered lands and called them "Islamic values."

The routed Hawazin and Thaqif tried to escape to Nakhla and Ta'if. Muhammad's cavalry followed those who took the road to Nakhla but avoided those who went to the passes towards Ta'if. Rabi'a bin Rafay, a young believer, took hold of the camel of the aforementioned old man Durayd bin al Simma. Because Durayd was in his howdah, Rabi'a thought he was lucky to have found a woman but when he made the camel kneel, he was frustrated to find the very old Durayd inside the howdah. Durayd asked him what he wanted and what his name was. Rabi'a told him his name and said that he wanted to kill him. Durayd taunted him, `Strike me above the spine and below the head, for that is the way I used to strike men. Then when you go to your mother, tell her that you have killed Durayd bin al Simma for the days when I used to protect your women.' When Rabi'a returned to his mother and told her that he had killed Durayd, she cried, mourned, and said, 'By God, he had rescued three of your mothers (i.e. step mothers or aunts) and grandmothers from men who had captured them.' The daughter of Durayd, Amara, mourned his death and Muhammad's murderous intrigues in the following verses:

> May God repay those who killed Durayd in the valley
> And may ingratitude rip them for what they do.
> May God give us the blood of their best men to drink.
> Many disasters you (*Durayd*) averted from them,
> When they (*assaulting tribes*) were at the brink of death.
> Many a woman of theirs you freed,
> And others you relieved from bonds.
> Many a men of Sulaym called you noble,
> As you helped them when they called you;
> They rewarded with such ingratitude and woe
> As melts the marrow in our bones.
> They said, 'We have killed Durayd.'
> 'True,' I said, and my tears flowed down my garment.
> Were it not for him (*Muhammad*),
> Who has dominated all the tribes (*i.e. make them fight each other*)
> Sulaym and Ka'ab would have faced a great army,
> Attacking them continuously wherever they were.

Muhammad sent Abu Amir al Ash'ari to chase the escapees but his men suffered heavy losses in the skirmishes, and Durayd's son Salama killed him by shooting an arrow at him. On hearing that the Banu Ri'ab had suffered heavy losses, Muhammad prayed, 'O God, compensate them for their losses.'

The retreating Hawazin chief, Malik bin Awf, stopped during the flight with some of his horsemen at a pass, and told them to wait until the weak ones and those left behind had caught up. Salama, the son of Durayd, escorted his wife to safety, and said:

> You forgot me until you were in trouble
> But you know that I protected you and walked behind you,
> Watching on all sides when every well-trained warrior
> Fled from his mother and did not return to help his friend.[404]

Muhammad's poet Abbas bin Mirdas celebrated the battle in a poem:

> Muhammad is the messenger who follows God's straight path
> He is true like Moses and has no rival in superiority.
> Evil was the state of the Thaqif in the valley,
> When we charged as lions and destroyed them,
> And blood flowed freely.
> In the former days, there was no battle like this;
> You would have never heard of such a day.
> We slew them in the dust by their flag
> Their chief was like a drunken stupid man
> He led them on the road to death as everyone could see
> He destroyed them and perished himself
> They gave him leadership when the bravest were fleeing
> Those who escaped suffocated with terror
> A multitude of them were slain
> It was not a place for the shy and the hesitant.

On his way out of the battle, Muhammad passed by the corpse of a woman whom Khalid bin Walid had killed and men had gathered around her. He sent word to Khalid forbidding him to kill children, women, and slaves because, as in Medina, he would distribute these among his jihadis; they would release women and children upon receipt of ransom money, and sell the slaves. In case there was no man left to come with a ransom, there were always jihadis eager to take these women home as slaves or wives. The Quraysh had not joined Muhammad for nothing. They had finally seen that his way of jihad was the shortest route to securing fertile land, wealth, slaves, women, and prestige. Hence, instead of making fun of his promises, as they had earlier, many were now accepting him as the messenger who "spoke the truth."

Muhammad sent Uyayna bin Hisn to raid the Banu Anbar, a sub-tribe of the Banu Tamim tribe. Uyayna did so, killed some men, and captured a number of men and women. In those days, Muhammad's wife A'isha told him that she had sworn that she would free a slave from the sons of Isma'il, and he said, 'We expect captives to be taken from the Banu Anbar tribe and we will give you one whom you can set free.' When they brought the prisoners, a deputation from the Banu Tamim rode along with them. They came to Muhammad and pleaded for the release of their tribesmen.

Muhammad liberated some without ransom and accepted ransom for others.[405]

When a group of men captured the tribal chief Thamama bin Athal al Hanafi, they did not know who he was until they brought him to Muhammad who recognized him as a great tribal chief and told his men that they must treat him honourably. He then went back to his house and told his family to send food to Thamama, and ordered them to take his she-camel to Thamama every night and morning so that he could drink as much milk as he wanted. Then he went to see Thamama and urged him to submit to Islam. Thamama warned him, `Enough is enough, Muhammad; if you kill me you kill one whose blood must be paid for; if you want ransom, ask what you want.' Muhammad would have had another man beheaded for such affront but he knew about the strength of Thamama's tribe and so he ordered his release. Thamama later became a believer.[406]

The Islamists provide selected examples to illustrate Muhammad's kindness to captives but ignore the reasons for which he had extended kindness to certain individuals. They also ignore examples of his cruelty to weaker tribes and persons. A closer study shows that he was usually kind only to those whom he needed to come to his side, such as the abovementioned Thamama.

Continuing with the aftermath of Hunayn, Muhammad ordered Khalid bin Walid to find a man named Bijad in his foster mother Halima's tribe, the Banu Sa'ad bin Bakr, and said, `If you get hold of Bijad, do not let him escape for he has done great wrong.' It is not known what Bijad had done to him but the event could have happened only when he was a child, sent to live with Halima.

When they caught Bijad and led him away with his family, they also took a woman, Shayma bint al Harith. Shayma pleaded that she had been Mohammed's foster-sister but the men did not believe her and treated her roughly as they brought her to him. When Shayma told Muhammad that she was his foster-sister, he asked for proof. Shayma said, `Look at the mark; it's the bite you gave me on my back when I used to carry you on my back.' Muhammad believed her, stretched out his robe for her to sit on, and offered her the choice of living with him in affection or going back to her people with gifts. She chose the latter. He gave her some camels and released a man and a woman from the captives of her tribe to go back with her.

The booty from Hunayn included around six thousand women and children, and a very large number of sheep and camels. Muhammad ordered to keep the captives and the looted property and animals under guard at al Ji'rana, to distribute later.

<u>The reasons for the relatives fighting each other, and the non-Quraysh fighting for the supremacy of the Quraysh: Economic chaos and starvation</u>

Hunayn was indeed a battle between relatives spread out in various tribes. The reports and the poetry of the period reflect this. For example, see Muhammad's poet Abbas bin Mirdas declaring:

> They attacked their kith and kin
> Seeking only to please God and Muhammad
> Charging in clouds of dust, smiting the heads of the unbelievers
> They did not hope for consideration of kinship
> But obedience to God and devotion to Muhammad.
> The night when Dahhak fought with the messenger's sword,
> And death was near, we defended brother against brother.[407]

One finds tribal relatives showing antipathy for kinship in verses such as, `The breast that fed them milk is dry,' in the following poem:

> On the day of Autas we fought fiercely
> Until the enemy cried, "Stop!"
> Hawazin appealed to the brotherhood between us
> But the breast that fed them milk, is dry.
> We left them like corpses of wild asses,
> Torn by wild beasts after being preyed upon.[408]

The poet Abdallah bin Mirdas had joined Muhammad but the woman he loved rejected Islam and bloodshed, as the following verses show:

> Finally, the last link with my beloved is broken!
> She has broken her promises though she had sworn by God.
> My beloved seeks unbelief and increases the separation,

But I am the follower of the prophet.
We trample the unbelievers shouting, `Slay! Slay!'
And sever their necks the way vegetables are sliced

One might question how tribal relatives could fight and kill each other without feeling guilty about it. One explanation is that guilt was overcome by the belief that bloodshed pleased God. God's messenger made sure that his jihadis prayed five times a day, and convinced them that God was happy with them. Evidence showing this is available in verses such as:

We left many a women, widows,
To mourn over their husbands' corpses
We seek the pleasure of God and not that of humans
To God belong the seen and the unseen.
The Sulaym have a lot to boast about
They are the people who helped God
They smote the unbelievers in Mecca's vale,
And left them dead like uprooted palms in the valley.
On Hunayn's day, our stand strengthened religion,
And with God that is recorded, to be rewarded.
We devoted our spears to God in the battlefield
We helped God and he made us victorious.
You will see no tribe large or small
Upon whom we have not left wound marks.
We helped God's messenger, and carried his flag,
We dyed it with blood, for red was its colour
We were his supporters in Islam.
We were the first to guard the messenger
And with intimacy, he summoned us first of all
God richly rewarded Prophet Muhammad
And strengthened him with victory, for God is his helper![409]

These verses and prayers show that guilt, if any, was overcome by the belief that murder and robbery were committed to please God, and hence justified. One might question that the quoted verses are not from Muhammad, in which case one needs referring to the Qur'anic verses to see how Muhammad suppressed the natural guilt of robbers and murderers. The Qur'an's main theme reflects in Sura 4 verse 48, which states that the greatest sin is to ascribe partners to God (i.e. allowing more than one faith), and that God may forgive all other sins such as banditry, rape, murder, deception, ethnic cleansing etc.:

> Surely God does not forgive that anything should be associated with Him (*i.e. shrines other than Ka'aba*), and forgives what is besides that to whomsoever He pleases. (Sura 4, verse 48)

Muhammad kept telling his jihadis that so long as they fought to abolish secular/multi-faith polytheism, God would forgive them for all they did, and he showed it in numerous examples by rewarding his most cruel and deceitful warriors with booty, women, and slaves.

One might also question the figures such as, for example, the twelve thousand men who allegedly participated in Muhammad's battles around Mecca, and ask how the early historians arrived at these figures: These historians used to collect reports from as many witnesses as possible, and then compare them with figures taken from reports such as:

> There are none like those who came to join
> And forge an inseparable bond with Muhammad.
> Deputations from the tribes Abu Qatan, Huzaba,
> And Abu'l Ghuyuth and Wasi' and al Miqna
> And the hundred added to nine hundred there;
> The Banu Awf and the Mukhashin brought six hundred
> And Khufaf brought four hundred;
> When our thousand helped the prophet,
> He handed us a fluttering flag.
> We drove off Hawazin that day with spears
> When even the messenger feared their bravery.
> We fought and, but for us, their bravery
> Would have injured the believers
> And they would have gained an upper hand.[410]

Another question arises; why the non-Quraysh, such as the Ansar, fought for the supremacy of the Quraysh? The events quoted in the following pages demonstrate that these mainly fought for booty other than for their devotion to Muhammad. This is also evident from the Qur'anic verses which repeatedly enunciate the rules for the distribution of booty and lure men with promises of booty to encourage them to participate in the raids.

Other than the Qur'an, the poetry of the times also states the same. For example, Abbas bin Mirdas boasted about gaining booty in his following verses:

> In God's guidance, you smite the wicked with every right.
> I swore a true oath to Muhammad,
> And left Hunayn's waterways streaming with blood.
> By God's command, we smote those we met.
> The Hawazin tried to escape on their beasts
> Loaded with their property they tried to save from us.[411]

One of the retreating Hawazin poets answered this boasting by taunting the "believer" mercenaries:

> You boast like a maid who struts in self-importance
> Wearing her mistress's hijab (female face cover)
> While below the waist, her body is naked.[412]

Each temple had a store of donations. Many reports and verses make it clear that these temples were targeted for their stores of donations. For example:

> Until the straight religion is established,
> And the idols, Laat and Uzz'a and Wudd are forgotten
> We plunder them for their necklaces and earrings.
> Do not help Laat, for God is about to destroy her
> The idols cannot help themselves
> Laat was burned in smoke and caught fire.
> When the messenger will descend on your land
> None of your people will be left there when he leaves.[413]

The main reasons compelling many to join Muhammad, as either believers or unbeliever allies, are traceable in the breakup of the regular economic activity in Mecca because of his raids and the ensuing disruption of trade and agriculture. In Mecca, he had around twelve thousand men with him who had given up on productive economic activity. In particular, the Ansar of Medina were newcomers to Mecca, and they lived off the looted cattle and property of the locals. Prayers and fasting alone could not put food in their bellies. Hence, on the pretext of dismantling of idols and spreading of Islam, these survived on the plunder of local tribes.

Many local people had to join in the plunder because they were starving. The evidence, which illustrates this, appears in numerous reports written in semi-poetic form as a matter of tradition (such as the Qur'an itself is in semi-poetic form), including the following:

> Mijdal, Mutali and Arik are deserted by its people
> And their cisterns are empty.
> We had homes, O Juml, when life was pleasant,
> But the turn of events has swallowed our tribe
> Poverty in alien lands has devastated us.
> Now far off is the home of her you long for
> And hostile tribes stand in the way.
> Talk no more of the days of youth
> Youth is gone and white locks have appeared.[414]

> When she saw her man whom the fierce heat of a torrid land
> Had left with blackened face and fleshless bones,
> You could see his leanness at the end of the night,
> As he was clad in his mail ready for a raid.
> I am always in the saddle of a thick short-haired mare,
> One day in quest of booty,
> Another, fighting along with the Ansar.
> How much fertile land have I travelled
> How much rough uneven ground at gentle pace
> That I might change her state of poverty,
> And she did not want me to return![415]

> They followed the messenger's religion
> While human affairs were disorderly
> They do not plant young palms in their fields
> And cows do not mow in their winter quarters
> But colts like eagles are kept in their courtyards
> Surrounded by multitudes of camels
> Their tribesmen wait for summons, armed and keen to fight.[416]

There is more than enough evidence to demonstrate that Muhammad's disdain for agriculture and peaceful production, coupled with his love for war and gathering the resources of war, had created a society in which thousands were forced to live on plunder and enslavement of the others.

Muhammad's tribal wars to enable his largely "unbeliever" Quraysh tribe to rule all Arabs

Muhammad's alliance with the "unbeliever" Quraysh betrays the propagandist assertion that he fought against the "unbelievers" to uphold monotheism. In fact, particularly after the conquest of Mecca, his wars were purely tribal wars fought to help his largely unbeliever tribe and its largely unbeliever allies to conquer other tribes living around Mecca. That is why his twelve thousand men comprised both believers and unbelievers. This also explains why he and his jihadis entered Mecca without a fight, and the Quraysh joined them to attack their rival tribes, particularly the Hawazin, the Thaqif, and those in Ta'if around Mecca. The evidence showing that the Quraysh joined him only to conquer and plunder their rival tribes is overwhelming. For example, see the following verses of a Hawazin poet:

> Do you not know that Quraysh have conquered Hawazin?
> O Quraysh, there was a time when we (*the Hawazin*),
> If we were furious, blood flowed because of our fury
> But now the Quraysh drive us like camels and peasants taunt us.

Those who were at the helm of affairs along with Muhammad, uncle Abbas, father-in-law Abu Sufyan, sons-in-law Ali and Uthman, fathers-in-law Umar and Abu Bakr, Khalid bin Walid etc. were all from the Quraysh tribes. The elite rulers related to each other through blood and kinship – not through piety or religious observance as the propagandists claim.

The "law of revenge" among the believers

The retreating Thaqif, who had bravely fought alongside the Hawazin, escaped to their relative tribes in Ta'if and closed the gates of the town. Muhammad decided to attack the people of Ta'if who had, since long before him, resisted the Quraysh attempts to gain regional supremacy. To fulfil his promise to the Quraysh that he would lead them to rule the entire region, he led his jihadis, and travelled through many settlements around Ta'if.

On his way, a mosque was hastily built and he prayed in it. Then he issued the law of retaliation for homicide among believers, for the following reasons: Until this time, Muhammadan law stated that a believer could not be killed in revenge, even if he had killed a believer. This was because Muhammad did not want to reduce the number of his jihadis but while he was more interested in making people submit to his rule, and thus raising a regular basis of taxation, his jihadis were more interested in acquiring quick booty and so they looted and killed believers as well. Muhammad did not like this, and now that he had too large a following to worry about reducing numbers, he ordered, `If a believer kills a believer, revenge will be due.' To show that he was serious about it, he brought this law into immediate effect: A believer of the Banu Layth had killed a believer of the Hudhayl tribe and Muhammad had the killer executed.[417]

The passing of the law of revenge among believers was prompted by an event that had taken place after the battle of Hunayn. Muhammad had sent a party of believers led by Abu Hadrad to Idam to coerce the locals to submit to him. Among the party was a man of the Khindif tribe, Muhallim bin Jaththama, whose sole purpose in joining the group was to seek booty. When the raiding party was in the valley of Idam, a man of the Ghatfan tribe, named Amir al Ashja'i, appeared on a camel with his belongings. As he passed by them, he greeted them as a believer would but Muhallim bin Jaththama killed him and took his camel and provisions.

The chiefs of the two tribes, al Aqra bin Habis of the Khindif and Uyayna bin Hisn of the Ghatfan, went up to Muhammad and quarrelled about the murder. The Ghatfan chief demanded vengeance for the blood of Amir while the Khindif tried to protect the killer, Muhallim, because of his tribal position among them. The dispute went on for a long time in front of Muhammad and Uyayna said, `O messenger, I would not let this killer go but I will make his women suffer the same grief which he made my women suffer.'

As he had done with Khalid bin Walid in a similar situation, Muhammad did not want to tie the hands of his assassins by setting examples of being tough on them. Hence, at first, he tried to brush off the issue with a mild "divine revelation:"

O ye who believe,
When you strike in the way of God
Investigate carefully:

If someone says to you, 'Peace be upon you'
Do not say, 'You are not a believer,'
Coveting his goods and property
God has plenty of booty for you.
You too were like them (*unbelievers*) before God helped you
Therefore, investigate carefully
For God knows all that you do. (Sura 4, verse 94)

But Uyayna would not give up without revenge. Muhammad did not want to lose the support of the Ghatfan, and therefore, to please Uyayna, he said, 'Accept fifty camels as blood-money on this journey and fifty more when we return from Ta'if,' which shows that he aimed to rob the people of Ta'if. Uyayna kept refusing the offer and a man of the Banu Layth, whose name was Mukaythir, supported him by telling Muhammad that the said murder had dissuaded people from submitting to Islam because, even after surrendering, they were killed. He said, 'O messenger, I can compare this murder, in these early days of Islam, with sheep that were coming with their leaders; the first was shot and the ones behind ran away. Let the Law of Blood stand today and leave blood-money for future events like this.'

Muhammad raised his hand and said, 'No, you must take fifty camels as blood-money on this expedition and fifty more when we return from Ta'if.'

The Khindif chief, al Aqra, then called the Ghatfan to a private meeting and blackmailed them by saying, 'You have opposed the messenger's decision about a dead man. Are you sure that the messenger will not curse you so that God too will curse you? I swear that if you do not accept the blood-money I will bring fifty men of the Banu Tamim who will call God to witness that your slain friend was an unbeliever who never prayed at all, and thus his blood will be disregarded.'

When the Ghatfan heard this, they thought that they would lose their hundred camels, and so they agreed to accept the blood money. In response, Muhammad pleased them by praying three times, 'O God! Do not forgive Muhallim.' Then he reprimanded Muhallim, 'You gave Amir security in God's name and then you killed him.'

Muhallim mysteriously died within a week and, when he was buried, his corpse was found the next day out of his grave. They buried him again but, again, someone dug him out. When it happened three times, people buried him far away and rolled rocks on his grave. When Muhammad heard about this he said, 'The earth has covered worse than him but God wants to give you a warning about what you must not do.'[418]

The raid on Ta'if

On his way to Ta'if, Muhammad passed by the abandoned fort of Malik bin Awf (the defeated Hawazin chief) and had it demolished. Then he passed by the property of a man of the Thaqif and sent him a message, 'Vacate this place or we will destroy your oasis.' The man refused to vacate his land and Muhammad had his oasis destroyed so that the people of Ta'if could not benefit from it.

He continued until he was near Ta'if and pitched his camp there, along with two tents for his wives who were with him. But he had placed the camp too close to the walls of Ta'if and the arrows shot by the people of Ta'if killed many of his jihadis. They could not break the walls or the gate because of this. Muhammad retreated, pitched his camp at a distance, and besieged Ta'if for some twenty days. Some of his men went under a testudo and tried to break the wall but, under cover of the arrows, some Thaqif men came out and pierced the testudo with rods of hot iron, which forced the jihadis to come out of the testudo. The Thaqif shot them with arrows and killed many more.

During the siege, some slaves from Ta'if found the opportunity to win freedom from their masters: They ran out to Muhammad and joined his ranks.

The Thaqif had seized the family of their traitor tribesman Marwan bin Qays because he had been helping Muhammad. Muhammad said to Marwan, 'In revenge for your family, seize the first man of your tribe that you meet.' Marwan seized a Thaqif man whose name was Ubayy bin Malik and held on to him until the Thaqif released his family. In response, Marwan released Ubayy and sent him back. A poet described Ubayy's arrest and release as follows:

O Ubayy, will you forget the kindness I showed you
On the day when Marwan tied you with a rope
And dragged you along?
You were as submissive as a well-trained beast,

And the messenger looked the other way.
The Thaqif came to get you released
When you had almost lost hope.[419]

Insider traitors used to raid their own tribes

In order to understand why a man would turn traitor to his own tribe and join Muhammad, the Islamists offer the explanation that Islam was a powerful religion and it changed people's hearts (i.e. turned them against their own tribes). However, there are two very significant reasons for which some men joined Muhammad against their own tribes: Firstly, a number of these were already either lone bandits or allied to small groups of bandits who had lost their tribe's protection. For example, Rafi' bin Abu Rafi' Ta'iy was a lone camel thief. He used to bury water in ostrich shells in various places in the desert. When he had driven the stolen camels in the desert, none dared to follow him because of fear of lack of water in the desert, while Rafi' had access to the water he had already stored. When Rafi' came to join Muhammad, the latter sent him to raid Dhatu'l Salasil under the leadership of Amru bin al 'As and Abu Bakr.[420]

Secondly, these men were underprivileged in their tribes and, hence, they had lost a sense of belonging to their tribe. Similar to what Muhammad had done, having failed to make it within their tribe, these would turn against it and join others to raid it. Again, like Muhammad, they bore grudges against the chiefs and well-off members of their tribes and, having once been insiders, had the best knowledge of their strengths and weaknesses. Muhammad would make maximum use of their knowledge and, when the target tribe had surrendered, he would appoint them to collect taxes from their people. Having been in a similar situation in the past, Muhammad could easily empathize with these men.

The siege of Ta'if

Muhammad's newer associates, the "unbeliever" former chiefs of Mecca, Abu Sufyan bin Harb and al Mughira bin Shu'ba, were related to many of those besieged inside the walls of Ta'if. The two men asked the besieged Thaqif to provide them security so that they could negotiate. The Thaqif agreed to talk but the two chiefs were afraid that if they went inside for negotiations, the

Thaqif would arrest them. To obtain more security, they called on their relative women of the Quraysh and the Banu Kinana, who were married to men in Ta'if, to come out of the walls and be their shields but the women refused to come out and the negotiations could not take place.

Having failed in both ways – breaking the walls or entering Ta'if through negotiations – Muhammad decided to adopt a long-term strategy to bring Ta'if to its knees. He decided to destroy the economy of Ta'if so that, once impoverished like his earlier victims, the tribes of Ta'if would have no choice but to join Muhammad in the plunder of the others. He ordered the destruction of the vineyards of Ta'if and so his men fell upon the vineyards. A recent convert-traitor, Ibn al Aswad bin Mas'ud, gave a suggestion. He said, `O messenger! My father and his brothers in Ta'if own these vineyards. There is no property more laborious to water, harder to cultivate, and more difficult to maintain than this one. If you cut down its trees, it will never be cultivated again. It is better that you take this property for yourself or leave it to your kinsmen.' Muhammad gave the property to Ibn al Aswad on promise that he would use its resources to keep raiding Ta'if – a strategy that, in time, would force Ibn al Aswad's father to submit to Muhammad.

When Muhammad became certain that he would not be able to conquer Ta'if at that point of time, and it was becoming harder to feed his jihadis on siege while he had a large store of looted livestock back at al Ji'rana, he decided to return to al Ji'rana. He used his mystic way of conveying his feelings by saying to Abu Bakr, `I dreamt that I was given a bowl of butter and a cock pecked at it and spilt it.' Abu Bakr understood that Muhammad wanted to lift the siege and so he said, `I think that you will not win from them today.'

At that moment, some women of Muhammad's closest associates came in and said, `O messenger of God, when God will give you victory over Ta'if, give us the jewellery of Badiya bint Ghaylan and al Fari'a bint Aqil, for these two have the best jewellery among the Thaqif women.' Muhammad said, `What if God does not grant me the Thaqif?' The disappointed women left and told Umar about what Muhammad had said. Umar rushed in and asked Muhammad if he had really said that. Muhammad confirmed that he had, and gave orders to dislodge the camp.

When the jihadis were retreating, the Ghatfan chief Uyayna bin Hisn said, `The Thaqif have held ground nobly and gloriously.' One of the believers cursed him, `God smite you, Uyayna! How come you praise the unbelievers for standing against the messenger when you have come to help the messenger?'

`I did not come to fight the Thaqif' Uyayna answered, `but I wanted Muhammad to conquer Ta'if so that I might grab a Thaqif girl whom I might tread (make pregnant) and she could bear me a son, for the Thaqif are known to produce clever children.'

Muhammad left Ta'if and stopped at al Ji'rana where, earlier, he had the captives of Hawazin locked up and their cattle and property stored. He was impressed with the defence that the people of Ta'if had put up and desired them to join forces with him. Hence, when his followers asked him to curse them, he prayed, `O God! Enable them to become believers.' However, he was not going to leave the conversion of the people of Ta'if solely in God's hands. He hatched another scheme as follows.

In order to split the people of Ta'if and win their best fighters to his side, he announced that if Malik bin Awf, the Hawazin chief now hiding in Ta'if, would come to him as a believer he would release his captive family, return his property to him, and give him a hundred camels. On hearing this, Malik quickly changed sides and secretly came out of Ta'if. Muhammad released his family, returned his property, and gave him a hundred camels. Then he put him in command of the tribes around Ta'if, with instructions to fight the Thaqif with the help of these tribes. Because of Malik's raids, none of the Ta'if flocks could come out of the town and this put the people of Ta'if in utter misery.[421] In raiding his former allies, Malik had lost his integrity but he now had the guilt-suppressing belief of being on God's side, plus the satisfaction of having his family and property back, not to mention a hundred camels.

The distribution of the booty from Hawazin and coercing people to become believers

As mentioned earlier, the captives from Hawazin were around six thousand women and children, and a very large number of sheep and camels. The escaped men of Hawazin, having heard about the return of family and property to Malik bin Awf, sent a deputation to Muhammad in al Ji'rana. These men wanted to surrender in exchange for the release of their women and children. They asked Muhammad to have pity on them for God's sake.

One of these men, Zuhayr abu Surad of the Banu Sa'ad bin Bakr – the tribe of Muhammad's foster mother Halima – pleaded, `O messenger of God, in the enclosures are your paternal and maternal aunts and the women who fed you and looked after you when you were a child. Had we been foster parents of your great ancestors, and fallen into this position in which you hold us now, we could hope for kindness and favour, and you are the most trustworthy man. Messenger of God, have pity on a people whom fate has frustrated and misfortune has shattered their lives.'

Muhammad knew that while in the past he could enslave and sell women and children of his non-relative tribes around Medina, he could not do the same in Mecca. The Quraysh had been marrying within the tribes around Mecca, and selling relatives, however distant, was totally against Arab values. He knew he would have to release the Hawazin women and children but he was in no mood to return the camels and cattle because he had a large number of allies waiting for the booty. Accordingly, he said to the Hawazin delegates, `Which of the two are dearest to you; your families or your cattle?' As expected, the delegates replied, `Do you give us choice between honour and cattle? Give us back our families for that is what we most desire.' But then another bizarre situation arose: Using their past training and experience of raids around Medina, the jihadis had already distributed many women and children amongst themselves. In addition, before raiding the Hawazin, to motivate his jihadis, Muhammad had allowed them to have sexual intercourse with the captive women under the previously mentioned law of "mut'a" (short-term marriage). It was not easy to have these women back.

Muhammad said to the delegates, `You can have those women and children back who were taken by my closest kin, the descendants of Abd al Muttalib, and me. About the rest, come to the mosque and, when I have prayed the noon prayer with my men, stand up and say, "We plead for the messenger's intercession with the believers, and the believers' intercession with the messenger for our children and our wives." I will then give you back my share of the women and children, and ask the believers to return your women and children.'

The Hawazin delegates did as Muhammad had instructed, and he said what he had promised to say. Then the Muhajirin and the Ansar stood up and said that they would return the women and children in their possession, but many other tribes refused to return the captives. To these tribes, Muhammad offered six camels from the booty for releasing each human captive. Thus, many women and children were returned to their men but for many captives there was no one to take them back because their men had died at the battle. From these, Muhammad gave a girl named Rayta bint Hilal to Ali, and another girl named Zaynab bint Hayyan to Uthman. He also gave a girl to Umar but Umar gave her to his son Abdallah who was a noble man and when her distant relatives came looking for her, he returned her.

The aforementioned Uyayna bin Hisn, who was disappointed at not getting a girl from Ta'if, was not eager to return his captive. He had taken an old woman of Hawazin, thinking that she was a person of high status in her tribe and her ransom would be high. When Muhammad called for the return of the captives at a price of six camels each, Uyayna refused to give the old woman back thinking she was worth more than six camels. Zuhayr abu Surad told Uyayna that six camels was a good price for the old woman because, as he said, her mouth was cold and her breasts flat; she could not conceive and her husband would not care to pay the ransom. Uyayna agreed and let her go for the six camels. Then Uyayna complained to al Aqra bin Habis about the low price paid for her and the latter said, `By God, you did not take her as a virgin in her prime years or even as a chubby middle aged!'[422]

About those who, by surrendering, sought the return of their confiscated lands, Abbas bin Mirdas said:

> Their fields and houses would have been divided,
> But for the right advice they were given.
> If they are guided to submit, they will become
> Leaders of men while time lasts.
> If they do not submit, we'll call for God's war
> In which they will have no helper.

About the resentment felt by those forced to submit, he said:

> Like a flock of sleep they had come, bleating, to surrender
> We said, 'Submit; we are your brethren,
> And our breasts are free from enmity.'
> But when they came to us they seemed
> Blind with hatred after peace had come.[423]

The above quoted events and verses reveal that people became believers mostly under coercion such as the threat of sword, or because their women and children had been captured, or they had no choice left. But the Islamists propagate that people "embraced Islam" because it was a better religion. The Qur'anic verses and those of Muhammad's own poets make it abundantly clear that fear of death and destruction was the primary reason for which the majority in Mecca uttered that he was the messenger of God. For example, see the following verses:

> Till you turn to submission and beg forgiveness
> And humbly seek protection,
> We will fight you with swords, not caring whom we fight,
> And whether we destroy ancient assets or new wealth.
> Many tribes of best races have allied with us
> If they think we are inferior, we will cut off their noses and ears
> With our polished Indian swords,
> And tie them and drive them to God and submission
> And those who do not stop from idolatry
> Will have to accept defeat.[424]

Muhammad gave generous gifts, though from the booty, to his newly allied chiefs of the following tribes: the Umayya, Abd al Dar, Makhzum, Adiy, Jumah, Sahm, Amir, Bakr, Kalab, Nasr, Sulaym, Ghatfan, and Tamim, among others. He gave hundred camels each to Abu Sufyan, his son Mu'awiya, Hakim bin Hazam, Harith bin Kilda of the Abd al Dar, Harith bin Hisham, Suhayl bin Amru, Huwaytib bin Abd al Uzz'a, Safwan bin Umayya, al Ala' Thaqafi – an ally of the Banu Zahra – Uyayna bin Hisn, al Aqra bin Habis, and Malik bin Awf, among others. He gave less than hundred camels each to the following Quraysh: Makhrama al Zuhri, Umayr Jumahi, Sa'id bin Yarbu, al Sahmi, and Hisham bin Amr of the Banu Amir bin Lu'ayy.[425] When he gave very few camels to his poet Abbas bin Mirdas, the latter felt jealous of Uyayna and al Aqra, and protested in his verses as follows:

> The booty I gained, when I charged on my horse,
> And kept the people awake lest they should sleep,
> And when they slept I kept watch,
> My share and that of Ubayd – my horse,
> Was handed over to Uyayna and al Aqra.

> Though I defended my people and risked myself,
> I was given only a few small camels
> Numbered by their four legs!

The verse, "my share and that of my horse," needs explanation: Because horsemen needed more resources than others, Muhammad had made a rule that a horse would have a share given to its owner.

Having listened to the poet's complaint, Muhammad said, `Take him away and cut off his tongue,' which meant, "Give him more to shut him up," and so they gave him some more camels.[426]

Another man complained to Muhammad, `You have given the unbelievers, Uyayna and al Aqra, a hundred camels each and left out the faithful Ju'ayl al Damri.' Muhammad answered, `By Him in whose hand is my soul, Ju'ayl is better than the whole world full of men like those two but I have treated those two generously so that they may become believers, and I have entrusted Ju'ayl to his faith.'

Another disgruntled man stood up and said, `Muhammad! I've seen what you have done today and I think you have been unjust.' Muhammad was furious and said, `If justice is not to be found with me then where will you find it?' The aggressive Umar, as usual, asked to be allowed to kill the objector but Muhammad said, `Leave him alone, for he may have committed followers.'

Muhammad had promised to give six camels for each captive to be released and thus secured the release of many women and children of the Hawazin. However, he had distributed the looted camels among more than forty most influential tribal chiefs and leaders of the jihadis, and kept a large number of cattle for himself to take to Medina with his men. Hence, he was unable to give six camels each to the commoners who had released their captives. Upon finding that he would not be able to fulfil his promise, he tried to ride away, but a large number of commoners followed him demanding that he gave them their share of the camels. These men were furious at his pandering to his tribal relatives and the already rich tribal chiefs at the cost of depriving the poor jihadis of a share. They forced him back against a tree and tore off his cloak. He shouted, `Give me back my cloak, men, for by God if I had anything I would distribute it among you; you have not found me mean or cowardly or false.' Then he decided to counterattack by accusing these men of stealing from the booty, and frighten them. He went to his camel, plucked a hair from its hump and held it in his fingers, saying, `Men, I have nothing but a fifth of the booty even to this hair, and this fifth is spent on your upkeep. So give back even the needle and the thread that you have stolen from the booty, for dishonesty will be a shame and the dishonest will be burned in hell on the resurrection day.' A disgruntled Ansari came with a ball of camel hair, saying, `O messenger, I took this thread ball to make a pad for my sore camel.' Muhammad told him to keep it but the man threw the ball away.

Muhammad gave little from the booty to the Ansar though these had been the major force behind his victories. He knew that in Mecca these had little knowledge of the local political situation and the least strength without him. They had no choice but to trust his judgement and so he ignored them whilst showering the Meccan chiefs with shares from the booty. The Ansar took the matter to heart and vented out their frustration. One of them said, `By God, since he came to Mecca, the messenger has been favouring only his kith and kin.'[427]

Hearing about the Ansar's frustration, Muhammad called their leader Sa'ad bin Ubaada, and told him to gather his people in an enclosure. Once they all gathered, he delivered a sermon, which shows his immense ability to manipulate people. He said, `O Ansar, what is this I hear of you? Do you think ill of me in your hearts? Did I not come to you when you were erring and God guided you? Were you not poor and God made you rich? Were you not enemies to each other and God softened your hearts?'

The Ansar were too embarrassed to speak out. Diplomatically, they said, `Yes indeed, God and His messenger are most kind and generous.' Muhammad wanted them to vent out their frustrations to the full, and so he said, `Why do not you answer me, O Ansar?' The Ansar insisted, `How should we answer you? Kindness and generosity belong to God and you – His messenger.'

Sensing the Ansar's hesitation, Muhammad began to speak on their behalf, as their advocate, `Had you so wished you could have said, and you would have spoken the truth and had been believed: "Muhammad! You came to us discredited and we believed you: You came to us deserted and we helped you: You came to us a fugitive and we took you in: You came to us poor and we comforted you." Are you disturbed because of the good things of this life by which I win over a people that they may become believers while I entrust you to your faith in me? Are you not satisfied that other men should take away flocks and herds while you take back with you the messenger of God? By Him in whose hand is the soul of Muhammad, but for the migration I would be one of the Ansar myself. If all men went one way and the Ansar another, I will follow the Ansar. O God! Have mercy on the Ansar, their sons, and the sons of their sons.'

The Ansar wept until tears rolled down their beards as they said, `We are satisfied with the messenger of God as our lot and portion.'[428]

Having thus satisfied the Ansar, Muhammad planned to return with them to Medina, taking with him the rest of the spoils to fund the journey. He left Attab bin Asid in Mecca, aided by Mu'adh bin Jabal, to instruct the people in religion and the Qur'an.

The Ka'ba was still a joint place of worship where unbelievers prayed in the traditional way while believers prayed in a slightly differentiated manner. The secular culture of Mecca was not dead yet and the Truce of Hudaybiya was still valid. As for Muhammad, he cleverly returned to Medina because he knew that the chaos he had created in Mecca would need time to turn into some kind of stability. People whom he had made to kill and rob each other would be taking revenge for some time to come and he did not want to be there to take the blame for not being able to pick up the pieces.

Continual persecution, buying traitors, and harassing the critics

The people of Ta'if kept their old religion but their days were numbered because, from Medina, Muhammad launched a terror campaign against them. In Arabia, in those days, poets played a major role (as do writers and media in modern times) in offering emotional support to people in choosing one or the other faith, and in fomenting trouble. The people of Ta'if had a great poet, named Ka'ab, whose poetry was a major moral force behind their religion. When Ka'ab's brother joined Muhammad, Ka'ab addressed him in his verses:

> Give my brother a message from me:
> For what reason has he (*Muhammad*) led you
> To a religion his (*Muhammad's*) fathers never held
> And your father never followed?
> Al Ma'mun (*Muhammad*) has filled your cup,

And made you drink again and again
May God forgive you for your error.

Note the notion in the last verse, that submitting to Muhammad was an error for which one needed God's forgiveness. Ka'ab had said in the 7th century what one cannot say in the 21st century without fear of being assassinated by the Islamists. In 2006, the Islamists forced even Pope Benedict to apologize for quoting the following: "Show me what Muhammad brought that was new and there you will find things only evil and inhuman such as his command to spread by sword the faith he preached." This passage was from "Dialogue Held with a Certain Persian, the Worthy Mouterizes, in Anakara of Galatia," written in 1391 as an expression of the views of the Byzantine emperor Manuel II Paleologus.

Offended by the above quoted poem, Muhammad ordered his men to assassinate Ka'ab. Ka'ab's brother sent a letter to him in which he wrote that Muhammad had had many critics killed in Mecca; the surviving unbeliever poets, Ibn al Ziba'ra and Hubayra bin abu Wahb had fled from Mecca. He wrote, `If you want to stay alive, come quickly to the messenger, for he does not kill those who come to him in repentance. If you cannot do that, then escape to some safe place.'

When Ka'ab received the message, he was terrified. People in Ta'if began to say that he was already dead. Finding no way out of fear, he composed an ode praising Muhammad, arrived in Medina, and begged forgiveness. Muhammad forgave him, listened to his love poems while sitting in his mosque, and greatly appreciated them. To the modern devout Muslim, this would be incredible because they believe that Islam forbids the composing of love poems. They could argue that these must be religious verses but when one reads them one can hardly call them religious:

> Su'ad is gone, and my heart is lovesick.
> Su'ad, when she came to say farewell,
> On the morn of my departure,
> Was like a gazelle with bright black, downcast eyes.
> When she smiles, you see her shining pearl-like teeth
> They seem to have bathed in a fragrant wine.
> She has a stuck-in belly and a lean chest,
> But from the back, you see a thickset bum
> You cannot say if she is short or tall.[429]

Muhammad maligns the Christians, as a pretext to raid their settlements on route to Damascus, and punishes the pacifists

The largely Zoroastrian Persians controlled regions now known as Iraq and Iran, among others. Initially, the Arabs directed their attacks on them at Qadisiya and Nehavend but only after Muhammad's death. In his lifetime, the Arabs directed their attacks on the Byzantine outposts at Yarmuk and Tabuk. The Christian Byzantines controlled regions now known as Turkey, Syria, Palestine, Jordan, and Egypt, among others. From Medina, Muhammad began attacking Christian settlements on route to Damascus.

Although we still find Arab Christian communities in some areas of Iraq, Egypt, Syria, Lebanon, and Palestine, it is rare to find a Jewish or Zoroastrian community in the now Muslim Middle East. Over the centuries of Muslim onslaughts, these either gradually fled to India and Europe, or joined one or the other among various sects of Islam.

The Christians of the Middle East differed among themselves in some points. Some said that Jesus was God; some said that he was the son of God; and some said that he was the third person of the Trinity with God and Mary. He was God because he used to raise the dead, heal the sick, tell about the unseen, make clay birds and then breathe into them so that they flew away. Against this belief, Muhammad had issued verses claiming that these miracles happened by the command of God, and Jesus himself was not God (see Sura 19: Mariam). The other Christians believed that Jesus was the son of God because he had no known father, and he spoke in the cradle and this is something that no child of Adam had ever done. Those who believed that Jesus was the third of the three sought evidence in that God says: "We have done, We have commanded, We have created and We have decreed," and they argued that if God were one he would have said, "I have done, I have created," and so on, but "We" referred to God, Jesus, and Mary. Concerning all these assertions, Muhammad issued hundreds of verses that one finds in Sura 3 and Sura 19, among others.

The Christians had often saved themselves from Muhammad's raids by pre-emptively submitting to his rule, exemplified by the following record. Sixty riders of the Christians of Najran came to Medina to submit and agree to pay taxes. Among them were fourteen of their nobles of whom three were in charge of the affairs; Abd al Maseeh (meaning the slave of Jesus) was their leader and chief whose opinion governed their policy; al Ayham was their administrator who saw to transport and general arrangements; and Abu Haritha bin Alqama was their bishop and scholar who controlled their schools. The Christian kings of Byzantium had honoured him, paid him a subsidy and given him servants, built churches for him and lavished honours on him because of his knowledge and zeal for Christianity.

The delegates came in their best dresses and the believers who saw them that day said that they never saw their like in any deputation that came afterwards. To match the status of these Christians, Muhammad too dressed up in elegant Yamani garments, cloaks, and mantles. When the time of their prayers came, they stood to pray in the mosque facing east towards Jerusalem in accordance with their faith, and Muhammad allowed them to do so.

When the two senior delegates spoke to him, Muhammad said to them, `Submit yourselves (*sal'lim*).' They said, `We have submitted.'

He said, `You have not submitted, so submit.' They said, `But we submitted before you.' By *sal'lim* Muhammad meant that they should become believers (*ma sal'lim*) while they took the literal meaning of the word which meant submitting to Muhammad's rule.

Muhammad said, `You lie. You call Jesus the son of God, you worship the Crucifix, you eat pork, and these are the things that hold you back from submission.' They said, `Muhammad, if not God then who is Jesus's father?'

Muhammad used their own arguments against them in reference to God to show them their error. For example, they believed that God has no associates in His authority and so there cannot be a Trinity; God cannot die whereas Jesus died and was crucified according to their doctrine; God is ever existent which means that He remains unceasingly in the place of His sovereignty whereas Jesus remained in Mary's womb for nine months. He claimed that he knew the things about which they differed, and he warned them, `Those who disbelieve in God's signs (i.e. Muhammad's verses) will have a severe punishment. God is Mighty, Vengeful, and He will take vengeance on all who deny

His signs after knowing about them and about what comes from Him in them. Nothing in heaven or earth is hidden from God,' i.e. God knew what they schemed when they made Jesus God and Lord knowing that Jesus was just a prophet, thus behaving with insolence and infidelity. Then he read his verses, `He it is who forms you in the womb as He pleases,' i.e. Jesus was one who was formed in the womb like every other child of Adam, so how could he be God when he had occupied such a place?

Speaking on behalf of God, Muhammad recited his verses, `I (God) gave Jesus power over those matters about which they say that he is God such as raising the dead, healing the sick, creating birds of clay, and telling the unseen. But some of My majesty and power I withheld from him such as appointing kings by a command where I wish, making the night to pass into day and the day into night and bringing forth the living from the dead and the dead from the living – all this I withheld from Jesus and gave him no power over it. Have they not a clear proof that if he were God, all that would be within his power, while they know that he fled from kings and because of them he moved about the country from town to town.'

Then he admonished and warned them and said, `If you love God, then follow me, God will love you and forgive your sins,' i.e. their past unbelief. `And God is Forgiving Merciful. Say: Obey God and His apostle,' for you know me and find me mentioned in your book. `But if you turn back, God does not love the unbelievers.'

To impress the Christians, Muhammad narrated whole biblical tales, with his own distortions, twists and turns, starting from Adam and moving on to Noah, Zachariah, Marry and Jesus, claiming that Jesus did not die on the cross but God lifted him up to the heavens, and ended his tales with these verses:

> Jesus was an apostle to the Israelites, and he said:
> I have come to you with signs from your God
> I make for you out of clay the figure of a bird,
> I breathe into it, and it becomes a bird by God's will
> And I heal those born blind, and the lepers,
> And I bring the dead back to life by God's will
> And I guide you in what to eat and what to store in your houses
> Surely therein is a sign for you if you believe
> I attest the Law that was before me
> And make lawful to you part of what was forbidden to you

I have come to you with a sign from your Lord
So fear God, and obey me.
When Jesus found unbelief on their part, he said
`Who will be my helpers to work for God?'
The disciples said, `We are God's helpers: We believe in God,
And bear witness that we have submitted
(*The unbelievers decided to kill Jesus and God lifted him to the heavens*)
And they plotted and God plotted, and God is the best plotter
Behold! God said, `O Jesus! I am going to cause you to die
And raise you to myself and purify you of the unbelievers
I will make your followers superior to those who reject faith
Till the Day of Resurrection, then all shall return to me,
And I will judge between you in matters in which you dispute
As to those who reject faith, I will punish them with terrible agony
In this world and in the next. (Sura 3, verses 49-56)

Muhammad did not give the Christians a chance to speak. If he had, their Bishop Alqama could point out that because God was omnipotent, He could easily come down to earth in human form for a few years and then die as a human. Either they were too scared for their lives because they were in his territory or he did not allow them to argue. Instead, he invited them to accept his apostolate or join him in a *"mubahala"* – a competition of curses in which both groups gather, along with their families, and jointly invoke God's curse upon the liars. He said, `To test if I am a true messenger or if you are true in denying me, bring your women and children and we shall bring ours. Then collectively we shall pray to God to send His curse upon those who are lying.' He even wrote this down in his "divine verses" as a command from God, with disguised death threats, as follows:

If any one disputes in this matter with you,
After full knowledge has come to you,
(*i.e. Jesus was not the son of God and Muhammad is God's messenger*)
Then say: Come! Let us summon our sons and your sons,
Our women and your women, ourselves and yourselves
And earnestly pray and invoke God's curse upon the liars!
This is the true account: There is no God except Allah.

But if they turn back (*from faith in Muhammad*)
Allah has full knowledge of those committed to sedition.
(Sura 3, verse 61-63)

The Christians addressed Muhammad by the endearing term "Abu'l Qasim" (the father of Qasim) and said, `O Abu'l Qasim, let us consult among ourselves; then we will come to you with our decision.'

They left him and consulted with Abd al Maseeh who was their chief and adviser, and asked him what his opinion was. Abd al Maseeh was one of those few who understood Muhammad's method of fulfilling his prophesies. He could see that if his people entered into such a competition, Muhammad's men would kill them and then spread word that their deaths were a curse from God. He said, `You know right well that Muhammad is adamant that he is a prophet and he has brought a decisive declaration about the nature of Jesus. You know too that those who ever invoked a curse on him have not seen their elders live and their young grow. If you do this, his men will exterminate you. But if you decide to adhere to Christianity and to maintain your doctrine about Jesus, then beg leave of this man and go home.'

They agreed with Abd al Maseeh, and he said to Muhammad, `We do not consider it appropriate to challenge you in a competition of curses. We want to return to our land but we would like you to send a man to collect taxes from us.' Umar was eager to be the governor of these well-off Christians but Muhammad appointed Abu Ubayda al Jarrah to govern them and collect taxes from them.[430]

Until this time, Muhammad had shown some respect for Christians probably because he had obtained his early education from scholars of the Bible such a Qis bin Sa'ada, Waraqa bin Noufal and Jabr, the Christian slave of the Banu Hadrami. Khadija's Christian relatives had also helped him in times of difficulty. He did not want the aggressive Umar to roughly treat the Christians of Najran, turn them into his slaves, or gradually expropriate their properties. He was correct in his judgement of Umar because, after his death, Umar expelled the remaining Jews from Medina and surrounding regions even though Muhammad had allowed them to stay as his serfs.

XXX

Muhammad directed his raids at the Byzantine Christians. He had heard that wars between the Byzantine and Persian empires had weakened both and he wanted to conquer each in turn. In the past, he had mostly caught his victims unaware, partly by telling his men that he was going to raid a place other than that he actually intended. However, this time, he had to inform his men that he was making for the Byzantines because the journey was long and they needed to prepare properly for it.

He began motivating his followers by labelling the Byzantines as, "the yellow people" (meaning bloodless or cowards) but he planned to raid the Byzantines in summer when the sun scorched the earth and his men hated travelling in the very hot desert. He asked Judd bin Qays, `Would you like to fight the yellow people?' Judd replied, `Could you allow me to stay behind because, by God, my people know that there is none more fond of women than me, and I am afraid that when I shall see women of the yellow people, I shall not be able to control myself.'

Tactfully, Muhammad allowed Judd to stay behind but used his indirect and fearful method of persuasion by revealing "divine verses" about men who wanted to stay behind.[431] These verses began with justification of his raid, luring his men by hinting at the gold, silver, and treasures, which the Christians had stored in their monasteries, and warnings of dire consequences for those who did not want to join him in this expedition. Accordingly, the following Qur'anic verses reflect a "big carrot and big stick" approach to war motivation, coupled with provocations against his target people by portraying them as perverts who hated Muhammad's "true religion:"

> The Jews believe that Aziz (*Ezra*) is the son of God
> The Christians believe that Essa (*Jesus*) is the son of God
> They say this for they heard it from earlier unbelievers
> May God destroy them! How perverse they are!
> They (*Christians*) have taken as their lords, beside God,
> Their priests, monks, and the messiah – son of Mary,
> Though he (*Jesus*) ordered them to worship only one God.
> They (*Christians*) subscribe to polytheism,
> And want to extinguish the light of God
> But God will uphold His light, though the unbelievers hate it.
> He has sent His messenger with guidance and true religion
> To dominate all religions, though the unbelievers hate this.

O Believers! Most priests and monks usurp people's wealth
And stop them from following God's way.
They hoard up gold and silver,
And do not spend it in God's way (*i.e. Muhammad's plans*).
Give them a message of grievous torture
On the day when their treasures shall be heated in hellfire
And their foreheads, sides, and backs shall be branded with it:
This is the treasure you stored for yourselves,
Now taste your treasures. (Sura 9, verses 30-35)

However, the lure of the treasures of gold and silver allegedly hoarded in Christian monasteries was not enough to motivate all men. Many did not want to participate in the raid on Tabuk, which they considered an unnecessary aggression against people who had no plans to attack Medina. As these pacifists requested to be left alone and said to Muhammad, `Please allow us to stay at home and not take part in any "fitna" (armed sedition),'[432] he responded by turning the argument upside down, and stating that the actual "fitna" was abstinence from the raids, and the pacifists will be burned in hellfire:

O Believers! What is the matter with you?
When you are told to travel, you cling heavily to earth.
If you do not travel, God will afflict you with a painful doom
He will replace you with other nations
He can do everything. (Sura 9, verses 38-39)

If it was a short journey and quick booty
They certainly would have followed.
But the journey is long and difficult,
And they swear by God that they do not have the strength
Actually, they are placing their lives at risk of death (*because*)
God knows that they are liars. (Sura 9, verse 42)

Those who believe in God and the Day of Judgement
Will not seek exemption from striving,
With their wealth and lives.
Those who seek permission to stay behind,
Believe neither in God nor in the Day of Judgement
Their hearts are full of doubts. (Sura 9, verses 44-45)

> Among them are those who say, `Grant me exemption
> And do not lead me to fitna (*armed sedition*)'
> Actually, they are already in the fitna [*of abstinence*]
> And hellfire is about to surround the unbelievers.
> (Sura 9, verse 49)

Despite Muhammad's exhortations, some men stayed behind. They had said to each other, `It is too hot to take such an expedition.' About these Muhammad said:

> Those left behind are glad that they stayed behind,
> And they were averse from striving in God's way
> With their wealth and their lives.
> And they said, `Do not go forth in the heat.'
> Say, `The fire of hell is much more hot.'
> Therefore, they shall laugh a little and cry a lot,
> In exchange for what they earned. (Sura 9, verses 81-82)

In the following verses, Muhammad shows a lack of knowledge of how men devised a system of months and years, because he states that God created these when He created the heavens and the earth:

> The number of months in the sight of God is twelve
> He ordained this when He created the heavens and the earth
> Of these, four are sacred; So do not be cruel to yourselves in them
> And fight the pagans all together as they fight you all together
> And know that God is with those who guard. (Sura 9, verse 36)

The richer men of Medina and those peasants who cultivated their lands, like every production-oriented man, knew that if they stayed long out of cultivation, trade, or commerce, they would no longer be self-sufficient and would have little choice but to turn into booty-seekers. Muhammad taunted them in his "divine verses." About the well off, he said:

> When a verse comes, stating that you should believe in God
> And fight alongside His messenger,
> The rich and influential come to seek exemption
> These are happy to be with their women and stay behind
> God has branded their hearts
> Therefore, they are unable to understand. (Sura 9, verses 86-87)

Then he cursed the hard working, poor and over-taxed peasants, who wanted to stay behind for cultivation, as follows:

> The desert peasants are the worst in unbelief and hypocrisy
> And more likely to be ignorant of God's commands,
> Which He sends to His messenger.
> When they are told to pay taxes, they treat it as a fine
> And they wish a disaster to fall upon you.
> But disaster is about to descend upon them
> Because God listens and knows. (Sura 9, verses, 97-98)

To prove that he was serious in fulfilling his prophesies, he ordered his devotees to burn the house of Suaylem, where the pacifists used to gather, at a time when these were inside the house. His devotee Talha bin Abaydallah and his gang set the house on fire. A few men tried to escape by jumping from the roof, but broke their limbs. Those who escaped, fled from Medina in fear for their lives.

There were many whom Muhammad had rewarded from the booty in Mecca to lure them to join him in more battles. But many were content with what they had and they did not want to go for more battles. When he embarked on his expedition to Tabuk, he vented out his frustration at these:

> And there are those who made a covenant with God:
> 'If He gives us out of His grace, we will spend it in His way (*jihad*)
> And we will certainly be good.'
> But when He gave them out of His grace,
> They became stingy and they turned back.
> So He has placed hypocrisy in their hearts as a consequence
> Till the day when they shall meet Him,
> Because they failed to do for God
> What they had promised to do for Him,
> And because they told lies.
> Do they not know that God knows their thoughts and secrets?
> And that God is the great knower of unseen things?
> They taunt those who spend in God's way,
> And pay taxes from their earnings, and they scoff at them.
> God will pay them back for their scoffing
> And they shall have a painful chastisement,
> Whether you (*Muhammad*) seek forgiveness for them or not.

Even if you ask forgiveness for them seventy times,
God will not forgive them.
This is because they disbelieve in God and His messenger,
And God does not guide a nation of wrongdoers.
(Sura 9, verses 75-80)

A large number of the Ansar were not happy since Muhammad had used them to conquer the tribes around Mecca but distributed the booty among his Meccan relatives. Hence, the army that went towards Tabuk was in fact two armies: Half the Ansar followed Abdallah bin Ubayy whom Muhammad had forced to join him by issuing threatening "divine verses" but he did not like raiding other people's lands. Hence, whilst travelling towards the Byzantines, Abdallah and his men would pitch their camp separately from Muhammad's camp.

Half way through, when men began to fall sick and faced sand storms, Abdallah and his men reasoned that they were not properly equipped for the expedition, and returned to Medina. These included many chiefs of the Medinian tribes, and they blamed Muhammad for his aggression and lust for power. Muhammad branded them as "hypocrites and doubters" and issued lengthy "divine revelations:"

And if they had really intended to travel on,
They would certainly have brought equipment for it.
But God did not like their coming with us,
So He stopped them, and said (*to them*):
Hold back with those who stayed behind.
Had they come along with you,
They would not have added to your strength
But only created disorder, hurrying to and fro in your midst
And sowing seeds of mistrust among you
And there are many who would have listened to them.
But God knows well those who do wrong.
In the past, they sought rebellion
And tried to undo our (*Muhammad's*) schemes.
But God's commandments prevailed
Although they hated them. (Sura 9, verses 46-48)

You (*the deserters*) wait for two things that might happen to us;
(*Victory or martyrdom*) Both are good for us.
We too wait for two things to happen to you:
God will punish you either directly or through our hands
So wait, and we too will wait. (Sura 9, verse 52)

And they swear by God that they are with you
But they are not with you.
They are a nation of hypocrites.
Had they found a refuge or a cave or a place to hide,
They would have broken all bonds with us
And rushed there in haste. (Sura 9, verses 56-57)

Doggedly Muhammad continued his journey and many either died or deserted. Each time a man deserted and Muhammad was informed, he would say, `Let him go, for if there is any good in him God will bring him back. If not, God has rid you of him.'

The more people began to lose faith in his miraculous powers, the more he realized the need to trace the "hypocrites" and punish them. Once, men were thirsty for several days. Then it began to rain. The believers said that God had sent the rain in response to Muhammad's prayers but the sceptics said, `But it was a passing cloud which would have come any way!' One of the sceptics used to follow Muhammad, trying to trace any signs of miraculous powers in him. A group of sceptics said one to another, `Do you think that fighting the Byzantines is like a war between the Arabs? By God the Byzantines will tie us up with ropes.' One of them warned them to keep their mouths shut and joked, `Keep quiet lest a verse came down from the heavens sentencing us to grievous torture.' This man, who was called Mukhashshin bin Humayyir, said, `I would rather receive a hundred lashes than have a verse descend about us.'

Muhammad found out about this conversation and he ordered Ammar bin Yasir to go to the sceptics and say to them, `You are already dead.' Then he added, `If they refuse to admit that they had cast doubts among men, tell them exactly what they had been saying.' The sceptics rushed to Muhammad and begged forgiveness saying, `O messenger, we were merely chatting in jest.' Mukhashshin bin Humayyir, the literal translation of whose name is "the rude son of a little ass," humbled himself in his efforts to be forgiven and said, `My name tells how foolish I am,' but

Muhammad was in no mood to tolerate doubts and jokes about his "divine powers" and "divine revelations." Accordingly, he issued the following verses:

> The hypocrites stay in fear lest a verse descends about them,
> Revealing that which is in their hearts.
> Tell them, 'Go on mocking, surely God will send what you fear.'
> And if you question them, they will certainly say:
> 'We were only joking and sporting.'
> Say to them, 'Were you laughing at God, His revelations,
> And His messenger? Do not make excuses:
> We know you have turned to unbelief after belief.
> We might forgive some, but some we will punish
> Because they are guilty.' (Sura 9, verses 64- 66)
>
> They swear by God that they said nothing
> But indeed they uttered blasphemy, after they had submitted
> And they meditated a plot which they were unable to carry out.
> They find faults in us
> Because God and His messenger enriched them out of grace.
> Therefore, if they repent, it will be good for them
> And if they revert, God will send a painful punishment to them
> In this world and in the hereafter,
> And they shall have no guardian or helper. (Sura 9, verse 74)

Mukhashshin was killed in the subsequent battle of Yamama but it is reported that his body was not found.

When Muhammad and his jihadis reached Tabuk, they began to stop the trade caravans and extort money from them, which they called "jizya" (unbelievers' tax). But the caravans were few and so they began to stop the local people from going to their wells until they were able to extort money from Yuhanna bin Ru'ba, the governor of Ayla, from the people of Jarba', and from the people of Adhruh. In exchange, Muhammad gave these people a document, as a guarantee from God and His messenger, stating that his men would not stop them from going to their wells or using roads, not raid their ships and caravans, and protect them and their men in Syria and Yemen. He also gave them a dire warning that should anyone of them break this "Treaty" by introducing some new factor, "his wealth shall not save him." In other words, he installed his jihadis as a self-appointed "protection and extortion force" in the area.

Then he sent Khalid bin Walid to the Christian ruler Ukaydir bin Abd al Malik at Duma. When Khalid's jihadis came within sight of Ukaydir's fort, they went into the cowshed and let the cows loose. Hearing the rubble, Ukaydir came out on his horse with his brother. Khalid's cavalry attacked the two, seized Ukaydir and killed his brother. Khalid stripped Ukaydir of his gown because it was made of brocade and laced with gold. He sent this expensive gown to Muhammad before he brought Ukaydir as a prisoner to him. When the believers saw Ukaydir's brocade gown, they rushed to touch and feel it for these Bedouins had not seen such an expensive dress in their lives. Muhammad did not like this and he said, `Do you admire this gown? By Him in whose hand is my life, the martyr Sa'ad bin Mu'adh's dusters in paradise are better than this.'

In captivity, Ukaydir had no choice but to arrange to pay extortion money to Muhammad. Then he was released and he returned to his town. A poet pictured Khalid's driving out the cows to seize Ukaydir as "God's way of helping" and said:

> Blessed is He (*God*) who drove out the cows
> I see God providing our leader with sight
> Those who stayed behind instead of travelling to Tabuk
> Tell them that we have orders to fight. [433]

Muhammad stayed in Tabuk for around ten nights and then returned to Medina. His conduct in Tabuk was no more than ordinary banditry and extortion. He had gained nothing other than some funds to be able to return but he had set an example for future attacks and gradual takeover of others' lands to build an empire. After his death, the Umayyads would continue to follow his examples, and eventually come to rule a large empire.

Upon his return, his devotees spread stories about how he had performed miracles, but when analysed, these turn out to be full of self-contradictions. For example, one story states that on the way, in a valley called al Mushaqaq, he ordered his forward troops not to drink water from its spring until his arrival. A number of those who reached first drank water so that when he arrived there was no water left for him. He cursed those who had drank the water and called for God's vengeance on them. Then he placed his hand on the rock, prayed, and water burst forth with a roar in such copious amounts that all were able to drink to their full: One cannot help noticing that if Muhammad was able to perform such miracles, why did he call for God's vengeance on those who had drank before him?

Back in Medina, and the social boycott of the pacifists

When Muhammad was preparing for the raid on Tabuk, twelve men who did not want to travel had come to him and tried to appease him by telling him that they had built a mosque. So far, there was only one mosque in Medina. For those who lived far from Muhammad's mosque it was not always possible to travel to it. This second mosque would enable the sick, the weak, and the old to pray near to their homes.[434] But Muhammad wanted all from near and far to pray with him so that he could have better control over them. These twelve men invited him to come to their mosque and pray for them, but he hated to pray in a mosque built outside his orders, especially when he wanted these men to join him in the raid on Tabuk.

While returning from Tabuk, when he was at a day's journey from Medina, he summoned Malik bin al Dukhshum and ordered him to go before him and burn down the second mosque. Malik and his men quickly went, lighted a palm branch, and then rushed into the mosque. They burned and destroyed it as people ran out. Muhammad then issued a "divine order" justifying that the mosque had been built to cause division among the believers, which would harm faith and promote unbelief:

> And some have made a mosque of harm and infidelity
> And of division among believers
> As an outpost for those who disobeyed God's messenger.
> They swear that they are well intentioned
> And God swears that they are liars.
> Never ever stand in that mosque
> Abide by the mosque you built in faith from the first day
> In it are men who love purity
> And God loves the pure. (Sura 9, verses 107-108)

He instructed his followers to excommunicate those who had stayed behind, and so they withdrew from them. The excluded men came to him, made excuses, and swore that they were telling the truth. As a punishment, he ordered them to give parts of their wealth to his devout followers. Because those who had stayed behind were mainly the prosperous ones or farmers, taking money from them was a profitable way to punish them. Accordingly, Muhammad issued his "divine revelations:"

> And others have confessed that they were wrong,
> They mixed a good deed with an evil one.
> Perhaps God will turn to them, God is Forgiving, Merciful.
> So take a part of their wealth, and cleanse them with this
> And pray for them. Surely, your prayer is a relief to them.
> And God is Hearing, Knowing. (Sura 9, verse 102-103)

However, three men said that they did not want to lie and they had no permissible excuse not to go to war. Although these were the honest ones, Muhammad decided to make an example of them, and he deferred their cases for further scrutiny. Until he could reach a final decision about them, no one was to speak to them. He tested the loyalty of one of them by sending him a forged letter through a Nabati trader from Syria who had come to sell goods in Medina. The letter seemed like it was from the Sultan of Ghassan written on a piece of silk, which read, `We hear that your master has treated you badly. God does not want to put you in humiliation and loss, so come to us and we will be generous to you.' However, the lured man was sensible enough to burn the letter.

After forty days, Muhammad decided to enhance the penalty, and he ordered the excluded men to separate from their wives. One of the men was so old that he could not survive without a servant, and so, upon the request of his wife, Muhammad allowed her to serve him food. Finally, after a social boycott and testing of fifty days, he forgave the three and issued a "divine revelation from God:" [435]

> Concerning the case of the three who had stayed behind,
> The earth narrowed around them despite its vastness
> And they became greatly stressed,
> And understood that there is no escape from God.
> They begged forgiveness, and God is the Forgiver and Merciful.
> (Sura 9, verse 118)

Although forgiveness (albeit for no crime) is good, in forgiving these men, Muhammad forgot that he had issued another "revelation from God," saying that God would never forgive those who had stayed back from war:

> When you will return to them, they will present their excuses.
> Tell them, 'Do not make excuses; I will never believe you,
> God has told me about you.'
> God and His messenger will see your doings
> Then you shall return
> To the Knower of the visible and the invisible
> Then He will inform you of what you did.
> They will swear by God, in order to be left alone
> So abandon them to themselves
> For these people are absolutely filthy
> And hell is their final abode,
> As a recompense for what they earned.
> They will swear so that you may be pleased with them
> But even if you are pleased with them
> God is not pleased with those who disobey. (Sura 9, verses 94-96)

<u>The details of Muhammad's taxes
and the means of extortion</u>

On his return from Tabuk, Muhammad received a messenger who had brought a letter from the bandit sultans of Himyar informing him that they had "accepted Islam." These bandit sultans were al Harith bin Abdu Kulal, Nu'aym bin Abdu Kulal, and al Nu'maan of the regions of Dhu Ru'ayn, Ma'afir and Hamadan respectively. In addition, the Zur'a Dhu Yazan tribe sent an emissary informing him of their submission to him. Muhammad, in his letter of reply, praised God and, after adding the usual salutations, wrote:

> Your messenger... informed us of your Islam and of your killing the *mushraykeen*. God has guided you in the right direction.

In other words, God wanted them "to kill the *mushraykeen*." In the letter, Muhammad demanded that now that these sultans were "believers," it was obligatory upon them to send a fifth of the booty, which he was to choose first before they divided it among others. He also demanded land tax (*u'shar*) payment, which was incumbent on all believers and defined as a tenth of the produce from land watered by spouts and rain, and a twentieth of the produce from land watered by bucket. The sultans were also to pay a cattle tax defined as follows:

> For every forty camels a milch camel;
> For every thirty camels a young male camel;
> For every five camels a sheep;
> For every ten camels two sheep;
> For every forty cows one cow;
> For every thirty cows a bull, a calf or a cow calf and;
> For every forty sheep, one sheep.

Muhammad defined believers as those who paid the said taxes, testified to his apostolate, and persecuted the *mushraykeen* (secular/multi-faith people). Only those thus defined could have a guarantee of safety from his men's attacks. Jews and Christians who did not want to convert had to pay, in addition to the mentioned taxes, *jizya* for every adult, male or female, free or slave, one full dinar or its equivalent in clothes. It did not matter how a slave could gather money to pay this tax because the purpose of *jizya* was to force people to become believers. Only *jizya* paying unbelievers could have the guarantee of safety from his men's attacks. He added that those who refused to pay it would be treated as his and God's enemies.

The letter further instructed the addressed to obey Muhammad's tax collectors, namely Mu'adh bin Jabal, Abdallah bin Zayd, Malik bin Ubaada, Uqba bin Nimr, Malik bin Murra and their assistants. The letter contained the following phrases:

> Collect the alms and the taxes from your provinces and hand them over to my messengers. Their leader is Mu'adh bin Jabal, and do not return him dissatisfied.

Muhammad's letter to the Zur'a Dhu Yazan tribe in the same region, Himyar, also stated:

> Malik bin Murra has told me that you were the first of Himyar to accept Islam and kill the *mushraykeen*. I congratulate you and order you to treat Himyar well and not to be false and

treacherous, for God's messenger is the patron of both your poor and rich ...

Though Muhammad was happy to take a fifth of the looted property, he kept his pride by stating that he did not take charity money:

> The alms are not lawful to Muhammad or his household; it is charity given to those believers who are poor or travellers.

In other words, with one-fifth of the booty, Muhammad was too rich to accept charity. Like a king, he wanted people to treat his appointees with respect and honour:

> Malik has brought the news and we shall keep secret what is confidential, and I order you to treat him well. I have sent to you some of the best of my religious and learned men, and you must respect them.

The "merit" of these "best of religious and learned men," may be judged from the following event:

> When Mu'adh was sent to the Yaman to preach, a woman came to him and asked, `O companion of God's messenger, what rights a husband has over his wife?' Mu'adh said, `Woe to you, a woman can never fulfil her husband's rights. Hence, do your utmost to fulfil his claims as best as you can.'
> The woman said, `By God, if you are the companion of God's messenger you must know the rights a husband has over his wife!'
> Mu'adh said, `If you find your husband in a state that pus and blood ran out of his nostrils, and you sucked it dry, you would still not have fulfilled your obligations to him.'[436]

Muhammad's instructions to his tax collectors, who went in the company of jihadis to enforce the collections, stipulated the following:

> When you dwell in a settlement, you can take provisions from the locals, and if the people disobey, then confiscate all you can, keep one-fifth for the prophet and the rest is yours.

Like any other oppressive king, Muhammad trained his jihadis to behave like imperial masters and instructed:

> Islam is always dominant and there is nothing higher then Islam. When you find Christians or Jews in your way, do not be the first to greet them, and do not give way but force them to give way to you. If one of them joins you, do not send him back but if one of you joins them, order them to send him back to you.[437]

The besieged people of Ta'if are divided, lured, and made to surrender, one by one

Life had been made unbearable for the besieged people of Ta'if. They could not come out of the town without fear of Muhammad's appointees around Ta'if attacking them. Consequently, one by one, men of the Thaqif tribe came to Medina to surrender.

One of these was a chief, named Urwa bin Mas'ud al Thaqafi. He and his brother al Aswad bin Mas'ud were in heavy debts to local people because Muhammad's men had taken their vineyards, which were located outside Ta'if. Urwa's relative, Abu Sufyan – who was also Muhammad's father-in-law – advised him to join Muhammad against the locals and then he would not need to pay off his debts. Earlier, his nephew (the son of al Aswad – hence called Ibn al Aswad) had betrayed his tribe and joined Muhammad in besieging the town for which Muhammad had granted him custody of the said vineyards.

Urwa went to see Muhammad but the latter told him that he would help him only if his people surrendered. Accordingly, Urwa returned to Ta'if, and told his people to become believers but they treated him as a traitor and killed him. To avoid inter-tribal revenge issue, the tribes of Ta'if – the Banu Malik and the Ahlaf – both claimed that one of their men had killed Urwa.

After the murder of Urwa, the Thaqif waited some months and then realized that they could no longer fight the booty-seekers besieging them. One of their leaders, Amr, said, 'We are in a fix. You have seen how this man (Muhammad) has taken hold of people. All Arabs have submitted to him and we lack the power to fight them.' Then people said one to another, 'Do you not see that your herds are not safe and none of you can go out without being butchered?' Hence, after conferring together, the Thaqif decided to travel to Medina and negotiate terms of surrender with Muhammad.

In Medina, the delegates were housed in a tent and Khalid bin Sa'id bin al 'Aas, a Meccan, acted as intermediary between them and Muhammad. The delegates were afraid that they would be poisoned and so they would not eat their food until Khalid ate some to reassure them. Their problem in surrendering was that they did not want to frighten their superstitious people by destroying the much-revered Temple of Laat until they had preached to their people and prepared them for it. Hence, they asked Muhammad for permission to keep their temple for three years so as not to hurt the feelings of women and children who loved Laat but Muhammad refused. Then they asked if they could keep it for one year but he refused. Finally, they asked if they could keep it for a month after their return home but he refused. The reason for refusing was that even a few days reprieve would enable the Thaqif to take away the jewels, gold, and precious beads that pilgrims had been donating at the temple over the decades.

Muhammad sent his new allies, the Meccan chiefs Abu Sufyan and al Mughira, to destroy the temple and confiscate its property and treasure. Abu Sufyan and al Mughira travelled with the Thaqif delegates and, when they neared Ta'if, Abu Sufyan stayed behind while al Mughira went up to the idol to dismantle it. When he struck Laat with a pickaxe, his tribesmen stood by to protect him from being killed the way Urwa had been killed earlier.

The women of Thaqif came out with their heads uncovered, mourning and crying over the destruction of their sacred idol, which they believed was their protector. When al Mughira had destroyed it and taken its jewels, gold and beads, he sent for Abu Sufyan. They sold the property of the temple and when al Mughira had collected the proceeds, Muhammad told him to give part of it to Urwa's son and nephew to pay off their fathers' debts. As usual, Muhammad had paid nothing from his own pocket and provided another precedent that becoming a believer allowed one to rob others with "divine" approval. In addition, he had brought the town of Ta'if, which had always rivalled Mecca, under the rule of the Meccan Quraysh.

The persecution of the remaining secular Meccans

With the surrender of Ta'if and the destruction of its Temple of Laat, the number of unbelievers had further reduced. Muhammad estimated that he was now in a position to subdue other local faiths as well and hand over control of the Ka'ba to his closest associates.

Under the rule of the secular Meccans, people used to donate voluntarily to the temples but Muhammad showed that he could gather lot more taxes through his appointees, by force if necessary. As the phrase in the following verses shows (see below, "They bought the revelations of God for a low price"), he was not happy with the amount of taxes he was receiving from his secular allies to justify maintaining secularism in Mecca. Though he had revived the Truce of Hudaybiya with the secular Meccans, which stipulated that people of all religions would be free to come to the Ka'ba and no one needed to fear during the sacred months, treaties had never been a barrier to his ambitions for long. Now, breaking his promises, he annulled the Truce of Hudaybiya in the following words of the Qur'an: [438]

> They bought the revelations of God for a low price (*i.e. less tax*)
> And barred men from God's way (*i.e. forcible extortion*)
> Evil is that which they do. (Sura 9, verse 9)

> God and His messenger declare that they are free from the Truce, Which they had made with the *mushraykeen* (secular/multi-faith).
> (*O mushraykeen!*) You have four months permission
> To walk around in this land,
> And know that you cannot weaken God,
> And God is about to humiliate you.
> God and His messenger announce to the people
> On the day of the greater pilgrimage (*hajj*)
> That God and His messenger dissolve their obligations (*the treaty*)
> With the *mushraykeen*.
> It is better for you to repent and seek forgiveness,
> And if you turn back, then know that you cannot weaken God.
> Inform the unbelievers about a grievous punishment for them.
> (Sura 9, verses 1-3)

In these verses he accused the secular/multi-faith Meccans of "barring men from God's way" when, in fact, he was about to bar all from Mecca except those who admitted to his apostolate and paid taxes to his men. He blamed others for his own deeds (breaking his promises) by fabricating – as he had always done with his victims – that they were conspiring against him. In his customary manner of cryptic utterances in a vague language, the so-claimed language of God, he revealed the following:

> How can the *mushraykeen* have a treaty
> With God and His messenger?
> Except those with whom you (*Muhammad*) made a contract
> In the Sacred House:
> If they keep their word, we will keep our word,
> Because God loves the dutiful. But how can it be?
> If they had enough support to dominate us,
> They would care neither for treaty nor for kinship.
> They convince you with their words but their hearts refuse
> And most of them are wrongdoers. (Sura 9, verses 7-8)

Apart from the Truce of Hudaybiya, Muhammad had also made specific contracts with certain tribes. For example, the Banu Bakr had entered into a ten-year contract, separate from others. Tactically, in order to confuse and split the secular people and avoid a possible alliance against him, Muhammad pledged to fulfil his specific contracts up to their expiry period:

> With those *mushraykeen* who have made treaties with us
> And they have not harmed us in the least,
> And not helped anyone to dominate us,
> We will complete the terms of the (*specific*) treaties
> Because God loves the dutiful. (Sura 9, verse 4)

On the day of the next hajj, when pilgrims of all faiths were performing the hajj, Ali stood up and declared that Muhammad had ordered him to proclaim that no unbeliever shall enter paradise, no *mushrik* shall make pilgrimage after that year, and no naked person shall walk around the Ka'ba. Reference to nakedness was added to equate the unbelievers with the profane. This strategy is still typical of Islamists who project all sorts of evils to non-Muslims.

Muhammad gave the unbelievers four months from the date of the proclamation to escape to safe places, for afterwards, as he said, there would be no treaty obligations.[439]

The seculars had not revoked the believers' right to pray in the Ka'ba and reside in Mecca, but now that Muhammad had the power, he gave them only four months in which the seculars were to either subscribe to his rule or die. Very aggressively, he declared:

> As soon as the months of exemption are over,
> Kill the *mushraykeen* wherever they are
> Arrest them, besiege them, and ambush them in every place
> If they repent, pray, and pay the taxes,
> Then leave a way out. (Sura 9, verse 5)
> And if they break their oaths (*i.e. refuse to pay taxes*)
> And slight your religion, then kill the leaders of unbelief,
> For they have no faith, so that they may stop. (Sura 9, verse 12)

The murder of the first critic, despite the critic's genius and well intentions, is the main weapon in all Islamic expansions. Muhammad's "divine commands" in this respect last to date. This forms the basis of the irreversible nature of Islamic consolidation and takeover of newer lands. In the above quoted verses, Muhammad had institutionalized the murders of critics and unbelievers as "God's Law." To prepare his men for this slaughter, he instigated them further and suppressed their guilt by hinting that "God forgives" in the following "divine verses:"

> Why do you not kill those who find faults in your religion?
> They expelled the messenger and they started it in the first place.
> Do you fear them when God is more worthy to be feared,
> If you are believers?
> Kill them! God will torture them through your hands,
> He will humiliate them, and help you against them
> And thus, cool the hearts of the believers
> And remove the rage in their hearts
> God forgives whom He wants. (Sura 9, verses 13-15)

As usual, he also hinted at the "rewards" for his best fighters:

> Do you think that you will be abandoned?
> God has not yet distinguished the best warriors amongst you,
> And those who do not revere anyone but God,
> His messenger, and the believers.
> God is aware of what you do. (Sura 9, verse 16)

The alliance between Muhammad and the secular Meccans had served him well. Now he wanted his closest associates to take control from the seculars. The secular Meccans argued, 'We do good deeds in the Sacred House, we feed and serve water to pilgrims, repair and maintain the building, and we have a right to pray in the Sacred House.' About these Muhammad issued "divine revelations," stating that his devotees and jihadis deserved to be posted to higher ranks in the governance of Mecca:

> It is not proper that *mushraykeen* should pray in God's mosques
> When they are themselves a testimony to their unbelief.
> Their (*good*) deeds are of no use
> For they are the eternal dwellers of hell. (Sura 9, verse 17)

> They think that serving water to pilgrims
> And tending the Sacred House
> Is as good as believing in God and the hereafter,
> And fighting in God's way:
> God does not hold these tasks equal
> And God does not guide a nation of wrongdoers.
> The believers who migrated and fought in God's way
> With their funds and their lives
> Are much superior in God's eyes
> And these will be placed higher. (Sura 9, verses 19-20)

In these verses, one notes the blasphemy in the declaration that fighting is much nobler an act in God's eyes compared to serving water to pilgrims and tending to the Sacred House.

However, there were barriers in expelling the unbelievers from Mecca: These were the friendships and tribal relationships between individual believers and unbelievers. Despite Muhammad's lures and exhortations, it was not easy for all of his men to break with the unbelievers because families too were split between believers and unbelievers. Accordingly, Muhammad decided to pitch father against son and brother against brother and, in order to force the remaining unbelievers to join in his expansionist wars, he banned all unbelievers from entering the Ka'ba:[440]

> O believers! The *mushraykeen* are absolutely filthy
> After this year, they shall not enter the Ka'ba. (Sura 9, verse 28)

> O believers! Do not respect your fathers and brothers
> If they hold unbelief (*in Muhammad*) dearer than belief
> The man who will respect them, will be a great sinner.
> If you love your fathers, sons, brothers, wives, families,
> And your earnings, and your trade,
> And you are afraid of losing it, and your houses,
> If you love these more than God and His messenger,
> And fighting in the way of God,
> Then wait until God brings about his command
> And God does not guide a nation of wrongdoers.
> (Sura 9, verse 23-24)

In saying this, Muhammad's Christian education apparently played a part because Jesus too had said, "If any man come to me and hate not his father, mother, wife, children, brothers and sisters, and his own life also, he cannot be my follower." Muhammad had not seen his father, he had no siblings and sons, his wives and daughters were believers and so it was easy for him to ask others to denounce their families but it was not easy for others especially when told that their kith and kin would be the fuel of the burning fires of hell.

The Meccans tried to tell Muhammad that stopping unbelievers from pilgrimage would reduce the hajj revenues; there would be fewer pilgrims, lesser donations, lesser sales in Meccan markets; they would cut themselves off from many places for trade, and this would diminish their livelihood. In response, he showed the objectors his way of making money:

> If you are afraid of poverty, God will make you rich if he wants,
> God knows all, God is wise:
> Fight those who do not believe in God and the hereafter,
> And do not forbid what God and His messenger forbid
> And do not acknowledge the religion of truth.

And fight the people of the book (*Jews and Christians*)
Until they pay the taxes with humble submission
And feel themselves subdued. (Sura 9, verses 28-29)

In other words, Muhammad was not content with the voluntary donations under the secular Meccan rule but he wanted his people to attack the unbelievers and make them pay extortionist taxes to his appointed officials, with submissiveness and utter humility.

Do not attend the funerals of the unbelievers

During these days, Abdallah bin Ubayy died. Muhammad had called him a hypocrite because he had tried to save the lives of his Jewish townsmen and stayed away from the battles of Uhud and Tabuk. However, he attended his funeral because Abdallah was the highly respected elder of the Ansar and had it not been for his kindness and hospitality, Muhammad would not be able to settle in Medina and launch his raids and conquests. The vengeful Umar tried to stop him from attending the funeral but he shunned him and stood by the grave until the burial of the body.[441] There was a reason for this: When Muhammad had migrated to Medina, with a handful of followers and in utter poverty, Abdallah had given him his shirt to wear. Now, proudly, Muhammad placed his shirt in Abdallah's grave to show that he did not owe him anything. In Arab tribal ethics, which Muhammad followed, receiving charity was an insult to a man of status but taking booty after killing and plunder was a noble act.

After attending the funeral, Muhammad regretted it and realized that attending the funerals of men he hated was no longer a political necessity. Accordingly, he issued the following "divine order:"

(*O Muhammad*) Never pray for one of them on his death,
And do not stand by his grave.
Until death, they denied God and His messenger,
They are evil-doers.
And do not be dazzled by their wealth and their children
Because God wants to punish them through these in this world
Until their souls depart,
And they remain unbelievers. (Sura 9, verses 84-85)

In Muhammad's mind, Abdallah was an "evil-doer" because he had valued the lives of his Jewish neighbours, abstained from raids on them, and hesitated in other banditry raids. After his funeral, Muhammad never attended the funeral of a pacifist.

The Islamists claim that the above quoted verses, like many other hateful and callous verses of the Qur'an, are God's words. An analysis paying attention to what God, by definition, stands for can only show that these verses are blasphemous.

More tribes are brought to Muhammad's rule

A situation of fear had arisen in which few people in Arabia felt safe from Muhammad's direct or indirect appointees and raiders. People expected that eventually Muhammad's men would either raid them or call upon them to submit and pay taxes.

Adiy bin Hatim, the chief of a Christian tribe, called the Ta'iy, had instructed his servant always to keep ready some of his well-trained and well-fed camels for escape, and to inform him as soon as he heard of Muhammad's jihadis approaching his tribe. One morning, the servant informed him that he had seen a cavalry coming upon them with flags, and found that they were Muhammad's troops. Adiy quickly boarded his family and children on the camels and escaped to join fellow Christians in Syria, but, in panic and haste, he left behind one of his sisters.

The jihadis raided Adiy's tribe and captured women and children, including Adiy's sister. They transported these to Medina and locked them in an enclosure near Muhammad's mosque so that, each time he went to pray, he could see them. When he passed by the prisoners, Adiy's sister stood up and addressed him in the way she was told, 'O messenger of God, my father is dead, and the man who should pay ransom for me has gone. If you have mercy on me, God will have mercy on you.' Muhammad asked who her man was, and when she said that it was Adiy bin Hatim, he scorned, 'The man who ran away from God and His messenger!' Then he went his way.

The event was repeated for three days each time when he passed by the prisoners until Adiy's sister lost all hope. However, because, either she had rekindled mercy in his heart, or he saw no opportunity to obtain a ransom, he finally decided to let her go. She waited until a trustworthy man was available to take her to Syria. Muhammad gave her clothing and some money for the journey and put her on a camel. As to why she was not sold as a slave, the Ta'iy were a wealthy and respected tribe and just as one could not sell a man of the Quraysh as a slave, the same rules applied to those belonging to the Ta'iy. Muhammad retained some respect for the Christians, because of his previously mentioned Christian teachers. In addition, he hoped that Adiy's sister would convince Adiy to return and submit to his rule.

When Adiy's sister reached Syria, she reprimanded him for abandoning her. Adiy was ashamed and sought forgiveness from her. She told him that some men of their tribe were already in Medina to submit to Muhammad, in order to get their lands back, and their families released. She advised him to be among the first to join Muhammad, get back his lands, and get his people freed.

When Adiy came to Medina, Muhammad treated him with respect and said, `Adiy, are you not half Christian because you live off on a quarter of your people's stock which you collect, though this is not permitted in Christianity?' Adiy admitted that Muhammad was right in his observation. Muhammad said, `Perhaps you see our poverty and this prevents you from joining our religion but, by God, wealth will soon flow so much that there will not be enough people to take it. If you think that we have enemies and we are few, or that power and sovereignty is with the Byzantines and Persians, by God you will soon hear that the white castles of Babylon have been opened upon us.'

Another deputation of Adiy's tribe, whose leader was Zaydu'l Khayl, had come to Muhammad and submitted to him before Adiy did so. Muhammad changed the name of Zaydu'l Khayl to Zaydu'l Khayr and allotted him some of the Ta'iy lands back, to collect and send taxes, and gave him a collector's charter. When Zayd left, Muhammad prayed, `I hope he would be safe from Medina fever,' but, on his way, Zaydu'l Khayl caught fever and died. His wife received the papers but, as they were no use to her (these were not ownership deeds but a collector's charter), she burnt them.[442] Then Muhammad appointed Adiy as his tax collector for the Ta'iy and the Banu Asad tribes.

The myths of "God's protection" and "God's curses"

Among the deputations that came to Medina was the Banu Amir tribe. Their chiefs, Amir bin al Tufayl, Arbad bin Qays and Jabbar bin Salma had come to see Muhammad but he refused to see them until they changed their religion. The delegates refused to convert and left. When they were gone, Muhammad prayed, `O God, rid me of Amir bin al Tufayl.'[443] On their way back, Amir said, `Muhammad treated us as if we were planning to raid him with squadrons and kill his Ansar. He failed to see that our horses were so exhausted that they had hardly brought us to Medina.'[444] In the way, Amir fell ill and died in the house of a woman of the Banu Salul. The second chief of the Banu Amir too died a day or two after he had reached his territory.

Muhammad heard about these deaths, and used the news to enhance fears in people's hearts by saying that Amir and Arbad had come to kill him but God had protected him and killed the two. He added that the second man was killed by a lightning strike.

In their propaganda campaigns, modern Islamists claim that Muhammad never cursed his enemies despite the fact that the Qur'an is replete with his curses. His above mentioned prayers, `O God, rid me of Amir bin al Tufayl,' and many more quoted earlier, illustrate that he cursed even those who had done no evil and posed no threat to him. He cursed Amir just for refusing to change his religion but people eulogized Amir, which shows that he was a fine man.

Muhammad's cursing Amir, and his subsequent death explain why his unbeliever visitors were afraid of eating his food until they had submitted to him and been accepted as believers. The Thaqif delegates were careful not to eat his food without testing it on one of his men. The believers spread word that Amir had died because of Muhammad's curse, but forgot to mention that Zaydu'l Khayl had died despite Muhammad's blessings.

The Islamists often claim that many of these men had intended to kill Muhammad and therefore they died. One often finds, in propagandist literature, that so and so, including Umar, Muhammad's closest associate, had come to kill him. The list is very long, starting with Abu Jahl, Muhammad's aunt – the wife of Abu Lahab – the Jews of Medina, Amir bin Tufayl, and so on but not a shred of evidence other than the myths spread by either Muhammad himself or his devotees, who wanted to show that he had divine protection. Their statements are usually self-contradictory because, if he had the privilege of divine protection, why would he curse and attack those who, he assumed, wanted to kill him, and why would he suspect, close to his death, that his wives had conspired to poison him? The most plausible explanation would be that, like every person who conspires to kill others, Muhammad was paranoid and feared that others – including his own wives – were conspiring to kill him.

Muhammad rules an Arabia run by bandits

Now that Muhammad had led the Quraysh to subdue the tribes around Mecca, people understood that it was time to submit to him before his jihadis raided them. Thus, as the Qur'an states in Sura al Nasr (the Help), people flocked to accept his religion, coming from all directions, and his poet Hassan bin Thabit described the situation as follows:

> We have killed so many with our sharp swords
> That people are obeying Muhammad's religion in batches.
> If you want to save your blood and your property
> From becoming our booty to be divided among our men,
> Then surrender and do not make partners to Allah.[445]

The deputations that came to Muhammad included the Banu Tamim. These were masters of plunder, as they themselves declared:

> We have plundered countless tribes
> In search of superiority, and we are generous.
> In times of dearth, we feed meat to the hungry.
> Our chiefs are like kings
> Therefore, we take a quarter from the booty.[446]

Among the new converts were the tribal chiefs al Aqra' and Uyayna, who had fought as Muhammad's allies at the battles of Hunayn and Ta'if. Muhammad had ignored their unbeliever status because, at that time, conquering was more important than belief. After the victories, he had generously rewarded them from the looted property, and thus won their hearts. Their egos flattered, they saw no reason now for staying away from him. When they joined his ranks, he entertained them and gave them valuable gifts but, because they had come to see him in a rude manner and shouted at him to come out when he was with his wives, he did not like their demeanour.[447] One of these even ridiculed another in their group in these words, `Your authority stems from your backside, at the bottom of your tail.'[448] Hence, when they had gone, Muhammad issued the following:

> O Believers! Do not raise your voices above that of the messenger,
> Nor shout when speaking to him as you shout one to another,
> Lest your deeds be turned to nothing, without you knowing it.
> They shouted for the messenger behind his private lodge,
> They have no sense. Had they been patient and waited for him,
> It would be better for them. (Sura 49, verses 3-5)

Then came the deputations of the Banu Sa'ad bin Bakr and the Abd al Qays. When al Jarud, the chief of the Abd al Qays, came to surrender, he said to Muhammad, `I have a debt. If I change my religion to yours will you guarantee to pay my debt?' Al Jarud had heard about valuable gifts given to many. Muhammad tactfully said, `Yes, I guarantee that God's guidance is better than what you earlier had.' However, when al Jarud asked for some camels to return home, he told him that he had none.[449]

Many chiefs and leaders came for specific and selfish reasons. Some wanted to secure positions as local chiefs in the new system or become tax collectors taking their share. One of these self-seekers was Farwa al Muradi from the region Kinda where his tribe, the Murad, had been defeated by a rival tribe, the Hamadan. The Murad tribe had lost many men at a battle, called al Razm, which had taken place between the two tribes. Farwa was upset at the misfortune that had befallen his people. He broke from the sultans of his region, and sought to install himself as a new sultan. Muhammad aided Farwa, appointed him the governor of Kinda, and, as usual, sent with him his man Khalid bin Sa'id to collect taxes.

However, many others tribes too were settled in Kinda, such as the Banu Zubayd. These differed in their political strategy towards Muhammad. One of their chiefs, Amr bin Ma'dikarib, had suggested that they should submit to him and secure their positions, but their senior chief named Qays bin Makshuh had refused to do so. The consequence of this split had been devastating because Farwa had taken the lead in submitting to Muhammad, and had himself installed as governor over the Banu Zubayd as well. Having not being able to tolerate Farwa's rule, Amr broke off with Qays, rode to Muhammad with some men of the Banu Zubayd, and submitted to him. When Qays heard of this, he was enraged and said that Amr had exceeded his authority.[450] Amr replied by deriding Qays:

> I ordered you to fear God
> But you went after pleasure like a young ass
> Whose lust beguiled him.

Despite his submission to Muhammad, Amr had to tolerate Farwa's rule over his tribe because Farwa had been the first to come to Muhammad. After Muhammad's death, Amr revolted and satirized Farwa's Islamic rule as:

> We found Farwa's rule, the worst of all,
> (*Like*) an ass sniffing at a female ass
> If you were to look at Abu Umayr (*Farwa's second name*)
> You would think he was a horse with its filthy discharge.[451]

It was not uncommon among Arabs to lampoon and satirize each other in this coarse manner. The above lines illustrate that converting to Islam did not improve the level of refinement in general. The Qur'an too reflects this coarse manner of speech, such as, "The unbelievers will bray like donkeys," and it contains lures to carnal pleasures, such as:

> Your wives are like your fields;
> So enter your fields the way you like. (Sura 2, verse 223)

The use of this kind of language reflects the coarse and lowly culture that produced it, and a testimony that these verses have nothing to do with God.

Seeing the benefit in yielding to Muhammad, more men from Kinda came to him. Among these was the son of the defiant Qays, named al Ash'ath bin Qays. He came with eighty riders, and when they went to see him, they had combed their long hair, and blackened their eyes with *kohl*. They wore robes with silk borders. Muhammad told them that his religion did not allow men to wear silk. They had no choice but to tear the borders off their robes and throw them away. To please him, al Ash'ath said that their mothers, like Muhammad's, were poor, but he replied, `We do not follow our mothers' lineage for this is tantamount to disowning our fathers.' To flatter him, al Ash'ath quickly followed suit and warned his men that if any of them said the same again, he would receive eighty lashes.

Another self-seeker was Surad who came to see Muhammad with a deputation from his al Azd tribe. Muhammad ordered them to attack their neighbours – the unbeliever tribes of the Yemen. Surad went with his Islamic duty to attack his neighbours and besieged the town of Jurash where the tribes of the Yemen lived. He besieged the town for a month but could not force entry. He then deceitfully withdrew to a nearby mountain called Shakar, and when the inhabitants of Jurash, thinking that he had left, came out of the town, he massacred a large number of them. Meanwhile the people of Jurash had sent two emissaries to Muhammad to plead with him to spare them the raids. While the emissaries were sitting with Muhammad, he cryptically told them, `Animals offered to God are being slaughtered near the mountain of Shakar.' The two emissaries did not understand his twisted language, and so they went to Abu Bakr who explained it to them, `Woe to you! The messenger has just announced to you the death of your people, so go back and ask him to pray to God to spare your people.' They did so, and Muhammad prayed, `O God remove the grief from them.'

When the two emissaries returned to their town, they found that Surad had massacred a number of them on the very day they were pleading with Muhammad; such was the efficient network of Muhammad's spies, and his disdain for the lives of the people whom he referred to as "Animals offered to God for slaughter." The terrified Jurash again sent a deputation to Muhammad telling him that they had submitted to him. In return, he allowed them to keep part of their land around their town, with boundaries for horses, camels, and ploughing oxen for grazing. By pitting the al Azd against the people of Jurash, Muhammad had succeeded in bringing Jurash under his control. One of the al Azd described their raid on the people of Jurash as follows:

> What a successful raid we had!
> With mules, horses and asses,
> We raided the "asses" of Jurash,
> To satisfy the malice I feel
> I do not care if they are believers or not.[452]

In the tenth year of Muhammad's migration to Medina, a deputation of the Banu Harith came to him. They had converted to Islam when Khalid bin Walid and his jihadis had raided them. Muhammad commented that they looked like Indians. Then he said, `Are you not the people who, when driven away, pushed forward?' The visitors remained silent. He repeated the words three times without getting an answer, and the fourth time one of the Banu Harith said, `Yes, we are,' and said it four times. Muhammad scorned, `If Khalid had not written to me that you had submitted without putting up a fight, I would throw your heads at your feet.' Then he asked them how they used to conquer those they fought. They said that they had never conquered anyone. `No, but you did defeat those who fought you,' Muhammad said. They replied, `We used to defeat those we fought because we were united and we never committed acts of injustice.' Muhammad condescended and appointed Qays bin al Hussein as their leader. When they had gone, he sent Amr bin Hazm to instruct them in religion and to collect taxes from them. His letter to Amr bin Hazm is a replica of the aforementioned instructions, which he had sent earlier to other tribes. The letter was about the ratio of sheep, cattle, camels and agricultural produce to be collected in taxes, and a fifth of all booty as his share. As usual, Jews and Christians, who wanted to keep their religions, were to pay a dinar or its equivalent in clothes on top of other taxes. In case they refused to pay, they would be treated as enemies of God, Muhammad, and the believers. The letter also stipulated instructions on how to perform the hajj and prayers, with a few additions: Muhammad disallowed men from twisting their hair to make pigtails that fell on the back of the neck, and from squatting in one garment in such a way as exposed their genitals. None but the pure were to touch the Qur'an; people were to run to the mosque when summoned, and wash their hands, feet, and faces when they went there.[453]

More revenue collectors and more prophets

Muhammad sent officials to the regions, where people had submitted, to superintend the collection of taxes and to arrange for the transportation of cattle and goods. He sent Ziyad bin Labid to collect from Hadramawt; Adiy bin Hatim to collect from the Ta'iy and the Banu Asad; Malik bin Nuwayra to collect from the Banu Hanzala; al Ala bin al Hadrami to collect from Bahrain, and Ali bin abu Talib to manage Najran. He divided the collection from the Banu Sa'ad between Zibriqan bin Badr and Qays bin Asim.

When he sent Abu Umayya to Sana'a as tax collector, another self-declared prophet al Ansi revolted against him:[454] Muhammad's declaration of apostolate was not unique. There had been other prophets in Arabia, and Al Ansi was not the only one. For example, the deputation of the Banu Hanifa came to Muhammad with a man called Musaylima bin Habib. When they submitted, Muhammad gave gifts to them and they left. Musaylima later claimed that he had become a partner in Muhammad's apostolate. He gathered a significant following,[455] which shows that other prophets too could succeed, and sent two messengers to Muhammad with a letter stating:

> From Musaylima, the messenger of Allah
> To Muhammad, the messenger of Allah.
> Peace upon you. I have been made partner with you in divine authority and so between us belongs half the land, and to the Quraysh the other half, but the Quraysh are a hostile people.

Obviously, at the time of writing this letter, Musaylima believed that either Muhammad was still fighting the Quraysh or it indicates that while Muhammad was collecting taxes from Medina and surrounding areas, the Quraysh kept the taxes they collected from Mecca and the surrounding areas. When Muhammad read this letter, he was furious and he asked the two messengers what they thought about Musaylima's claim to apostolate. The messengers said that they believed the same as Musaylima. Muhammad replied, `By God, were it not that a messenger is not to be killed, I would behead the two of you!' Then he wrote back to Musaylima as follows:

> From Muhammad, the messenger of Allah,
> To Musaylima al *Kazaab (the liar)*.
> Peace is for those who follow the guidance. The earth belongs to Allah and He lets it to those of His men who are pious.[456]

Muhammad sanctifies the pagan rituals

In the tenth year of migration, Muhammad performed his last hajj and instructed the pilgrims in the pagan rituals of hajj, such as circulating around the square stone building and kissing the black stone, which he had learned from his childhood. However, he presented and sanctified these acts as "Islamic."

During the hajj, Ali came from the Yaman with a large quantity of extorted linen to present to Muhammad. In his rush to meet him, Ali left one of his men in charge of his jihadis but gave little instructions about what was to be done with the linen. The man in charge decided to make everyone look presentable. When Ali returned and found the jihadis dressed in new sheets of cloth, he asked what had happened, and the man in-charge said that he had dressed the men so that they might appear seemly when they mingled with other people. Ali ordered them to take off the sheets and put them back with the other booty. The jihadis expressed resentment and complained to Muhammad who told them not to complain because, as he said, Ali was scrupulous about the goods that belonged to God.

During the hajj, Muhammad addressed a crowd of around ten thousand that gathered there. This is known as his famous "farewell sermon" and various reports state that he said the following:

> You have rights over your wives and they have rights over you. You have the right that they should not defile your bed and behave shamelessly. If they do, you are allowed to leave them in separate beds, and to beat them but not with severity. If they refrain from these things, they have the right to food and clothing. Lay injunctions on women kindly, for they depend on you, because they do not own property. You have taken them only on trust from God, and you have made lawful (halaal) their private parts with the words of God. The child belongs to the one in whose bed it was born and the adulterer must be stoned.
>
> God has assigned fixed shares of the heirs, and, hence, leaving a will to transfer your property the way you like is not lawful. He who becomes father to one who is not his real son, and the slave who changes his master to one who is not his master, on them rests the curse of God, the angels, and men.[457]

The said curse on "he who becomes father to one who is not his real son," indicates that Muhammad was still obsessed with the damage to his reputation he had caused by marrying his foster son's wife. In trying to rebuild his reputation, he abrogated the noble Arab tradition of adopting children and leaving inheritance for them. The parts of the sermon about women, and the return of the stoning penalty for adultery, show that he was upset at his wives neglecting him in his old age and worried that other men might take advantage of this. This is described in the following narrations.

As Muhammad grows old, he forbids men from seeing his wives

Since Khadija's death, Muhammad had used the traditional Arab freedom to meet and marry many women. He was very choosy and particular about checking the women fully before marriage. When he sent Umm Saleem to check a certain woman thoroughly, he instructed her: `Smell her mouth and scrutinize her neck from both sides.'[458]

Many men in Medina kept casting doubts about why he had so many wives and slave women. They said that if he could have many wives and slave women, they too could do the same. To dissuade them from imitating him, he issued the following "orders from God:"

> O prophet, We have made lawful for you
> The wives to whom you have paid dowries
> And the slave women whom God has given you as booty
> And the daughters of your paternal uncles and aunts
> And of your maternal uncles and aunts, who fled with you
> And any believing woman who gives herself to the prophet
> And whom the prophet wishes to take in marriage.
> This privilege is yours alone, granted to no other believer.
> We (*God*) know what We have ordained for them
> About their wives and their slave women.
> We grant you these privileges so that none may blame you.
> God is Forgiving and Merciful. (Sura 33, verse 50)

Another problem was that some men had begun to take interest in his wives. These would come to meet him, have meals with him, and look for excuses to talk to his wives. During one such meal, a man touched A'isha's hand.[459] This greatly offended Muhammad and he issued more "divine verses:"

> O Believers! Do not enter the dwellings of the prophet
> For a meal early, waiting while the meal is being cooked.
> Enter when you are called in
> And leave as soon as you have eaten.
> Do not engage in banter for this hurts the prophet,
> And he is embarrassed to ask you to leave
> But God is not embarrassed in telling the right thing.
> When you ask the prophet's wives for something,
> Speak to them from behind a curtain
> This is purer for your and their hearts. (Sura 33, verse 53)

As he was growing old, he feared that men would try to befriend his wives on pretext of sharing the latter's grievances, mentioned earlier in this work, and with a view to marry them after his death. Hence, he added the following verses to the above:

> It is not right for you to annoy God's messenger
> Nor shall you ever wed his widows after him at any time.
> This will surely be a grave offence in the sight of God.
> Whether you do something openly or in secrecy
> God has knowledge of all things. (Sura 33, verses 53-54)

Then he commanded his wives to cover themselves when they went out, and not appear in front of other men. In public, they were not supposed to shake their feet or talk in coquettish manners that would catch other men's attention.[460] He also gave the following dire warnings to those who spread scandals about his marital issues:

> Those who speak ill of God and His messenger,
> Shall be cursed by God in this life and in the hereafter
> He has prepared for them a humiliating punishment.
> Those who slander believing men and women undeservedly
> Shall bear the guilt of false accusation and manifest sin.
> O prophet, say to your wives, daughters,
> And the women of the believers
> To draw their cloaks close round them
> That is proper, so that they may be recognized and not annoyed.

If the hypocrites and those who have tainted hearts,
And the scandalmongers of Medina will not stop,
We will set you over them,
And they shall not be your neighbours but for a little while
Cursed, wherever they will be found
Seized, and slain with a fierce slaughter.
Such has been the way of God with people before
And you shall not find any change in God's ways.
(Sura 33, verses 57-63)

Muhammad falls ill and dies, while his associates fight amongst themselves for power

After his last hajj, Muhammad returned to Medina only to find it in turmoil, with three large groups bitterly contesting each other for power. The first group comprised the earlier Meccan migrants, the Muhajirin, who were Muhammad's veteran followers. The second group consisted of the recent Meccan converts, called the "Talq'a." These were his tribal relatives and major leaders of the Quraysh. The third group comprised his Medinian Ansar followers.

The gulf between the three groups was widening to the level of animosity. The first and second groups held claims of the Quraysh superiority in ruling people whilst the Ansar, led by Sa'ad bin Ubaada, demanded a proper share in the governance of Arabia.

Muhammad was becoming increasingly unhappy with these horrible social circumstances in the creation of which he had played the key role. He was certain that the Quraysh would be the future rulers, and he confirmed this by his declarations, `We (the Quraysh) are the rulers whilst you (the Ansar) can be the ministers (*Ana Emir wa untuma wazir*);' and, `The Arabic of the Quraysh tribe is the most superior and holy because God spoke in this dialect.' But his Medinian followers were confused by his other statements, such as, `An Arab is not superior to an Ajmi (Iraqis and Persians), and an Ajmi is not superior to an Arab;' and, `All believers are equal as brothers.' To allay the fears of the Ansar, Muhammad advised his veteran Quraysh followers to be kind to them and preached:

> O Muhajirin! Be kind to the Ansar, for while other converts are increasing in number, the Ansar are becoming a minority. The

Ansar have always been my comfort and support. So treat their good men well and forgive those of them who err.[461]

However, the Muhajirin still saw the Ansar as their main rivals because both groups were planning to rule after him. Muhammad felt so dejected that the dead seemed to him happier than the living. In the middle of one night, he took his slave Abu Muwayhiba, and went to the graveyard called Baqi al Gharqad. There he stood among the graves and spoke to the dead, 'O people of the graves! You are much happier and much better off than those alive for it is among the living that conflicts have appeared like clouds of darkness, one after the other, the last being worse than the first.' Then he turned to his slave and said, 'God has given me two options; the first is to take the keys of the treasures of this world, have a long life, and then enter paradise. The second is to meet my Lord and live in paradise now.' The slave asked him to take the first option but he said that he had chosen the latter. Then he prayed for the dead and, when he came home, his terminal illness began with a severe headache. His wife A'isha too had headache and she was saying, 'O my head!' Muhammad said, 'No A'isha, O *my* head! If only you were to die before me so that I could wrap you in shroud and pray over you and bury you!' A'isha did not like this and replied, 'If I died before you, and you buried me, you would return to my house and spend a bridal night with one of your wives.' This was a taunt at his many marriages and slave women.

Muhammad smiled and when he went around seeing his nine wives one by one, the pain overtook him until he fell in the house of Maymuna. He called his wives, asked their permission to be nursed in A'isha's house, and they agreed.[462] His cousins, al Fadl bin Abbas and Ali, brought him to A'isha's home in a state that his head was bound in a cloth and he dragged his feet. A'isha had not been on speaking terms with Ali since the day she had faced accusations of adultery and Ali had beaten her slave woman to coerce her to tell the truth.

Muhammad's illness worsened but he was not willing to give up. He went to the mosque with his head bound, and sat in the pulpit. There he said a long prayer for those who had died at the battle of Uhud. Then, in his customary obscure manner, he said, 'God has given one of his servants the choice between this world and that which is with God, and the servant has chosen the latter.'

Abu Bakr, who was good at deciphering Muhammad's language, correctly guessed that he referred to his own death, and he wept, saying, `We and our children will be your ransom to bring you back.' Muhammad replied by saying that Abu Bakr was his best friend.

Even at this stage, Muhammad would not give up sending raid parties. A lifetime habit was not easy to give up, and he could not take rest. He planned to send a force under the command of Osama bin Zayd bin Haritha towards Syria, into the territory of the Balq'a and al Darum, in the land of Palestine. When he found that people were procrastinating in joining the expedition, he came to the mosque with his head bound, and sat in the pulpit. After pushing the people to depart, he returned and his pain became severe. To please him, Osama and his army went out a stop from Medina and stayed there to wait and see what would happen to him.

As his illness grew, he suspected that his wives were conspiring against him. Umm Salama, Maymuna, and some other women, along with uncle Abbas, forced him to take a medicine when his condition grew worse. He did not like this and, when he temporarily recovered, he ordered that all the women in the house should take the same medicine. Abbas said, `We were afraid that you would get pleurisy.' Muhammad replied, `God will not afflict me with pleurisy because pleurisy comes from Satan, and God will not let Satan overpower me. Except my uncle, force everyone in the house to take this medicine.' He wanted to see if the medicine had been poisoned. Maymuna was fasting but she too was forced to take the medicine.

Some people wondered why Muhammad, who had performed miracles, could not cure his illness or stop his death. For these he said, `A prophet does not die without being given the choice.' In other words, he wanted to show that he was still in control of the situation.

Tibri states that on the ninth day of Muhammad's illness, he mustered enough strength and asked A'isha to summon Ali. A'isha wanted him to see her father rather than Ali and so she said, `Why don't you see Abu Bakr instead?' Then he asked Hifza, Umar's daughter, to summon Ali but she replied, `Why don't you see Umar instead?' It might seem heartless to ignore a dying man's wish but both A'isha and Hifza were worried about their future. They knew that no one would marry them because Muhammad had forbidden it. Their futures would depend on their fathers' provisions and they were worried that if Muhammad nominated Ali as his successor, the Hashimis would be in charge and the lower tribes of their fathers, Banu Adiy and Banu Tamim, would be ignored. Hence, the two women called in their fathers and they came. When Muhammad saw Abu Bakr and Umar, he appeared to recover somewhat and said, `Bring writing materials that I may dictate something for you, after which you will not be led into error.' Abu Bakr and Umar, known to be amongst his most faithful companions, did nothing. Instead of calling for a scribe, they voiced concerns that this would put strain on him. Instead of helping him make his dying wishes known, they kept asking him and everyone to remain silent. Disappointed, Muhammad said, `Leave me alone. Do not quarrel in my presence.' As he whispered, because of weakness, Umar used his loud voice to full advantage and shouted, `The messenger of God is overcome by pain. We have the Qur'an, God's book, and that is sufficient for us.' In plain words he meant, `We do not want to hear his last words,' but the Islamists quote Umar's statement as an example of his absolute faith in the Qur'an.

When Muhammad was unable to lead the prayers, he ordered A'isha to tell her father, Abu Bakr, to lead the prayers but A'isha did not want people to think that Abu Bakr was trying to take Muhammad's place, lest they turned against him. Hence, she made excuses, saying to him that Abu Bakr had a weak voice, he was too emotional, and he wept much when reading the Qur'an. Muhammad repeated his order and A'isha repeated her objection at which he accused her of being treacherous like Youssef's (*Joseph's*) brothers. The story of Joseph, in the Qur'an, states that his brothers were jealous of him because their father loved him more. The brothers threw him into a well, brought his shirt to their father, with animal blood on it, and told him that wolves had eaten him. However, a passing caravan, which had stopped to draw water from the well, pulled Joseph out.

Upon Abu Bakr's refusal, Umar stood up to lead the prayers and, in his enthusiasm, he very loudly shouted, `Allah O Akbar' (God is Great). Muhammad did not like this and said, twice over, `Allah and the believers forbid it.' He was upset that his own wives and companions had begun to disobey him and he had no power left to do anything about it.

Though some reports suggest that Muhammad wanted to appoint Ali as his successor, others state that he had said, `It is the same if I appoint a successor or leave people to select one by themselves.' Although this did not help prevent the conflicts that arose after his death, if he did so, he would have had good reasons for it: He understood his men well enough to know that as soon as he would appoint a successor, it would alienate the disappointed candidates and their tribes, and trigger the conflicts even before his death. This would have undermined his claim to apostolate. He wanted to die in peace as the messenger and leader of all Arab tribes and he wanted everyone to keep coming to him and doing favours in the hope that he would appoint them as his successor.

When his illness became severe, he was unable to speak. He would lift his hand upwards and then bring it down upon him, pointing to God and then to himself. On the day of his death, he felt better in the morning. He lifted the curtain on A'isha's door, which opened in the mosque, and stood at the door to see if Abu Bakr was leading the prayers and found him sitting on the pulpit. Abu Bakr moved from his place to make room for him but he pushed him back, saying, 'Lead the men in prayers.' He sat and prayed in a sitting posture, on the right side of Abu Bakr. When he had ended his prayers, he turned to the men and spoke to them in a loud voice that could be heard from outside the mosque, 'O men! The fire has been kindled, and rebellions come like the darkness of the night. By God, you cannot blame me for I allow only what the Qur'an allows, and forbid only what the Qur'an forbids.'

When he had finished, Abu Bakr said to him, 'O messenger of God, I see that this morning you enjoy the favour and blessings of God. Today is the day of my wife, Bint Kharija. May I go to her?' He allowed and Abu Bakr went to see his wife.

The shrewd uncle Abbas had guessed that Muhammad was to die soon and that his morning reprieve was like the last fluttering of a flame. It was time for all to secure their future positions. Accordingly, Abbas took his nephew Ali in privacy and said to him, 'Ali, three nights from now you will be a slave of our rivals (either the Ansar or the Umayyads). I swear by God that I recognized death in Muhammad's face as I used to recognize it in the faces of the sons of Abd al Muttalib. So let us go to him and ask for the succession; if it is to be granted to us, we shall know it, and if it is to go to others, we will request him to instruct the people to treat us well.'

Ali answered, 'By God, I will not ask Muhammad for succession because if he withheld it from us, none after him will give it to us.'

Muhammad came back from the mosque and lay in A'isha's lap. She later reported, `I found him heavy in my lap and as I looked into his face, his eyes were fixed and he was saying, "No, the most exalted companion is of paradise." I said, "You were given the choice to live or meet God and you have chosen God, who sent the truth to you!"

He died in A'isha's lap in the heat of the noon on Monday, June 8, 632. She would say, using the Arabic euphemism, `His head lay between my lungs and my lips when it became very heavy and I saw the empty gaze of death in his eyes.' She laid his head on a pillow, and stood beating her breast and slapping her face, in the traditional way of mourning, and the other women too broke into terrible, piercing howls.

When the news spread that Muhammad was dead, men and women alike slapped their faces, beat their chests with clenched fists, raked their fingernails over their foreheads until blood streaked down their eyes, and scooped up handfuls of dust and poured it over their hair. Umar panicked and tried to hide the news by shouting, `The hypocrites allege that the messenger is dead, but, by God, he is not dead: He has gone to his Lord, as Moses went away from his people for forty days, returning to them after they had said that he had died. By God, the messenger will return as Moses returned and will cut off the hands and feet of men who allege that the messenger is dead.'

Abu Bakr stopped Umar and said, `Gently Umar, be quiet,' but Umar refused and went on shouting. When Abu Bakr saw that Umar would not be silent, he went forward to the people who came to him, and addressed them, `O men, if you worshiped Muhammad, he is dead: If you worship God, God is alive, immortal.' Then he recited this verse, `Muhammad is nothing but a messenger. Messengers have passed away before him. Can it be that if he were to die or be killed, you would turn back on your heels? He who turns back does no harm to God, and God will reward the grateful.'

People did not know that this verse had come down until Abu Bakr recited it. Hearing the verse, Umar was dumbfounded with the realization that Muhammad was dead. His legs became lifeless, he fell to the ground, and almost fainted.[463]

Ali, Zubayr bin al Awwam and Talha bin Abaydallah took over A'isha's room, and she moved to Hifza's room. They prepared

Muhammad for the grave by washing him and wrapping him in his shroud but others were busy thinking about their future.

XXX

A group of the Ansar gathered around their leader, Sa'ad bin Ubaada, at Thaqifa Banu Sa'ida, planning how to take power in their hands. The Muhajirin gathered around Abu Bakr and Umar. An informant came, told them that the Ansar had gathered to choose a new leader for the believers, and said, `If you want to take charge of the people, take it now before the Ansar's action becomes serious.'

Umar and Abu Bakr decided to gather their men and go to the Ansar to see what they were doing. On their way, they met two sympathizers who warned them not to go to the Ansar but make their own decision separately. Umar insisted on meeting the Ansar and found them in the tent. In the middle of the tent was a man wrapped up in a blanket. In answer to Umar's inquiry, the Ansar told him that he was Sa'ad bin Ubaada and that he was ill. Sa'ad bin Ubaada was one of the first Khazraj Medinians who had travelled to Mecca and secretly sworn allegiance to Muhammad at al Aqaba. The Quraysh had chased and arrested him and given him a good beating. Since then, he had always bore grudge against the Quraysh. On the day Muhammad and his jihadis had marched into Mecca, Sa'ad had raised the slogan, `This is the day of raid – today the Ka'ba will be fair game.' Muhammad had ordered Ali and Khalid bin Walid to take the flag from Sa'ad and lead the others in entering Mecca. Now, Sa'ad did not want to be ruled by the Quraysh but be the leader himself. However, his illness made it easy for Umar to do what follows.

When all had sat down, an Ansar speaker pronounced God's praise and said, `We are God's helpers and the regiment of Islam. You, O Muhajirin, are like our family for you came to settle among us but now you are trying to cut us off and wrest authority from us.'

Umar had come fully prepared. He knew that the Muhajirin were the only bridge between the powerful Umayyads and Ansar, and that the Ansar would have to take a subordinate place. He had prepared a harsh speech but Abu Bakr told him not to speak because this would cause conflict. Hence, when the Ansar speaker had finished, Abu Bakr rose and said, `All the good words that you said about yourselves you deserve them. But the Arabs will accept only the Quraysh as rulers because they are traditionally known as the best of the Arabs in blood and country. Therefore, in your own interest, I offer you one of these two men: Accept the one you like.' Thus speaking, he took hold of Umar's hand and that of Abu Ubayda bin al Jarrah, who was sitting with them. The Ansar were not impressed and one of them said, `Let us have one ruler from us and one from the Quraysh.'

Altercation broke out and voices were raised until, when a complete breach was to be feared, Umar stood up and said, `Stretch out your hand, Abu Bakr.' He did so, and Umar paid him homage; the Muhajirin followed, and then some of the Ansar hesitatingly joined. Then Umar aggressively jumped on the sick Sa'ad bin Ubaada, and trampled him under his feet. Someone shouted that Umar had killed Sa'ad, and Umar replied, `God killed him.'[464]

This was the first blood among Muhammad's companions who had sought power after his death, and countless more were to follow, each to be justified, following Muhammad's tradition, as having sanctioned by God. Both the killer and the victim were his closest aides and blood was shed when his body was still waiting burial.

Abbas had urged Ali to abandon his vigil over the body, offering to keep watch in his place while Ali asserted his claim to leadership but Ali had refused. He stayed with Muhammad's body and as the light faded on Tuesday evening, the news arrived that the first caliph would not be Ali but Abu Bakr.

By now, a full day and half had passed since the death and the June heat was causing the body to putrefy. Because the dessert heat quickly rots a corpse, custom decreed that a body be buried within twenty-four hours but with all the clan leaders and believers busy in scheming for leadership, Ali and Abbas had decided to wait. When they heard that power had gone to Abu Bakr, they did not want to wait, for this would give Abu Bakr a chance to use Muhammad's funeral to score points and confirm himself as his true successor.

In the small hours of the Wednesday morning, sleeping in Hifza's room, A'isha was woken by scraping sounds echoing around the courtyard of the mosque. She did not get up to investigate the noise, which she later discovered was the sound of pickaxes and shovels digging into the soil in her room – just a few doors down. Muhammad had once said, `No prophet dies unless he is buried where he died.' Accordingly, they dug the grave at the foot of the sleeping platform on which he had died in A'isha's room. When it was deep enough, they tipped up the pallet holding the shrouded body and slid it down into the grave so that it faced toward Mecca. Then they covered it with earth and laid a simple slab of stone on top. There was no funeral, ritual, mass procession, crowd of mourners or eulogies. They buried the body in the silence of night.

The next day people came to see the grave and prayed over it: First came the men, then the women, then the children, and then the slaves. A'isha regretted the way they dealt with Muhammad's body and said that they did not properly wash him. She used to say, `Had I known what I knew later, none but his wives would have washed him but we were told nothing about the burial of the messenger though we heard the sound of the pickaxes in the mid of the Wednesday night.'[465]

Muhammad's poet, Hassan bin Thabit, was from the Ansar and he described the Quraysh takeover of power, and the consequent poverty that befell Ansar as follows:

> Since the messenger was buried in his grave
> Misery has befallen the Ansar
> They have been barred from all towns
> And their faces have turned grey.
> Tell the poor that generosity is gone
> With the prophet who departed in the morn.
> Where is he who gave me a saddled camel?
> And my family's rations when rain did not fall?
> The day they laid Muhammad in his grave,
> And covered him with earth,
> The booty was divided to the exclusion of the Ansar
> And the Quraysh squandered it openly within themselves.
> Your wives have no curtains in their tents
> Like nuns they put on coarse garments of hair
> Certain of misery after happiness
> O best of men, I was as if in a river
> Without which I have become lonely in my thirst.[466]

The verses show how the Quraysh abandoned the Ansar to their lowly peasant status as the former took control of the affairs.

As people heard of Muhammad's death, they began to revert to their former religions[467] under the belief that his jihadis would no longer attack them. However, Abu Bakr quickly stepped into Muhammad's shoes, launched raiding parties, and forced people back into paying taxes to his rule. Abu Bakr and his successors also sent raiding parties into new lands and re-established the system of jihad and the distribution of booty. Thus the Islamic age of living off banditry, called the Khilafa (caliphate) and euphemised as "spreading Islam and God's rule," was carried into the coming centuries. The following pages provide a summary of the conduct of Muhammad's relatives who ruled after him in the name of Khilafa.

Appendix I: Arab-Islamic Imperialism Summarized Highlights of the Khilafa Despotism of Muhammad's Relatives

Abu Bakr, the first caliph (634-636 CE) ignores the murder of Sa'ad bin Ubaada

The next day, Abu Bakr sat in the pulpit in the mosque and people swore fealty to him. He justified his assumption of authority by saying that he had no other choice because he was afraid that Muhammad's community would split up. Then he delivered a sermon in which he wowed to carry on fighting in the name of God, and thus continue the tradition set by Muhammad.

Tribal affiliations and prejudices had always played a major role in the Arab political decision-making. Accordingly, when Muhammad died, his prominent associates came close to fighting each other. The situation was nothing like the Islamists' claims that the believers chose their caliphs because of their piety and adherence to religion. From the larger Quraysh tribe, there were four most likely candidates for the post of caliph. These were Muhammad's two fathers-in-law, Abu Bakr and Umar, and his two sons-in-law, Ali and Uthman. As stated above, while Ali was busy in arranging for Muhammad's burial, Umar took lead in murdering the Ansar candidate, Sa'ad bin Ubaada, and then made the others to swear fealty to Abu Bakr.[468] The reason Umar had hastily nominated Abu Bakr was that the latter was a simpleton whom he could easily manipulate. In addition, Abu Bakr had the support of a number of Medinians. A few days after becoming the caliph, Abu Bakr took a few carpets and went to the market to sell them. Umar stopped him and said, `What are you doing?' Abu Bakr replied, `I have to earn a living.' `That is not the way,' Umar told him, `You have to act as a ruler now.' Then he told him to take an annual stipend of four thousand dirhams from the treasury.

In exchange for Umar's support, Abu Bakr did nothing to investigate the murder of Sa'ad bin Ubaada. It was obvious that he did not want to apply the law of revenge on Umar for killing a veteran believer. Two years later, he repaid more of Umar's favour by nominating him as his successor. Both Umar and Abu Bakr belonged to the weaker Quraysh tribes, Banu Adiy and Banu Tamim respectively, and were afraid that if the Umayyads took over, they would start taking revenge for their men killed in Badr and Uhud. Hence, they colluded to keep the Umayyad's from taking power.

The stronger Meccan tribes held the weaker tribes in contempt and so they resented Abu Bakr's taking the post without any consultation with them. The Umayyads in particular were angry, and their chief Abu Sufyan came to see Ali and said, `How come this man from our smallest tribe has become the caliph? We would rather have a Hashimi, particularly you, in the top post and, if you are so willing, I shall fill the valley with cavalry and infantry.'[469] Because the Umayyads had always rivalled the Hashimis in ruling Mecca, Ali was able to see the insincerity behind Abu Sufyan's offer of support. He saw this offer as an Umayyad attempt to make the Hashimis fight the other Quraysh tribes and grab the power back for themselves. He refused to start a new war and said that he did not want to divide the believers.

On their part, Abu Bakr and Umar did not want Ali to have enough resources to be able to gather men around him. Accordingly, they refused Ali's wife, Fatima (Muhammad's daughter), her share from the income of the occupied Jewish lands of Fadak.[470] When Fatima protested and said that, before his death, Muhammad had bequeathed Fadak to her, Abu Bakr said that close to his death, Muhammad was not in his right mind.

Abu Bakr died within two years of his appointment and, as he had willed, Umar took over the Khilafa rule.

<u>Umar, the second caliph (636-644 CE): The beginning of the colonization of Bilaad al Shaam and Persia</u>

Because Umar had impulsively imposed the rule of Abu Bakr upon people, he was fully aware of the threat of someone else doing the same against his rule. To stop this from happening, he declared, `The one who stands for the post of caliph without consultation, and the one who swears allegiance to him, both will be executed.'[471] Thus, he prohibited exactly what he had done.

Because Umar belonged to a small and weak tribe, the Banu Adiy, he had no choice but to win support of the most powerful Umayyads by granting all ruling posts to them, and almost no significant position to his own tribesmen.[472] Fortunately, the Umayyads were more interested in conquering the fertile and rich lands of Bilaad al Shaam and Persia (now called Syria, Palestine,

Israel, Jordan, Lebanon, Egypt, Iraq and Iran) than to bother taking Medina from him.

Even before Muhammad was born, well-connected Meccan merchants had established roots in the lands and cities in which they traded. They owned estates, mansions, farms and orchards in Egypt, Damascus, Palestine and Iraq and there were Arab settlements in the lands of Byzantium and Persia. These two empires had been at war, intermittently though, for eight hundred years. They had thoroughly depleted their resources, and lost much of their strength and control over regions. In 627, when Muhammad held off Abu Sufyan's siege of Medina, Heraclius won victory over the Persians at Nineveh, in what is now northern Iraq. Three months later his army sacked the palace of Chosroe in the Persian capital of Ctesiphon, close to the future city of Baghdad, thus provoking the emperor's son to kill his own father. At the time of the Truce of Hudaybiya between Muhammad and Abu Sufyan, the younger Chosroe sued for peace with Heraclius but the Byzantine emperor pursued his advantage and ousted the Persians from Egypt, Syria, Palestine, and Anatolia. He made a triumphal re-entry into Constantinople in August 629.[473]

However, although Heraclius had forced the Persian empire to the verge of collapse, the long military conflict had left his own realm very weak. Byzantine control of the far-flung Christian empire was more tenuous than ever. The two great empires had essentially fought each other to exhaustion and they became easy prey to Arab jihadis.

In the year 634, Arab forces took Damascus. In 636, they defeated Heraclius at Yarmuk, to the southeast of the Sea of Galilee. In 638, they took Qadisiya, in southern Iraq, from the Persians. One year later, they conquered Jerusalem and by the year 640, they controlled both Egypt and Anatolia.

When Jerusalem fell to the Arabs, Umar went to visit the city. He ordered the construction of a mosque in place of the Jewish Temple of Solomon, which the Arab raiders had reduced to a rubbish heap.[474]

When Armenia and Egypt fell to the Umayyad commander Amr bin al Aas, Umar played his part in the burning down of the great library of Alexandria; his message to the commanders on the Egyptian front was clear, 'We have the Qur'an; we do not need other books.'

Fanatical Islamists around the world, particularly the Wahhabis of Saudi Arabia, Pakistan, Afghanistan, and Algeria, still revere and follow Umar's message. These do not read books other than Islamist propaganda books and, when they recite the Qur'an, they leave its understanding and interpretation to the propagandist preachers.

The Umayyads enslave the Syrians, Egyptians, Iraqis, and Persians in the name of Islam

As the Umayyads began to establish their rule in Syria, Egypt, and Iraq, hoards of jihadis entered the conquered lands to rob the locals[475] and take slaves and concubines, which they called their reward from God in return for doing jihad. In this process, they found support from the earlier Arab migrants who had been settling in these countries since long. The conquerors would hoard looted goods and transport them along with slaves and concubines on horses, donkeys, and camels, to Damascus, which the Umayyads declared as their capital. They sent little to Caliph Umar in Medina, which disaffected the Medinian Ansar from the empire.

To protect the caravans of goods on route from Persia to central Arabia and Syria, the Umayyads established two military camps in Iraq. These camps later grew to become the towns of Kufa and Basra. The dispossessed Iraqis, Persians, and nomads began settling around these two encampments. They were willing to lift and store goods or pack them for onward transportation but the Arabs mainly used slaves for such jobs. However, it was next to impossible for the rulers to find literate men and so these were highly valued and appointed as the collectors of goods and taxes. Although the jihadis were engaged in organised robbery of the vanquished, if a servant stole as much as a sack of grain from the stores, they would amputate his hand under the Shari'a, which they applied to non-Muslims as well. Many embraced Islam out of fear of persecution[476] because the jihadis would confiscate non-Muslims' properties on pretext that the latter were insulting Islam and the Qur'an, and would spare their lives only if the victims converted to Islam. In support of their forced conversions to Islam, they could quote Muhammad's saying:

> I am commanded to fight the people until they say, "There is no God but Allah, and Muhammad is His messenger." Once they

say it, their blood and property are protected except when there is a legal right.[477]

Once they had established their rule, the imperialists allowed submissive and hardworking non-Muslims, particularly Christians and Zoroastrians, to live as *dhimmi* (non-Muslim subjects). Experts in agriculture and trade, the dhimmis could make enough money to pay the *jizya* tax. Upon seeing that non-Muslims converting to Islam meant lesser revenues, many Arab rulers subsequently banned conversion to Islam. The argument was that if converted to Islam, the new Muslims would not work as hard as they did to pay *jizya* in order to protect their faith. Afterwards, the Umayyads imposed *jizya* on newer Muslims too and declared that they had done so because these were converting to Islam only to avoid the *jizya*. Some officials once wrote to Hajjaj bin Youssef, the governor of Iraq, that because of conversions to Islam, new Muslims were settling in Kufa and Basra and this was reducing the revenues. Hajjaj ordered his officials to expel the newer Muslims from the towns and force them to pay *jizya*.

Not only did the imperialists force the non-Muslims to pay *jizya*, they also made fun of their cultures and beliefs. They portrayed the Zoroastrians as stupid enough to worship fire, having sunk to the degradation of letting vultures eat their dead, and subjected them to gross humiliation and taunts. Being unable to fight back, the Zoroastrians gradually migrated out of their Persian homeland to India, where some Indian Rajas granted them asylum. The details of this tragic cleansing of Zoroastrians from Persia and their migration and settling in India are available in the book titled, "Beyond Belief" by the Nobel Laureate V. S. Naipal.

The Arab imperialists forced Arabic language on all conquered people, calling it "the language of God" and branding other languages as inferior.[478] For centuries, they did not allow the Persian converts to pray in Persian. Conversion to Islam was no guarantee that the conquered would become equal to the conquerors. The conquerors wanted to enslave the Ajmis (Iraqis and Persians) and were blatantly racist.[479] Even after converting, the Ajmis could not lead in prayers in mosques or take up a higher post such as that of a judge.[480] If Ajmis participated in jihad alongside their masters, they did not receive a share in the booty.[481] Non-Arab men were not allowed to marry Arab women but Arab men could enslave non-Arab women or marry them without the consent of their parents, have children from them, and then refuse to father them. Children of Arab fathers and Ajmi mothers were called "hajieen" (faulty) and, therefore, deprived of inheritance. This was simply an extension of the previously described Muhammadan permission to rape captive women.

In one reported incident, an Arab married off his daughter to an Ajmi. The local Umayyad governor immediately had the couple divorced. The Ajmi bridegroom was beaten, and his head, eyebrows, and beard were shaven off as a penalty for marrying an Arab woman. Even after fourteen centuries, the Saudis have kept this tradition alive; they do not allow Saudi women to marry non-Arabs even if the latter are Muslims.

Through such oppression and blatant racism, the Umayyads bred hatred in the hearts of the Persians that was to explode later.[482]

(644 CE) An oppressed Persian slave stabs and kills Umar

Umar paid the ultimate price for his ruthlessness: He rejected the pleas of a badly exploited Persian slave, Abu Lu'lwa, who stabbed and killed him,[483] and then committed suicide.

Furious at his father's murder, Umar's son Abaydallah ran wild and slew Abu Lu'lwa's daughter, another Persian named Hurmuzan, and a Christian named Jaffina. After slaying Jaffina, he used his sword to carve the sign of the Crucifix on the victim's forehead.[484] The three victims had nothing to do with Umar's murder. Sa'ad bin abi Waqqas, an early follower of Muhammad, restrained Abaydallah and locked him up to stop him from shedding more blood.

Uthman, the third caliph (644-656 CE), begins by disregarding the Islamic law of revenge

After Umar, the Umayyads managed to place their tribesman Uthman as the caliph. The selection of Uthman against Ali – a Hashimi – was made easy by Abd al Rehmaan bin Awf, the chief of the selection committee who was also Uthman's father-in-law. Abd al Rehmaan rejected Ali on grounds that Ali had expressed his intention to make changes to the way Abu Bakr and Umar had run the empire, while Uthman had said that he would maintain the status quo. In other words, the Umayyads wanted to keep the high posts, which Umar had granted to them, so that they could remain the chief custodians of the booty they gathered from the conquered lands. Accordingly, after assuming the post of caliph, Uthman kept all the higher posts with the Umayyads. He repaid Umar's past favours to the Umayyads by releasing his son Abaydallah without any punishment. He justified this by declaring, `O believers! A few days ago, Abaydallah's father Umar was murdered. While it is true that Abaydallah has killed three innocent persons, if I get him executed, we will lose the support of the Banu Adiy tribe.' As a special concession, Uthman paid blood-money from his own purse to the relatives of the victims though it caused great resentment among many, especially the friends of Hurmuzan. Uthman warned the critics to stay away from Abaydallah but a friend of Hurmuzan waited for the right moment and killed Abaydallah at a battle in which both were supposed to be on the same side against the "unbelievers."

Because Uthman appointed his Umayyad tribesmen as governors from Khurasan (in Persia) to North Africa,[485] it enriched them beyond proportions, bred jealousy among the other tribes[486] and, as the subsequent events showed, caused murderous internecine wars between the Umayyads, the Alawites (Ali's descendants), and the Abbasids (descendants of Muhammad's uncle Abbas).

When the Arab armies returned to Medina with booties from conquests in North Africa, Uthman bestowed the entire first booty, worth half million dinars, to his cousin Marwan bin al Hakam. The entire second booty went to his second cousin named Abdallah bin Sa'ad bin abi S'rah.[487] People saw this as gross insult to Prophet Muhammad who had hated both these men: Marwan's father, al Hakam used to imitate and ridicule Muhammad's mannerisms in speech. Marwan too was less than obsequious, and Muhammad had banished him from Medina. About the second man, Muhammad had condemned Abdallah bin Sa'ad to death for making fun of his "divine revelations" but, at Uthman's request, granted him a last minute reprieve. Uthman was a rare Umayyad who had supported Muhammad at a time when his other tribesmen had been making fun of Muhammad. The tribe had joined Muhammad only after the fall of Mecca, largely as his unbeliever allies. Now Uthman had placed these men at the helm of the Khilafa.

A highly respected associate of Muhammad, Abuzar Ghifari, criticized Uthman's nepotism and the accumulation of wealth in a few hands within one tribe.[488] He called these acts sinful. Uthman exiled him and he died in misery, on a caravan route, with no one to bury him but fellow travellers. This horrible treatment of a man who had been Muhammad's close associate caused widespread resentment.

(651 CE) Uthman assembles and edits the Qur'an

Muhammad had left a legacy of verses that many of his followers had either memorized by heart or engraved on bark, clay tablets, and palm leaves. Part of the scribed stock had been kept at Ali's house, and the rest stored at A'isha's lodge, but she had passed it on to her father Abu Bakr when they buried Muhammad in her room. When Abu Bakr had died, it had been passed on to Umar. When Umar had died, it was stored at the house of his daughter Hifza.

During the fourteen years of Abu Bakr and Umar's rule, Ali had compiled the first Qur'an. He was best suited to do so because, since childhood, he had always been with Muhammad and participated in his life. Ali had presented his Qur'an first to Abu Bakr and then to Umar for circulation across the empire but both had refused to accept it, fearing that Ali would subsequently use this achievement to claim the Hashimis' right to rule the Khilafa empire. They were content with the verses that they had acquired either directly from Muhammad or through their daughters, who had been Muhammad's wives.

The Umayyads had mostly laughed at Muhammad's revelations during his lifetime but now, with their empire expanding from Syria to North Africa, they realized that the Qur'an was the best tool ever invented to subjugate people by controlling their minds. Hence, Uthman set himself the task of collecting the Qur'anic material from wherever it lay, and provide a standardized Qur'an. He took the stock of verses from Hifza and gathered those companions of Muhammad who remembered part or all of his verses by heart. Then he instructed these men to compile the Qur'an. The compilation took around five years. He then edited and selected the final version,[489] after burning down the verses he did not want to include because, he said, he did not recall Muhammad ever having said those verses. The resulting Qur'an was not large enough to satisfy him. He then added to it segments of Biblical scriptures[490] that had been largely orally transmitted to the peninsular Arabs, and their copies were available in Medina and Mecca from the local Christian and Jewish scholars. These scriptures consisted of the stories of Mary (*Maryam*), Joseph (*Youssef*), Jonah (*Younas*), Abraham (*Ibrahim*), the Israelites (*Bani Israel*), and Noah (*Nuh*). By adding these scriptures, with minor alterations, Uthman wanted to make the Qur'an more voluminous and credible enough to look like a "holy book." It is also possible that Muhammad himself had adapted some of these and had them scribed in his lifetime, and Uthman obtained them from where they lay.

Uthman did not value Ali's input though this would have provided more authenticity to the resultant Qur'an. It is reported that he did not consult Ali because he wanted to exclude the verses that Muhammad had said in Ali's favour. These verses could raise Ali's status above that of the other three caliphs of the period.

The burning down of a part of Qur'anic verses caused great controversy among Muhammad's former associates because they still had variant versions of Muhammad's sayings, which they believed were genuine words of God. The disagreement grew so much that pupils and teachers of Qur'an ended up killing each other. When Uthman found out about this, he said, `Here in my presence, you lie in the Qur'an and make it full of mistakes, so those who are in faraway lands, they must be doing more than this.' To stop devotees from killing each other over this issue, Uthman had his Qur'an officially circulated, and he ordered that any other Qur'anic material should be destroyed.[491]

The Islamists claim that the present Qur'an is exactly in the form as revealed to Muhammad, and God has always protected it. Most naïve Muslims believe that it descended from the heavens in one piece. However, the earliest records show that Uthman collated and edited the Qur'anic material, destroyed parts of it, messed up with the chronological order of the verses and then, to make it thicker, he added the variant versions of Jewish and Christian scriptures that were available in written form, on parchment.

The strongest evidence, showing that the present Qur'an is not in the form as Muhammad had it scribed, is its chronological disorder: The chapters (suras) which Muhammad uttered in his early days in Mecca are located at the end of the present Qur'an. Rather than arranging the suras chronologically, Uthman had them arranged more or less by length – from longest to shortest. This means that one who wants to match the suras with Muhammad's life has to read the Qur'an backwards – starting from the end towards the beginning. One also needs to keep in mind that, as explained above, Muhammad did not utter all of the Jewish and Christian parts of the Qur'an, though he might have read pieces of these to his followers during his sermons, or to his opponents when engaged in theological debates.

To record his objections, Ali wrote his book, "Nahj'l Balagha," in which he lamented at the dishonesty and greed of the three caliphs, Abu Bakr, Umar, and Uthman, who had usurped his right to be the caliph and he had kept quiet for the sake of unity among believers.[492]

(656 CE) Abu Bakr's son murders Uthman

In Egypt, the Umayyads ruled with an iron fist, and the greed of their tax collectors knew no bounds. The oppression left the Egyptians with no choice but to rebel.[493] Around two thousand Egyptians travelled to Medina to protest.[494] Abu Bakr's son (A'isha's brother), named Muhammad bin Abu Bakr (shortened here as Ibn Abu Bakr), took advantage of the situation. He led the rebellion and brutally killed Uthman.[495] The reasons for which he did so are as follows:

When Abu Bakr had died, Ali had taken Ibn Abu Bakr home and fostered him. Upon coming of age, because of being the son of the first caliph, Ibn Abu Bakr had been persistently asking Uthman to appoint him to a high post but Uthman did not want to strengthen a non-Umayyad. In addition, it was expected of Uthman to suspect that Ibn-Abu Bakr would take sides with his foster father Ali. However, Ibn-Abu Bakr kept pestering Uthman.

Uthman's chief advisor, the notorious Marwan bin al Hakam, played a cruel trick on Ibn Abu Bakr to get rid of him. He sent him to Egypt saying that he had sent orders of his appointment as the governor of Egypt but, on his way to Egypt, Ibn Abu Bakr discovered that the orders stated, "Execute him as soon as he arrives in Egypt." This enraged him. Realizing that he would not be safe back in Medina, he carried on his journey. When he reached Egypt, he hid from the authorities and joined the local rebels.[496] Subsequently, he was able to lead the rebels and, under his command, they marched into Medina.

The rebels rioted and protested in Medina for several days and besieged Uthman in his house. Finally, some of these broke into the house and Ibn Abu Bakr slew Uthman. Uthman's wife Na'ila had her fingers severed when she tried to protect her husband from the strikes of the sword. Marwan escaped to Damascus.

It is noteworthy how two thousand rebels were able to take over Medina and slay the caliph, while others turned a blind eye. The only warriors who could save Uthman were his own tribesmen, the Umayyads, but they were busy in ruling the conquered regions far away from Medina, and their leader Mu'awiya (Abu Sufyan's son) governed them from Damascus. The other tribes, including the Hashimis (represented by Ali and Abbas), had become indifferent to Uthman's plight because he had seldom done them any favours. Out of old companionship, Ali did send his sons, Hassn and Hussein, to save Uthman but they were outnumbered.

The majority of the Medinians had already abandoned Uthman, and new local claimants for the post of caliph had emerged. These were Zubayr bin al Awwam and Talha bin Abaydallah who had been Muhammad's close associates.

For three days, Uthman's corpse decayed in his house as no one dared to bury it in the presence of the rebels in the town.[497] Afterwards, Nu'maan bin Bashir transported Uthman's blood-stained robe and the severed fingers of his wife Na'ila to Mu'awiya in Damascus. Mu'awiya displayed these gruesome exhibits in public to provoke vengeance among his Umayyad tribesmen.

Ali and Mu'awiya become rival caliphs (656-660 CE)

Uthman had laid the foundations of the Umayyad dynasty by appointing Mu'awiya – the son of Abu Sufyan and Hind, and brother of Muhammad's wife Umm Habiba – the governor of Bilaad al Shaam, comprising what are now Syria, Palestine, Israel, Jordan and Lebanon.[498] The region was fertile and rich and generated vast amounts of wealth and taxes.[499] Mu'awiya was supposed to send major share of the taxes and booty to Medina, the capital of the empire, but instead he had stored most of it for himself in Damascus. Thus, he was able to raise a strong warrior force of several thousand. He was powerful enough to challenge the caliph in Medina.

After the murder of Uthman, Ali declared that he was the caliph but the Umayyads refused to swear fealty to him. They declared a rival caliphate with its capital in Damascus[500] and

Mu'awiya as the new caliph. For all the "holiness" of the House of Allah, Mecca, and Medina – the prophet's town – the Umayyads shifted the capital to where there was more wealth, and stopped sending a share to Medina. Without a share of booty and taxes from the conquered regions, Ali could not raise an army to match that of Mu'awiya.

Because Uthman and Mu'awiya were both from the Umayyad tribe, Mu'awiya swore to avenge Uthman's blood. Accordingly, he demanded that Ali should arrest and transport the slayers of Uthman to Damascus for execution, but Ali had little means to do so because Ibn Abu Bakr had fled to Egypt, and two rival claimants, Zubayr bin al Awwam and Talha bin Abaydallah, had gathered an army to fight against him. A'isha supported them because Talha was her father's cousin, and she had always hated Ali since the Afak event when some people had accused her of adultery and Ali had beaten her slave to extract the truth. In short, three tribal groups, led by Ali, Mu'awiya, and A'isha held claims to the caliphate.

A'isha leads an army against Ali: Talha and Zubayr are killed

A battle took place between A'isha and Ali's armies. It is known as "the battle of the Camel" because A'isha led the army whilst riding a camel, and was brought down when one of Ali's men severed the camel's legs. When A'isha fell, an old man lifted her up and respectfully said, `Mother! Are you hurt?' A'isha rebuffed him saying, `I am too young to be your mother.' The old man replied, `But the prophet had said, "My wives are the mothers of all believers," and that is why I addressed you as "mother."

Around ten thousand men died on both sides, including Zubayr and Talha.[501] Ali won the battle and respectfully sent A'isha to her home. Now there remained only two main contenders for the post of caliph: Ali and Mu'awiya.

Ali and Mu'awiya fight for power

Ali appointed Abaydallah bin Abbas as his governor for Yemen while, in parallel, Mu'awiya appointed Yusayr bin abi Aratt. Both appointees arrived in Yemen with orders from their respective caliphs. To scare Abaydallah and drive him out of Yemen, Yusayr seized his two little sons and slaughtered them. Their mother lost sanity because of grief. A woman of the Banu Kinana tribe, who watched the slaughter, screamed and shouted, 'Before Islam, they used to spare children's lives – and you call it the period of darkness in which Islam brought light.'[502]

Many battles took place between the armies of Ali and Mu'awiya, and scores of Muhammad's former associates died on both sides. During the battle of Siffin, one of the earliest and venerated believers, whose name was Ammar bin Yasir, was killed while fighting against Mu'awiya. Muhammad had prophesied about Ammar that an unjust group would kill him. When Mu'awiya was told that his soldiers had killed Ammar and hence, according to the prophecy, Mu'awiya's cause was unjust, he replied, 'We did not kill Ammar but those who brought him in front of our spears.' Thus, Mu'awiya twisted the whole argument and laid the blame of Ammar's death on Ali.

When it seemed that no one would be able to win, Mu'awiya resorted to the use of deceit. Upon his instructions, his men raised a copy of the Qur'an on a spearhead and shouted that it was unlawful for believers to kill believers, and they should consult the Qur'an to decide between the two sides. Ali respected Mu'awiya's attempt to truce, and ordered his warriors to stop fighting. Meanwhile, word had spread among Ali's warriors that Mu'awiya was rich while Ali had little money to pay them. Then Ali made another mistake and appointed Abu Musa al Ash'ari to negotiate on his behalf. Abu Musa was a pious man but he was a simpleton compared to Amr bin al 'Aas, who represented Mu'awiya in the negotiations.

Amr tricked Abu Musa[503] by convincing him that the root cause of the bloodshed were Ali and Mu'awiya and, therefore, both should be declared ineligible for the post of caliph. According to the decision reached by the two, both were to declare that they dismissed their respective caliphs and ask people to choose a third person. Having agreed so, Abu Musa stood up in the assembly and declared that Ali was unfit for the post of caliph. Then Amr stood up and, instead of disqualifying Mu'awiya as agreed, said, 'I agree with Abu Musa to remove Ali from the post of caliph.'

Behind the scenes, Mu'awiya kept bribing many of Ali's men. Even Ali's brother, Aqeel, took money from Mu'awiya and joined his camp.[504] Before Ali had time to tell his warriors what really had happened, most of them had gone.

(660 CE) The Khwarij turn into bandits and murder Ali

One faction of Ali's army, known as the Khwarij, was the most disaffected by these circumstances. These had joined Ali for booty but Ali could neither pay them nor gather booty from conquests. Mu'awiya too had returned to Damascus and considered them unworthy of his attention. The Khwarij deserted Ali and declared that he had been unwise in appointing such a stupid delegate as Abu Musa. Then they sent an assassin, named Ibn Maljum, who stabbed Ali and killed him right in the mosque when he was leading the prayers.[505] This shows that Ali's brother, Aqeel, had actually been wise in taking money from Mu'awiya and joining his camp, thus saving his life.

Poverty and hopelessness drove the Khwarij to become bandits who robbed all regardless of faith. To justify this, they declared that all great believers, including and after Uthman, Muhammad's main associates, his wife A'isha, Ali, Mu'awiya, and so on, were actually infidels, and those who considered these major figures of Islam as believers, were infidels too. Accordingly, they declared it lawful to attack and kill fellow Muslims, including women and children, and seize their properties.[506] Then they went further and declared that killing men and enslaving women and children was mandatory, because God did not sanctify booty if its rightful owner was alive.[507] One of their sects permitted the execution of even those who had surrendered and received contracts of safe conduct. In support of this, they would quote Muhammad's examples, available in the Qur'an:

> And if you fear treachery on the part of a people,
> Then throw back their contracts to them
> So as to be their equals
> Surely God does not love the treacherous. (Sura 8, verse 58)

> It is not suitable for the prophet to take captives
> Until he has made enough slaughter in the land. (Sura 8, verse 67)

Infighting considerably weakened the Khwarij[508] but their incursions against the Umayyad strongholds continued. Because they were no match to Mu'awiya's well-paid Syrian warriors, they turned their attention to the almost unprotected Mecca. In 746 CE Abu Hamza al Kharji, a Khwarij commander, attacked Mecca when the pilgrims were performing hajj. Rabi'a ibn Abd al Rehmaan (a teacher of the famous Imam Malik) and some Meccan nobles made a peace treaty with them but the Khwarij defied it, entered Mecca and killed many, especially those from the Quraysh[509] because they believed that the Quraysh had done the greatest harm to the people of the region.[510] Their grudge against Ali and Mu'awiya had extended to the entire Quraysh and their hometown, Mecca.

Mu'awiya (661-680 CE) executes Abu Bakr's son and condemns the Shiites

After Ali's murder, his followers, known as the Shiites, refused to swear fealty to Mu'awiya. Each side argued that the other had strayed from the true path of Islam. The extreme Shiites believed that Ali was the most supreme creation of God and that anyone who valued other associates of Muhammad over Ali was condemned to hell.[511]

On the other hand, from the pulpits of their mosques, the Umayyads slandered Ali and passed collective curses upon his progeny. To protest against this, Umm Salama, Muhammad's widow, wrote a letter to Mu'awiya in which she wrote the following:

> You stand on the pulpit in the mosque and hurl the worst invective at Ali and his family. This act is actually tantamount to hurling abuses at Allah and His messenger because I testify that Allah and His messenger loved Ali.[512]

Mu'awiya launched a campaign to find those who had killed Uthman. Ali had appointed Ibn Abu Bakr as the governor of Egypt but he had not yet succeeded in raising a strong warrior force. Mu'awiya's men hunted him down, executed him, placed his corpse in a donkey's hide and burnt it. Amru bin al Haq, a former associate of Muhammad, had also participated in the rebellion against Uthman. Mu'awiya's men traced him in Iraq. He hid in a cave but a snake bit him and he died. Mu'awiya's men cut his head off and took it to Ziyad, the governor of Iraq. Ziyad dispatched it to Mu'awiya, who placed it on public display in Damascus, and then sent it to Amru's widow. His men threw the severed head in her lap.

Ziyad, the governor of Iraq, was the son of Abu Sufyan from a slave girl named Sumayya. Because Abu Sufyan had not declared him as his son, people called him, `Ziyad bin Abihay' (Ziyad – the son of his father). Ziyad became a brutal military commander and initially fought on Ali's side against his half-brother Mu'awiya. When Mu'awiya heard about Ziyad's over-powering military skills, he called upon him with witnesses who testified that Abu Sufyan had relations with Ziyad's mother and, therefore, Ziyad was his half-brother. Mu'awiya restored Ziyad's status as a family member among the Umayyads. Ziyad was so grateful that he spent the rest of his life serving Mu'awiya's caliphate. Initially, Mu'awiya appointed Ziyad as the governor of Kufa and Basra. When Ziyad came to deliver his first sermon in the Kufa mosque, some men threw pebbles at him. In fury, he ordered his soldiers to close the mosque doors. Then he had the men arrested, and their hands amputated.[513]

Mu'awiya continued his verbal and military campaigns against the Shiites. In Kufa, a man named Hujar bin Adiy could not tolerate the use of mosque pulpit to slander Ali. He began to stand up in the mosque and, whilst the others sent curses upon Ali in a chorus, he would praise him and criticize Mu'awiya. Ziyad arrested Hujar bin Adiy and his twelve friends and transported them to Damascus where Mu'awiya had eight of them beheaded, and a ninth, named Abd al Rehmaan bin Hassan, buried alive in sand.[514]

Mu'awiya wanted to nominate his son, Yazid, as his heir. His governors bribed the influential tribal chiefs and members of the *shura* (advisory body) to nominate him. Mu'awiya sent a hundred thousand dirhams to Abdallah bin Umar – the son of the second Caliph Umar – to entice him to support the nomination but he refused to take the money. During the session of the *shura* held to nominate his heir, Mu'awiya placed a guard with bare sword behind each member and thus intimidated them to agree to his will.

The sixth caliph Yazid (680-683 CE) and the slaughter of Muhammad's grandson

When Yazid became the caliph, he appointed Abaydallah ibn Ziyad (often written as Ibn Ziyad) – the son of the above-mentioned Ziyad – as the governor of Kufa. Yazid and Ibn Ziyad both proved to be as brutal as their fathers had been in running the empire.

Ali's son Hussein (Muhammad's grandson) refused to swear allegiance to Yazid. Hussein's brother Hassn had realized the futility of rising up against the Umayyads and resigned in favour of Mu'awiya,[515] who generously rewarded him. With this money, Hassn passed his time in marrying and divorcing until he had married more than a hundred times, and one of his wives poisoned him to death.[516] It is reported that Mu'awiya had encouraged her to do so by promising that he would get her married to Yazid, the future caliph.

When Yazid became the caliph, Hussein declared that Yazid's rule was ill begotten and unjust. He began his journey to Kufa where, according to his cousin, Muslim bin Aqeel, he could find support. Yazid sent an army, led by Amr bin Sa'ad bin abi Waqqas, which stopped Hussein and his family at Karbala. Hussein was travelling with around thirty-two cavalry, forty infantry, and the women and children of his family. The Umayyad army comprised four hundred soldiers who could easily arrest and transport them to Damascus. Hussein pleaded with the soldiers to either take them to Yazid's court, where he hoped for better treatment, or allow them to migrate out of the empire but Amr insisted on taking them to Governor Ibn Ziyad, who had already executed Hussein's cousin Muslim bin Aqeel.

When Hussein and his men refused to go to Ibn Ziyad, Yazid's soldiers killed them one by one, stripped the corpses of their dresses, and ran horses over them. After looting the belongings of the victims, they severed the heads of the corpses, undressed the women, and transported them to Kufa. Ibn Ziyad put the severed heads on public display, stood on the pulpit in the Kufa mosque, and declared:

> Praise God Who revealed the truth and exposed the impostors
> He granted victory to the Ruler of Believers Yazid and his men
> And killed Hussein – the son of Ali
> Liar – the son of a liar, and his Shiites (*followers*).

After the declaration, he dispatched the severed heads and the captured Hashimi women to Yazid in Damascus, who displayed these in his court[517] to prove that he had crushed the rebellion. It did not matter much to him that his men had slaughtered the grandson of their prophet – the founder of their religion – and a large number of his family. One needs to recall that Yazid was the grandson of Abu Sufyan and Hind whom Muhammad had forced to surrender to him. Now Yazid had avenged his grandparents.

The gruesome nature of the battles and murders narrated above make it clear that most of Muhammad's associates saw each other more as tribal enemies than as fellow believers or Muslims. The Islamists claim that Muhammad brought enlightenment to entire humanity. The conduct of his closest relatives and associates shows that he was unable to enlighten even them.

The Caliph's army plunders Medina and Mecca

The massacre of Hussein and his family enraged the people of Medina, predominantly the Ansar. They declared that Yazid was sinful and hence unfit for the post of caliph. They expelled his governor from Medina and appointed Abdallah bin Hanzala as their new chief. In response, Yazid sent twelve thousand warriors, led by Muslim bin Aqaba al Mari, to attack Medina. He instructed them to allow three days to the Medinians to surrender. If they would not, they were to be massacred and the town was to be plundered for three days. The Medinians refused to surrender and hence the famous battle of Hara took place.

Yazid's warriors conquered Medina and plundered the town for three days during which time they killed seven hundred prominent citizens and around ten thousand people. They chained the children of the Ansar and humiliated them,[518] entered people's homes and raped their women. The historian Ibn Katheer estimated that around a thousand women were raped in those three days.

After plundering Medina, Yazid's army attacked Mecca. As people took shelter in the Ka'ba, under the traditional belief that no one would attack them in the "House of Allah," the army used catapults to hurl stones at it, after which they set fire to it. The fire greatly damaged the Ka'ba and one of its walls collapsed. Some traditions quote other reasons for the fire, but all historians confirm that the army bombarded the Ka'ba with stones by using catapults.[519]

These events defy the Islamist claim that whosoever would try to attack the Ka'ba would face the wrath of God. The Qur'an states that, in the pre-Islamic period, when Abraha had tried to attack the Ka'ba, God had sent birds carrying deadly stones in their beaks, which they threw at his army and decimated it. But in those days the Ka'ba was a multi-faith shrine. Assuming that this Qur'anic story is true, the only logical explanation for the destruction of the

Ka'ba at Muslim hands would be that it lost its "divine protection" after it was turned into an exclusively Muslim shrine.

Caliph Abd al Malik (685-705 CE) plans to construct another Ka'ba in Jerusalem

After Yazid, his son Mu'awiya II ruled for a brief period (683-684 CE) but Marwan bin al Hakam side-lined him and took power in his own hands. Marwan was the Umayyad whom Muhammad had hated but Uthman had appointed as his chief adviser. After Uthman's murder, Marwan had escaped to Damascus and had since been advising the Umayyads on how to rule. Now he usurped the caliphate for himself, and after a year (684-685 CE), passed it on to his son Abd al Malik.

Because the Umayyads ruled from Damascus, they could not have Islamic legitimacy unless they controlled Mecca and Medina as well. At that time, these "holy towns" were ruled by Abdallah bin Zubayr whose father Zubayr bin al Awwam had been a claimant to the post of caliph, and Ali's men had killed him at the "Battle of the Camel."

The Umayyads could have full control of Mecca and Medina only if they expelled the Abbasids, the Alawites, and all other claimants to the caliphate from the "holy land." Considering this an impossible task, Abd al Malik planned to construct another "House of Allah" in Jerusalem, which was in his control. He believed that he could divert the pilgrim business from Mecca[520] to Jerusalem through propaganda that "the real House of Allah" was in Jerusalem. Abd al Malik's said plan shows that many in those days understood that "holiness" was only a state of mind. They also knew that, through propaganda, "holiness" could be directed at one or the other object. In plain words, they knew that the House of God in Mecca was not really the House of God. Such depth of understanding would be hard to find these days among more than one billion Muslims, many of whom would not hesitate from killing one for suggesting anything like that.

As Abd al Malik worked with his engineers on the design of the new Ka'aba, one of his governors, Hajjaj bin Youssef, challenged him by saying that he could conquer Mecca and Medina if he had twelve thousand Syrian warriors. As a last resort, Abd al Malik agreed to it.

Hajjaj bin Youssef

Hajjaj bin Youssef, Caliph Abd al Malik's governor of Iraq and Persia, was the Islamic equivalent of Ivan the Terrible. Caliph Umar bin Abd al Aziz (described later) once said about him, "the most evil man in this world."[521] When he began as governor, he came to Kufa mosque to deliver his first sermon with his face covered. He stood speechless on the pulpit for so long that the natives began to whisper to each other, cursing the Umayyads for sending a dumb governor who would not show his face. After having generated enough suspense and tension among the audience, he slowly uncovered his face and declared:

I am a famous and experienced man. Do you recognise me O people of Kufa? I have just taken charge but I already see blood and I smell it. I see that the crop of your heads has ripened and harvest time is approaching fast. I see necks, beards and headdresses smeared in blood. The Ruler of Believers has sent me to crush you because you are the vilest people on earth and I am the most deadly of his arrows.'[522]

When Hajjaj died, there were around fifty thousand men and thirty thousand women in his dungeons. A hundred and thirty thousand had already died in these prisons[523] because there was no adequate system of feeding or clothing prisoners. Sometimes the guards would take the prisoners out to beg for food.[524] When they died and had no relatives to bury the bodies, they dumped them in unmarked graves. In oppression, the 20th century regime of Saddam Hussein was not much different from that of Hajjaj in the 7th century.

It was on Hajjaj's orders that scholars added pronunciation aides to the words of the Qur'an. The Islamists always praise Hajjaj for his services to the Qur'an but overlook the fact that if Arabic was the language of God, it would not require these corrections decades after Muhammad's death. However, the holiness and perfection of Arabic is another Arab imperialist myth. The imperialists would persecute those who tried to show that Arabic was a weak language that required improvement but when their own man Hajjaj changed it in punctuation and pronunciation, they hailed it as a great achievement.

Hajjaj uses catapults to bombard the Ka'ba

Traditionally, Arabs used to abstain from fighting in the month of hajj. However, to gain the maximum advantage of surprise, Hajjaj's army besieged Mecca during the hajj. They fixed huge catapults on the mount Abu Qubays and began bombarding the Ka'ba with heavy stones. At this, Abdallah bin Umar (the son of Umar) came out to see Hajjaj and pleaded with him to stop the bombardment until the pilgrims, who had travelled from far, could complete the hajj. Hajjaj allowed the pilgrims to leave Mecca, and resumed the bombardment.

After conquering Mecca and Medina, his soldiers raped women, looted and plundered, and beheaded the local chiefs. They placed the severed head of the local leader Nu'maan bin Bashir in his wife's lap, displayed the heads of Abdallah bin Zubayr, Abdallah bin Safwan, and A'mara bin Hazam in Mecca, Medina, and then transported these to Damascus for further exhibition. In Mecca, they hung the corpses of the slaughtered on crosses fixed at public places and left them to decay. They transported the head of Mus'ab bin Zubayr to Kufa and Egypt for public exhibition, and then to Damascus. Afterwards, Caliph Abd al Malik decided to transport it to all cities of Syria for exhibition but his wife, Aatika bint Yazid, confronted him and said, `You have had your bloody sports for too long. Has your heart not cooled down? You have killed all the rebels. What's the point in putting their heads on display?' She had the severed head dismounted, washed and then buried.[525]

Walid bin Abd al Malik (705-715 CE): Further persecution of the Abbasids and Alawites

When Abd al Malik died, his son Walid bin Abd al Malik (705-715 CE) carried on the persecution of the Alawites and Abbasids who held claims to the caliphate on grounds of being the descendants of Ali and Abbas respectively. Walid banished the Abbasid chief Ali bin Abdallah to the village Hamayma in Persia and exiled his tribe from Mecca and Medina. The Abbasids scattered in Persia and Syria. However, the main victims of the Umayyads were the Alawites because the former had snatched the caliphate directly from Ali, and five generations of Ali's progeny had refused to swear allegiance to successive Umayyad rulers.

Hence, later in history, Walid's brother, Hisham bin Abd al Malik (724-743 CE) had Hussein's grandson Zayd bin Ali crucified in Kufa. Then, in 743 CE, he had Zayd's son Yahiya executed. In 748 CE, Caliph Marwan II executed Yahiya's son Abdallah.[526]

Umar bin Abd al Aziz, a rare noble caliph (717-720 CE) is poisoned by his own family

On Walid's death, his brother Suleiman bin Abd al Malik (715-717 CE) became the caliph. When Suleiman died, upon his will, his cousin Umar bin Abd al Aziz took over. Umar had been the governor of Medina when Walid bin Abd al Malik was the caliph. Upon the latter's orders, Umar had committed an atrocity that changed his life forever. He had Khubayb, the son of Abdallah bin Zubayr, flogged, immersed in icy cold water, and then made to stand at the door of the Prophet's Mosque all day in severe cold. When Khubayb died of this torture, it traumatized him and his heart changed. He resigned and became a truly God-fearing man.[527]

When he took over as caliph, he ordered that Arab rulers should live within their honestly earned incomes, and stop the loot and plunder of non-Muslims. He tried to take care of people's rights by protecting their honour, lives and property.[528] He relinquished his inheritance and donated it, along with his wife's jewellery and precious stones, to the treasury. He began confiscating the ill-begotten properties of his relatives and others among the ruling Umayyads. He replaced cruel governors and officials with kinder ones, abolished unfair taxes, and sent instructions to governors not to amputate hands or execute people without his prior approval. However, his family did not want to give up a life of luxury, and they poisoned him within two years of his rule. After his death, it was back to the ways of the earlier caliphs and their warriors living off the pillage of non-Muslims.[529]

The Abbasids seize the caliphate from the Umayyads

Around 748 CE, the last Umayyad ruler Marwan was fighting on many fronts. First, the Alawites and the Abbasids had raised forces against him. Second, in Khurasan, a Persian by the name of Abu Muslim had recruited a massive rebel army. Egypt, Iraq and Persia had stopped sending taxes and goods and it was hard to pay the soldiers. In Damascus, the Arab tribes fought among themselves for the distribution of diminishing booty and taxes: Adnani, Qahtani, Yemeni, Mazri, Azd, Tamim, Kalb, and Qays tribes had groups that attacked each other. These were not willing even to pray together and had separated their mosques.[530] These divisions among the Umayyad allies made it relatively easy for the Abbasids and Alawites to take over but, without the help of the Persian Abu Muslim and his Khurasani fighters, it would be hard to defeat the Umayyads. Alongside the Arab commander Abu Awn, he defeated Marwan at the battle of Great Zab and murdered him in Egypt.[531] By around 750 CE, the joint forces of the Abbasids, Alawites and Persians had defeated the Umayyads in several places in Iraq, Syria, Egypt and Central Arabia, and appointed Abbasid governors.

After capturing Damascus, the Abbasids and their allies ran wild and massacred fifty thousand people. For seventy days, they used the Grand Umayyad Mosque as a stable for their horses. They dug the corpses of the Umayyad caliphs Mu'awiya, Yazid, Abd al Malik, Hisham and others out of their graves. When they found that the corpse of caliph Hisham had not decayed much, they flogged it, hanged it for public exhibition for days, and then burned it. They slaughtered every Umayyad child they could lay hands on. After the massacre, they spread carpets over half-alive bodies and ate their meals whilst listening to the groans and moans of the dying. In Basra, after the massacre of the Umayyads, the victorious dragged the corpses from their legs in streets, and dogs ate the remains. When they conquered Mecca and Medina, they repeated similar barbarism.[532]

After the Umayyad defeat, infighting broke between the Abbasids and the Alawites. The Alawites were the first to put up a government in Kufa but Abu Muslim had their wazir, Abu Salama, and his Alawite appointees assassinated.[533] He made people swear allegiance to the Abbasids rather than to the Alawites.[534] Otherwise, the post of the caliph would have gone to the Alawite claimant Nafs Zakiya – the great grandson of Muhammad's grandson Hassn.

<u>Al Saffah, the first Abbasid caliph (750-754 CE)
slaughters the Alawites of Mosul</u>

The Umayyad caliph Walid bin Abd al Malik had banished the Abbasid chief Ali bin Abdallah (grandson of Muhammad's uncle

Abbas) to a far-flung corner of Persia, but Ali bin Abdallah had prospered and had twenty-two sons[535] whom he had trained to take revenge from the Umayyads. Now his grandson Abu'l Abbas al Saffah became the first Abbasid caliph. He appointed his uncle, Da'ud bin Ali, as the governor of Kufa.

The last Umayyad Caliph Marwan had executed al Saffah's brother Ibrahim, and his father Muhammad bin Ali had died of grief. Now that Da'ud bin Ali, the brother of Muhammad bin Ali, had become the governor of Kufa, he slaughtered the entire Umayyad population in Kufa in revenge. Afterwards, al Saffah and Da'ud stood on the pulpit in the Kufa Mosque and declared to the Iraqis and Persians that they would not be cruel to them. Al Saffah narrated the atrocities that the Umayyads had inflicted upon them and said, `I hope that you do not receive the same wounds from our tribe.' Then Da'ud stood on the pulpit and said:

> We have taken power neither to collect gold and wealth nor to construct palaces with streams for ourselves in your towns. We have taken power because it was our right as the kin of Prophet Muhammad. The Umayyads had usurped our right and hounded our cousins – the Alawites. They also oppressed you, humiliated you, and expropriated public properties. Now we will govern you in accordance with the guidance provided by the Holy Qur'an, and the trust of Prophet Muhammad and our ancestor Abbas, who was his uncle.[536] The Holy Book, God, His prophet, and Abbas guarantee your peace and security. By the Holy Ka'ba, we will not harass you. The Arabs and the Ajmis have nothing to fear.[537]

However, al Saffah was a cruel and deceitful man. He sent a contract of safe conduct to the last Umayyad governor of Wasit called Yazid bin Hubayra. Yazid believed in al Saffah's word of honour and surrendered but al Saffah executed him.[538]

The Alawites of Mosul refused to swear allegiance to al Saffah, and he sent his brother Yahiya to crush them. When Yahiya reached Mosul with his warriors, he sent his men to announce, all through the town, that he would grant amnesty to those who would gather in the central mosque of Mosul. Several thousand men came to the mosque to seek amnesty. Yahiya had them disarmed and, at the same time, placed his soldiers at the mosque gates. Then they locked the gates and massacred the disarmed Alawites.

When the news reached the homes of the victims, their families began to mourn. All night Yahiya listened to the screams and cries of women and children in the town, and was so irritated that he ordered his warriors to slaughter them. The warriors were given free reign over the town and they ran amuck, killing old men, women and children, looting houses and raping women.

Among Yahiya's warriors, four thousand were Persians who, along with others, had raped the Arab women of Mosul. An old Arab woman approached Yahiya in a street, grabbed the bridle of his horse, and shouted, `You are from the descendants of the prophet's uncle. You and the Alawites both are from the Hashimi clan of the prophet. Do you not feel the least shame that your Persian soldiers are raping Hashimi women? Do you bring aliens to rape your own women?' Thus, the old woman successfully triggered Yahiya's tribal instincts and he quickly sent in orders to his Persian contingent to gather in the mosque for distribution of the booty. When these gathered, Yahiya had them disarmed and ordered his Arab soldiers to massacre them.

Shi'a Islam

The Alawites were never able to become rulers of the Arab-Islamic empire. One by one, first the Umayyads tortured and slaughtered their generations, and, later, when the Abbasids took over the caliphate, they did the same to them. In a period of around seventy years, all successors to Ali were either killed or they went into hiding for fear of their lives. Hence the Shiites, the followers of Ali and his progeny, have had the largest share of martyrs (albeit at Muslim hands) to mourn. Intermittently, the Shiites have faced massacres in various Muslim countries right up to modern times.

The earlier Persian sympathy for Ali, his son Hussein, and his later progeny, because of their sequential murders, lasts to date among the Shiites. The heroes of Shi'a Islam did not conquer but were hounded and executed. Hence, Shi'a Islam derives passion from the melodrama its preachers generate around the murders of Ali and his progeny – no less potent in emotional appeal than Jesus's crucifixion.

It is noteworthy that Ali's progeny are the blood descendants of Muhammad, whose daughter Fatima was Ali's wife. Hence, the greatest irony of Islam is that Muslim rulers, who, by the very premise of their religion, were supposed to respect its founder's descendants, killed them. This fact alone reveals the fallacy of the term "History of Islam." Explanation follows in Appendix II.

The legacy of Muhammad and his relatives

The narration of the history of the rule of Muhammad's relatives can be carried on to cover another century but this is beyond the scope of this book. It should suffice to state that, after Muhammad's death, his successors carried on this process of subjugation (Islam) to the remaining Arabia, Yemen, Jordon, Iraq, Iran, Egypt, Syria, Palestine, Turkey, Central Asia, parts of Africa and India, and even Spain. Following Muhammadan patterns described in this book, over the coming centuries, the conquerors gradually and systematically cleansed the permanently colonized regions of their pre-Islamic faiths, ideologies, multi-cultural societies, and secular cultures. They raided Hindu and Buddhist temples in parts of India and eliminated Buddhism from large parts of southeast and central Asia. India's secular civilization, which absorbed the cultures of migrants and invaders alike, received a major distortion when extremist Muslims geographically split India because they did not want to coexist with other faiths. The creation of Pakistan (the Land of the Pure) in 1947 entailed unrivalled bloodshed when Hindus and Sikhs were forced to leave the Muslim majority areas. The "Land of the Pure" then became a hotbed of intermittent violence as the hate propagated against non-Muslims consumed the Muslims themselves.

At present Wahhabis, Shiites, and Sunnis in many Muslim countries often blast each other's' mosques with explosives amidst other violent sectarian engagements.

In the early centuries after Muhammad, the conquerors were Arabs but, later, Turkish, Persian, and Central Asian rulers also followed the pattern of ruling other people in the name of Islam. The Turkish Ottoman empire too was called "Khilafa" but the Turks actually oppressed the Arabs in the name of Islam and Khilafa – the idiom, "to the doctor, his own medicine" befits this situation. By the time the Arabs revolted against the Turkish Khilafa and won their freedom from it, they had learned the lesson and stopped using the word "Khilafa." They substituted it with titles that are more appropriate: "Sultanate", "Emirate," and "Memlikat" – the meaning of each of these titles is "Kingdom."

Appendix II:
The fallacies of "Islamic History"

Because the aforementioned Arab tribes used religious pretexts as excuses to take power, to expropriate other people's lands, and to expand their empire (Khilafa), their history has falsely come to be known as "Islamic History" in the religious sense of the word "Islam." In order to understand this, one needs to look at the following:

- The so-called "Islamic History" is based on the axiom, among others, that Muhammad fought against the Meccan "unbelievers" and brought them to believe in one God. But the fact is that when the Meccan tribes, predominantly the Umayyads and the Banu Makhzum, refused to submit to Muhammad, it was not because they were "unbelievers" but because they did not want to follow a Hashimi so-called "messenger" or "prophet."
- The so-called "Islamic History" claims that the period of the caliphates of Abu Bakr, Umar, Uthman and Ali was the period of best governance in the history of humanity. When one looks at the facts that three of these caliphs were murdered by "Muslims," two on tribal issues (Uthman and Ali), the absurdity of the said claim becomes obvious. A logical explanation of the history of the period is that the said caliphates were based on tribal loyalties and rivalries. Yet, believing that the caliphate (Khilafa) was a Godly way of governance, there are an estimated one million supporters of the "Khilafa Movement" within Europe alone.
- The so-called "Islamic History" claims that Muhammad's closest people were the most pious believers who were given the good news that they would live in paradise forever. However, the fact remains that these people behaved in an appallingly immoral manner. For example, Muhammad's wife A'isha led an army against his cousin/son-in-law Ali: The issue between them was not religious but tribal and personal rivalry. Again, those who killed Hussein did not see him as the grandson of the "holy prophet" but as a Hashimi challenging the Umayyad empire. Likewise, the descendants of Muhammad's relatives and companions, Talha, Zubayr,

Mu'awiya, Ali and Abbas kept fighting against each other for nearly two centuries.

If we analyse the abovementioned key events and other historical events described in this book, it becomes obvious that the "History of Islam" is in fact the history of the rivalries, power struggles, and battles between the Arab tribes, and that the propagated Islamist history is based on the following historical inaccuracies:

<u>Propaganda: Muhammad brought the Arabs to worship one God</u>
<u>Reality: The Arabs worshipped one God long before Muhammad</u>

Modern Islamists propagate a "black and white" history in which the Arabian society before Islam is shown to be in the darkness of ignorance (*ja'hal'iyya*) into which Islam brought enlightenment. They declare that Muhammad brought worship of one God to the Arabs who were polytheists, atheists, idolaters, Christians, Zoroastrians or Jews. But one finds in the old records that, in the pre-Islamic multi-faith Arabia, the vast majority of people did worship one God long before Muhammad. This is evident from the following few examples:

- The Qur'an itself states that the so-called *mushraykeen*, whom Muhammad declared as unbelievers, actually believed in one God:

    And if you ask them who created the heavens and the earth
    And made the sun and the moon subservient,
    They will certainly say, God. Why are they then turning away?
    And if you ask them who sends down water from the clouds,
    And gives life to earth with it, after its death,
    They will certainly say, God. Say: All praise belongs to God.
    And when they ride in their ships, they call upon God,
    Being sincerely obedient to Him. (Sura 29, verses 61, 63, 65)

- In Arab literature, diction and written correspondence, one finds that the pre-Islamic Arabs frequently referred to Allah as "the one God;" for example, almost all letters written by the so-called *mushraykeen* and quoted in history books use phrases such as, "We swear by Allah," "In the name of Allah," etc. On top of their letters they used to write, "In the name of Allah" (*Bayismak Allah*).[539] The famous poet Zayd bin Amr began to call Allah "The Gracious, the Merciful." Mohammad borrowed this from Zayd and began to use the phrase, "In the name of Allah, the Gracious, the Merciful."

- The most interesting evidence illustrating that the "unbelievers" (*kuffar*) actually believed in one God is that when Muhammad fought against them, both sides used to raise the same slogan, "In the name of Allah." Even Abu Jahl, branded as "the chief enemy of Islam," used to pray to Allah, and fought in Allah's name.[540]

<u>Propaganda: Pre-Islamic Arabia was the land of depravity and sin</u>
<u>Reality: There was freedom of conscience in pre-Islamic Arabia, and Abraham's monotheistic religion had already taken roots</u>

The Islamists state that Muhammad brought enlightenment to an Arabia of corruption, debauchery, sin, brutality and barbarism. The earliest Arab records show that Arabia before Islam was a multi-religious, more enlightened, and more tolerant society than it is now. This is particularly true of Saudi Arabia where Islam originated both as a religion and as an imperial force. For example, before Islam, Arabs allowed and respected all faiths, such as the monotheistic Ahnaf, Christians, Jews, Zoroastrians and atheists (*dahriya*) who did not believe in life after death.[541] This meant that Arabs were free to discuss various faiths and philosophies as a prerequisite to develop great intellects through debate. The worst tragedy for Arabia has been the fact that Muhammad abolished this great freedom of speech, faith and conscience. Rather than improving upon the social situation he found, he laid the essential foundation that created and perpetuated poverty, thus forcing his followers to become bandits, imperial invaders or soldiers of imperial invaders. Even in modern times, because the Islamic community does not allow a Muslim to give up Islam without facing the death penalty, the most humane born-Muslims have no option but to live as nominal Muslims.

Propaganda: Muhammad blessed entire humanity
Reality: Muhammad sanctified the worst among the pre-existing Arab cultural practices

The Islamists claim that the religions before Muhammad were flawed and he brought in a better religion. In-depth analyses of these religions show that after acquiring expert knowledge of the Hanafi faith, Judaism and Christianity, Muhammad mixed the noble aspects of these religions with the worst cultural practices of his times, and assembled his religion out of these: His prayer format came from the Hanafi faith, and he borrowed fasting from the Quraysh and Judaism.[542] The direction of prayers initially towards Jerusalem made the Quraysh believe that he had become a Christian.[543] He borrowed so much from the Torah that the Jews initially thought he was one of them. Circumcision was customary in pre-Islamic Arabia as a matter of masculine honour, and banning pork came from Judaism. The rituals and formations of the hajj, and animal sacrifices were pre-Islamic practices. Alongside, he picked and sanctified the most brutal tribal practices such as robbery and enslavement of weaker tribes (jihad), stoning to death and flogging for adultery and fornication respectively (only when done with non-slaves), revenge for murder, and amputation for petty thefts. Muhammad sanctified these existing practices as God's law. For example, see the following:

> O you who believe, it has been written for you to take revenge of the killed: A free man for a free man, a slave for a slave and a woman for a woman; but if the brother of the slain is willing to forgive, then pay the blood money generously. And there is life for you in revenge, O men of understanding, that you may guard yourselves. (Sura 2, verses 178-180)

The verses imply that if a free man kills a slave or a woman, the victim's heirs can take the life of one of the killer's slaves or women – unless the killer is rich enough to pay and be free. Ancient Arab records show that the Arabs practised this law long before Muhammad and, therefore, God could not have possibly sent it to him. The Arabs believed that if a man was killed and his relatives did not avenge him, an owl would emerge from his skull and keep screaming, "Give me blood! Give me blood." The law of retaliation had existed in pre-Islamic Judaic, Babylonian and Roman legal codes too but only the killer could be killed in revenge.

If Caliph Uthman had disregarded this law of revenge the way he disregarded the law about stoning the adulterers when assembling the Qur'an, reformists like Imam Abu Hanifa would have the choice of making better laws such as, "Investigate who the killer is, and punish him/her only." The said law of revenge is so unjust that even Islamic states do not implement it despite their claims that they derive their laws from the Qur'an.

Appendix III:
What can good-natured Muslims do?

Reviving the Hanafi Faith

Ultimately, there is a way for civilized Muslims whereby they can adapt to the tolerant and secular modern world and maintain the gentler aspects of their Islamic heritage. The way is to revive the Hanafi (also called Hanifi) faith that is historically proved as the benign monotheistic Arab religion which was developing when Muhammad was still young. As narrated at the beginning of this book, his tribesmen Wirqa bin Noufal, Abdallah bin Jahsh, Zayd bin Amr bin Nafeel and Uthman bin al Hawayrith had abandoned the superstitious use of idols. Zayd went to Syria in search of a true religion and met Christian and Jewish leaders. He and Umayya bin abi Asalat, the famous poet, finally resolved on a faith that was known as the Hanafi faith [*Deen-a-Hanifi*] and considered to be the faith of Abraham, the common father of all Jews and Arabs. The famous orators Qis bin Sa'ada, Qays bin Nashba, and Abuzar Ghifari also had abandoned the use of idols before Muhammad did so. Those who did not use idols and followed the Hanafi faith were called Ahnaf, they were respected and allowed to preach and train others.

Anything noble and exalted found in Islam, the belief in one God, the prayer formats, fasting, charity, and hajj, was present in the Hanafi faith, if not in other contemporary faiths. The Ahnaf believed that Prophet Abraham practiced the Hanafi faith when his search for the true God led him to abandon the use of idols, fire, and other material symbols as manifestations of God. Before and during Muhammad's life, the Ahnaf included many Quraysh elders and preachers from whom Muhammad learnt in his youth and admired. The Hanafi faith did not allow murder on religious grounds and preached love and fraternity between faiths. Christians, Jews, Zoroastrians, and people of other faiths were historically welcomed by the Quraysh to participate in the hajj.

Because the Hanafi faith was an Arab religion, in reviving it, Muslims will highlight their cherished Arab traditions and religious heritage. However, in order to revive this tolerant, secular, and gentle religion, they will have to purge their teachings of the violence-generating ungodly clauses which checked the positive and progressive reformative tendencies of what is known as "Classical Islam." Any impartial expert in the 7th century Arab culture would know that the violence and hate-breeding clauses are the product of the primitive Arab-Bedouin culture and, as such, have nothing to do with God. Once these have been declared as cultural values and not God's words and commandments, one could hope to revive the great and noble Hanafi religion.

I am fully aware that reverting to the Hanafi faith is easier said than done but it is not impossible: The Qur'an and the old Arabic books still contain the noble verses of the Ahnaf. Competent scholars can collate them and recompose modern Islam back to its original Hanafi spirit. Modification of beliefs is not without precedence because as previously mentioned, Muhammad's associates too disagreed about the variant versions of the Qur'anic scriptures and, to end these disputes, Caliph Uthman had the Qur'an officially collated, and ordered the burning of all Qur'anic scriptural material other than that he approved of.

Also, during the Abbasid Khilafa, Imam Abu Hanifa and his students had major parts of Islamic legislation reverted to its relatively benign origins in the Hanafi faith, such as instituting respect for other religions and permission for non-conformism to prevalent beliefs and values. The majority of Muslims accepted much of this reversion and therefore, in the regions where Hanafi Jurisprudence is practiced, such as in Turkey and parts of India, Muslim behaviour has progressed toward greater tolerance. In these regions, Muslims generally abstain from jihad, and do not seek dire penalties though in recent times, many have been lured by Saudi money and preaching to convert to the most violent and extremist sect of the Wahhabis – the followers of the Saudi preacher Muhammad bin Abd al Wahhab (1703-1792).

Epilogue: Was Muhammad a Man of God?

A holistic study of Islam raises serious questions about why a growing number of more than a billion people believe in a religion that, empirically, turns out to be the harsh cultural practices of primitive Arabian tribes. These tribes lived in the hostile climatic conditions of the desert and were often forced, either by starvation or by greed, to raid the neighbouring agriculturist sedentary societies. The earliest Arab-Islamic records and the Qur'an itself build the strongest case to prove that, contrary to his claims, Muhammad could not be farthest from anything resembling a man of God. In fact, one may judge him against his own definition of what constitutes rebellion against God. Muhammad had said:

> There are three types of men most rebellious to God:
> Firstly, those who kill in the Ka'ba;
> Secondly, those who kill a man who has not killed, and;
> Thirdly, those who kill in prejudice.[544]

As described in the previous pages, Muhammad committed all the above-mentioned acts:

- Firstly, he ordered and supervised the execution of a poet in the Ka'ba when he entered Mecca as an ally of those he called "the unbelievers;"
- Secondly, through his secret and planned raids, he instigated and supervised the murders of thousands of innocent Jews, Christians, the so-called "mushraykeen," and people of weaker tribes, and;
- Thirdly, he had the vast majority of his victims killed in sheer prejudice.

During his twenty-three years of "apostolate," Muhammad arranged for banditry raids, secret assassinations, ransom taking, kidnappings, slave trading, ethnic cleansing, inter-tribal wars, and murderous expeditions. Of these raids, the number of well recorded and documented, discussed by the Qur'an itself, is thirty-eight. He personally took part in twenty-seven raids and battles. In nine of these, given below, he was directly engaged in killing:

The battle of Badr;
The battle of Uhud;
The battle of Ahzaab, also called al Khendaq (the Trench);
The massacre of the Qurayza;
The *Sa'ria* (surprise raid) on the Mustalaq;
The massacre of the Khyber Jews;
The occupation of Mecca;
The battle of Hunayn; and
The battle of Ta'if.[545]

There are well-documented accounts of thirty-seven raids with names of those who led the raids, the details of victims and the property looted and distributed, including the distribution and selling of taken slaves. By all accounts, Muhammad's behaviour was that of a traditional Arab tribal chief, bandit, slave trader, ransom kidnapper – certainly not that of a God-fearing man. Yet the Islamists quote Muhammad's battle victories as testimony to his apostolate and justify them on grounds that God wanted him to succeed by any means. The fact is that anyone, who is prepared to use such cutthroat and brutal tactics as he used, would have succeeded: Emir Mu'awiya used the same methods as Muhammad did, and succeeded in establishing the vast Umayyad empire.

It is well known that many kings started as bandits and came to rule vast territories. If Muhammad had claimed that he was a king, one could place him amongst the greatest of kings. But the deceit lies in his claim that he was sent by God as the messenger: If messengers were to kill and plunder, sell slaves, hold captives for ransom, allow rape of slave women, and develop systems of extortion, how does one differentiate between a man of God and an earthly king?

The above stated assertions rely on evidence derived not only from the earliest histories but also from the Qur'an and its exposition by Muslim scholars. Regarding the ethnic cleansing of the Jews from Arabia, some Islamists argue that the Jews left of their own will, which is arguing against the descriptions in the Qur'an itself. While the Islamists can hide the earliest history books, they cannot hide the Qur'an for it is available all over the world.

In Muhammad's defence, one might argue that there was little else he could do in a society in which, supposedly, the evils he engaged in were rampant. However, one must point out that Muhammad could have taken the side of the pacifists and hard workers like, for example, the Jews, and those he called the "hypocrites." Far from joining them, he passed curses and punishments on those who did not want to attack the others.

There is enough evidence to conclude that Muhammad, at times, equated himself with God and, at others, considered himself as God's most favourite messenger. He presented his version of the Arab tribal law as God's law, had those killed who tried to reveal his deceptions, camouflaged banditry, atrocity, rape, and slavery under the cloak of prayers and rituals, and then shunned responsibility for his doing by saying that God's schemes had to succeed. One can hardly imagine a worse blasphemy than this.

Muhammad's extreme aggression changed the face of Arabia for worse. Pre-Islamic Arabia was a multi-faith, tolerant, secular and, hence, intellectually stronger society until Islamic fascism silenced its greatest men, some of whom are mentioned in this book. However, defying their own earliest books, and the Qur'anic testimony, the Islamists assert that Muhammad was the most moral person that ever walked the face of earth. He was God's chosen and most favourite. Muslims cannot speak his name without affixing to it the most reverential title, "Whom God Praises and Protects." One who dares to say, "Muhammad," without the reverential titles, faces heavy reprimands from others and expulsion from Islam. A slightest hint that he was not as perfect as presented may lead to the murder of the "disrespectful." For centuries, globally, Islamists have been deceiving a quarter of humanity and committing murders of those who want to tell the truth about Muhammad. There seems no end in sight.

XXX

As mentioned in the introduction to this work, the very first histories of Islam and the biographies of Muhammad were written by great and skilled Arab researchers within a century of his death. These researchers have been named in the introduction. Upon reading these books, it becomes obvious that these sons of the soil were motivated by a thirst for true knowledge, untainted by any propagandist requirements. However, instead of presenting these old books as they are, the 20th and 21st century Islamic propagandist books take short pieces from these and add a vast amount of devotional propaganda for reasons given below.

In most Muslim countries, the vast majority does not read the earliest Islamic books. In fact, the old books of Islam have become a barrier to the propagandists' work and so they actively seek to discredit and destroy them. Popular 20th century propagandists such as Suleiman Nidvi and Shibli Nu'maani from Pakistan criticized the 7th and 8th century earliest researchers for not presenting Muhammad as the noblest and wisest prophet of all. In their devotion to Muhammad, they even accused the earliest researchers of lying where they found a description of Muhammad more befitting that of a tribal warlord than that of a prophet. In such criticism, they forget that in the present times a true scholar of Islam can infer logically only from the earliest sources.

After doubting the veracity of the earliest researchers, the propagandists invent an ideal of Muhammad supported neither by historical evidence nor by the Qur'an but by blind zeal alone. However, reverential and devotional modification of the original serves the propagandists by winning followers and income generating ventures (donations from wealthy and devout Muslims) albeit at the cost of truth and genuine intellectual progress. By discrediting the earliest sources and not making them available, we mislead ourselves about Muhammad's life and the real history of the period. Many modern western writers too, some very prestigious, have taken money and awards from the oil-rich Arabs to whitewash Muhammad's oldest biographies. In doing so, they have nourished their bellies at the cost of honesty in disseminating knowledge.

The earliest books were written by near-contemporary Arabs in a society where robbery as well as generosity, battles as well as forgiveness, keeping harems full of concubines, slavery, regularized adultery in the form of temporary marriages and enslavement of women alongside freedom for upper class women, were common practices. Tribal chiefs were admired for possessing large numbers of slaves, concubines, cattle and property, for showing high skills in battle and plunder, and for generosity to their tribesmen and guests. Coward and tight-fisted chiefs were lampooned as well. Thus the norms and values for which the Arabs praised and followed Muhammad, make it necessary for the modern propagandists, who live in very different cultural and ethical contexts, to hide the old books. Instead of translating them in modern languages, they adapt selected pieces from them to aggrandize Muhammad as the prophet for all ages and God's chosen. They euphemise or reinterpret primitive tribal injunctions, such as secret assassination of critics, cutting the hands of thieves or stoning adulterers to death, as the word of God and a panacea to the ills of all modern problems. They deceive almost one fourth of the world through new Islamic preaching such as the claim that modern scientific concepts have been derived from the Qur'an. That there is no shred of evidence to prove this, or that the evidence points to the Qur'an as being the most irrational and violence-generating book ever written, is of no importance to the propagandists who seek to check any realistic study of Islam simply by silencing the researcher. Throughout the fourteen centuries of Islam, one finds bits and pieces of literary records of the murdered brilliant Arab, Iraqi, Persian and Indian scholars, including the great jurist Imam Abu Hanifa, who tried to save their secular and tolerant cultures by pointing that the Qur'an was a reflection of a primitive society and not the eternal word of God. The effect of their arguments and philosophies was often curbed by destroying their books and executing the philosophers. Starting from Muhammad, Islamic rulers and bigots among the public have seldom spared intellectuals who refused to serve the Islamic regime and/or ideologically challenged it. Even writing about noble themes in poetic or semi-poetic form was construed as an attempt to undermine the supremacy of the Qur'an and hence sinful. This murderous tradition has been carried into modern times: Amnesty International and similar organizations have widely reported on many intellectuals in Muslim countries imprisoned, murdered, tortured, or on the run. These are not safe even in Europe. In the last half century, through massacres, cleansing, and plunder of property, the Islamists have sabotaged the reformist movements of Ahmadis in Pakistan and Bahais in Iran.

Bertrand Russell once wrote that if a hundred great minds of Europe had been killed in infancy, modern civilization would not have come into existence. The words aptly explain the intellectual stagnation in the Muslim world.

THE END

Notes on research, references, and translations from Arabic and Urdu texts to English

This work is based on extensive readings about historical events, individuals, groups, forms of societies and the material and cognitive conditions that existed in the past, coupled with profound and regular observations of identical conditions in Muslim cultures that retain elements of these. I have made all possible efforts to present historical facts as found in quoted records but further logical extensions of events reproduced by historians were indispensable in order to provide analyses, detail, and insight into the said periods. References quoted in this work point to bare events found in the quoted books. The responsibility for explanation, interpretation of euphemisms, and logical extension of the referred events or narrations lies with the author of this work.

In order to avoid the frequent Muslim allegation that non-Muslim bibliographical sources on Islam and Islamic history are biased or prejudiced, I have used only those bibliographic sources that are considered authentic by mainstream Muslims and Islamists alike.

The translations from Arabic and Urdu prose and poetry, or any other texts, have been done by the author of this book unless otherwise mentioned in the endnotes. These and the quotes from the Qur'an have been reproduced with utmost care taken for their direct and contextual meanings – the way they were originally understood.

Acknowledgements

I thank Ali Sina for reading part of this book, suggesting improvements, and for his highly appreciative comments. I also thank Ibn Warraq for agreeing to write a review of this book if Prometheus agreed to publish it, and Tony Heron for proofreading and suggesting improvements in the use of language and grammar.

The title painting is one of many miniatures commissioned by the Turkish Ottoman ruler Murad III (1574-1595) to illustrate the epic "Siyar-i-Nabi" (The Life of the Prophet) written by Mustafa Darir in Turkish language by around 1388 CE upon the wish of Sultan Barquq, the Mamluk ruler in Cairo, Egypt.

ABOUT THE AUTHOR

Dr Shameem has been conducting research for this book for the last forty years, from authentic old Islamic records. Although his purpose in writing it is to promote understanding of what is termed "Islamic history," as found in its earliest sources, the Islamists may construe it, against all historical evidence, as insults to the main figures and tenets of Islam. He states, `I have repeatedly narrated pieces from Muhammad's life to groups of audience, and keenly observed their expressions and reactions. When I narrate reports of the events that took place, many in the audience are suspicious, dismayed, and amazed, while others show distrust. When I offer my conclusion that Islam, meaning surrender, in its early centuries, was the morality or immorality of the Arab tribal warlords and bandits, most Muslims show intense emotion. Those full of blind devotion would probably want to kill me for these conclusions – but not for narrating the events. This is because when they read about these, they tend to applaud Muslim successes in battles and, their victory over other religions, without trying to go deeper and realize that real morality does not lay in subjugating and forcing others to follow ill-conceived ideals. I have also met intelligent readers who have found for themselves that the history of Islam in its early centuries is the history of tribal wars and banditry in the guise of a fabricated religion borrowed from the earlier religions.'

The mildest criticism against this book could be that it will not help, because, as it is said, Islam can contribute positively if it is presented as noble and great, which spread through preaching and kindness. To this, the author's reply is that while this book may be destroyed, the Qur'an and Sira will always be there for the terrorists to read and apply literally, where they can.

SELECTED BIBLIOGRAPHY

Arabic

Hassn, Ibrahim H. *Tareekh al Islam*. Cairo: Maktaba al Nahzat'l Masria, 10th edition, 1985.

English

Abu Zahra, Muhammad. *The Four Imams*. Translation into English by A'isha Bewley. London: Dar al Taqwa, 2001.

Al Isma'il, Tahia. *The Life of Muhammad*. London: Ta Ha Publishers, 1 Wynne Road, SW9 0BB, 1998.

Guillaume, A. *The Life of Muhammad, A translation of Ibn Ishaq's Sirat Rasul Allah*. Karachi: Oxford University Press, Pakistan, 16th Impression, 2003.

Hazleton, L. *The First Muslim*. New York: Riverhead Books, 2013.

Holden, D., and Johns, R. *The House of Saud*. London: Pan Books Ltd., 1982.

Holt, P. M., Lambton, A. K. S., and Lewis, B. (eds.) *The Cambridge History of Islam, vol. 1A*. London: Cambridge University Press, 1970.

Ibn Warraq (ed.) *What the Koran Really Says: Language, text and commentary*. New York: Prometheus Books, 2002.

_____. *Why I am Not a Muslim*. New York: Prometheus Books, 2003.

Lester, Toby. "What is the Koran," *The Atlantic Monthly, January 1999*. http://www.theatlantic.com/issues/99jan/koran2.htm

Lings, Martin. *Muhammad, his life based on the earliest sources*. Cambridge U.K. Islamic Texts Society, 1991.

Mackey, Sandra. *Saudis: Inside the Desert Kingdom*. USA: Signet, Penguin Books, 1990.

Masood, Steven. *The Bible and the Qur'an: A question of integrity*. UK, USA: Authentic Media, 2002.

O'Neil, Sean and McGrory, Daniel. *The Suicide Factory: Abu Hamza and the Finsbury Park Mosque*. UK: HarperCollins Publishers, 2006.

Patai, Raphael. *The Arab Mind*. New York: Charles Scribner's Sons, 1973.

Robinson, Adam. bin *Laden: Behind the Mask of the Terrorist*. Edinburgh: Mainstream Publishing, 2007.

Sasson, Jean. *Princess*. Bantam Books, 2004.

———————. *Daughters of Arabia*. Bantam Books, 2004.

———————. *Desert Royal*. Bantam Books, 2004.

Trifkovic, Serge. *The Sword of the Prophet*. Boston, MA: Regina Orthodox Press, 2002.

Urdu

Abu Zahra, Muhammad. *Hayyat-a-Imam Abu Hanifa* (*The Life of Imam Abu Hanifa*). Translation from Arabic by Prof. Ghulam Ahmad Hariri. India: A'ataqad Publishing House, New Delhi-2, July 1987.

Ali, Imam. *Nahj'l Balagha*. (First written in the 7th century and printed regularly by many publishers in India, Iran, and Pakistan).

Al Qur'an (*The Qur'an*), Urdu translation and interpretation. Saudi Arabia: King Fahd Qur'an Printing Complex, (regularly published).

Asqalani, Hafiz Ahmad Ibn Hajr. *Bulugh'l Maram*. Translation from Arabic by Maulana Abd al Tawab. Multan, Pakistan: Faruqi Kutab Khana, Bohr Gate, 3rd edition, 1983. (Written between 773-825 CE).

Bukhari, Imam. *Sahih al Bukhari.* Collection of hadeeth. (First written in the 9th century and printed regularly by many publishers, worldwide).

Da'ira Mu'arif al Islamiya (Islamic encyclopaedia), Pakistan: (regularly published).

Hussein, Tu'a. *Al Fitna tul Kubra, Uthman (Uthman, the greatest sedition).* Karachi: Nafees Academy, 5th edition, March 1976.

———. *Ali wa Banu (Ali and his sons).* Karachi: Nafees Academy, 5th edition, March 1976.

Ibn Hisham. *Syrah Ibn Hisham.* Translation from Arabic by Maulana Abd al Jalil Sadiqi. India: A'ataqad Publishing House, New Delhi-2, August 1982. (First written in the 8th century).

Moudoodi, Abu'l A'la. *Khilafat-o-Malukiat (Khilafa and Tyranny).* Lahore: Idaara Tarjuman'l Qur'an, Urdu Bazaar, 25th edn. July 2000.

———. *Syrat Sarwar-a-Aalm (Biography of the saviour of the world).* Lahore: Idaara Tarjuman'l Qur'an, 7th edition, August 1999.

Nu'maani, Allama Shibli, and Nidvi, Allama Suleiman. *Syrat-al-Nabi (The prophet's biography).* Lahore: Maktaba Medina, Urdu Bazaar, 1980.

Zyat, Ahmad Hassn. *Tareekh Adab al Arabi (History of the Arabic literature).* Translation from Arabic by Abd al Rehmaan Surti. Lahore: Sheikh Ghulam Ali and Sons, Chowk Anarkali, June 1961.

References and Notes

1. Nu'maani, vol. 1, p. 298.
2. Hazleton, p. 39.
3. Ibn Hisham, vol. 1, p. 216-217.
4. Ibn Hisham, vol. 1, p. 108-109.
5. Nu'maani, vol. 1, p. 299.
6. Guillaume, p. 38.
7. Ibn Hisham, vol. 1, p. 109.
8. Ibn Hisham, vol. 1, p. 43 to 55.
9. Ibn Hisham, vol. 1, p. 61-63.
10. Ibn Hisham, vol. 1, p. 80-91.
11. Ibn Hisham, vol. 1, p. 162.
12. Ibn Hisham, vol. 1, p. 208.
13. Nu'maani, vol. 1, p. 132 to 134.
14. Ibn Hisham, vol. 1, p. 138-157 & p. 293-297.
15. Hazleton, p. 21.
16. Nu'maani, vol. 1, p. 112.
17. Ibn Hisham, vol. 1, p. 456.
18. Ibn Hisham, vol. 1, p. 270.
19. Nu'maani, vol. 1, p. 134.
20. Nu'maani, vol. 1, p. 113.
21. Nu'maani, vol. 1, p. 117.
22. Nu'maani, vol. 1, p. 121-122.
23. Nu'maani, vol. 2, p. 238.
24. Ibn Hisham, vol. 2, p. 789.
25. Al-Isma'il, p. 193 to 195.
26. Ibn Hisham, vol. 1, p. 181.
27. Guillaume, p. 68-69.
28. Ibn Hisham, vol. 1, p. 211-212.
29. Al-Isma'il, p. 193.
30. Ibn Hisham, vol. 1, p. 272.
31. Nu'maani, vol. 1, p. 118-121.
32. Nu'maani, vol. 1, p. 121-129.
33. Nu'maani, vol. 1, p. 84, & Ibn Hisham, vol. 1, p. 247-249.
34. Nu'maani, vol. 1, p. 83.
35. Asqalani, p. 128.
36. Nu'maani, vol. 1, p. 128-129.
37. The Qur'an, p. 1722.
38. Ibn Hisham, vol. 1, p. 319.
39. Ibn Hisham, vol. 1, p. 406.
40. Ibn Hisham, vol. 1, p. 284-285.
41. Ibn Hisham, vol. 1, p. 293.

[42] Nu'maani, vol. 1, p. 130, & Ibn Hisham, vol. 1, p. 432-433.
[43] Ibn Hisham, vol. 1, p. 306.
[44] Ibn Hisham, vol. 1, p. 431-434.
[45] Nu'maani, vol. 1, p. 131-132.
[46] Ibn Hisham, vol. 1, p. 730.
[47] Ibn Hisham, vol. 1, p. 321-322.
[48] Ibn Hisham, vol. 1, p. 427-429.
[49] Guillaume, p. 163-165.
[50] Ibn Hisham, vol. 1, p. 286-287.
[51] Ibn Hisham, vol. 1, p. 344-346.
[52] Ibn Hisham, vol. 1, p. 249-257.
[53] Zyat, p. 65-67.
[54] Nu'maani, vol. 1, p. 121-123.
[55] Nu'maani, vol. 1, p. 134, & Ibn Hisham, vol. 1, p. 347.
[56] Ibn Hisham, vol. 1, p. 404-408.
[57] Ibn Hisham, vol. 1, p. 402-404, 515-517, 522-523, & vol. 2, p. 330.
[58] Guillaume, p. 145.
[59] Ibn Hisham, vol. 1, p. 350-354 & 382.
[60] Ibn Hisham, vol. 1, p. 760-763.
[61] Ibn Hisham, vol. 1, p. 278-279.
[62] Nu'maani, vol. 1, p. 131.
[63] Guillaume, p. 151-152.
[64] Nu'maani, vol. 1, p. 147-148.
[65] The Qur'an, p. 1750.
[66] Ibn Hisham, vol. 1, p. 398-400.
[67] Ibn Hisham, vol. 1, p. 140.
[68] Nu'maani, vol. 1, p. 148.
[69] Guillaume, p. 160-161.
[70] Ibn Hisham, vol. 1, p. 410-411.
[71] Guillaume, p. 172-173.
[72] Ibn Hisham, vol. 1, p. 465.
[73] Ibn Hisham, vol. 1, p. 466-467.
[74] Guillaume, p. 191-192.
[75] Nu'maani, vol. 1, p. 149-150.
[76] Ibn Hisham, vol. 1, p. 405-406.
[77] Nu'maani, vol. 1, p. 110, & Ibn Hisham, vol. 2, p. 80.
[78] Nu'maani, vol. 2, p. 251.
[79] Moudoodi (*Syrat*), vol. 2, p. 625-626.
[80] Guillaume, p. 161.
[81] Ibn Hisham, vol. 1, p. 385-389.
[82] Nu'maani, vol. 1, p. 151, & Ibn Hisham, vol. 1, p. 419.
[83] Guillaume, p. 193-195.
[84] Ibn Hisham, vol. 1, p. 189.
[85] Ibn Hisham, vol. 1, p. 606.
[86] Nu'maani, vol. 1, p. 156.

[87] Ibn Hisham, vol. 1, p. 606.
[88] Bukhari.
[89] Nu'maani, vol. 1, p. 156-159.
[90] Moudoodi (*Syrat*), vol. 2, p. 701, & Ibn Hisham, vol. 1, p. 489.
[91] Ibn Hisham, vol. 1, p. 744-745.
[92] Moudoodi (*Syrat*), vol. 2, p. 703.
[93] Nu'maani, vol. 1, p. 156-157, & Ibn Hisham, vol. 1, p. p.235 & 477-479.
[94] Guillaume, p. 199.
[95] Guillaume, p. 203-204.
[96] Ibn Hisham, vol. 1, p. 479.
[97] Nu'maani, vol. 1, p. 159, & Ibn Hisham, vol. 1, p. 491-492.
[98] Ibn Hisham, vol. 1, p. 495-497.
[99] Ibn Hisham, vol. 1, p. 302.
[100] Ibn Hisham, vol. 1, p. 495-497.
[101] Nu'maani, vol. 1, p. 160, & Guillaume p. 205-206.
[102] Ibn Hisham, vol. 1, p. 498.
[103] Nu'maani, vol. 1, p. 164, & Ibn Hisham, vol. 1, p. 543.
[104] Ibn Hisham, vol. 1, p. 554-561.
[105] Nu'maani, vol. 1, p. 175-176.
[106] The Qur'an, p. 57-58.
[107] Asqalani, p. 391.
[108] Nu'maani, vol. 1, p. 179.
[109] Ibn Hisham, vol. 1, p. 606.
[110] Nu'maani, vol. 1, p. 173-174.
[111] Asqalani, p. 209.
[112] Ibn Hisham, vol. 2, p. 374 & p. 400.
[113] Ibn Hisham, vol. 1, p. 588.
[114] Ibn Hisham, vol. 2, p. 772-774.
[115] Ibn Hisham, vol. 2, p. 750-752.
[116] Ibn Hisham, vol. 2, p. 776.
[117] Ibn Hisham, vol. 2, p. 779.
[118] Asqalani, p. 260.
[119] Asqalani, p. 265.
[120] Asqalani, p. 446.
[121] Asqalani, p. 259.
[122] Ibn Hisham, vol. 1, p. 357.
[123] Asqalani, p. 259.
[124] Abu Zahra (*The Four Imams*), p. 48-49.
[125] Asqalani, p. 444-445.
[126] Asqalani, p. 323.
[127] Asqalani, p. 371.
[128] Asqalani, p. 442.
[129] Abu Zahra (*Hayyat*), p. 461.
[130] Moudoodi (*Khilafat*), p. 171, 175.
[131] Abu Zahra (*Hayyat*), p. 545-546.

[132] Guillaume, p. 256.
[133] Guillaume, p. 270.
[134] Ibn Hisham, vol. 2, p. 780-783, & Guillaume, p. 675.
[135] Ibn Hisham, vol. 1, p. 673-675.
[136] Ibn Hisham, vol. 1, p. 578-581.
[137] Ibn Hisham, vol. 2, p. 72-73.
[138] Ibn Hisham, vol. 1, p. 580-581.
[139] Ibn Hisham, vol. 2, p. 760-763.
[140] Part of the translation comes from Guillaume, p. 666.
[141] Ibn Hisham, vol. 1, p. 573.
[142] Nu'maani, vol. 1, p. 158.
[143] Nu'maani, vol. 1, p. 177, & the Qur'an, p. 57-58.
[144] Ibn Hisham, vol. 1, p. 575-576.
[145] Asqalani, p. 390-391.
[146] Ibn Hisham, vol. 1, p. 622-644.
[147] Ibn Hisham, vol. 1, p. 642-649.
[148] Nu'maani, vol. 1, p. 178-179, & Abu Zahra (*The Four Imams*), p. 57.
[149] Ibn Hisham, vol. 1, p. 620-623.
[150] Ibn Hisham, vol. 1, p. 466 & 531.
[151] Ibn Hisham, vol. 1, p. 692-693.
[152] Asqalani, p. 274.
[153] Asqalani, p. 417.
[154] Asqalani, p. 402.
[155] Nu'maani, vol. 1, 183-184.
[156] Nu'maani, vol. 1, p. 301.
[157] Ibn Hisham, vol. 2, p. 339-341.
[158] Ibn Hisham, vol. 1, p. 680-683.
[159] Asqalani, p. 384-386.
[160] Asqalani, p. 403-407.
[161] Asqalani, p. 149.
[162] Asqalani, p. 154.
[163] Asqalani, p. 148.
[164] Asqalani, p. 162-167.
[165] Ibn Hisham, vol. 1, p. 589-590.
[166] Asqalani, p. 63-66.
[167] Asqalani, p. 71.
[168] Abu Zahra (*Hayyat*), p. 417.
[169] Asqalani, p. 69.
[170] Asqalani, p. 123.
[171] Asqalani, p. 113.
[172] Ibn Hisham, vol. 1, p. 582-583.
[173] Asqalani, p. 182-183.
[174] Asqalani, p. 132-135.
[175] Asqalani, p. 106-107.
[176] Asqalani, p. 182.

[177] Asqalani, p. 188.
[178] Ibn Hisham, vol. 1, p. 375.
[179] Asqalani, p. 155-156.
[180] Asqalani, p. 196.
[181] Asqalani, p. 128.
[182] Asqalani, p. 122.
[183] Asqalani, p. 126.
[184] Asqalani, p. 404.
[185] Nu'maani, vol. 1, p. 237-238.
[186] Al-Isma'il, p. 203, & Nu'maani, vol. 1, p. 239.
[187] Ibn Hisham, vol. 2, p. 350-353.
[188] Nu'maani, vol. 1, p. 239.
[189] Asqalani, p. 388-390.
[190] Abu Zahra (*Hayyat*), p. 567.
[191] Asqalani, p. 353-367.
[192] Asqalani, p. 188-189.
[193] Asqalani, p. 288-387.
[194] Asqalani, p. 354.
[195] Asqalani, p. 392.
[196] Asqalani, p. 388.
[197] Asqalani, p. 332.
[198] Asqalani, p. 328.
[199] Asqalani, p. 386-387-393.
[200] Asqalani, p. 354-355.
[201] Asqalani, p. 201.
[202] Asqalani, p. 404-407.
[203] Asqalani, p. 410-412.
[204] Asqalani, p. 324-325.
[205] Asqalani, p. 329 & 350.
[206] The Qur'an, p. 215.
[207] Asqalani, p. 410.
[208] Ibn Hisham, vol. 1, p. 694-695.
[209] Nu'maani, vol. 1, p. 185.
[210] Ibn Hisham, vol. 2, p. 192-195.
[211] Ibn Hisham, vol. 1, p. 696-697 & 745.
[212] Zyat, p. 176-177.
[213] Ibn Hisham, vol. 1, p. 700.
[214] Ibn Hisham, vol. 1, p. 709.
[215] Ibn Hisham, vol. 2, p. 620.
[216] Ibn Hisham, vol. 1, p. 533-534.
[217] Ibn Hisham, vol. 2, p. 333.
[218] Ibn Hisham, vol. 1, p. 706-709.
[219] Nu'maani, vol. 1, p. 202, 206, 207, 210.
[220] Nu'maani, vol. 1, p. 188, & Ibn Hisham, vol. 1, p. 716-717.
[221] Ibn Hisham, vol. 1, p. 710-716.

[222] Nu'maani, vol. 1, p. 189-190, & Ibn Hisham, vol. 1, p. 719.
[223] Nu'maani, vol. 1, p. 190-192, & Ibn Hisham, vol. 1, p. 730-731.
[224] Nu'maani, vol. 1, p. 187, & Ibn Hisham, vol. 1, p. 712-713.
[225] Ibn Hisham, vol. 1, p. 760-763.
[226] Ibn Hisham, vol. 1, p. 722-723.
[227] Moudoodi (*Syrat*), vol. 2, p. 703.
[228] Nu'maani, vol. 1, p. 195, & Ibn Hisham, vol. 1, p. 757.
[229] Nu'maani, vol. 1, p. 191, & Ibn Hisham, vol. 1, p. 723-725.
[230] Nu'maani, vol. 1, p. 181.
[231] Nu'maani, vol. 1, p. 191-192.
[232] Ibn Hisham, vol. 1, p. 726-727
[233] Ibn Hisham, vol. 1, p. 733-735.
[234] Asqalani, p. 409.
[235] Ibn Hisham, vol. 1, p. 733.
[236] Nu'maani, vol. 1, p. 189.
[237] Ibn Hisham, vol. 1, p. 737.
[238] Ibn Hisham, vol. 1, p. 721-722.
[239] Ibn Hisham, vol. 1, p. 739 & 768.
[240] Ibn Hisham, vol. 1, p. 741-743.
[241] Nu'maani, vol. 1, p. 194.
[242] Ibn Hisham, vol. 1, p. 745-751.
[243] Ibn Hisham, vol. 1, p. 756-757.
[244] Asqalani, p. 271.
[245] Asqalani, p. 105-106.
[246] Asqalani, p. 266.
[247] Ibn Hisham, vol. 1, p. 636-641.
[248] Ibn Hisham, vol. 1, p. 597-605.
[249] Ibn Hisham, vol. 1, p. 632-634.
[250] Ibn Hisham, vol. 2, p. 35, & Nu'maani, vol. 1, p. 233-234.
[251] Ibn Hisham, vol. 2, p. 23-38.
[252] Ibn Hisham, vol. 1, p. 637.
[253] Nu'maani, vol. 1, p. 180-181.
[254] Guillaume, p. 279.
[255] Ibn Hisham, vol. 1, p. 623, & vol. 2, p. 24.
[256] Ibn Hisham, vol. 2, p. 24-25.
[257] Ibn Hisham, vol. 2, p. 25.
[258] Ibn Hisham, vol. 2, p. 346-349.
[259] Ibn Hisham, vol. 1, p. 457-461.
[260] Ibn Hisham, vol. 2, p. 21.
[261] Nu'maani, vol. 1, p. 211, & Ibn Hisham, vol. 2, p. 22.
[262] Ibn Hisham, vol. 1, p. 486-487.
[263] Asqalani, p. 412-413.
[264] Asqalani, p. 333-334.
[265] Asqalani, p. 102-103.
[266] Ibn Hisham, vol. 2, p. 27.

[267] Ibn Hisham, vol. 2, p. 40-46.
[268] Ibn Hisham, vol. 2, p. 62-65.
[269] Ibn Hisham, vol. 2, p. 67-71.
[270] Ibn Hisham, vol. 2, p. 167-168.
[271] Ibn Hisham, vol. 2, p. 77-78.
[272] Ibn Hisham, vol. 2, p. 80.
[273] Ibn Hisham, vol. 2, p. 50-54.
[274] Asqalani, p. 188.
[275] Ibn Hisham, vol. 2, p. 83-84.
[276] Ibn Hisham, vol. 1, p. 584.
[277] Ibn Hisham, vol. 2, p. 71.
[278] Ibn Hisham, vol. 1, p. 581.
[279] Ibn Hisham, vol. 2, p. 89-90.
[280] Ibn Hisham, vol. 2, p. 111-112.
[281] Ibn Hisham, vol. 1, p. 576.
[282] Ibn Hisham, vol. 2, p. 86-88.
[283] Ibn Hisham, vol. 2, p. 372.
[284] Nu'maani, vol. 2, p. 244, & Al-Isma'il, p. 200.
[285] Ibn Hisham, vol. 2, p. 752.
[286] Ibn Hisham, vol. 2, p. 208-215.
[287] Ibn Hisham, vol. 1, p. 586-587, & vol. 2, p. 216.
[288] Ibn Hisham, vol. 2, p. 216.
[289] Asqalani, p. 413.
[290] Ibn Hisham, vol. 2, p. 216-217.
[291] Ibn Hisham, vol. 2, p. 220-232.
[292] Guillaume, p. 450.
[293] Ibn Hisham, vol. 2, p. 235.
[294] Ibn Hisham, vol. 2, p. 253-260.
[295] Guillaume, p. 453
[296] Ibn Hisham, vol. 1, p. 581, & vol. 2, p. 256-257.
[297] Ibn Hisham, vol. 2, p. 265-268.
[298] Nu'maani, vol. 1, p. 233 & 246.
[299] Nu'maani, vol. 1, p. 245-251.
[300] Ibn Hisham, vol. 2, p. 752.
[301] Ibn Hisham, vol. 2, p. 271-272.
[302] Ibn Hisham, vol. 1, p. 585.
[303] Ibn Hisham, vol. 2, p. 271-273.
[304] Ibn Hisham, vol. 2, p. 323.
[305] Ibn Hisham, vol. 2, p. 273-277.
[306] Asqalani, p. 283.
[307] Ibn Hisham, vol. 2, p. 278-281.
[308] Nu'maani, vol. 1, p. 250-251.
[309] Ibn Hisham, vol. 2, p. 282.
[310] Ibn Hisham, vol. 2, p. 680-682.
[311] Ibn Hisham, vol. 2, p. 322-323.

[312] Translation of this verse by Guillaume.
[313] Ibn Hisham, vol. 2, p. 776-779.
[314] Nu'maani, vol. 1, p. 267.
[315] Ibn Hisham, vol. 2, p. 364.
[316] Ibn Hisham, vol. 1, p. 33.
[317] Ibn Hisham, vol. 2, p. 380.
[318] Ibn Hisham, vol. 2, p. 368-375.
[319] Ibn Hisham, vol. 2, p. 327-379.
[320] Ibn Hisham, vol. 2, p. 381.
[321] Ibn Hisham, vol. 2, p. 376-378.
[322] Ibn Hisham, vol. 1, p. 466 & 531.
[323] Nu'maani, vol. 1, p. 284.
[324] Ibn Hisham, vol. 2, p. 327-329.
[325] Nu'maani, vol. 1, p. 270-271.
[326] Nu'maani, vol. 1, p. 283.
[327] Ibn Hisham, vol. 2, p. 393-394.
[328] Ibn Hisham, vol. 1, p. 721.
[329] Ibn Hisham, vol. 2, p. 401.
[330] Ibn Hisham, vol. 2, p. 394-397.
[331] Ibn Hisham, vol. 2, p. 403-404.
[332] Nu'maani, vol. 1, p. 277.
[333] Ibn Hisham, vol. 2, p. 408-409-416-417-418
[334] Ibn Hisham, vol. 2, p. 399-402-403.
[335] Nu'maani, vol. 1, p. 280.
[336] Ibn Hisham, vol. 2, p. 407.
[337] Nu'maani, vol. 1, p. 283, & Ibn Hisham, vol. 2, p. 395-396.
[338] Ibn Hisham, vol. 2, p. 402.
[339] Nu'maani, vol. 2, p. 248.
[340] Al-Isma'il, p. 204, & Ibn Hisham, vol. 2, p. 402.
[341] Ibn Hisham, vol. 2, p. 395.
[342] Nu'maani, vol. 1, p. 278-279.
[343] Ibn Hisham, vol. 2, p. 405-406.
[344] Al-Isma'il, p. 205.
[345] Asqalani, p. 318-319.
[346] Nu'maani, vol. 1, p. 283-284.
[347] Asqalani, p. 361.
[348] Ibn Hisham, vol. 2, p. 405, 410.
[349] Ibn Hisham, vol. 2, p. 396.
[350] Ibn Hisham, vol. 2, p. 405.
[351] Ibn Hisham, vol. 2, p. 421-422.
[352] Ibn Hisham, vol. 2, p. 403-404.
[353] Ibn Hisham, vol. 2, p. 422.
[354] Nu'maani, vol. 1, p. 278.
[355] Nu'maani, vol. 1, p. 283.
[356] Ibn Hisham, vol. 2, p. 411-412.

[357] Ibn Hisham, vol. 2, p. 354-357.
[358] Ibn Hisham, vol. 2, p. 357-359 and Guillaume, p. 494-499.
[359] Ibn Hisham, vol. 2, p. 362-365.
[360] Ibn Hisham, vol. 2, p. 359-367, & Asqalani, p. 393.
[361] Nu'maani, vol. 1, p. 252-253.
[362] Al-Isma'il, p. 201, & Nu'maani, vol. 1, p. 252.
[363] World Islamic Heritage, Saudi Arabia.
[364] Abu Zahra (*Hayyat*), p. 562.
[365] Nu'maani, vol. 1, p. 268.
[366] Al-Isma'il, p. 206.
[367] Nu'maani, p. vol. 2, 257.
[368] Moudoodi (*Khilafat*), p. 305.
[369] Nu'maani, vol. 2, p. 257.
[370] Al-Isma'il, p. 205, & Nu'maani, vol. 2, p. 248.
[371] Nu'maani, vol. 2, p. 248.
[372] Nu'maani, vol. 2, p. 256-257.
[373] Nu'maani, vol. 1, p. 312-316-317.
[374] The Qur'an, p. 1598.
[375] Nu'maani, vol. 1, p. 311-315.
[376] Asqalani, p. 351.
[377] Asqalani, p. 333.
[378] Nu'maani, vol. 1, p. 312-313.
[379] Nu'maani, vol. 2, p. 247.
[380] Ibn Hisham, vol. 2, p. 433-436.
[381] Ibn Hisham, vol. 2, p. 445-446.
[382] Ibn Hisham, vol. 2, p. 763.
[383] Ibn Hisham, vol. 2, p. 446-448.
[384] Ibn Hisham, vol. 2, p. 758-759.
[385] Guillaume, p. 665.
[386] Ibn Hisham, vol. 2, p. 451-454.
[387] Ibn Hisham, vol. 2, p. 459-468.
[388] Ibn Hisham, vol. 2, p. 469-484.
[389] Ibn Hisham, vol. 2, p. 482-483.
[390] Guillaume, 549.
[391] Asqalani, p. 409.
[392] Asqalani, p. 372.
[393] Nu'maani, vol. 1, p. 296-297.
[394] Ibn Hisham, vol. 2, p. 485-487.
[395] Ibn Hisham, vol. 2, p. 500-501.
[396] Guillaume, p. 552
[397] Ibn Hisham, vol. 2, p. 504.
[398] Guillaume, p. 555.
[399] Ibn Hisham, vol. 2, p. 514-519
[400] Ibn Hisham, vol. 2, p. 522-532.
[401] Ibn Hisham, vol. 2, p. 549-550.

[402] Ibn Hisham, vol. 2, p. 532-536.
[403] Guillaume, p. 572.
[404] Ibn Hisham, vol. 2, p. 537-546.
[405] Ibn Hisham, vol. 2, p. 763.
[406] Ibn Hisham, vol. 2, p. 783.
[407] Ibn Hisham, vol. 2, p. 547-558.
[408] Ibn Hisham, vol. 2, p. 565-566.
[409] Ibn Hisham, vol. 2, p. 559-569.
[410] Ibn Hisham, vol. 2, p. 555-556.
[411] Ibn Hisham, vol. 2, p. 562-569.
[412] Ibn Hisham, vol. 2, p. 552.
[413] Ibn Hisham, vol. 2, p. 581-584.
[414] Ibn Hisham, vol. 2, p. 557-562.
[415] Guillaume, p. 584.
[416] Ibn Hisham, vol. 2, p. 562.
[417] Ibn Hisham, vol. 2, p. 576-584.
[418] Ibn Hisham, vol. 2, p. 769-772.
[419] Ibn Hisham, vol. 2, p. 584-588
[420] Ibn Hisham, vol. 2, p. 766.
[421] Ibn Hisham, vol. 2, p. 585-595.
[422] Guillaume, p. 593.
[423] Ibn Hisham, vol. 2, p. 537-541.
[424] Ibn Hisham, vol. 2, p. 581-582.
[425] Ibn Hisham, vol. 2, p. 596-598.
[426] Guillaume, p. 595.
[427] Ibn Hisham, vol. 2, p. 595-603.
[428] Guillaume, p. 596-597.
[429] Ibn Hisham, vol. 2, p. 603-619.
[430] Ibn Hisham, vol. 1, p. 654-672.
[431] Ibn Hisham, vol. 2, p. 620-621.
[432] Ibn Hisham, vol. 1, p. 586.
[433] Ibn Hisham, vol. 2, p. 623-633.
[434] Nu'maani, vol. 1, p. 320.
[435] Ibn Hisham, vol. 2, p. 635-646.
[436] Ibn Hisham, vol. 2, p. 725-728.
[437] Asqalani, p. 414-415 & 449.
[438] Ibn Hisham, vol. 2, p. 647-655.
[439] Ibn Hisham, vol. 2, p. 655-662.
[440] Nu'maani, vol. 1, p. 321.
[441] Ibn Hisham, vol. 2, p. 669-670.
[442] Ibn Hisham, vol. 2, p. 711-716.
[443] Ibn Hisham, vol. 2, p. 698-699.
[444] Guillaume, p. 632.
[445] Ibn Hisham, vol. 2, p. 696-700.
[446] Ibn Hisham, vol. 2, p. 690-695.

[447] Ibn Hisham, vol. 2, p. 685-697.
[448] Guillaume, p. 631.
[449] Ibn Hisham, vol. 2, p. 706-709.
[450] Ibn Hisham, vol. 2, p. 717-721.
[451] Guillaume, p. 640-641.
[452] Ibn Hisham, vol. 2, p. 722-725.
[453] Ibn Hisham, vol. 2, p. 731-734.
[454] Ibn Hisham, vol. 2, p. 738.
[455] Ibn Hisham, vol. 2, p. 710-711.
[456] Ibn Hisham, vol. 2, p. 739.
[457] Ibn Hisham, vol. 2, p. 740-745.
[458] Asqalani, p. 317.
[459] Nu'maani, vol. 2, p. 240.
[460] Nu'maani, vol. 1, p. 254.
[461] Ibn Hisham, vol. 2, p. 798.
[462] Ibn Hisham, vol. 2, p. 787-789.
[463] Ibn Hisham, vol. 2, p. 794-805.
[464] Ibn Hisham, vol. 2, p. 806-810.
[465] Ibn Hisham, vol. 2, p. 814-818, & Guillaume, p. 687-688.
[466] Ibn Hisham, vol. 2, p. 827-829, & Guillaume, p. 689-690.
[467] Ibn Hisham, vol. 2, p. 818.
[468] Ibn Hisham, vol. 2, p. 806-810.
[469] Moudoodi (*Khilafat*), p. 97.
[470] Moudoodi (*Khilafat*), p. 162.
[471] Moudoodi (*Khilafat*), p. 85.
[472] Moudoodi (*Khilafat*), p. 98.
[473] Hazleton, p. 266-268
[474] Holt et al., p. 62.
[475] Moudoodi (*Khilafat*), p. 107 & 174.
[476] Abu Zahra (*Hayyat*), p. 266.
[477] Abu Zahra (*The Four Imams*), p. 58.
[478] Zyat, p. 21-27.
[479] Moudoodi (*Khilafat*), p. 162-163, 170, & Hussein, Tu'a (*Al Fitna*), p. 130.
[480] Moudoodi (*Khilafat*), p. 170.
[481] Abu Zahra (*Hayyat*), p. 142.
[482] Moudoodi (*Khilafat*), p. 170-171.
[483] Hassn, (Arabic section), p. 255, & Hussein, Tu'a (*Al Fitna*), p. 21.
[484] Hussein, Tu'a (*Al Fitna*), p. 90.
[485] Moudoodi (*Khilafat*), p. 109.
[486] Moudoodi (*Khilafat*), p. 98-100.
[487] Moudoodi (*Khilafat*), p. 106 to 108.
[488] Nu'maani, vol. 1, p. 129.
[489] Zyat, p. 163-164.
[490] Abu Zahra (*Hayyat*) (Urdu), p. 422.
[491] Zyat, p. 164; Masood, p. 29-31.

[492] Ali, Imam, Chapter: *Khutbah-a-Shaqshaqiyya*.
[493] Hussein, Tu'a (*Al Fitna*), p. 156-160.
[494] Moudoodi (*Khilafat*), p. 106-120.
[495] Hussein, Tu'a (*Al Fitna*), p. 263, & Moudoodi (*Khilafat*), p. 146.
[496] Hussein, Tu'a (*Al Fitna*), p. 163-167.
[497] Moudoodi (*Khilafat*), p. 117 to 119, & Hussein, Tu'a (*Al Fitna*), p. 263.
[498] Moudoodi (*Khilafat*), p. 115.
[499] Hussein, Tu'a (*Al Fitna*), p. 151-156
[500] Hussein, Tu'a (*Ali wa Banu*), p. 338-347.
[501] Moudoodi (*Khilafat*), p. 124-129, 131.
[502] Moudoodi (*Khilafat*), p. 176.
[503] Moudoodi (*Khilafat*), p. 134-145, 209.
[504] Moudoodi (*Khilafat*), p. 309.
[505] Hassn, (*Tareekh al Islam*) (Arabic), p. 279.
[506] Moudoodi (*Khilafat*), p. 214-215.
[507] Abu Zahra (*Hayyat*), p. 231-232, 234.
[508] Abu Zahra (*Hayyat*), p. 228-230.
[509] Abu Zahra (*The Four Imams*), p. 22.
[510] Abu Zahra (*Hayyat*), p. 222.
[511] Moudoodi (*Khilafat*), p. 212-213.
[512] Abu Zahra (*Hayyat*), p. 144-145, & Moudoodi (*Khilafat*), p. 174.
[513] Moudoodi (*Khilafat*), p. 175-178.
[514] Moudoodi (*Khilafat*), p. 164-165.
[515] Moudoodi (*Khilafat*), p. 148-153.
[516] Zyat, p. 211.
[517] Moudoodi (*Khilafat*), p. 179 to 181.
[518] Abu Zahra (*The Four Imams*), p. 22.
[519] Moudoodi (*Khilafat*), p. 181-184, & Abu Zahra (*Hayyat*), p. 210
[520] Holt et al., p. 100.
[521] Moudoodi (*Khilafat*), p. 185-187.
[522] Zyat p. 291-293.
[523] Moudoodi (*Khilafat*), p. 186, & Zyat, p. 292.
[524] Moudoodi (*Khilafat*), p. 296.
[525] Moudoodi (*Khilafat*), p. 178-179 & 184-185.
[526] Abu Zahra (*Hayyat*), p. 144.
[527] Moudoodi (*Khilafat*), p. 187.
[528] Abu Zahra (*The Four Imams*), p. 21.
[529] Moudoodi (*Khilafat*), p. 161-163 & 187-191
[530] Moudoodi (*Khilafat*), p. 171, 172 & 196.
[531] Holt et al., pp. 102, 106.
[532] Moudoodi (*Khilafat*), p. 193.
[533] Holt et al., p. 106-107.
[534] Holt et al., p. 102.
[535] Zyat, p. 317
[536] Moudoodi (*Khilafat*), p. 192.

[537] Zyat, p. 321.
[538] Moudoodi (*Khilafat*), p. 193.
[539] Nu'maani, vol. 1, p. 259.
[540] Ibn Hisham, vol. 1, p. 771.
[541] Nu'maani, vol. 1, p. 81-83.
[542] Nu'maani, vol. 2, p. 73-74.
[543] Nu'maani, vol. 1, p. 133.
[544] Asqalani, p. 378 379.
[545] Ibn Hisham, vol. 2, p. 749.

Printed in Great Britain
by Amazon